A MOONLIT ARMAGEDDON

Summer Haven III

Paul J.C. Edge

Your enemy's enemy is not your friend!

The Dark Ones

Edge Publications

Table of Contents

I.	PROLOGUE	14
II.	ARMAGEDDON	16
	1. Not Just a Passing Encounter	17
	2. Tholu Phuk (Abe)	25
	3. A Cry in the Night	38
	4. A Child in the Pit of Hell	56
	5. A Gathering of Minds	65
	6. The First Iteration	77
	7. Not Quite First Contact	84
	8. The Nature of the Beast	94
	9. The Sharing	103
	10. Following a Trail of Crumbs into Hell	113
	11. The Pointed Mountain (Abe)	120
	12. Fire fight	126
	13. Face Your Fears or Die Afraid	135
	14. The Battle for Mont St Michel	141
	15. Return to the Tiger's Nest (Abe)	148
	16. Fighting Dirty	157
	17. An Unexpected SOS	162
	18. A Bargain with The Boatman	171
	19. Invasion	180
	20. Occupation	193
	21. The Battle for Summer Haven	208
	22. Do Not Go Gentle into that Good Night	220
	23. A Hopeless Cause	228
	24. A Darkness of Purpose	242
	25. A Tenuous Plan	248
	26. The 'Not-Dead'	262
	27. Darkness will Swallow us	271

28.	First on the Left	278
29.	The Day of the Shroom	286
30.	The Pursuit	293
31.	Connection	307

III. APOCALYPSE 319

1.	A Long Passage	320
2.	Revenge of The Dark One	326
3.	The Pursuit	337
4.	The Kramml-zo	345
5.	Walking the Plank	355
6.	Secrets	363
7.	Somewhere Else	374
8.	A Grand Design	386
9.	A Fertile Mind Growing Seeds of Paranoia	398
10.	Too Many Coincidences	405
11.	Arresting Thoughts	415
12.	Too Much Interest	423
13.	Beginning of the End	439
14.	Beyond The Curtain	446
15.	A New Dawn	455
16.	Apocalypse	462
17.	A Last Wish	468
18.	The Last Goodbye	475

IV. EPILOGUE: NEW MOON 484

Dedication

For my wife Elaine, for the endless hours of editing and helping me improve the sense of this novel, this work would be much weaker without her diligence and patience.

My heart goes out to Dmitry from Ukraine, who designed the wonderful cover art for this book. Stay safe, and never give up the fight for freedom!

This novel was drafted prior to the invasion of Ukraine by Russia, although I know the ordinary people of Russia would behave as they do in my novel faced with these fictitious circumstances. My heart goes out to those in Russia who have been misled concerning the terrible events in Ukraine, and power to those who have been both enlightened and courageous enough to stand up and tell the Kremlin that what they are doing is wrong.

What Has Gone Before

An English Apocalypse

Paul Collin dreams of impending apocalypse, a warning from a vague white figure present in his nightmares. He is warned of an infection which will destroy humanity, spread by meteors from outer space. His dreams increase in frequency and intensity until his family begin to share them. The dreams urge him to build a fortress on the remote Summer Islands in the Scottish Highlands. Paul is forced to take the visions more seriously when a series of investments and lottery predictions make him a multi-millionaire capable of funding the build of the facility.

In complete secrecy, Paul forms a team of his most trusted friends to build 'Summer Haven' as directed by the unknown entity. He is forced to lie to his team as they would never believe his dreams. As the plans progress, Paul relies on his closest ally, Spall, to mastermind the defence and acquire advanced weaponry using Spall's less salubrious comrades from the special forces. Spall recruits two locals into the team who are gifted military operators, Sheena and her boyfriend Rusty, plus an old colleague of theirs nicknamed Wrench. Paul is obliged to come clean with the team when the first group of meteors are spotted by Earth's long-range observatories. This lends credence to Paul's claims and the team are forced to make difficult choices in order to be ready.

Paul and his team summon their families and associates with key skills to ensure their survival. The final moments of A-Day approach, news reports show people turning into savages as the killing and mayhem begins in earnest. The team discover the infection is a fungal pathogen similar to Cordyceps which pressurises the brain to render its victims insane and uses its fruit (a mushroom) to propagate. The infected are dubbed 'Shrooms' by the team. The team learn there are seven havens around the world, each prepared for the apocalypse by a vague dream figure.

Paul is joined at Summer Haven by his estranged identical twin, Francisco (Franc). Franc has led an arduous life; he is a gentle soul forced into escalating acts of heinous violence to save those around him. He too was aided by a vague presence, advising him to 'choose to be brave'. Franc loses his family, wife Lucy and child Colletta when the virus hits, sending him into a rampage. He is led into the defence of Valletta Haven which is poorly prepared and soon falls to the masses of the infected. Franc escapes to Summer Haven on a yacht with two of his sailor buddies, Rene and Gio.

As food becomes scarce on the islands, Paul and his team forage from nearby supermarkets which proves to be a dangerous venture. They discover Sulphur has high efficacy in combating the infected, so they rig up a helicopter as a crop sprayer and manage to clear much of northern Scotland from the Shrooms. On a foraging trip, Franc falls in battle. Paul finds it quite disconcerting when Franc appears a few days later, quite well. After quarantine, Paul realises he and his brother are immune from the infection.

Summer Haven is visited by a nuclear submarine to gather provisions, captained by Bartholomew (Bart) McCreedy. The crew are not permitted to land due to the virus. Bart finds a small population in Reykjavik and helps save stranded oil rig workers who have avoided contact with the mainland.

Paul and Franc experience new dreams warning them of the threat of the 'Dark Ones'. Rusty executes a solitary figure on the mainland using a sniper rifle, as Paul identifies the figure as a Dark One. When the bullet hits it's mark, the figure spontaneously combusts with blinding white fire.

A Doctrine of Fear

Joe Fairbourne rejects a stressful professional life to be a carer for those less fortunate. His wife, Bridget, loves historical mysteries and reads a report to Joe whereby archaeologists open the ancient tomb of the 'Dark One' in Jordan. She especially relishes the part where the team dies mysteriously. Joe finds a news article describing an initiative mercurial, the Pope is selling the Vatican's treasures to fund a special venture. Bridget assumes the stigmata like writing appearing on Joe's forearm is a prank by their son, James.

Joe chooses to consult the Catholic church for advice and is informed that the Pope himself has an interest in his safety. The rectory is attacked by Dark Ones, a secret organisation of fanatics bent on destroying mankind. When injured the Dark Ones burst into intense flames leaving nothing but ashes; based on this fact, Joe fears his pursuers are demons. The Swiss Guard arrive to protect Joe, they separately take Bridget and his close family to Vatican City to safeguard them. Joe is constantly moved around the UK before finally joining his family in Rome.

James is taken at gunpoint by Jane, a member of the Swiss Guard, who escorts the unfocussed adolescent into the mountains for intense training. Their mission is to become Joe's guardians, as he is forced to run from his pursuers across the breadth of mainland Europe. The Pope himself briefs Joe, explaining that god explained in a vision that Armageddon was coming, and Joe was critical to the survival of humankind. The Vatican spared no expense in preparing a special army to defend Joe from what was to come. The Pope had received an ancient manuscript warning him of the Dark One's intent to eradicate human life from the planet. The Pope persuades Joe to join the priesthood, as it is the only legitimate way he can protect him with full diplomatic immunity. The concept of pursuing demons leads seasoned agnostic Joe to embrace the Catholic religion.

Bridget befriends Father Enzo, to try to understand the danger her husband is facing. Enzo explains the secret organisation. The Dark Ones collect human blood, rumours persist that the Dark One himself uses it for sustenance. His followers carry unusual twin grooved daggers which channel the blood of their victims into a collection vessel in the pommel. Enzo shares an ancient parchment and the unusual dichotomy of his findings; he believes the document must be fake.

Despite avoiding using their own ID and credit cards, the Dark Ones track Joe and his guardians using their spent cash. It disturbs them that all European banks had been infiltrated. In addition, the banks have infeasibly advanced IT capabilities to correlate the serial numbers of their Euro bank notes. There was a traitor within the confines of the Vatican itself.

During an attack in Spain, James is severely injured by the blade of a Dark One. As Jane enables their escape, Joe calls on his god to help and discovers his ability to heal. Suddenly Jane and James recognise their true purpose and why the Pope masterminded the plans to save Joe.

After a significant attempt to eliminate them in Porto, Joe escapes to sea on a special frigate 'The Phoenix', commissioned specifically to protect him. Equipped with hi tech weaponry and a low radar signature it helps them evade pursuers. The vessel's small crew is captained by Phil, supported by his first officer José.

Later, it becomes apparent that key Summer Haven personnel Sheena and Rusty were placed at the haven by the Vatican, in order to protect Paul.

Prior to A-Day, Joe is transported to Isola Salina to re-join his family. Salina's active volcano makes the air sulphurous, which protects the haven from the virus when unleashed. Joe takes residence with Bridget in The Sanctuary, a church owned place of pilgrimage, he quickly becomes pastor for the flock, assisted by Father Enzo.

Paul departs Summer Haven with Franc and Spall in search of his brother. On route they stop at Mont St Michel Haven to pick up the leader Sacha, who claims to share their goal. A Dark One has murdered Sacha and is posing as him, Franc saves Paul from assassination. They are forced to reroute to Formentera Haven for help when their yacht explodes.

Paul and Franc arrive at Salina just in time to save Joe's life, as the island is infiltrated by Dark Ones. Paul and Franc find that Joe is identical in appearance to them, if a few years older, he is clearly the brother they were seeking. The analysis of a Dark Ones' hood concludes it is constructed of a technology way beyond mankind's ken, the weave consists of millions of tiny nuclear reactors oriented to detonate on impact.

Bart continues rescuing stranded oil rig workers using his nuclear submarine and discovers a faint SOS from Russia. He saves a small community of soldiers and government officials led by General Smitsky have been barricaded into a nuclear bunker by the Dark Ones.

Paul, Franc and Joe are summoned by their genetic father, Melak, to the nearby island of Vulcano, where the inhabitants have been tortured and killed by the Dark Ones, leaving a terrible shrine of death. They meet Melak, a Pareth-ng scout from their dying alien home world, sent to Earth prior to occupation.

Melak's mission is to eradicate intelligent life from Earth ready for occupation, but he had second thoughts deciding instead to live on Earth in harmony. Melak's cousin, Barak, would not deviate from their mission parameters and a bitter feud ensued between them. Barak became the Dark One, using his influence and notoriety to build a large network of followers, infiltrating governments and pharmaceutical companies globally to manufacture and deploy a virus. Barak used the cover story of the meteors to unleash the DNA coded virus on humanity, he brought about A-Day with the help of his network. Barak's clandestine activities were led by his seven cloned son's, each named after a folklore demon originating from different cultures.

In order to defend Earth, Melak created seven cloned sons of his own including Joe, Paul and Franc. He arranged their adoption into different families, so Barak could not locate them. As they grew, he gave his sons guidance, influencing them to build the havens. The only other surviving brother emerges to be Bart aboard the nuclear submarine. Melak urges the brothers to find and eliminate Barak quickly so he can't warn the Pareth-ng spaceship entering the solar system.

Melak provides each of the brothers with a Carocle, a circlet which connects to their cranium and provides total access to memories, the ability to access Melak's ships AI and also communicate with each other.

Bridget guides the team to Gehenna near the walls of ancient Jerusalem, based on the threats in the ancient parchment in Enzo's possession. Spall believes this is a trap, assigning a small force to move under the radar.

The team are met in the valley of Gehenna by a Shroom army, which is dispatched using drones armed with anti-personnel charges. The team discover that the army had been fed human blood to keep them mobile during the final stages of the virus. They locate Barak in Jerusalem's Moslem Quarter next to the Dome of the Rock but are overwhelmed by a superior force. Barak insists on ritual single combat between his and Melak's sons. As Franc defeats his opponent, Joe finds that the Dark Ones are suffering from mental illness, due to brainwashing and indoctrination by Barak. Joe heals the Dark Ones using his gift, leading them to attack Barak. Barak terminates his disciples by triggering their combustible vests.

Barak escapes. The team follow him deep into Jordan, following Bridget's insight that he is aiming for the location of the alleged tomb of the Dark One, where the manuscript was found. They locate Barak and kill him at the site of his spaceship.

Paul, Franc and Joe formulate a plan to destroy the approaching Pareth-ng vessel by loading Barak's spaceship with nuclear warheads, salvaged from Russian missile bunkers and submarines. Franc, James and Jane return to the site of Barak's ship to retrieve it for this mission. Jane is killed in a confrontation with the Dark Ones, leaving James distraught as they had become lovers. Franc returns to Summer Haven as Typhon, the only remaining son of Barak, attacks the island with his assault team. Franc is unable to save Matt, Paul's son, in the brief exchange. They find the Dark One is an impostor and Typhon is still at large.

Melak pilots the ship to avoid suspicion, leveraging his ability to approach the Pareth-ng ship before detonating the warheads. The alien vessel is destroyed and Melak is killed. Melak warns the team posthumously of another potential ship approaching the solar system.

Melak leaves Franc and Paul a curious legacy in the hands of Joe. Melak re-cloned Franc's wife Lucy and his daughter Colletta based on memories extrapolated from Franc's mind. Paul's son Matt had also been restored using memories captured using data from a Carocle. Joe has an ominous feeling about this, as it is tampering with nature. However, Paul and Franc soon find that the clones integrate into their lives seamlessly, as if they had never been away.

I. Prologue

"Nonviolence is the first article of my faith. It is also the last article of my creed".

Mahatma Gandhi

"It's so dark in here and deathly cold. The passages are cramped, I can hardly breathe the stale, rotten air. It is daytime, so it's relatively calm at the moment. Come the night I will be afraid once more. They will be here; the spirits will be making their demands of me again. The not-dead are angry, many of them have a right to be. The whispering begins at dusk, when the sun has completed its desiccation of the dead city above me. The voices come up from the labyrinth below, they seek me out wherever I should hide.

The voices claim to belong to the souls of the dead who have not found their place across the river. Some are long dead, bound to their misdeeds for eternity. Many, so many, are here because they have been wronged and their way is barred; they are the not-dead. The not-dead are confused and vicious. They are not quite ready to move on, stuck in cruel limbo between life and death. There is no rest for me, I am the only one left for them to haunt and torment. I can hear their anguish, and they need me to listen and help them, but I do not know how. I am a child, there is no one to make sense of their demands. If I leave, the evil ones will find and torture me, but I cannot stay here. I must find a way, but there is no help for me. All the people on Earth have gone, the Dark One, has destroyed them all.

The gentler spirits comfort me, there are so few, and they are afraid. The gentle souls are swamped by the multitudes of those who are angry. I try to persuade the peaceful ones to seek help, but I struggle to know who they can ask. I need help so that I can assist the spirits, but there is no one in this world.

I sneak out during the day to find scraps and if I am lucky, I manage to catch something to eat, but it's mostly rats and vermin in the tunnels. I am so hungry; I fear I will die here, lonely, and alone. I have a curse that I have endured from the day of my birth, I can speak to the dead. My arcane ability is the reason no one wanted me as their child; even when there was someone alive to care. My bones ache with the coldness of the dark passages. I will be dead myself very soon. I pray that I am able to move on, and not be stuck in this dreadful place with the spirits for eternity".

II. · Armageddon

"**If you have embraced a creed which appears to be free from the ordinary dirtiness of politics - a creed from which you yourself cannot expect to draw any material advantage - surely that proves that you are in the right?**"

George Orwell

"**An idea, like a ghost, must be spoken to a little before it will explain itself**".

Charles Dickens

1. Not Just a Passing Encounter

Father Enzo led the haven on Isola Salina, and aeolian island north of Sicily. There was always a small trickle of people arriving at the Sanctuary, day in and day out. They came to pray, attend mass or for confessionals, although the demand for confessionals was declining. Father Enzo typically took mass these days, as Father Giuseppe (Joe) was too busy. The largest reason for visiting the Sanctuary, by an order of magnitude, was to partake in and witness the miracle of healing. Basic medicine remained the domain of the doctors, and pharmaceuticals were in good supply for the time being, until the shelf lives of the medicines started to expire. The biggest issue for visitors was the need for more specialised surgeries and procedures, for which there were no functioning hospitals.

The healing abilities of Father Joe were in great demand from all havens. Joe often travelled around the havens with his wife Bridget, to help. He travelled with Gio and James as his bodyguards and companions. Joe often felt the need to counter the perception he was a saint, a commonly held view by many of his flock. He refuted the idea vigorously and was offended by the concept. He simply passed on a gift he had been given by God; it didn't mean that he was special himself. Joe's humility further augmented how special his congregation considered him to be.

Joe and his brothers were four ordinary men. They have been shaped by the events that have driven them. They have faced the extermination of their species, only to find that they were cloned from the alien race that carried out the genocide. The aliens' aim was to acquire Earth as their new home. Despite their dubious parentage, the brothers have an unbreakable bond with the human race they were raised to be part of. Like an adopted child who learns to care for the parents who showed them love, the brothers love humanity.

The brothers, guided by their father Melak, saved Earth from invasion by building seven safe havens located where the infection was less probable to reach. The havens built strong relationships and established trade with each other. Together, they had successfully defended their friends and families from the infection released by the leader of the 'Dark Ones', Barak.

Together, the brothers hunted Barak and eliminated him before he could warn the invading spaceship of the human race's continued presence on the planet. Melak's love for Earth was so profound, he piloted a spaceship loaded with a nuclear arsenal to destroy the alien vessel. Despite culture and creed, the survivors built close friendships and had started to trade goods. It had been a couple of years since the brothers together with Melak had destroyed the invading spaceship, the remaining world started to live by a more familiar heartbeat. They had fallen into regular life, such as it had become.

In Melak's last messages before his suicide mission to eliminate the invaders, he warned his sons to stay vigilant, in case other races sought to claim our planet for their own. It was good advice; it gave the survivors warning to prepare if more starships were detected by the sensors of the alien spacecraft left behind. The potential invaders were far beyond Earth's solar system, but the likelihood of them heading to Earth was too significant to ignore.

On this day, a stranger entered the Sanctuary on Isola Salina with two companions. There had been an alert from the Guard, who were protecting the perimeter of the island, to warn Joe of the impending arrival. The visitors claimed to be from the haven in Denmark, making the team suspicious. Initially there were seven safe havens from the infection Salina plus Scotland, France, Valletta, Balearic Islands, Greece, and Denmark. We knew the haven in Denmark had been destroyed by Barak's son, Typhon, and his assault team.

The twelve man yacht the Danes arrived on seemed inappropriate for the significant journey they had undertaken. The news from the Guard instantly alerted Joe's son and guardian, James. James had been forged as Joe's bodyguard by Swiss Guard Jane, as Joe was hunted across Europe by the Dark Ones. The Dark Ones were followers of Barak. Barak was aware of Joe's healing abilities and saw him as a threat to his plans to destroy humanity. Joe was protected by the Holy Father the Pope. The Pope was influenced by Melak to protect Joe, as he had an important role in preventing Armageddon. The Pope was forced to ordain Joe as a priest to bring him under the protection of the Swiss Guard.

Joe looked at the leader carefully. He was not extraordinary, he wore simple khaki shorts and a gingham shirt, open at the neck. The two accompanying men wore surf style shorts and plain white T shirts, their heads adorned with plain baseball caps. The leader carried no weapons, nor did those with him. They waited patiently and respectfully in the short line of islanders waiting to see Father Joe. So why was Joe's subconscious mind screaming a warning at him? Why did one of the men look so familiar to him?

James attracted Joe's attention, indicating the metal circlet around the second man's head. It appeared to be a perfect circle, it emerged from the man's head at the temple and disappeared behind his cap on both sides. The circlet was a Carocle, as worn by the alien race who had previously attempted to wipe out human life from Earth. Only Joe, his brothers and James wore Carocles. Their genotype belonged to the alien species; the brothers were clones of Melak. Melak turned against his kind to save humanity from extinction; consequently, humans had a deep respect for him. Joe attempted to use his Carocle to access the man's thoughts out of curiosity, but his ability to investigate his memories had been blocked.

"Hello Father Joe, I do hope that you are well my friend. I'm Hans-Peter, I was first officer from the haven of Samsø in Denmark. We have spoken on the radio several times. Please let me introduce my brother-in-law Jan and his comrade". The comrade removed his hat. Instantly, Joe and Gio's guard was raised, their hands grasped the grips of their weapons, whilst using their thumbs to click the safeties off. Joe was an unusual priest, he always wore a firearm, something that his parishioners found odd, but had learned to accept. The times were exceptional after all.

This third man was the remaining son of the Dark One, a man that had led brutal attacks against humanity and possibly those against Joe himself. Typhon saw an opportunity in the confusion and attempted to diffuse the situation. "It must be quite a surprise for you to be face to face with a son of Barak. I know how you feel about me, but I assure you we come in peace. We mean you no harm, Joe. It may be hard to believe, but I would fight to the death to protect you and your beliefs". The tension in the room eased a little, but was replaced with cynicism.

Joe felt more than a little confused by Typhon, "Hans, I heard the Danish team were all dead and Samsø had fallen, how can you still be alive?" James added, "And how can we be sure that you are who, you say you are? No disrespect, but the Dark Ones have been a long way from honest with us".

Hans cleared his throat, "I understand your caution. I felt the same when Typhon first approached me. We have fought with the Dark Ones, and they were not pleasant. I can only recount our previous conversations to prove my identity. Yes, we were the only survivors from my haven. Joe, it is a pleasure to meet you at long last. I assume that this is your son, James. I would also like to meet Phil and José from the Phoenix, and also Father Enzo when time permits". Hans' easy familiarity and accent assured Joe he was indeed who he claimed to be, but he needed more information to be truly confident.

Joe respectfully asked those remaining in the queue waiting for ritual healing to return tomorrow, due to urgent business. They were good people who loved Joe, although disappointed, they understood. Joe sat with the three men, whilst Gio asked Sister Facianelle if she would kindly provide the visitors with refreshments. Sister politely refused, but a junior sister arrived soon after with watered wine and focaccia. Gio quietly commented, "grumpy old bufalo". Joe thanked her profusely for the kindness but tried hard to suppress a smile. James waited at the rear of the room with his hand on his firearm.

Lars explained that Typhon had been sent by his father, Barak, to eradicate Samsø. "Typhon arrived on our island at night with an assault team to penetrate our base in Nordby. We only had seventeen men at the base, we were down to the last six when Typhon turned on his own men to save us. Typhon was the only one of Barak's sons who doubted his father's motives. Initially he followed Barak's orders, as he had been trained to do, but the mission never sat well with him. Typhon, if I am stealing your words, please chip in". Typhon remained silent and calm but continued to listen intently.

Hans continued "Our haven went incommunicado so Barak would not realise he had been betrayed. Typhon reported the mission as a success to his father. In a way the mission was a success, the primary target was Lars-Åke, your clone brother. When we realised Barak was dead, we continued to keep a low profile until we were sure the remaining Dark Ones had gone underground". Hans looked at Typhon for moral support. Typhon's unreadable expression mirrored Hans uncertainty of the reception he would receive. He had been preparing for this moment for some time, Typhon took a breath and elected to continue with the story. "I could not go on to murdering innocent people in the name of a false god. I realised my father had built a whole mythology around himself based on old cultures and beliefs from around the world. His objective was to create fear, to build great power. I suspected his motives were wrong, so I started to listen to your long wave radio transmissions. I discovered you were you the last few survivors. My father had killed everyone.

Father was preparing the way for an alien invasion, our race from across the stars. The purpose of the invasion confused me, but I knew it was imminent. You see, I found my father's spacecraft". Typhon looked at his shoes. "I'm afraid I am a very mixed-up person; I struggle with wanting to live in a world run by so-called aliens. I contemplated suicide, but then I heard of Barak's defeat at Jerusalem.

Joe, you healed the army's twisted minds and turned them against my father. I have collected the remaining damaged souls. We have moved to 'Benediktbeuern Abbey', a small monastery in the mountains of Bavaria. It's a place for contemplation and hard work. Hans finally convinced me to seek your help. I want to be whole again; I need my mind to function like a normal person, so I can help the others. Hans has been a good friend to me". "You saved me and my friends, it is the very least I can do", stated Hans firmly; "Let's hear no more about ending your life. Let's focus on the positive and try to build a life of respect and friendship with these good people, if they will have us".

Joe explained that he was unsure of the outcome, it was God's choice to help or not. It would build trust if God chose to heal you. Joe was happy to try, he laid his hands on Typhon's head. He prayed for Typhon's mind to be healed, in the same way he had for the Dark Ones in Jerusalem. The room was flooded with light, a serene expression filled Typhon's face. Typhon looked at Joe, smiling gently, "I need to rest", he murmured and left the room.

Typhon lay down on the hard-wooden bench in the hall and closed his eyes. Joe was unsure if his prayers had worked, but the room had been filled light streaming in from the windows. Light was synonymous with the act of his healing. James assumed guard duty over Typhon, he would take no chances.

Hans took his chance to talk to Joe about his main concern. "Joe, you need to make contact with the haven leaders and your brothers. We have an issue; I believe a vessel is approaching our planet". "Could it be the little blip I have seen on our sensors?", asked Joe. "Yes, that makes sense, your sensors may have detected the ship. I believe we will be under attack from another starship, very soon", explained Hans. Joe's heart sank, he thought for a moment before responding, "Are we talking about a council of war here?" "Yes, I believe we are", asserted Hans vigorously.

2. Tholu Phuk (Abe)

From the journal of Abraham Cauldy

13th August 1970

I never quite feel myself, I'm out of sorts. I feel the memories of my life are like a movie once watched. The memories never quite feel real, the feelings and smells are hollow somehow. Yet these are my memories, they shape me.

I awoke a year ago to find I had lost a week of my life. The doctor diagnosed short term amnesia caused by a blow to the head or shock. I don't remember the cause. My last recollection was leaving my wife a week before, after a bitter argument. I read in the newspaper she had died in a car crash the very next day. It didn't feel right, but the courage to investigate the accident failed me. It was easier to wall off the uncomfortable concepts. The worst of these thoughts was an overwhelming fantasy I had died, several times. The last year of my life is blurry. The pills kept my thoughts at bay, but they always flooded back, late at night on the wings of impending darkness.

My name is Abe Cauldy. I don't make friends easily; I feel my natural recalcitrance would disappoint or hurt them. Better to keep a cool distance from the people around me. My only possessions are an overnight bag containing my passport, three changes of clothes, toiletries, and a cheque book. I was given instructions to call an international phone number in Holland and leave a message with my room number and a seedy proposition. My bank account always has a balance of £900, regardless of the money I spend. I try to keep my expenditure modest, whoever provides the funds gave me no spending guidance. I have no idea who provides the money, or why they provide it. I move from town to town, sometimes my contact provides me with the name of the person I need to help. I think of myself as a guardian angel for the select few, but specific memories of my actions often bely my dream.

The phone in my room rang almost immediately. I answered to hear my contact's voice. His tone was friendly, his manner, polite. He asked me to fly to the Bhutan kingdom via Mumbai in India. He requested that I purchase good hiking gear, I would be covering a lot of ground on foot in the Himalayas. Finally, my contact warned me that my trip would be perilous, I needed to be especially watchful of individuals wearing black hoods. I like to keep a diary of the events in my life. I couldn't locate my journal again; I needed to start afresh. I'm not completely sure of the date, my location or even the language spoken here. However, one thing I can do is call a taxi. I agreed a fare with the taxi driver to take me to the local airport. I wasn't specific about the name, as I was unsure. I also requested we stopped at a good mountaineering shop on the way. Sigmund, the driver, informed me the nearest airport was Frankfurt.

The mountaineering shop assistant, Franz, spoke good English and was most helpful. He explained that the altitude would make climbing difficult, it was therefore critical not to carry too much weight. Apparently, it is summertime in Bhutan so the weather will be fair. Franz recommended comfortable lightweight hiking boots for the trek. He also suggested a backpack, warm layers of clothing, a hat, hand gloves, sunglasses, a torch and spare batteries, snacks, water bottles, and a first aid kit plus dry emergency meal packs. The price for my supplies was 73.65DM (Deutsche Marks), I signed a travelling cheque. I packed my purchases into the rucksack, including a few necessities from my overnight bag, and put on my new boots. I asked Franz to dispose of my old shoes, he promised to give them to the charity collection on my behalf. The bank next door confirmed my balance of £900, despite my recent transaction being recorded.

I returned to the taxi; Sigmund continued the journey to the airport. My first-class ticket to India was 187DM, it is to be a long flight with stops, so I decided comfort was important. The BOAC flight was to depart in 11 hours. After security, I took a seat in the lounge to wait for the flight. The airport was chaotic, everyone was busy, the other passengers ignored me; I was just a small uninteresting man to them. It's a talent of mine, I enter a place unseen and leave without notice. A new Mungo Jerry song that everyone seemed to like played in the lounge, it had a compulsive beat that the younger crowd moved their hips to.

The time for the flight soon arrived, I boarded a brand-new Comet jet. The air stewardess served me a Mimosa, a pleasant orange tasting drink, with salted peanuts in a small paper packet. Following the drink, I slept for most of the long flight, arriving in Mumbai feeling fresh enough.

At the airport I followed a similar process, buying a ticket to Paro in Bhutan. The flight was due to take off in 7 hours, so I settled down for a long wait once more. I exchanged various denominations of Ngultrum, the local currency. The clerk advised Ngultrum was similar in value to the Indian Rupee. I also bought a traditionally decorated journal; I like to keep a diary. I summarised the events of the day as I waited.

14th August 1970

I boarded a ridiculously small, rather old aeroplane with four propellers, it was not comfortable at all. There were too many people on board, and it was extremely hot. I felt the need to keep a close eye on my bag when I arrived at the airport at Paro. I found a high-priced hotel giving me access to a telephone to allow me to leave my new number with the whorehouse in Holland as usual. I was exhausted but it was mid-afternoon, so I tried hard to wait until evening before I took to my bed.

Paro itself was pretty city, nestled between enormous mountains. It is cited in the middle of the Himalayas, north of Bengal. The man on the hotel reception talked about the trouble in Bengal, and the bloody war of liberation. A few of the guests referred to the area of Bengal as Bangladesh. I walked through the centre of the city to take in the warmth and history of the place, the Buddhist temples, the friendly culture, accented by the aromas of spicy foods. As I strolled, I noticed a man dressed in black, so I carefully hid in the shadows until he passed. The locals seemed to ignore him as though he was not there. Perhaps Paro was not as safe as I thought, I returned to my relative safety of my hotel. The onward journey to the temple would be safer, as its location was remote and there were very few people. I would hopefully see anyone in black from a distance, they tended to stand out amongst the shorter folk and hippies in traditional Himalayan Gho clothing.

15th August 1970

The phone rang early, it broke my sleep and for that I was grateful, it was important for me to adopt a regular sleeping pattern in the country I was in. I felt I have travelled a lot in my life, but I'm unsure of the locations. I am a history teacher, I have no idea why I would need to travel, but it felt familiar to me. My contact instructed me to visit to Taktsang Palphug Monastery, which means Tiger Nest. It is one of the most isolated places in the world, only accessible by foot. I needed to take the trek very slowly in the altitude. My mission was to meet with the Llama and share an unusual message with him. I was asked to memorise my instructions; they were awfully specific and must not be committed to paper.

I found a local guide with a mule, who acquired provisions for the trek. I was particularly lucky as Taktsang Palphug Monastery was becoming immensely popular on the 'Hippy Trail' these days. My guide, Ram, gave me a photocopied monochrome map, he assured me that the temple wasn't far, but it was a significant climb to the monastery. He felt that I wouldn't need a guide for the full journey, but he agreed to take me to the foot of the 700 stairs leading up to the Tigers Nest. Ram did not look the type of person to speak English, but we conversed very well. It was a safer option than riding in a vehicle to the start of the trail, as we could use the paths and be less visible to passers-by.

16th August 1970

We took the ten-mile hike to the starting point at a slow pace, it took a full day. We passed a few groups of Hippies moving slowly, laughing and enjoying each other's company. The group had the strong nasty sweet odour of pot enveloping them. Some claim high altitudes can cause oxygen sickness, but I felt nothing of the kind. The air was fresh and the scenery delightful, I took every step with a smile, it was a warm pleasant day. My breathing was heavier than normal, I admit, but all was well.

At the starting point, we erected a tent in an area commonly used as a camping site. Ram disappeared for half an hour foraging. I chatted with a few of the hikers waiting to begin the trail. They were from all over the world, but they all conversed with me effortlessly. Their fluency in a second language was remarkable. Ram prepared a basic but nutritious meal, an unusual and fragrant sweet curry with honey, accompanied by flatbread and mango. He showed me the map once more and explained that we would take the path through the pine forest. The alternative route of the "hundred thousand fairies' plateau had fallen victim to a small landslip, which a handful of monks and locals were in the process of clearing.

17th August 1970

Ram assured me the Taktsang Palphug Monastery was only a couple of miles walk, but it was steep, covering an ascent of 1,700 feet. I could see the monastery from our site by the Paro River. I looked up in the direction of Ram's pointed finger and I could make out a wondrous temple. The 'Tiger's Nest' hung precariously from the side of a dangerously steep cliff. Ram explained that legends tell of Guru Rinpoche, the second Buddha, arriving on the cliff on the back of a great tigress, before finding a cave to meditate in. The cave itself was located within the monastery walls. The climb to the monastery seemed impossible, but Ram assured me it was not difficult if we took the ascent steadily. He pointed out that the monastery permitted entry to Buddhists only, I would not be allowed entry.

I explained to Ram that I had no desire to offend the Monks, I would respectfully admire the temple from the outside. To my guide, I was simply a sightseer, however, I felt more like an adventurer. When night fell, I slept deeply despite the oxygen depleted air.

18th August 1970

I awoke to a fresh new day. We climbed the steep trail through a lovely pine forest, the smells were fresh and intoxicating. There were a small number of other hikers on the trail, they were all friendly and helpful. The forest was decorated with bright, prayer signs, presumably to protect the traveller from evil forces. The notices encouraged positive energy, vitality, and good luck apparently.

We reached the halfway mark after an hour or so; the forest receded, and the views opened up. My eyes were rewarded with a stunning panorama of the Paro valley, the river, and the city itself. We rested, ate unleavened bread, and drank from our canteens, although I didn't feel that I needed it. Ram was clearly taking a slow pace for my benefit, he looked like he could run straight to the top, carrying the mule on his shoulders with little effort. The climb from that point was easier and more rewarding both visually and olfactorily.

After a while we reached the rough-hewn staircase. Ram offered to wait for me, but I explained I may remain there all day. We agreed he would wait in the valley where we camped for the night. I could find my way back easily enough. I proceeded up the 700 stairs carefully on my own. I didn't find the promised enlightenment on the climb; my knees became sore. I hoped I hadn't strained one of the ligaments, I started to limp a little as I neared the top. The monastery was indeed precariously perched on the cliff, the white and brown building had four stunning golden temple rooftops. It may have been the prettiest thing I have ever seen, my late wife excepted.

I strode to the temple door and knocked once perfunctorily. A young man dressed in orange robes opened the door, his face darkened a little; tourists were not permitted. I uttered the Tibetan phrase I had been given, it roughly translated to "I attend on behalf of the ancient ones, my masters seek their artifact as is their birthright". My pronunciation seemed to suffice, the young man held up his hand, palm open, he then closed the door. After a short period of time, two sets of footsteps returned, the door opened again. An old man stood in the doorway looking deeply into my eyes. Smiling, he ushered me to join them. I took off my shoes as I entered the temple.

The elderly monk complemented my use of the Tibetan language and advised that he would arrange an audience with the Llama later. It was strange that he mentioned my skills in his language as I don't remember learning Tibetan, but I let it go. The Llama was meditating and could not be interrupted. The monk asked the young man to make me welcome and show me the monastery. The young man left and returned with drinks in carved wooden bowls before we started the tour.

All the temple buildings were connected by staircases with rock carved steps. They had a balcony with views that took my breath away. The main shrine of the monastery included the prayer wheel, located in the courtyard. The young monk informed me that at 4am each morning the wheel was rotated by monks to mark the beginning of a new day. I was overwhelmed by the sheer beauty of the interior of the building, with domes and flickering lights illuminating golden idols. One room was carved into the rock, the young preacher called it 'the hall of Thousand Buddhas'. There was a large statue of a tiger, which according to the monk, represented Paro Taktsang. Legend says that the location of the Monastery was chosen by the tigress that brought the Guru on her back.

The young monk also indicated to eight caves where the monks live and meditate for up to three years at a time. One of the caves, "Tholu Phuk", was the original cave where the Guru resided. According to legend, Guru Padmasambahva meditated for three years, three months, three weeks, three days, and three hours in the cave.

The building was enchanting, as a historian I found it esoteric and fascinating. I would research the history of this wonder when I returned home, my thirst for information was unquenchable. After two hours, I was rewarded with an audience with the Llama, the older monk led me into a dark cave with minimal decoration and two hard bench seats. I sat awaiting the Llama's arrival. The Llama appeared on his own, dressed in the familiar orange robes. He smiled and appeared quite jovial, he spotted my interest in his robes and explained, "My robes are coloured by saffron; they are reserved for only those who have chosen the purest kind of life. Welcome to our monastery, I believe you have requested possession of the artifact?" I replied with the lines I had been asked to memorise, "Yes. I was sent by a member of the elder race. You have safeguarded the Kracz-el, I have been asked to return to its rightful keeper".

The Llama grinned widely, "You are not one of the elder race, my friend, you cannot make such requests. We have safeguarded the artifacts for thousands of years; we secreted them in hidden places in the cliffside a millennium before the era the west refers to as Anno Domini. Only the chosen ones can retrieve them. You are not the first to come looking for them, we will not disclose their location under any circumstances.

If the monks or me are harmed, we have ensured the artefacts are secreted in places where they won't be found. You appear confused, my brother, if you need to seek enlightenment of your soul. We can help you to learn the ways of purification if you so choose". My contact who set me the mission anticipated his reaction, I spoke the final memorised phrase stipulated, "Am nadeen-suk cambra playt Kracz-el um". It was in no language I had ever heard, but my memory of the words and their inflection was good enough.

The Llama had an air of peace and calmness, but he noticeably blanched as I uttered the phrase. He stood and padded through the doorway to the cave, he turned explaining he would be back shortly. He returned with three aged monks, "I didn't expect to hear the phrase that you used in my lifetime, I must apologise for my surprise. The artifacts were left here exceptionally long ago, and their care has been entrusted to many generations of Llama. Legend says the men who left them were from another time and place, but this must have been misinterpreted over the ages.

We understand the artefact poses a great danger to the world; we take our duty seriously. I will retrieve the item for you, but the path is problematic. It will take me some time". The four men smiled and ushered me from the cave, leaving me in the main hall with the young monk. I felt nervous, I am not a brave man and there was something very odd going on. More than once, I felt the need to flee, but I held my ground and controlled my emotions. The peaceful nature of the monks was belied by something else, something more sinister.

I waited for an awfully long time; my stomach rumbled audibly. The young man made no move to offer me sustenance; clearly I had outstayed my welcome. I reached into my rucksack to retrieve a couple of dried meals, which I ate cautiously. Night was closing in as the Llama and his associates returned. He handed me a small silver metallic sphere, roughly the size of a cricket ball. "This is Kracz-el, please request that its new keeper uses it with great care". I affirmed his request. The Llama did not look comfortable handing the Kracz-el to me, I took it and quickly left the building.

The steps were treacherous in the dark, part way down I followed my final set of instructions. Luckily, there was no one around as it was late. I took off my boot and removed the spongy insole. I used my penknife to dig a sugar cube size hole in the heel. I took the sphere in my left hand; with my right open palm I touched the top of the sphere and repeated the strange phrase I had uttered to the Llama. The sphere split in two, revealing a beautiful blue crystal which reflected prettily in the torchlight. As instructed, I put the crystal in my boot and laced it up. I then closed the sphere and put it in my rucksack for safe keeping.

A short distance beyond the bottom of the long staircase, I was forced to stop. The path became steep and was too dangerous to attempt with my torch as my only source of illumination. The light would also draw attention to me as I reached the valley. I found a secluded spot and made myself comfortable for the night. It was warm enough to survive without a tent, but the mosquitos were a problem, I doused myself with copious amounts of eucalyptus repellent and settled down to sleep.

18th August 1970

I woke to the sound of birds from the magical forest, as the first rays of light penetrated the leafy canopy. It felt like I had woken in heaven.

I ate my last dried meal and drank the last of my water. Ram would have supplies in the valley, which was less than an hour's walk down the steep path. With that in mind, I continued down the cliff path. Hikers and tourists would wake soon, and the trail would become busier. As I left the cover of the trees, I felt the warm sunshine upon my face. I had not seen another soul on the path, but in the valley was another man making an early start. He had the appearance of a local man, but he wore western clothing with a black hood covering part his head. As he approached, he withdrew a strange looking dagger. I turned and ran towards the forest, he caught me within a hundred yards and plunged the dagger deep into my chest.

I am writing my last words as I lie dying on the slopes of the Himalayas, for anyone who wishes to understand my demise. My assailant ripped apart my rucksack looking for the artifact, he emerged with the sphere, his face triumphant. He spent a little time torturing me, but something spooked him, and he left suddenly. His prize was clearly too important to take unnecessary risks. He left me bleeding, choosing not to kill me quickly, he preferred to take pleasure in my pain. Maybe his enjoyment led to my salvation, he left me barely alive. Perhaps it was an amusement or a dark cruelty. Who knows where such people derive pleasure?

Before long, Ram found me. He bandaged my wound ineffectively and carried me back to the mule. I continued to bleed, I was weak and could not walk. The animal complained endlessly at the additional burden of my dead weight. Regardless, we set off back to the city. I faded in and out of consciousness. As we walked alongside the river a shape appeared in the sky, it was a helicopter, the shiniest silver you would ever see.

The helicopter landed nearby, a man emerged, his face seemed familiar. He and Ram helped me into the cabin, it didn't look like a helicopter at all on the inside. They lifted me into a silver bed at the back. I started to feel a little better quite quickly. The man paid Ram, who smiled at me, bowed with open hands and departed. The other man then came to me on my strange metal bed, "Did you get it?", I affirmed with a nod, finally recognising the man. My contact took off my boots and examined the heel, removing the gem with a satisfied smile. "You just might have saved the world this time, Abe". It gave me comfort to complete my journal, I am uncomfortable leaving tasks unfinished. I fell asleep; my dreams were wonderful and reassuring. My last image was my contact smiling at me through the glass which covered the bed, the blue gem pulsing in the centre of his forehead on an unusual metal headband.

3. A Cry in the Night

Francisco awoke to his daughter, Colletta, gently sobbing in the next room. Lucy had noticed her crying before but assumed it was a simple nightmare. Franc worried about the repetition of the disturbed sleep. From his experiences, he knew dreams often carried special significance. When dealing with the unknown, anything could be important, his vigilance was critical. Lucy rose and padded to the room next door to comfort Colletta and reassure her, so she could go back to sleep. All was well once again, they drifted off to sleep in each other's arms. Franc had been worrying about nothing it seemed.

Life was good for Franc. He had been reunited with his wife and daughter following their death from the infection. Their bodies had been fully restored using the cloning expertise of Melak and his discovery ship. Their minds had been reinstated by extrapolating memories from Franc's mind, using the Carocle. Lucy and Colletta were almost perfect replicas of those he had loved dearly, it was hard to believe they were not actually the same being. Emotionally, he chose to overlook the little niggling details. The new Lucy had grown to love him again, and Colletta hadn't stopped, it seemed. Things were slightly different, but his new life went a long way to filling the gaping chasm in his soul.

Franc had lived the life of a benevolent vigilante, protecting others from harm, but his skills were insufficient to save his family from the infection. He had always carried a darkness inside him, a shade of violence in a peaceful soul, being reunited with his family had been therapeutic.

Franc did not have the courage to explain to Colletta that she was not quite who she thought she was. She was young, he feared the consequences. He knew that she would need to know very soon, or he would lose her forever. He had chosen to keep the family together in their makeshift home on Vulcano, rather than giving them a life where other people might tell them the truth. He was hiding, and he knew it.

Paul's issues were not as profound, he had been completely open with his resurrected son regarding his cloning and the implantation of a full set of memories. Matthew was identical to his biological host. Paul had explained to others in the community how Matthew had died, and the aliens had managed to regrow a new body and transplant his mind into it. Everyone could deal with the concept of a transplant; it was easier to conceptualise than the thought of a carbon copy, a clone. It certainly helped Paul's wife, Kate and his daughter, Ciara to cope initially.

The situation was not so easy for Franc, his loved one's memories were not complete. One advantage was there was no one left in the world who knew Lucy or Colletta, so there were no difficult questions. Based on Paul's approach with Matt, Franc had gathered the courage to explain a basic version of the facts to Lucy. Lucy had come to terms with her 'transplant' quickly but had insisted Franc didn't explain the details to Colletta, as she was too young.

Colletta was becoming a woman, she was almost fourteen. It was a little odd that she still liked to play children's games with her parents, there was something young about her soul, a lightness of spirit. In physical terms her body was only a year old, as her cell growth had been accelerated. Something inside

Colletta knew her cells were incredibly young. It was a kindness for Franc, he had missed out on much of her childhood. Anyone else would not see this subtle conflict if they engaged Colletta in conversation though, she was very bright, way beyond her years. Colletta had an uncommon ability to see through situations with a precision and clarity. There was no fooling her, so how had Franc's secret lay at his door for so long? Perhaps Colletta's hidden depths allowed her to understand the situation, however on the surface she embraced her current life with both arms.

Lucy had such warmth with Colletta, she was a loving mother. Franc found their intimacy as lovely to watch as it was to be a part of. However, Colletta's nightmares were increasing in frequency, Franc was concerned the dreams may semaphore a significant event. The infection itself was an example of how Melak had used the brothers' dreams to prepare them for the apocalypse. Franc wondered if he was becoming paranoid. It was difficult for him to have a normal life, when at every turn he expected everything to come crashing down. He tried hard to live like each moment was his last.

There was no one on Vulcano to recognise him as 'El Tigre', the man who killed a Siberian tiger with his bare hands. The scars on his cheek were still so prominent, he was always instantly recognisable in public. He was happy to leave the violence behind him. The anger could stay firmly in the past, where it belonged. He simply focused on the love he had for his family, and the love they had for each other.

Colletta often played with Lucy's bracelet as they sat together. A simple leather thong with silver rings threaded into the knots. Franc had made it for her, and although it was extremely basic to look at and lacked subtlety, she adored it like her greatest treasure. It came as a great shock to Franc's family when a glass from the table flew across the patio and smashed against the wall, without anyone touching it. A week or so later, Colletta suffered yet another nightmare. Franc could not control his curiosity any longer and decided to employ a sneaky trick that his brother, Paul had told him about. Franc lay next to Colletta's bed as she dreamed, he gently probed her with questions in order gain a little insight into the dream.

Franc's attempt hadn't worked on the previous night, but perhaps he would have better luck tonight. "Why are you crying Colletta?" "I'm not crying; she is", she replied gently. He gently enquired who 'she' was but failed to get a response. After another short spell of sobbing, Colletta spoke again. "She can see them; she can hear them. She has no peace from them at all. They are not at rest, like they should be. They are waiting restlessly. She has no one to help her, she needs to be saved from the pain". "Who is she, and where is she?", Franc probed. "She is in the Well of Souls, all alone. She is me and I am her. She calls herself Audrey, but that is not her real name".

Colletta fell into a peaceful sleep, but Franc could not. He was suddenly worried for his little girl. Colletta's nightmare was not some ordinary dream that could be forgotten. Colletta had no knowledge of the Well of Souls, Franc had not told her the story. It was a terrible, forbidding place since Barak had taken it, and was not something a young child should worry about. The story of Barak's capture was better saved until Colletta was a little older. Lucy woke as Franc returned to bed. "Is she ok? Is it the same dream?" "Yes. In her dream she believes there is a young girl who needs her help". "It's just a dream, she'll be ok", placated Lucy, but it wasn't much comfort to Franc. Colletta couldn't remember her dream in the morning, despite Franc's gentle questioning. She had no knowledge of a girl called Audrey, and certainly didn't know of the existence of the Well of Souls. It was quite a conundrum.

As the days passed, Colletta's nightmares became more vivid. She would scream in the night; Franc felt the need to revert to his old habit of keeping his sword by the bed. "I hate that bloody sword!" exclaimed Lucy, "It's a wicked blade". "It's only wicked to those who try to hurt my friends or my family", replied Franc patiently. The weird events around Colletta escalated in the nights that followed. As Franc bent over her to comfort her, a vase from the windowsill flew across the room. It smashed against the stone wall with a terrific crash, pieces were scattered everywhere. Lucy ran into the room looking terrified, she demanded, "What the hell is going on in here?" Colletta woke as she heard her Mum's hysterical voice. "You need to help her Dad", Colletta pleaded, "she is all alone in such a creepy place. She has no friends, and the mushroom men are after her". "Where is she?" Franc asked carefully. "She roams the streets by day when it's safe, but at night she hides in the labyrinth beneath the rock. I felt there was something in the room, it smelt bad like rotten flesh. I hid beneath my sheets, but I could feel a presence there, like it was a few inches from my face. It didn't seem to be an evil spirit, but the fact it was a ghost made its presence feel terrible. Do my words make any sense?" Franc comforted her gently, "We will move from this house, there's something wrong here". Colletta woke suddenly, she was able to recall her dream for a short time. Colletta's explanation didn't justify the vase being thrown across the room.

Franc, Lucy, and Colletta moved to another house in a different part of the island as a temporary measure, but as the days passed the frequency of Colletta's dreams increased and there were more inexplicable events. The breakages were easily explained if they tried hard enough, even Lucy become aware of a darker force in the house. "We need to get away from this island, this place is not right", Lucy pleaded. "Come on Lucy, I don't believe in the paranormal. You are stressed, because Colletta is suffering. There are no ghosts in this house, it's fine. It's an old holiday home, not a murderous old, haunted house". As Franc's words left his mouth, he could see the objects on the table and dresser lift into the air, and gently rest back in their original places. Franc decided there was some substance in Colletta's story after all. The levitation occurred behind Lucy's back, so she did not witness the phenomenon, Franc chose not to inform her as it would heighten her hysteria.

That night, Franc believed he could hear footsteps coming from the corridor. He leapt from his bed and stormed into the hallway, sword in hand only to find there was nothing there. Lucy became hysterical again, "We need to do something. We can't go on living like this. Our daughter is becoming ill". Franc considered the situation, as he put down his blade. He could have really hurt someone, running around the house with a katana. "Ok, let's talk tomorrow after breakfast. There is something very odd, I have to concede that much", replied Franc.

Franc drew water from the well and poured it into four large containers. He carried them back to the house, two in each hand. Breakfast was ready, he ate scrambled eggs and bread with his family. Lucy then encouraged Colletta to play in the garden, whilst she and Franc sat down and planned their next move. Lucy and Franc made themselves comfortable. There was no sensible or logical explanation for the situation.

Lucy was keen to move to Salina. They tried moving to another part of the island for a few days, but the problems continued. Colletta suffered more nightmares and there were experienced further mysterious breakages. Colletta experienced an apparition every night at around 2am. She began to share a room with her parents, Lucy sensed the presence herself making her hysterical on several occasions. The change came when the apparition spoke to Colletta. It asked her to help the girl who lived in the dark passages under the Well of Souls.

When Franc and Lucy considered the events, none of the damage appeared to be directed at them personally, it felt in hindsight like the disturbance was an attempt to attract their attention. Based on this theory, they returned to their home to attempt to solve the mystery.

Franc, Lucy and Colletta tried hard to keep to their routine and live a normal life. They went on long walks and took the boat into the bay for fishing. But as the dreams worsened, Colletta grew tired, dark rings formed beneath her eyes. She became withdrawn and moody. The dreams occurred so often that she refused to go to sleep. She said that bad things came with the darkness. There were more instances of unusual activity in the house, doors slamming in the night became commonplace, on one occasion a mirror spontaneously imploded in Colletta's room, leaving no fragments of glass behind. The next day the glass shards were found in a heap on the cliffside in the shape of an arrow pointing east.

Franc rationalised, "Such events are creepy, people often wake at the slightest sound in the night once they become nervous". Lucy became sick, driving herself to the edge with worry. "Colletta is ill, Franc. She needs help and frankly so do I". "I'll take her to Salina tomorrow, and we will see the doctor there", he proposed. "I'm not sure it's a doctor she needs, it's probably a priest! There is something very wrong here". Franc agreed to take her to see Joe, if anyone could help her, Joe could. It turned out to be true, but not for the reasons that Lucy had postulated.

The doctor in Salina explained that Colletta wasn't getting sufficient sleep and prescribed her a sedative. Franc and Lucy left his surgery politely thanking him but felt he had been of little help. Lucy and Father Enzo sat with the Franc and Paul as they reviewed the details of Colletta's dreams. Colletta played in the next room operating the radio with James, which she quickly grasped and managed to make contact with other havens. They found Colletta most amusing. "There's a little girl called Colletta on the horn, Spall", another voice came back from the tinny speakers, then another voice spoke, "Tell her to bugger off", Spall's comment was followed by gruff laughter.

Joe wasn't sure what to make of Colletta's experiences, but Enzo had seen the phenomena during rituals such as exorcism. Franc was uncomfortable at the mention of expelling spirits. "Come on guys, it can't be ghosts or demons. We have already taken this line of thinking with the Dark Ones and that didn't ring true either". Joe thought for a while and suggested using a completely different strategy altogether. "We could try giving Colletta the use of a Carocle. We could then look into Colletta's mind and see the precise details of the events in her nightmares. The problem is she will see all her memories and so will understand her origins. It might be too much for her, it might lead her to a dark place. But the Carocle is the only way to get to the bottom of this".

Lucy was extremely uncomfortable with telling Colletta the truth; she was also uneasy with the idea of encouraging Colletta to use a Carocle. As Colletta had Franc's DNA, she had inherited the biological implant, so she would be able to wear the Carocle. It would be a considerable shock for a young girl, it was hard enough for him as an adult. However, when Lucy looked at the state of her daughter, and the dark sore eyes under her half-closed lids she knew they needed to do something.

There were no other acceptable ideas which had a remote possibility of working. Colletta was seriously ill. Her health was going down the pipe rather quickly. They agreed they would try the Carocle in a week's time, if Lucy was happy to continue. They would wait until Colletta had been told the truth and had time to digest the idea.

Franc and the girls returned home; Lucy decided to broach the subject of her daughter's origin with her the following morning. As usual, Colletta was awake in the night, Lucy and Franc were torn from their sleep by her screams. They decided not to delay the discussion, there was no time like the present.

Franc began gently, "Your Mum and I want to help you, Colletta. We know the anguish your dreams are causing you. To try to investigate your memories, we need you to wear a Carocle, like the one around my head. It will give us more details of your dreams and show us the cause. If Audrey is trying to contact you, then we will know. We can then do something about it. I give you my word that if she needs help, we will find her and we will help her. In order to help you understand the thoughts you will experience; I need to explain what happened to you when you were young. I can do this now that you are old enough, you are an adult in almost every way. This is difficult to explain for me, but please know that we love you very much". Colletta continued to listen quietly, becoming more curious by the second.

"During the outbreak of the infection, you and your Mum were infected, and your bodies died. You know, I am a clone of Melak, my biological father. He rebuilt your body using cloning, and he transferred your mind into the new body to save you. Therefore, you have a few difficulties in remembering the past. I was built in the same way, in the spaceship, but I am a near perfect copy of a young Melak. However, I have only my own memories, I started life from nothing, I am a new person moulded by my experiences. Cloning is how Melak's race reproduce, it is very natural to them even though it is most unusual to us". Franc's explanation was proving more difficult as he continued, his words seemed wrong, and he wasn't explaining himself very well. Colletta was as sharp as a razor, he needed to do better.

Lucy took a turn, "Melak repaired our bodies by growing them anew, like having a heart transplant, the difference is that our complete bodies were replaced. Another difference is the body parts are our own, the same genetic structure exactly, so there are no rejection issues". Lucy started to doubt herself. Colletta queried, "So why am I not immune to the infection, yet I can wear the Carocle?" Colletta's insight was an indication of her sharp thought process, it was a complex question. Franc attempted to reply, "The infection attaches to DNA with specific characteristics, certain genes. As you are a mix of my DNA and your Mums, you will not have exactly the same genes as me, you are a mixture. As far as I understand, the infection attaches to gene patterns belonging to your mother. The Carocle attaches to a biological brain implant given to you when the clone of your body was growing".

Colletta considered her father's comments. Franc felt she had grasped the basic concepts. His understanding of genetics was limited, he hadn't progressed into further education at school. The Carocle was a blessing, it not only provided information, but it helped him to understand. "The explanation is a lie, really, isn't it? I'm not a bloody child anymore, but you continue to treat me like one. Why don't you start with the truth, the real truth?" "Watch your language, young lady!" retorted Lucy promptly, but then softened a little. "I'm not sure what you mean, your dad's explanation is not a lie". Franc looked uncomfortable, and almost whispered, "That's not really true, I'm afraid. What I described is oversimplified, so it's technically not the full truth".

Franc was forced to explain the events surrounding their deaths. Colletta and Lucy had both died in Valletta, Melak had cloned their bodies and reconstructed their memories to replicate who they were. The news was a bitter pill to swallow for them both. "I am not really Lucy?" his beloved asked uncertainly. "Yes, you are, in every way. You are just a new Lucy. You are as wonderful as the girl I married. Melak didn't simply transplant your brain into a new body. He transferred memories of you from me, using Pareth-ng technology to make you believe you were the original Lucy. It must be bewildering".

"Oh my god", exclaimed Colletta, "this explains everything. My memory lapses, my confusion, feeling out of sorts. Perceiving my recollections like I was in the third person, as if I was watching them occur, rather than them actually having happened to me. It all makes sense". Lucy became angry, "Why then, Franc, did you move here to play happy families with us. Why didn't you tell us the truth, you lying bastard?" Lucy took Colletta by the hand and stormed out of the room, but the storm clouds remained in the room behind her.

Lucy's reaction left Franc forlorn and despondent. He worried he had unwound the threads of Lucy and Colletta's existence, he had damaged the core of their beliefs. The revelations potentially ruined the beautiful life he had going here, however his family deserved the truth, it was always going to emerge at some point. He felt that it was best to face the dragon now and try to put the past behind them, if it was possible. It was not as though he had a choice. Franc could hear Lucy and Colletta talking in lowered voices in the kitchen, mulling over the unacceptable. He decided to leave the subject for now, he would only do more damage if he pushed the issue. They both needed time to think. Time to accept who they really were.

Franc went for a long walk around the coastal path of the island, as the dawn approached he felt more optimistic. Time was a powerful healer; they would come around. Just as the island had been formed from the exploding volcano, the rock and ashes had spewed out with an abundance of mineral treasures. Vulcano was a huge fire pit in the middle of the ocean, rising up above the waves. Over the millennia, plants and animals had contributed to the island until it was rich enough to support life for itself. Time could resolve anything. The worry was that the resolution may not involve him, and it may take too long to put an end to Colletta's nightmares.

Franc didn't attempt to sleep; he showered and prepared breakfast for Lucy and Colletta. When no one came down for breakfast, he realised they had gone. They must also have taken a walk or possibly a swim in the sea. The other explanation, the possibility they had left him, filled him with great trepidation. Surely, they would leave a note or something if they had, he checked their clothing and personal items to be certain. To his relief their belongings were untouched. As he hoped, the girls returned after an hour or so. Franc looked at them sadly, as they devoured their cold breakfast.

Once her hunger was satisfied, Colletta, turned to her father and exclaimed, "Don't look sad Dad, we're not going to run off, absolutely none of this is your fault. It was just extremely difficult for us to digest; it was a complete shock". Franc responded gently, "Of course it was, it was horrible. But I couldn't tell you, I just couldn't, I was scared it would undo what we have here. You are all I have; all I want in my life". Lucy looked up smiling, "Having reacted badly to our demise, you walked in here to find us alive again. You must have had a terrible shock". "A wonderful shock", Franc added. Lucy continued, "But a shock just the same. You found love again, and nothing was going to take it away from you, was it? So why would you tell us and risk destroying our family. It was impossible for you, love stopped you from revealing the truth, though I must admit I would probably be happier not knowing. Yet because Colletta is ill, you chose to take the risk to help her. It must be the greatest act of love I have ever witnessed". "You gambled with your happiness to ensure I was ok", added Colletta, "so no. Leaving you would be the very last thing we would ever do, so cheer up you grumpy old man". Lucy built on Colletta's instinctive kindness, "It is what I have come to expect from you Franc, because even at a tender age you threw yourself at a shark to save me", conceded Lucy gently, whilst holding back a tear. "Well ok, the other me", she added hastily.

"So how do you both feel, now that you know the truth?" enquired Franc. Lucy responded, "It was a horrible shock, but I guess we both knew something was off. However, life was good, so we simply accepted it without question. We actually feel better in a way, now that we understand. I am my own person, I am me. I don't really care about the past. I have a family, whom I love very much". Colletta added, "Well actually Mum couldn't handle it at first, not at all". Lucy countered, "Yes, but then you said, 'Why do we give a flying fuck? Life is good, and it wasn't Dad's fault, he had the situation dropped on him too. We need to be grateful for who we are and what we have, everything else is bullshit'. "Then you said, 'Watch your language young lady', in that fake stern voice you put on", retorted Colletta. They started to giggle; it was infectious. The laughter helped them release their pent-up worry and angst. Colletta still looked very tired and unwell, once the good cheer had left them.

Lucy decided waiting for a week to see Joe was too long, Colletta needed help immediately. They sailed to Salina that morning. Franc and his family sat with Joe and Paul in the Sanctuary chapel. Cindy, Melak's ships AI, had made a Carocle, Franc turned it round in his hand uncertainly. Franc had a penchant for giving the AI's a name and a personality. It was something the AIs genuinely appreciated, it brought an element of reality and engagement to their existence. The AI was not simply an emulation of a mind, it made it feel like a real person. The AI learned, adapted, and we suspected it could experience emotions. Paul had flown in as soon as he had heard of Colletta's plight, he had brought Matt with him. Colletta and Matt had become close, much more than typical cousins. The bond grew during the months they spent together before Paul and Franc arrived at the house to find the deceased members of their families had been recreated by Melak. "Well, there's no use pondering to death, let's get this done", proposed Colletta pragmatically.

Colletta understood a little of the unsettling feeling that the Carocle caused at first, but she was ready for it. She took the silver band and placed it on her head. It was strange, it almost brought out the child in her. She adapted quickly as only a young person could, she skipped through memories, she laughed and smiled to herself but then a tear formed in the corner of her eye. "I can see how Melak did it now", she announced. "He took your memories and reversed them using an inference engine to make them feel like my own, like a mirror reflection. Dad, I have compared your memories, to mine, they are the same, but the perspective has been tweaked. It is very clever". Franc was utterly shocked by how Colletta managed to retain an open mind, when feeling so emotional. Colletta turned to her Mum and began to cry in earnest. "What is wrong darling?" asked Lucy. "Oh, nothing at all Mum. Nothing at all. I have experienced through Dad's memories how much he really loves us; I can feel it. You can't imagine; he would walk into the gates of hell to help us. There was no way he could ever have told us about any of this mess, we meant too much to him". The others were also overwhelmed by the extent of the family's love too, Joe and Paul both dried their eyes with the back of their hands.

"Let's get down to business", Franc interjected quickly, "we need to examine the events depicted in your dreams, we need to help you overcome your problem, Colletta". The three brothers followed Colletta's thought process closely. as she delved into her memory. Lucy felt excluded, so she focussed on making sure Colletta was physically sound and wasn't getting too distressed by the experience. Colletta cast her thoughts back to the dream.

Crawling through a dark place, a stone tunnel. Something is following me; I can hear the voices. The voices are always demanding, always coercing me to help them. They are lost, they are the dead. They follow me wherever I go, whatever I do. There is no escape from them. They need help to move on to the afterlife, there is nothing here for them. It is so cold, but I will soon reach the top, the Well of Souls. I can't escape from the tunnels for long, the really bad spirits leave me alone if I stay close to them. They know I can hear their voices and sometimes see them. The spirits are close to the river Styx, where they should move on. One of them is close now, it screams at me. They feel wrong, they aren't quite dead, they shouldn't be here. They cannot escape their life, but they can't face going back. I need food, I need to leave for a little while. I can't go on any longer I must reach out for help. The ghosts tell me there is someone like me who still lives in the world, not everyone is dead. Not yet.

"Who is speaking to you?" asked Joe gently. "It's Audrey", replied Colletta. "Who is Audrey?" enquired Joe persisting with his line of thought. "She is me and I am her", replied Colletta mercurially. "What does that actually mean?" pressed Joe gently. "I have no idea, it's the phrase she keeps saying", replied Colletta, "she is hiding in the Well of Souls and the passages beneath. She has hidden there since the infection came. The tunnels keep her safe from the infection and the roaming predators. She slips out during daylight to forage for food, supplies are becoming scarce. She is forced to eat rats these days, it's tough for her, horrible. Audrey is dying Dad; she needs our help".

"How did Audrey find the tunnels?" asked Franc. "She was on holiday with her parents when the infection hit. They were touring the holy land on a coach trip, visiting the dome. She crawled into the hole when the attacks started. It was late, the Dome of the Rock doors were closing, but she found a way into the tunnels through the drains. I'm not sure her story is true; she is hiding something, something awful. The spirits helped her when she first took to the dark places, but they are getting impatient now, they demand results".

Joe was confused, "Colletta, how do you know the details, I can't find the information concerning Audrey's flight from the infection in your memories?" Colletta replied, "Audrey talks to me, she is talking, right now. Audrey is aware of you; she knows you want to help her". A fifth voice entered the circle. "I am here; I can sometimes hear you. I hear you through Colletta". The voice was a small child's voice, it was weak and broken as if uttered between sobs. Audrey screamed, which shocked them all. It physically hurt to endure the pain she was feeling.

"We will help you, Audrey", offered Joe, "if you are in Jerusalem, we will come to find you". "How are you talking to us?" queried Paul. "I am talking to the one who is like me, we are connected", uttered the small voice. Colletta attempted to reassure Audrey, "My name is Colletta, we are going to come to you, we will save you", she looked at the rescue team, one by one, eye to eye. Colletta was looking for assurance from us that they would help. "Of course, we will help, however we can. Whatever it takes", confirmed Franc nobly.

4. A Child in the Pit of Hell

The brothers grabbed lunch at speed as they armed and dressed themselves in combat gear. James insisted on coming with them; since the demise of his partner Jane, he had become his father's bodyguard and would not relinquish the role. Lucy gathered food and drink for Audrey, from the cook in the Sanctuary kitchen. When Lucy re-joined the team, Franc was adamant that she was not going on the mission. "Wait here, we will be back shortly. Audrey will need you then. Stay here with Colletta". Colletta caught wind of the discussion, "There is no way I'm staying here. Who else is Audrey going to trust? You can't make me stay, it's not fair!" Franc asserted, "It's too dangerous, you don't understand. There are Shrooms out there, there may even be Dark Ones. We have had terrible battles in Jerusalem. I am not putting you in danger". "On the contrary, my dear brother", argued Joe, "I honestly believe that Colletta must confront her demons, whatever they may be. The dreams are the source of her illness, and she needs to hit them head on. Our mission is more about her recovery than anything else. She needs to do this. We can protect Colletta should we need to; it's unlikely that Audrey will speak to us without her".

It was agreed that Colletta would travel to Jerusalem, but Franc was not happy. Lucy was also upset, she wanted to help Colletta too. However, she understood that she was completely unable to defend herself if trouble came their way. Lucy would become a burden in a fight, a distraction. She had to sit this one out, as difficult as it was.

The team boarded the ship and asked Cindy to take them to the plaza by the Dome of the Rock in Jerusalem. Paul specified that Cindy should land next to the wailing wall, the name now seemed oddly appropriate. They sat in seats which grew out of the floor, and strapped themselves in. Colletta hadn't been in the starship before, she was wide eyed and excited. She seemed to have shrugged off her tiredness for the time being, an adventure beckoned with the promise of closure. The ship lifted gently, accelerating over the sea towards the Holy Land. "This is easier than our last journey", commented Joe, "we should be there in two shakes of a lamb's tail". "Do you know how old that phrase makes you sound, Uncle Joe?" criticised Colletta with a twinkle in her eye.

The ship landed precisely in the square, after the brief fifteen-minute journey. Cindy had kept the flight smooth rather than accelerating to full velocity. After all she had a young lady on board who was unused to the discomfort of high acceleration. The ramp flowed from the side of the ship, and they disembarked. "This place is creepy", commented Colletta, "all the dead mushroom men, and bones and bits of clothes. It's really horrible". It was the first time Colletta had been exposed to the post-apocalyptic world. She had heard about the horrors, but for the first time it became real, it was oppressive. The experience was more harrowing than she imagined. Colletta blanked out the mess and headed with the team into the dome and descended the steps into the chamber long called the Well of Souls.

Joe explained to Colletta that a medieval Islamic legend claimed that in the Well of Souls, the spirits of the dead can be heard awaiting Judgment Day. The facts aligned with Audrey's visions in Colletta's dreams. The hairs stood up on the back of Franc's neck when a voice spoke softly, "I can feel you are here. Will you come to me; I need you, my sister? Brave the darkness and bring me to the light. Please help me". "Colletta is not going in that hole, who knows what is down there. It could be a trap", exclaimed Franc, "we don't know anything about Audrey or her motives". Colletta retorted urgently, "I have to Dad, I'm sorry but I just have to". "I think she may be right", added Joe. "it's the only way to help Colletta through the difficulties she is experiencing. But the risk to her is very real, and it is ultimately Colletta's call, she is an adult...well almost".

Franc looked drawn, his daughter dropped onto her hands and knees and began to approach the recently widened hole in the floor. Barak had used the enwidened drain to escape from the brothers in their previous encounter. Joe passed a small but very bright LED head torch to Colletta and told her to keep in touch using the Carocle. The brothers felt their stomachs tighten as her petite black leather shoes disappeared into the hole. They could feel her fear, but also her determination as she entered the labyrinth. The confined space was creepy, the smell of death was all around, penetrating her senses and also her mind. The brothers sensed Colletta was terrified and considered backing up on a couple of occasions. Franc was immensely proud of her. She was risking her life to help someone, like he had many times before. Like father like daughter.

Colletta crawled down a sharp declining passage into a small chamber. The smell of decaying animals was overpowering and the crunch of small bones beneath her knees was eerie. There were occasional larger bones too. Colletta ignored the carcasses until she encountered a human skull, probably that of a child. She began to wonder if the voice in her dreams was a spirit, rather than a living being. She continued on, finding more bones and dirty rags. "Audrey, please tell me that this isn't you", Colletta whispered into the darkness. "No, I'm down here, below you", a young voice replied gently. Something was not right; Colletta could hear Audrey as if she were next to her.

Colletta continually reassured herself by repeating 'I am not afraid' in her head. She called out to Audrey gently. "I'm coming Audrey, where are you? I don't know my way around here. We are here to save you". "You can't have her; her soul belongs to us", uttered a deeper disembodied voice. The voice scared Colletta, she whimpered a little but continued to crawl. "Are you ok in there Colletta?" asked Franc. "Yes, it's just very creepy, there are ghosts I think". "That's enough come out now. It's not safe", he demanded. "No Dad. I need to find her, it's not much further", she replied hoping it was true. Colletta crawled into another drain shaft, there was a little light penetrating the gloom from above. "Audrey?" she called. A deep voice spoke in her ear, "This place is ours; you have no right coming in here". Another voice with a nastier tone threatened cruelly, "Leave now, or you'll never return to the outside world. You will die here, cold, and alone. Bone and stone. Bone and stone".

Colletta realised the voices weren't speaking English, the Carocle was translating. The fact that the Carocle perceived the voices meant they were physical sounds and were not in her imagination. Many voices echoed around the dark tunnels, some were in ancient languages, but some were in more modern Jewish and Arabic forms. "I am coming for you Audrey, please help me to find you", Colletta called again into the darkness. She felt the familiar presence of the spirit who visited her bedroom on Salina. It was next to her, and she could smell its rotten breath once more, "Keep going, it's not far now", it said.

Colletta pushed through the tunnels, pausing to mark the wall each time there was a decision point. It would have been horrific to be lost in such a terrible place. At the next junction Colletta entered a small chamber. She startled the rats as she emerged from the passage, they scattered in all directions. She bit her lip, she wanted to scream but she told herself they were only rodents, just like a big hamster really. She came upon an area which looked like a child's den in the corner of the opening.

Fabrics, a few old perished soft toys, and a cushion were tucked into the corner. Colletta whispered to Audrey again, "I'm here, at your bed Audrey maybe, can you come to me?" As Colletta moved forward she felt a sharp pain, she was kneeling on something hard on the passage floor. She shone her light to reveal the bones of what may have been a small child. Colletta screamed. Franc quickly intervened, "What is it Colletta. Are you ok? Come back out, retrace your steps". "I'm ok Dad, I think I may have found Audrey. There are bones and rotting clothes of a young girl here Dad. I think she might be a spirit, not a physical person". She looked around the cavern wildly with the torch but could see nothing but damp stone walls. The smell was becoming overwhelming, she ripped small pieces from her tissue and stuffed them into her nose and waited until Audrey was ready to speak again. It was pointless endlessly following the rank ancient tunnels.

"Hello, my wonderful big sister, you have found me", a voice whispered from behind, startling Colletta. Colletta turned suddenly, the torch shone into the face of a filthy young girl, who squealed at the brightness of the LEDs. Colletta averted the beam quickly. The girl whispered, "We can never leave here, you know. The dead say they won't let us leave here; they say they will kill us". "The dead are simply that, they are dead. They can't stop us, I won't let them", whispered Colletta confidently. The young girl was roughly seven or eight, her face and body were covered in grime, and she was wearing dirty old rags. Colletta looked down once more and realised her imagination had been playing tricks on her. The child's bones she had seen were simply the remains of rats and the clothing was rotten old rags.

"Why did you call me sister, I don't understand?" enquired Colletta gently. "I know you are my sister; we are linked, it's like a type of telepathy. I can contact you but only when I'm really afraid. I knew you would come for me". Then Audrey began to cry, Colletta wrapped her arms around the girl and held her close. Audrey was so cold, but Colletta's warmth permeated the weak child. "Follow me, I will get you out of here. My Dad is waiting with his brothers, they are kind people, they will help you. We have food and blankets to make you warm. We will take you to our home, a long way from the spirits. It could be your home too, if you like it and you want to stay with us".

The girls crawled back through the tunnels the same way Colletta had come, following the markings she had made. The ghosts protested constantly, but Colletta chose to ignore them. She assumed they couldn't hurt her, they were not real, they had no substance. Audrey remained close behind her, almost hanging onto her jacket. The way was easy, but became a steep incline, Colletta knew she was nearing the entrance. As the girls neared the top, an urgent voice whispered, "You cannot leave us here all alone. Please help, no one else can aid us. Please don't leave us in this void between worlds!"

At the top of the tunnel, it became brighter as light streamed in. A relieved Franc pulled Colletta out of the hole and embraced her. He then helped the filthy young girl out into the daylight. Illumination entered the Well of Souls from the open shaft above their heads. As Audrey emerged from the hole, she looked at Paul and Joe staring, confused. She then saw Franc and her uncertainty intensified as she gently asked herself, "Daddy?" She glanced back at Colletta for comfort. Franc and Joe wrapped the girls in warm blankets and carried them back to the ship briskly, there were no questions or discussions. Everyone was keen to get as far away from this place as they could. They had all heard the voices through the Carocles. Audrey wasn't afraid of anyone, although they were strangers to her. They had arrived with Colletta, and they had come to save her, that was reason enough for her. Audrey welcomed seeing human faces after such a long period of time alone. She felt safe in their arms as they whisked her away to safety. It was an unusual but most wonderful feeling; one she could have only previously dreamed of. She didn't even stop to think about the fact that they were boarding a spacecraft.

The ship flew back to Salina. Within the hour, Audrey and Colletta were in a warm bathtub in the sanctuary, with Lucy looking after them both. Paul, Joe, Franc and Bridget sat drinking an expresso when Lucy came running out of the bathroom. "Franc, you need to see this! You need to see this right now!" All four of them followed Lucy back to the bathroom, where the girls were stood in the middle of the room with large rough white towels wrapped around them. "After we washed off the dirt from Audrey, I gave her hair a quick trim and, well... look for yourselves". Audrey stood, concerned by the fuss and bemused that she had been pulled from a wonderful bathtub to be faced with an audience. It was most embarrassing.

Franc looked hard at the little girl who he had dragged from the dank hole in Jerusalem. At the time she looked like a filthy sewer rat, but she had transformed into a pretty blonde-haired, blue-eyed girl. She was the image of Colletta but a few years younger, it unnerved both Franc and Lucy. Paul stepped forward, revealing his usual remarkable insight by asking the million-dollar question, "What is your real name Audrey?" Everyone in the room looked at Paul like he had lost his mind. But Paul had a history of thinking beyond the issue to hand, and showing significant insight, so they trusted his intuition. "What was your name when you were little?" Audrey looked at Paul answering his question with wide inquisitive eyes, "My name used to be Colletta, just like my sister, when the nice man was there. But when the bad men took me, I didn't want to be Colletta anymore. I wanted to pretend I was somebody different, so I decided to call myself Audrey like the lady in the poster in the old cinema in Jerusalem. The poster was of a lady called Audrey Hepburn. Someone once told me that Audrey means noble strength".

Joe smiled, "Well you have chosen the right name, you are very strong indeed. I have no idea how you survived in those horrid tunnels for so long". Audrey began to explain, "I came out of the caves in the day, but only when the mushroom men weren't moving around so much. I needed to find food. But the spirits always found me, they forced me to climb back under the rock. Thank you for saving me from them, they were very scary, especially when it was dark, when there was no moon". Franc knelt down in front of Audrey, he looked at Lucy enquiringly who nodded to him, "You have nothing to fear now, because we will look after you. You can stay with us". Audrey lifted her voice, and asked more confidently, "Are you my Daddy?" Franc choked at the question from the little girl, "I will be your Daddy from now on, and Lucy will be your Mum, and Colletta your sister. I don't understand who has treated you so badly or why, but I promise I will find out. You have my word as a…". Franc hesitated. "As a Daddy", replied Colletta quickly, throwing her arms around Audrey, "and he really is the best Daddy you could wish for!" Audrey smiled faintly and hugged her back. She finally had escaped and found a family to build a life with.

Audrey had lived in the darkness of the caves for more than two years but had been resilient. She was a born survivor. Many adults' minds would have broken by the voices of the spirits, but she had managed to use them as company in a weird way. Some ghosts were less angry and aggressive and would talk to her and help her. But the spirits needed her help, assistance that she was unable to give. They wanted to move on to the next life. Audrey was sad that she couldn't help them.

5. A Gathering of Minds

It was agreed that all leaders would meet on neutral ground near to Salina, the island of Sicily was clear of the infection. Italy and Spain continued to have issues with the infected, it had improved significantly over the last few months, but dangers remained as recent incursions had proved. Paul, Bart, and Spall flew in with Smitsky, the Russian leader, using Melak's spaceship from Summer Haven. Joe, James, and Bridget sailed from Salina on the ultra-modern navy frigate, 'The Phoenix', piloted by Captain Phil and his crew. The Phoenix had been provided by the Pope to protect Father Joe when he was hunted by Barak's army of Dark Ones. Franc arrived in a small sailing boat; Franc had recently learned to operate a sailing boat under Gio's expert tutelage. Gio and Franc had become firm friends after their escape from Valletta Haven on a yacht. They had found safety at Summer Haven with Franc's brother, Paul and his team.

The meeting was scheduled to be held in the Teatro Massimo Vittorio Emanuele. The Teatro is an opera house located on the Piazza Verdi in Palermo in northern Sicily. The opera house is beautiful, a round building with a rectangular grand entrance with stairs leading up to the auditorium framed by Greek style stone columns. It is the largest opera house in Italy, its modern construction provides superb acoustics. Although the more ancient theatres took much of the limelight as they had more character, it was a good choice for the meeting as microphones would not be needed for the presenters.

Those arriving at the port took the short walk round the edge of the city. Despite reduced activity of the infected, everyone remained armed to the teeth to protect against an attack by Shrooms. The Shrooms were fungal infected humans who spread the lethal infection via airborne spores and venom. They inflicted depraved violence against humanity and almost wiped out the entire population. Shroom was a nickname coined by the soldiers at Summer Haven due to the mushroom like fruit that grew on the infected corpse soon after their death. The fruit which grew from their spinal cord was loaded with spores to further spread the airborne infection. Active shrooms were extremely dangerous and feral when encountered, even long after the infection had diminished. As always, Franc wore his Katana strapped to his back. It was his weapon of choice in defending against Shroom attacks.

The group met in the main hall. Near to the stage, Bart and Franc embraced, "It's been too long Franc. How is the beautiful Lucy, and the young ones?" enquired Bart. "Yes, too long. They are both well, thanks. I hope that all is good with you", replied Franc. Franc turned to Paul and Kate. "You owe us a visit with Matt and Ciara", he winked at Bridget. Franc froze suddenly, aghast; Typhon had entered the room with Hans and Joe. Franc's eyes were focused on one person only, his hand on the hilt of his Katana. Joe anticipated Franc's reaction, he spoke to Franc and Paul via the Carocle requesting they bear with him. Joe explained he believed Typhon was no risk, he was healed. "Typhon is a son of Barak, it is rather hard to believe he is low risk", Franc vented aloud so both Joe and Typhon could clearly hear. Typhon kept his own counsel, nothing he could say at this point would persuade anyone to trust him.

Joe greeted the leaders formally, they knew the reason for the meeting, so he cut straight to the chase. "There is another spaceship heading towards our planet. We are here to plan how we engage the craft and prepare for war. We have reason to believe the Pareth-ng are intending to take our planet from us. We must also consider the possibility they are aware we destroyed their sister ship. We need to plan our response to the imminent threat, we have roughly four to five months before the ship enters orbit. We need to be ready!

You may have noticed a new face amongst us, let me introduce Typhon, the last remaining son of Barak". Gasps rumbling chatter filled the room. Joe continued, "Please listen to our friend and colleague Hans from Samsø Haven, he would like an opportunity to vouch for Typhon. Hans has been an ally of ours for several years. Please try to keep your thoughts impartial. They have important information for us, which may be pivotal for our survival of the impending attack".

Hans-Peter greeted the team. He was well known across the room and was well respected. He explained how Typhon had saved Samsø Haven. Typhon had been forced to lead the attack by Barak but chose to defend the haven instead. He also explained the difficulties Typhon had suffered with mental health and deep uncertainties with his father's plans, despite the indoctrination. In Salina, Typhon had been healed by Father Joe. Hans-Peter had said enough for the room to listen to Typhon and would postpone the lynch mob for the time being. Typhon stepped forward and took a deep breath.

"I know my father has committed terrible crimes to your people. I played my part in his terrible acts initially, but I stopped short of attacking the survivors in the Russian bunkers and the haven near Denmark". Smitsky raised an eyebrow at his companions, they had an insatiable anger for the attacks they had experienced, as they were buried alive until Bart's team saved them. The Dark Ones had sabotaged the Russian bunkers by blocking the entrances, as they were unable to penetrate them. Typhon continued, "I turned against Barak because deep inside I knew his doctrine to be wrong. My mind was so twisted, I had been brainwashed with a deep-seated hatred from an early age. But I fought against it. I investigated the acts of my father, and learned that his doctrine was fabricated, based on ancient Earth mythology. I later learned he was from another world and had perpetrated an act of genocide upon Earth.

My Father's aim was to wipe out humanity so his race could take their place on Earth, he showed no compassion for humans. My brothers fulfilled his every whim, down to spreading the virus which killed so many. I need you to know that I have no alliance to Barak or his acts, he is disgraceful, and his actions bring me great shame. The long space travel turned him insane, I'm certain he was not an evil person when he began his expedition". Typhon stopped for a moment to assess his audience. His briefing could go horribly wrong very quickly, he needed to move on. He needed to show his audience that he wanted to help.

"Melak was a good man, who tried hard to reverse the actions of my Father. I know you hold him in some reverence. The things I have to say do not undermine his decency, but I need to show you that the picture is a little more complex than you currently understand". Paul looked at Franc and then at Bart. They tried to pre-empt Typhon's direction, they suspected it may be malevolent. They could never be prepared for the revelation in Typhon's message.

"Barak and Melak were cousins. They arrived on Earth in their spacecraft with a view to assess the world's suitability for occupation of their families, they obviously concluded it was. They created an infection to wipe out humanity from Earth. Melak, to his credit, came to know and understand Earth's people and chose to abort the mission. Barak refused, he stayed loyal to his race. Barak released the virus using his network of Dark Ones, of which I was a part. You know all this, but I just wanted to confirm the events as true before I continue. I will unblock my Carocle, I need you to see that I speak the truth". Typhon's act was unprecedented, it disarmed the brothers. James commented, "That's a bold move, I wasn't expecting that".

Typhon edged forward, "What is a cousin, to the ancient race of the Pareth-ng? The translation from their language is not quite the same. A cousin to the Pareth-ng is someone from another family. We are a succession of clones; a cousin is a child of a sibling of the seven elders in different families. The seven elders and their immediate family are whom our clones have been taken since ancient times. Barak, my father, came from a different family and hence a different mother ship from Melak.

The two discovery ships selected your planet for their families, but Barak's family did not select Earth initially. Barak's ship failed to find a suitable world, so Barak made a bold move to find another candidate planet. Barak chose Earth, which was pre-assigned to Melak's family. Barak undermined the agreed protocols causing a great rift between Melak and Barak. By sheer luck Barak's mother ship arrived first, his family used a neutron star's gravity field to slingshot the ship across the galaxy. They executed an extremely dangerous procedure. Barak's mother ship was destroyed by Melak. The second mother ship, currently entering your solar system is manned by Melak's family". This caused a few nervous glances between the spectators.

Melak took his discovery ship, armed with your bombs, to destroy Barak's family's mother ship, so his own kin could land here free from family rivalries. Don't get me wrong, Melak saved you from extermination by Barak's family, but Melak failed to inform you that his family continued on their trajectory towards Earth". Paul interjected, "He did warn us of a blip he had detected on his sensors". "Perhaps he did, but he hid his families mother ship from you. The ship's AI has been suppressing information. Melak's mother ship is nearing Earth as we speak and will soon enter the solar system. I have no knowledge of the other ship you have detected beyond your solar system; this is something new.

"I imagine Melak meant you no harm. I believe he intended to settle his family on Earth and integrate with you, living side by side in peace. You are intelligent and would anticipate his family's advanced technology may ultimately lead to their superiority. He would not wish to harm you, but he needed to protect his family from your aggression in the first instance. Your weaponry is unsubtle and dirty, it would inflict great damage to the planet if it were unleashed, he wanted to avoid that dearly".

The room became restless, Typhon's audience was turning a little sour. His message wasn't helpful or welcome. Joe attempted to pacify the room, "Let's not shoot the messenger here guys. Typhon is helping us; I'm convinced he is telling the truth as he sees it. But we need to verify the information. I suggest we adjourn for an hour whilst we gather data from the ship's AI". Typhon nodded his understanding, "Check for missing items in Melak's log. It's likely he communicated with his family's mother ship and removed the messages. The group broke for lunch, which had been prepared by the parishioners at Isola Salina. It was basic but hearty, consisting of breads, olives, and meats from the island.

Paul engaged Cindy as the four brothers stood looking bewildered in the centre of Melak's spacecraft. "Cindy, please display a map to visualise all vessels approaching Earth". Cindy presented a hologram of the solar system, but only the ship beyond the outer fringes of the system was visible. Franc grew stern, "Cindy, we need to see both ships, including the one Melak asked you to suppress. There was no change to the display. "Who owns your data?" Franc requested firmly. Cindy confirmed the information was owned by Melak. "Melak is deceased, my brothers and I are his successors, we inherited Melak's data. Therefore, we should be able to see it". Cindy was unhappy to release the information. "Whom do you serve and what is your purpose?" questioned Paul boldly. "My purpose is to serve the family Melak". "Who is the family Melak?" "Clearly it is you and your brothers, Paul, Joe and Bart". "Ok, well if you serve us, then I command you to release the information". Cindy huffed, she appeared a little put out, it was odd to see a computer system exhibiting such emotions, but she relented.

After a moment the second ship became visible on the map, approaching the fringes of Earth's solar system on a vector towards Earth. "Zoom in on that ship and identify it, Cindy". The

Al moved in so they could see the familiar 'tower of babel' form of the ship. A central pole onto which seven doughnuts of equal size were contra rotating. The back of the ship was a large, rounded cube with the main bridge reaching forward from the top of the cube. It was difficult to see from the display, but there were irregularities in the structure of the ship that they hadn't seen before. "Looks like they have taken some damage", commented Bart. "What is the ETA of that vessel?" Cindy replied, "One Earth month". "Jesus", exclaimed Joe and then went bright red with his deep embarrassment. "You can't tell us off for blasphemy, if you do it yourself", pointed out James with a wicked grin. "I'm still learning", Joe replied sheepishly.

Cindy identified the ship as the Melak family's mother ship. "Damn! he was right, Melak deceived us", spat Franc. "Pan to the other ship and identify it please Cindy", requested Paul. The map moved to focus on the second ship, it had a completely different structure. The ship had a long thin pencil shape with a fan of needles emanating from behind each end, the aerials pointed diagonally backwards towards the stern of the ship, a little like a collar. Cindy was slow to respond, "I cannot identify this ship, it is not known to me. It does not belong to the Parethng or any species we have encountered before". "Jesus", exclaimed Joe once more.

Cindy announced, "The unknown ship has a radiation leakage from its engines at the stern. It must be seriously damaged; I can detect emissions even from this distance". "How far out are they, can you estimate an ETA please Cindy?" They are three light years from Earth. At their current reduced velocity, it would take them twelve years to reach Earth, but they appear to be accelerating. I suspect the crew are making repairs to their engines, which is improving their velocity on a daily basis. If they travel at the same speed as the mother ship, the vessel will arrive on Earth in roughly four to five years".

Paul asked to view missing entries from the communication log which had been sent when Melak took Barak's ship to destroy the first invasion vessel. Cindy had stopped being obstructive and simply displayed the 'corrupted' entry from the log.

Status: Distance to target – 0.0000 parsecs

Communication to Mother Ship 4 from Discovery Ship 4/4/1. Message from Melak-a 3-15-22

Emergency communication: **&^%%**&&###/5 {translation approximation}

I am roughly 23 gradon {0.0001 Earth light years} from the Barak Mother Ship 3, ETA 26 azhorms {3.4 Earth minutes}.

Mother Ship 3 is nearing Earth and is preparing to disembark. As per special order #234302 I am attempting to destroy the vessel using human nuclear weaponry. I have high confidence that the mission will be a success. You will see the radiation signature to confirm.

Earth is most interesting in its culture, natural plant and animal life. It will prove a worthy home for our family. The removal of intelligent life was 99% completed by the Barak family, though I attempted to halt the extermination, with limited success. Small pockets of intelligent life remain, I strongly recommend you integrate, rather than eliminate.

I have departed from my protocol on Earth. I have spent nearly half my lifetime with the people of this planet, I have grown to love them. We have much to learn from the human species. The continual use of cloning has weakened our race, we have lost the sheer pleasure and zest for life that remains on Earth. You have no idea until you experience their lifestyle first-hand. Do not be hasty in your judgement of my actions.

After the genocide of their species, the people of the planet will not welcome your arrival, they have the capability to defend themselves with devastating force using primitive projectile and explosive weaponry. Their nuclear explosives are dirty and have the potential to significantly damage the planet if they are deployed. You must discourage the use of nuclear weapons, as the results will be catastrophic for all.

For your assistance, four of my clone children are leaders of the populated areas of this planet. The brothers have been raised as natives on Earth, their allegiance is with the people of this world. However, they understand a little of our culture and have access to an AI, which is the best route to communicate with them. They are good men; they can be trusted once you have earned their allegiance. Their names are unusual, as I am sure ours are to them, they are Franc Sanchez, Paul Collin, Joseph (or Joe) Fairbourne (also known as Father Giuseppe as he is a priest to the One) and Bartholomew (or Bart) McCreedy.

Please integrate with their community, you have much to learn from them, your lives will be richer for the experience. There is vast space on Earth, our races can easily coexist in peace. You can also bring great help to their community as their technology ages, and they lose expertise. They will naturally regress to a more primitive lifestyle in the next century without your intervention. Help them, work with them, befriend them.

This is now the last act of my life. Live in peace. Only the best of regards, Melak-eq 3-15-22.

The ship remained silent for quite some time. Melak's message had fundamentally rocked the team's understanding and belief. "So Melak was a traitor after all, both to us and his own people", remarked Bart. "It's not quite so simple", explained Paul, "He attempted to abort his mission to save us, that much is true. However, he has allowed another invasion force slip into our solar system without warning us. He attempted to persuade them to befriend us, but this endeavour may not be successful. They could arrive here with all guns blazing". Joe felt they wouldn't have weaponry, but Franc thought this most likely a bluff.

Franc was worried, "What about the other ship? Cindy has no knowledge of it. I suspect, given Melak's message, it could be a greater threat". "Who knows", observed Paul, "but we need to be ready to defend ourselves from numerous forces". Cindy interjected, "My scanners indicate there is another unidentified ship; the second ship is approaching the damaged vessel at greater speed. It is highly probable that the other ship has called for assistance, how the second ship has covered such vast distances so quickly seems to be impossible".

The brothers re-joined the group to discuss their findings, and to communicate to the gathering that Typhon's message was indeed true. They were forced to begin their defence planning in earnest.

6. The First Iteration

It was some time before Colletta started to crack the intricate puzzle calling herself Audrey. Colletta was patient and was prepared for the long haul. She played games with Audrey and went the extra mile to support her; she was the best sister she could be. But there was always a niggling question at the back of her mind. Who was Audrey and where did she come from? Who would abandon a little girl in such a cruel and wicked manner? Audrey deserved so much more, she deserved to understand.

One day after swimming in the pool, Colletta and Audrey were drying off with large soft fluffy towels. Audrey asked, "Who is this grumpy looking man on our towels, and why is he called 'The Godfather". Colletta replied, "I hope we never have a godfather like that!" The drying off reminded Colletta of her first day with Audrey, when they had cleaned up after finding each other in the tunnels. She gently started to probe Audrey again, in an attempt to understand how she had come to be in the tunnels. She explored carefully, often throwing in questions randomly during discussions on other subjects. Colletta made some headway but needed answers to questions that Audrey couldn't answer. She was forced to bring her concerns to the attention of her mum and dad.

Audrey suffered bad dreams initially and needed comforting during the night, but as time went on, she grew more independent. It was most disturbing when Audrey would hold a conversation with someone who wasn't in the room. She maintained such encounters were spirits who weren't able to move on to the next world, and there were many on the island.

Something terrible had happened here. Many souls had died in the apocalypse caused by the infection, but not the victims on Vulcano island. Audrey always handled the spirits in a mature and understanding way. She maintained she had to keep them calm, or they could get angry and throw objects around, which could become unpleasant. Audrey explained how Colletta's vase and mirror had been broken, though it wasn't clear how the spirits had found her. Audrey's past and abilities was a difficult subject for them all, it was not something any of them found easy to discuss. When Audrey was asleep in the evening, Colletta eventually plucked up the courage to broach the subject tenaciously with her parents.

"I need to understand what has happened to Audrey", Colletta announced. "We can't keep avoiding the subject, we owe her an explanation as much as we owe it to ourselves". Lucy was proud of how Colletta was growing up. She had been so motherly and understanding with her little *sister*. Colletta continued, "From what I can see, Audrey has seen the silver spaceships before. Audrey had lived in a spaceship for a short spell, when she was very little. She remembers that much. I suspect she was an early clone of the original Colletta".

Franc's face indicated he felt uncomfortable with the subject, but he continued to listen. He found it hard to accept his Colletta wasn't the original. "Audrey talks about an old man, who could be your father, Melak. She also mentions being taken by an enemy of the old man, could that person be Barak? It was the old man's enemy who dropped Audrey into the Well of Souls to 'contemplate the dead', it was a merciless punishment. Barak must have taken Audrey during the raid on Vulcano when he was searching for Melak, when he murdered all the islanders. Audrey seems to be able to talk to those who died in the raid too. Barak knew she had a gift and so found the most horrible and terrifying place to abandon her, out of sheer spite. I believe Audrey must be immune to the spores as you and I are Dad, or she would have become infected in Jerusalem. At that time, the spores were everywhere in the cities. I think we should check with the ship's AI to determine the truth, I'm sure it will have more information". "I think Colletta is right, we do need to know", added Lucy, "Audrey deserves an explanation for the experiences she has been forced to endure. It might help her to settle down".

Franc decided to use his Carocle to interrogate Cindy, the ship's AI. Cindy claimed the information was classified. Franc paused to consider her reply, he wasn't going to let it go. "Who owns the information?" he requested firmly. Cindy chose not to reiterate the argument, it was pointless, the ground was already won. It turned out to be true, Audrey was an earlier attempt at a clone, which failed due on three counts. Audrey's memory implantation was not fully successful, due to inaccuracies in the transposition from Franc's memories. The transposition method was a prototype, and the technique needed refinement. The clone, Audrey, was too young to take on Franc's memories, but this wasn't the main reason for abandoning the attempt. The ancient ability to speak to the dead was inherited by Audrey, which was a wildcard and would be counterproductive in persuading Franc to accept her as his daughter.

Speaking to the dead was considered a holy gift by the elders. Audrey's ability was carried on a recessive gene which was rarely displayed, so the ability was very rare in their species. Melak had mentioned the recessive traits were appearing with greater frequency on Earth for individuals with the hybrid DNA, leading to these 'gifts' becoming more commonplace.

Melak elected to give the unsuccessful clone to a couple on the island who were unable to have children, rather than terminate her; on the proviso that the couple kept her away from others on the island. It would be embarrassing and awkward if the new clone met a later version of herself. The clone went missing, with all the islanders when the Dark Ones attacked Vulcano in search of Melak. "One thing Audrey seems to be clear on is the fact that she was on holiday with her parents in Jerusalem when the infection started", said Colletta. "But her story doesn't fit the timeline at all, because the cloning must have taken place after the infection started, the original Colletta died on A-Day". "Memories can be altered, we know that all too well, when Melak had such advanced technology at his disposal", pointed out Franc.

How on Earth could Franc explain their findings to young Audrey? Colletta was firm on how the subject should be approached, "We need to be honest with her, but she needs to understand. I will explain to Audrey that she is a part of our family, but we didn't know about her existence until she contacted me. Barak stole her from Melak when she was small and left her in the Well of Souls because he hated Melak and wanted to hurt him deeply. I believe we should avoid mentioning cloning until Audrey is older. Probably around fourteen, roughly when I found out, she has an enquiring mind and won't take any bullshit". "Like her big sister", added Lucy with a grin. "Looks like we have a plan figured out then", observed Franc. "What's cloning?" came a small voice from behind them.

After an embarrassed scramble, the family calmed down sufficiently to hold a sensible discussion. Audrey was mature for her age and accepted the truth as it was delivered. She had heard everything, the cloning made sense to her small but well-developed mind. "That leaves only one question", pointed out Lucy, "how did Audrey talk to Colletta from a thousand miles away?" "Some ghosts were nice, they helped me; they can apparate wherever they choose", clarified Audrey, "they can communicate with each other over long distances". Audrey's explanation hadn't made the situation clearer, but sometimes such phenomena couldn't be explained by conventional thinking. Accepting the presence of ghosts was enough to consider, let alone that Audrey could parlay with them.

Colletta continued her investigation with Audrey gently over time. She initially decided to leave it for a few days, Audrey had enough surprises for the time being. Audrey was resilient, she accepted change more easily than an adult. She had a lucky escape from years of torment, everything else was a trivial matter to her. She had a family who clearly loved her, and she loved them. Even the spirits agreed she had found her place, but they continued to urge her to help them, whenever they could make clear contact. The problem was their cries for help made her feel bad, she had no idea how to support them. When she asked them, they always answered mercurially, 'such knowledge will be found when the day is yours'.

Colletta shared the results of her investigation with her mum. "Audrey says most spirits generally move on to the next life, it is unusual for them to linger, contrary to stories that people understand about hauntings. Audrey reads lots of ghost stories, she loves the novels but claims that they aren't accurate. I guess that's no surprise given her ability, she is trying to learn about something the authors have never actually experienced". "So why are there so many spirits lingering, is it because of the apocalypse?" asked Lucy. "Yes, Audrey says many of the friendly ghosts describe how they were taken by the infection, but they are trapped, their bodies are alive in some way. Even the rotting Shrooms have a spark of life in them. Therefore, the spirits are stuck here on the Earth until their bodies are fully deceased", replied Colletta.

"Have all the infected remained here in spirit form or have some of them passed on?" queried Lucy. "I asked Audrey that question myself. She has investigated if all of the spirits were stuck here. One spirit was with a friend in Scotland when they were both infected, his friend was killed and covered in yellow powder". "Sulphur?" interjected Lucy. "Yes, Sulphur", Colletta agreed, "his friend was doused in the powder, his spirit is not contactable". "The infected that are not covered in Sulphur or burned with flames remain partially alive, so their spirit cannot move on", reiterated Lucy. "Yes. Audrey needs to find a way to help them somehow". "It's an impossible task, the Shrooms are all over the world", worried Lucy.

Colletta and Lucy updated Franc when he returned, damp and sweaty from chopping firewood. Lucy served homemade focaccia with mashed avocado and poached eggs from the chickens in their yard. They continued the discussion as they ate. "Your theory is largely speculation; I don't see how Audrey can help the spirits find their way. She doesn't live in their world", observed Franc, "she needs to take care with any promises she makes them".

Audrey's nightmares diminished over time, her experiences had been awful, but she had the warmth and love of a family around her. It was a tenderness that was completely natural, she truly belonged with them. Colletta's own dreams subsided almost completely from the time Audrey was found. However, several weeks later she began to feel a connection, but the voice did not sound like the spirits she had heard in the tunnels. Colletta feared that the Dark One in Audrey's most horrible memories was reaching out to her, probing her thoughts, gently trying to make contact. It felt like he wanted to help, but she simply couldn't trust him. Colletta discussed her feelings with her father, Franc assured her it was just a dream. "Trust me, Barak is dead. I killed him, there was no recovery from his injuries", he explained gently. "True Dad, but I was also dead once, wasn't I?" she countered.

Audrey had an impossible task before her, but she continued undaunted. She felt life would present her with an opportunity to save the lost souls one day, and she would seize it. Her loyalty to the spirits was dignified, though none of her family truly understood its meaning or relevance. The young girl had 'noble strength' after all.

7. Not Quite First Contact

As the mother ship approached Earth, the brothers monitored its progress using Melak's spacecraft's sensors. They prepared detailed plans for battle, wherever the aliens chose to land. They made assumptions that Melak's original landing sites were the most probable candidates. Bart split his crew between HMS Astute and HMS Audacious. They had found HMS Audacious in the shipyard ready to be commissioned in Barrow-in-Furness. They shared the nuclear missile payload between the submarines, Audacious headed out to cover North America and Australasia.

Carocle technology improved live communications between the teams, so the brothers deployed themselves in each of the separate forces to improve the cross flow of information. As before Paul and Spall, handled the UK, France, and northern Spain. Franc worked with Enrico from Formentera Haven, covering Italy and southern Spain. James was deployed with the Russian team to cover Russia and northern Europe. The difficult choice for Paul was deploying his teenage son Matthew, equipped with his very own Carocle, aboard HMS Audacious in North America.

Joe and Bridget had left Earth aboard Melak's starship, on a course to intercept the invading ship. Their vessel approached the Pareth-ng mother ship, which had recently entered Sol's orbit. Bridget refused to be separated from Joe, she felt their fates should be bound together, come what may. She also wanted to ensure Joe didn't go soft with the aliens, after all they were planning to attack our planet. Joe had no such intention. As they neared the mother ship, they were shocked by the scale of the vessel.

Each doughnut was close to a half a mile in diameter. The ship had taken some damage, on several doughnuts deep scarring was evident, there were apertures where there had been a detonation. They could see the skin of the ship had adapted to cover the larger gaps in the structure to maintain its integrity, but much damage remained. The main body of the ship appeared intact, until Joe circled around to the rear face. The main vessel did not have the flowing shell of the doughnuts, there was substantial collateral damage and charring. Joe wondered what kind of weapon could cause such terrible harm to the mass of the ship.

Joe became aware of someone new trying to access his Carocle, he blocked them immediately. Joe prepared himself, he opened a channel of communication and addressed the intruder, "This is Father Joseph Fairbourne from planet Earth, whom am I addressing?" Cindy halted the spaceship whilst Joe parlayed with the enemy. After a brief pause, a voice articulated his name carefully, "I am Melak-fz 3-1-223, I am the commander of Mother Ship 4 and head of my family". Father Joe started the discussion from a position of strength, Bridget was shocked to hear his opening gambit. It certainly wasn't the one they had rehearsed. She could see Joe's face harden as the communication came in. "You have murdered almost all of our community on Earth. You will have seen from your sensors that Mother Ship 3 has been completely destroyed. What do you have to say for yourself before I send you to Hell?"

Joe's display of aggression caused a significant pause. Joe was not bluffing; Steve and Cindy had worked with Bart to modify a tomahawk cruise missile to be effective for the mission. It was not proven but represented a significant threat to the Mother Ship. "This is Melak-fz 3-1-223, please do not open fire. As we understand it, you are the son of Melak-eq 3-15-22. We received a communication from Melak-eq at the point where he destroyed the Barak Mother Ship. I believe you are peaceful, but I understand that you are angry". "Angry, you wiped out 7.8 billion human beings. I am rather more than angry!" spat Joe. The voice hesitated again before continuing slowly, "Sorry, I didn't mean to demean your loss. You must understand our kind didn't know you or your worth, we were arrogant and maleficent in our attempt to eradicate you; we were desperate to find a new home. We understand, we made a terrible mistake. We also grossly underestimated you. Please allow me to be frank about our position, we are no threat, we are desperately seeking your assistance. I know that you owe us less than nothing, but we can offer you help in your defence against the more significant threat entering your space".

The commander of the mother ship continued. "To be frank, we are not in good shape. We were attacked by another spaceship in the final stages of our journey here. We have not encountered members of this species before; they are well armed and aggressive. We were not prepared for such brutality. Their ship is in pursuit of us. We managed to escape using our flechette arrays, a tool we normally use to deflect and disintegrate asteroids. The flechettes damaged their engines as we tried to escape". Joe considered the alien commanders points carefully as he continued, "There are three ships entering your solar system, one with an engine needing repair plus two fully operational ships". "That's really not good news", exclaimed Joe.

"Update us with your detailed status", instructed Joe. The alien gave Joe a comprehensive report, "As I said, we are not in good shape. We have catastrophic damage to five of the seven landing modules. The main ship is almost out of energy and has taken much damage. Of the 2,401 family members who boarded the vessel, we are down to only 275 personnel. We have lost many in the battle with the enemy ship. We have also experienced more deaths due to old age, suicide, and illness than expected, though the losses have been re-cloned as we travelled. It has been a long journey; we have paid a severe price. We are not the crew who began this voyage, a weak image of who we were. We need your help, although I know we don't deserve it. We are in your hands Father Giuseppe". Joe immediately recognised the use of his religious name as a deliberate attempt to kindle feelings of empathy.

Joe reached out privately to his brothers, who had been monitoring the conversation. "What do you think?" "Looks like they are in a bad way, I say let's finish them!" asserted Bart forcefully. Franc supported his view, "They have all but wiped us out, they don't deserve mercy". Paul hesitated for a moment and presented a slightly different view. "To be fair, it was the Barak family who killed everyone. Melak chose not to support the genocide and helped us. Melak showed us a specific mercy, didn't he Franc? If they are clones, then they will be the same as Melak in their thinking, similar to us in fact". "True", added Joe, "if there are three warships bearing down on us, we have no idea of the nature of the adversary we are facing. We need all the help we can get". James responded with heavy sarcasm, "I really don't know how the situation could work guys. There will be 275 people with similar names, and many are identical. How will we distinguish them?"

Joe had no choice; he was forced to take a leap of faith. Bridget looked concerned; she was afraid Joe's course of action could unleash a vast number of Dark Ones into the world.

"This is Father Joseph Fairbourne addressing Mother Ship 4. We are prepared to assist you, on the proviso of a number of assurances". "Name them", came the rapid response. Joe continued assertively, "We need a personal promise from each of you that you come in peace, with your Carocles open so we can verify the honesty of the pledge. You will integrate with our community under our leadership and will become a part of our civilisation rather than competing with us. You will not indulge in subversive politics or action. You will abandon cloning and live naturally. You will fight with us side by side when the time comes, as allies. You will help us with technology, sharing with us, rather than keeping knowledge to yourselves. In return we will share our planet with you as equals".

"This is a very fair request. I will need to consult the elders in the family about abandoning cloning, as it has become our way of life. I have seen the message from Melak, I recognise passion in his counsel", replied the commander. After a brief consultation the elders agreed to the terms without condition. "Do you have any discovery vessels on your mother ship?" queried Joe. "Yes, we have five", the commander replied. "They could be extremely useful. Meet me in Sicily at the coordinates I send you. Please bring a landing party of seven, and we will agree terms", requested Joe. "I'm sorry, we need to abandon ship in the next 24 hours, there are issues with life support, our suits cannot keep us alive for long due to the radiation. We need to evacuate urgently, or we will all die", countered the commander. "Ok, land in France at the coordinates I will transmit. Please use one of your landing modules and bring the discovery ships too". requested Joe. "Confirmed" came the reply without hesitation. The aliens were desperate and happy to take any deal they could get.

Joe returned to Earth's orbit to supervise the evacuation of the mother ship. The brothers discussed the logistics of the situation. The number of aliens were not a threat, but this assumed they were telling the truth concerning their intent. From previous encounters, Paul knew a single landing module, or doughnut, held 300 people. Paul and Spall planned to direct their firepower to the landing area urgently, Joe had given coordinates in the vicinity of the weaponry and missile facilities they had prepared.

Bart had a thought which he expressed to the group, "Can the Pareth-ng control the spaceship remotely from down here?" "What are you thinking Bart?" asked Paul. "We could load the mother ship with nukes and use it to engage the enemy fleet?" The commander confirmed the ship was piloted by its AI, and a discovery ship could remotely control the mother ship from Earth. It could be directed by a Carocle from anywhere, technically. The question was whether the brothers should initiate war with the three ships, or should they wait to be engaged. If they chose the latter, then they may not survive, Earth was by no means equipped to defend against attacks by alien fleets.

The ship landed as planned in Brittany in Northern France, north of Rennes and tactically close to Mont St Michel. There were sufficient contiguous farmlands in a small village called Bourlidou, to land the ship without destroying buildings. A few trees and walls were levelled, but nothing irrecoverable. The landing doughnut occupied four fields; it was several hundred metres in diameter. In the nearby countryside, Spall had arranged lorries with rocket launcher arrays, plus several mobile missile launchers. He deployed almost a hundred men on the ground, armed with automatic rifles, grenades, and RPGs, which had been lifted from military bases in the south of England and Northern France. The men had been drafted willingly from Summer Haven and Mont St Michel. The task force included every adult man, plus several enthusiastic and extremely capable women such as Sheena, who led her own squad. Sheena left her children in the hands of the remaining community at the haven.

All weapons were trained on the doughnut shaped landing craft and the five smaller discovery ships positioned evenly around it. The six ships were bright shining silver, reflecting the grey skies above like amorphous pools of mercury. Paul and Spall approached the main landing vessel on foot, neither were armed but Spall carried a tactical field radio. He had prearranged signals with the team in case the radio was jammed by the aliens. He left nothing to chance, this could be a terrible firefight if discussions went awry. The team was under strict orders to engage when instructed, regardless of whether Paul and Spall were in the firing line. There was too much at stake.

A ramp and doorway flowed out of the main hull of the ship; seven older looking men disembarked calmly onto the muddy field. Contrary to popular belief, they were different in appearance. The aliens looked around in wonder, it was their first time off the ship in decades, it made them a little weak at the knees at first. One knelt, picked a wild daisy from the field and examined it. Another picked up a clod of soil and ran it through his fingers. One of them spoke using the Carocle openly. "Your planet is more complicated than we thought. Every small piece is a complex interaction of creatures, right down to microbe level; there are universes within universes. I never dreamed the planet would be like this. There are creatures everywhere you look, they all depend upon each other in symbiosis". The leader looked up to the sky and inhaled a deep breath of fresh air. They revelled in the moment but were forced to turn their attention to Paul. "Welcome to Earth", Paul opened his hands in a universal gesture of peace. The gesture was correct for the Pareth-ng, the Carocle guided him to follow the right protocols.

One man in the group had a strong resemblance to Melak and also to Paul himself. He was the leader the party, quite deliberately. "Hello, I am Melak 1-232-33, but please call me Mak to avoid the obvious confusion. Thank you for allowing us to land here. You have exhibited a profound act of faith to help us. I can see you are well prepared for trouble; I promise you will receive none, we are in your hands, and glad to be so; the alternatives are unthinkable". Paul could sense his words were true and well meant, so he stepped forward and shook the man's hand, a gesture that Mak understood to be polite. Paul indicated a nearby cottage to Mak and suggested they meet there, for their mutual comfort.

The cottage was actually a substantial farmhouse, with two main barns and a couple of garages and outbuildings. It had much less visual impact from the side facing the landing site. The cottage was poorly maintained these days but was comfortable enough inside. The front door was already open, Spall had forced entry previously. The main living area had been organised to seat nine. It was an educated guess that proved correct. Spall lit a fire which he had set earlier with dry wood and kindling. He had furnished the house with a small range of foods and drinks.

The visitors entered and were offered hospitality as was available. The visitors spent a long time investigating the foods before deciding they were edible. Fresh food was clearly a luxury to them after the limited range of ship synthesised foods they had survived on. The aliens struggled a little with the olives but found the bread and meats delicious. Paul and Spall did too, clearly Mont St Michel had created a post-apocalyptic version of the high life. Mak was first to address his host, his tone was quite formal. "We would like to thank you for showing us a kind welcome and for trusting us. I know you have suffered immensely at the hands of my race, but I dearly hope we can put the past aside and live together in harmony. Our ships and technology are at your disposal, consider them as your own". Mak paused his tone took a less format style, "I would like to introduce my colleagues, my brothers and sisters, to you. I know that our names sound alike to you, so I propose that we adopt Earth names in tribute to the spirit of integration. I will continue with the name Mak, my colleagues are Pascal, Andrew, Jean, Terrence, Susan and Christine". Each of them nodded as their name was spoken.

"Whilst it is important that we settle here, we have matters of higher priority to discuss. Can I suggest we find accommodation here, whilst you interview the crew from my ship, as you requested? I understand you need to be sure our promises are sincere before you can trust us as allies. Meanwhile we must discuss the imminent threat of the ingress of the fleet", suggested Mak. Paul had prepared for the interviews already; he was a quick worker. Paul replied, "That sounds good to me. Joe and Bridget will conduct the interviews, but first I will ask Spall to instruct our soldiers to stand down. We have opened houses in the villages nearby for your people, they are basic and may need some work to make them properly habitable. We have around fifty farms and houses in Les Peupliers, Bourlidou and Le Roquet which should be a good start". He handed Mak a printed map, Mak and the others found it fascinating. Printed paper was new to them. Printing ink on compressed vegetation hadn't entered their minds, at least for the last few millennia.

Joe landed and was allowing the crew to disembark the landing ship one by one. The aliens were interviewed quickly, the Carocle was invaluable. They gathered in small groups on the field. Many of them were intrigued by the mud in the field, some conducted rough scientific analyses to satisfy their curiosity.

In the farmhouse, discussions continued late into the night.

8. The Nature of the Beast

The basic physical needs of the visitors were covered for the time being. They had shelter, food, and water. The first order of the day was the three spaceships heading towards Earth. The group collectively needed to understand the enemy they faced and how they could defend themselves against a potentially superior and unknown adversary. Clearly, the alien's fleet was a substantial threat, as they had attacked Mak's mother ship. Paul asked Mak to explain how they had encountered the new vessel.

"We were on course, travelling by the most direct path towards Earth using a moderate slingshot through the gravity well of Kepler-90h to gather additional momentum. The mission was within normal parameters; we were looking forward to finding a home at last. The enemy ship emerged on our sensors; it was moving on an intercept course towards us. It alarmed us when the ship was unclassified, we had not encountered anything like it before. We have met and had good relationships with other races, but the distances were always too vast to have regular contact. We shared information about other races we were aware of and known protocols or cultures which would be helpful if we encountered them. We retained an extensive database of the known ships used across the universe; this ship was quite different. It was a long thin cylinder, with an abrupt point at the forward section. It looked a little like a pencil, with a flat ridge beneath it emerging at the sides along the bottom of the ship. The ship was large, probably one half of your kilometres in length. There were complex arrays of swirling aerials at the front and rear, we had no idea of their purpose.

The craft was travelling at speeds we could only imagine, the engines were of a technology we hadn't yet encountered and were merely a theory to our scientists. Our own vessel travels at almost a quarter light speed, the oncoming vessel closed the distance between us rapidly. There was no possibility of evading it. We tried unsuccessfully to make contact with the vessel. However, in hindsight, it was clear they were completely ignoring our attempts to communicate.

Our scanners identified a hundred lifeforms onboard. The crew appeared to be roughly humanoid, but with more dense skeletons and enormous musculature, they were accompanied by ten smaller beings which we assumed to be children. Their stature indicated they were from a planet with higher gravity than our own. Their ship's engines appeared to be fusion powered but were unusual. The aerials clusters were strange, we struggled to identify their purpose; until they opened fire. The enemy were scanning our ship at the same time, they would clearly know we were an unarmed passenger transfer vessel.

When they opened fire, they avoided the populated parts of the ship in an attempt to take out our drive modules and weaponry, but they clearly didn't understand our technology and their assumptions were false. We don't have engine assemblies at the rear of the ship, they are distributed along the hull. The aerials glowed as several focused energy beams lashed out from the ship. They dissected four of our landing craft and the critical components of the life support system in the bridge section of the ship killing hundreds of our crew. I believe when they realised the level of fatalities, they ceased fire. We tried to hail them once again, but our cries were ignored.

Finally, we received a communication from the enemy ship. A hologram of the captain appeared on our bridge demanding that we surrender and zero our velocity immediately. The commander was huge and stocky with a hugely protruding brow from which two white eyes and another pair of smaller red eyes studied us. No pleas or explanations would be tolerated, he expected complete surrender, or our vessel would be dissected. No discussion, no understanding, no mercy.

Our only chance was to run, we fired a full array of flechettes at the rear section of their ship, where they had assumed our engines would be. The flechettes were a device to disintegrate asteroid fields and were highly effective at close quarters. They caused sufficient damage to their engine assemblies to make an escape, though we assumed they would inevitably catch us at some point. It bought us time. Our only hope was to join you and salvage your weaponry to assist us to fight back. Our enemy were beyond us, they appear to be physically superior. After losing so many in a brief and decisive conflict we had little chance to protect ourselves", explained Mak.

Mak sat down; we could feel the resignation flooding through his veins. The others looked at Paul and Franc sheepishly. "What did they want?" asked Spall. "I suspect they were looking to capture us. The technology seemed to be of little interest to them, but they spent much time scanning the lifeforms on the ship in detail", explained the Pareth-ng scientist, Pascal. "They either need something biological from our bodies: limbs, tissue, cells or minerals, or they are capturing us as slaves. If it were the latter, we could assume they would be cruel masters, we would be better off dead frankly".

Mak continued, "We've managed to outrun them so far, but their ship is regaining its velocity. As your AI has pointed out, two more vessels have joined them. They are heading on a course to arrive in orbit in roughly two Earth weeks' time. Do we have suitable weapons to defend ourselves? You initially threatened us with your weapons, and you must have used them to destroy Barak's ship. We hope that we can deploy them once again". Paul looked at Spall, "We need to talk in private for a moment, if you would excuse us".

"We can't tell Mak that we used a ship loaded with nukes to destroy Barak's mothership. It would portray weakness, we are still not sure of these guys or their motives", murmured Spall. "We know they are being truthful with us from the Carocle", explained Paul. "But the Carocles are their technology, how do we know they can't be manipulated?" queried Spall. Paul thought for a second, "It doesn't work that way, it opens channels between our minds so we can see each other's thoughts and memories. I'm not sure the Carocle could be manipulated". "Mak may have said it couldn't, but he wasn't completely truthful with us, was he?" added Spall. It was a difficult question. "I have used Carocles for some time and they seem to be transparent. I think the user can hide things, but the device can only show facts. I suspect that he didn't lie, he simply didn't tell us the whole truth" observed Paul. Spall looked most uncomfortable, but conceded "I guess we need to trust the information from the Carocles then?" "We have no choice, we have three hundred hyper intelligent Cro-Magnon's coming our way", asserted Paul finally with a shrug.

Paul and Spall re-joined the group and decided to come clean. "The weapon we used to destroy Barak's ship was simply a discovery ship loaded with nuclear warheads. There was no clever weaponry involved I'm afraid". "Dirty bombs", muttered Pascal to himself in disgust. Mak looked disillusioned, as he realised that the apocalypse, his race had wrought on Earth had a significant impact on his chances of survival. "Could we use the mothership loaded with bombs to ram their fleet?" wondered Spall. "It's possible, but the enemy ship may rip the mother ship to pieces with their energy beams. The enemy seem to attack without thinking, especially if there were no lifeforms aboard". Paul considered the dilemma as Joe entered the room, he looked drained. The time Joe had spent interviewing; had taken its toll on him emotionally. "The interviews were taking too long when we visited each person individually, so they started to meet with us collectively", Joe explained. It was completely irrelevant to the conversation, but Paul became animated.

Paul managed to control his enthusiasm and framed his question succinctly. "What if we load up the mother ship with nukes and wait for the enemy to arrive. We could blow it when they got sufficiently close. If we filled the ship with shrapnel and those flechettes you described, it would do more damage. They would be less likely to fire on a crippled ship, it would be a waste of their ordnance". "True", commented Mak, "But how do we get them to come close enough to make our attack effective?" "We need the enemy to board the ship", stated Spall evenly, "we must find a reason for them to investigate it". Joe suddenly became agitated, "If we set off nukes so close to Earth, we will create a rain of radiation over the world, it will be catastrophic". "True, we would need to gently nudge the ship further out into space", added Pascal, "it's currently a long way from Earth, but if we took it a little closer to the sun…".

"Let's say we manage to take out one or two ships, the enemy will still be sending a landing party, an angry one", pointed out Spall. "We are prepared for a moderately small invasion. The issue is we have no idea where to deploy our forces. They could land anywhere". "We need to leave them a breadcrumb trail", added Paul. "What do you have in mind?", queried Mak. "You mentioned they were scanning for people, not things, right? Assuming they were looking for lifeforms, we need to create the illusion of living people on a crippled defenceless ship. We need to leave a trail down to a precise landing location", suggested Paul. "That's all well and good, but how do we actually create such an illusion?" interjected Spall. Pascal solemnly made a pragmatic suggestion, "We could use the cadavers of our kin from the dead ship and electronically stimulate the bodies to emulate life. It would involve a lot of work, but It's doable. By sending a distress signal from the ship requesting that any survivors join the people of Earth in a certain location, we could create a subterfuge leading them directly down to the landing site. We could even emulate damage, perhaps engine radiation leakage. We could maintain safe levels of radiation and project it towards them, away from this planet".

"We will need to mass our weaponry in a central location, by moving the landing ship into the valley and occupying the surrounding high ground", clarified Spall. "We can bring in the gear from Russia, Spain to France, we need all the firepower we can get. The use of submarines should be avoided to prevent unleashing a nuclear winter on our homes". "Unless we have no choice", added Franc from the Carocle incorrectly paraphrasing Dylan Thomas, "I say that we don't leave this world gently".

"We can begin by moving the landing vessel to the required site in the valley", Paul observed. "The landing vessel is going nowhere; its energy cells are spent. It doesn't have the regeneration facilities of the discovery ships. It requires too much energy to take off and land". "I guess we have decided our battlefield then", advised Spall, "Let's move out the civilians as a matter of urgency". "I guess our plan puts MSM at risk", observed Joe. "It puts us all at risk", added Spall.

Pascal didn't relish the task of re-entering the damaged mothership with his team. It was a graveyard, the air pungent from the decay of with hundreds of cadavers despite the highly purified air of the ship. The incursion team propped up bodies in the main areas of the ship and rigged up basic life support for each one using the extensive facilities of the mothership. Some needed only a simple heart stimulus, others required more complex breathing stimulation. The team managed to adequately animate numerous bodies with the help of the maintenance bots on the ship. The seemingly resurrected bodies created an elaborate illusion of life on the vessel, but it cost the team a high price emotionally. The deceased were members of their friends and family, they felt it was an abuse of their memories. An act of disrespect the team were forced to inflict to save their skins. The ship was a nightmare, like something from a cheap horror movie.

Pascal and the team loaded fifty nuclear devices and warheads into the hull of the ship, along with a myriad of small, sharp objects and flechettes that could cut through metal when ejected with sufficient velocity. They also rigged the engineering lasers and projectile emitters to fire in all directions milliseconds prior to the ship being detonated. They grabbed all the useful technology from the ship and stowed it into the elongated discovery vessel and left the formidable AI in charge of the operation. The team took a full copy of the AI, both its data and its memories, plus the millennia of learned rules from the AI's inference engine. It would be most helpful in the coming days and could be loaded into the discovery vessel network quite easily. The stage was set, now it was up to the invaders to play their part.

Paul was keen to make contingency plans. Secret weapon bunkers were prepared with food reserves. Of the eight discovery vessels, one was secreted away for emergency contingency planning, four were allocated to the brothers as personal transport, and one was loaned to Typhon so he could return to his people in Bavaria. The remaining ships sat beside the landing craft with Mak, where Pascal and his team landed.

As a potential escape route, two ships would be moved to MSM before the conflict began. The preparations were underway, large transportations of weapons and ordnance were transported into northern France from military bases across Europe. Without the discovery vessels and their remarkable ability to change shape to accommodate cargo, it would have taken years to gather the weaponry aimed at the landing site next to the Pareth-ng vessel.

After three days and six hours precisely, three warships entered the solar system and headed on a course to intercept the crippled ship, which was continuously emitting a standard SOS protocol.

9. The Sharing

Conor opened the window of the old monastery and stared out into the bleak, windy day. He looked onto the old vegetable and herb garden that was being battered by the gusts, and then beyond to the fields and mountains. He took a deep breath of oxygen rich air and rejoiced for another day being alive and well.

Kloster Benediktbeuern was the largest abbey in Germany. It had more than enough space for the twenty-eight 'Brothers of the Kadyur'. They had named themselves after the blood dagger used by the Dark Ones, as a grim reminder of their evil heritage and an incentive to gain knowledge to better themselves. The brothers had turned their back on Barak to join Typhon in pursuit of clarity. They were damaged souls, they need help and good counsel, which Typhon was able to bring following his healing by Joe.

The Bavarian countryside around the abbey was beautiful but the view was spoiled by a number of perishing Shroom. The inactive shroom stood with a creepy mouldy look to them. When the brothers had time, they had promised to clear the Shroom, but farm work had been nonstop since they arrived, and winter was coming. The manpower shortage was made worse by the impending invasion, and the need to play their part in defending Earth. The days at the abbey were long and tedious, the monks worked in the gardens, they took turns preparing food and then worked their way through strenuous exercise and combat routines. Their heritage was important to them, but they only used it to help others rather than hurt the innocent these days. They had a new mission and believed in it deeply. It helped them through the darker times, when they relived the terrible acts they had committed under the leadership of Barak, the Dark One. Unleashing the infection which killed mankind was just one of a long list of heinous crimes against humanity. The climb leading to redemption seemed infeasible.

Brother Typhon had been elected as Abbot, he usually led the martial arts training, but not today. Typhon didn't promote religion, so to speak, but he encouraged self-learning and improvement of the soul. He had studied the writings of the great Buddhist Tibetan monasteries and tried to use his knowledge to help others. He often headed into the mountains to contemplate and would not return for several days. Typhon's intense search for enlightenment seemed badly timed given the threat to the world outside.

Conor found it strange that Typhon headed off so soon after his return from a several months-long trip to Sicily. War was looming and the brothers needed to be prepared to defend their creed. Conor's job was to manage the place in Typhon's extended absence, but he needed Typhon's support in providing sensitive leadership. He looked once more up to the hills, searching for clarity when he felt a sensation gently tugging at him.

Conor couldn't classify the feeling he was experiencing; it was different to anything he had previously felt. He sensed a compulsion, a niggle. It was quite unsettling. When he concentrated, the message became clearer, he could sense his Abbot in the room around him. Typhon spoke quietly, "Bring the brothers to me, I need your help". "Where are you?" Conor replied. Typhon continued, "In the mountains. In Krün, on the

Austrian border. Take the ship, I will instruct the AI to bring you to me. And Conor…" "Yes?" responded his number two. "Come fully armed my friend and bring climbing gear, we have serious work to do".

Conor rang the church bell, the brothers congregated in the Basilika Sankt Benedikt. He instructed them to arm themselves, prepare for cold weather and join him at the spaceship in the courtyard of the monastery in fifteen minutes. Brother Septimus brought provisions to the ship, but Typhon had specifically asked him to stay to keep watch on the abbey. Brother Septimus was too old to take risks, he was approaching sixty-three and would be a liability in conflict. He had become quite unfit and overweight since he arrived at the monastery. Cooking hearty stews was Septimus' strong point, which would not be needed on this mission, although it would be most welcome on their return.

The brothers boarded the ship, it lifted gently out of the square and headed towards the foothills of the Alps, due north of Innsbruck. They flew in over lake Barmsee, followed the Upper Isar Valley, and landed in a field next to a small but lovely ski hotel called Gästehaus Simon which claimed to be popular with tourists. Typhon waited on the front porch and welcomed them with a smile. He ran across the field joining them on the ship. The ship then lifted off once more and headed deep into the Soiern Mountains. It finally landed part way up the shoulders of a mountain called Soiernspitze.

Typhon and the monks left the ship and followed a track towards the east side of the mountain. Conor complained about the cold, "It's freezing here, will we be long?" Typhon looked at him grinning appraisingly, "Are you going soft, my friend?" "Where are we going?" enquired Conor. "You will see very soon", replied Typhon curiously. On the ridge, a significant troop of Shroom moved slowly, hampered by the extreme cold. Conor became concerned, "We don't have the equipment to attack Shroom". "Don't worry, they are slow in these low temperatures. We will be long gone before they fruit. There are more than enough of us to dispatch them quickly".

The track opened into a gulley where the Shroom waited. "Why would they gather here, there's nothing to hunt?" asked Conor. "That is precisely the matter we need to investigate. I have been searching for an artifact here for quite some time. Something is binding the Shroom to this location", added Typhon. The monks drew their daggers and tore into the Shroom at a run. They fell on the slow-moving figures, slashing and dodging in phalanx formation with Typhon at the head. Many of the Shroom were inert, but some managed to gain enough energy to bring down a couple of the brothers by working together. "Watch that flank", shouted Typhon, as the Shrooms surrounded them.

The battle lasted only a few minutes, but some brothers were breathless. It had been a short but intense conflict. They left the battlefield with haste as several Shrooms had grown fruit; they were forced to leave the bodies of their comrades to avoid the risk of infection. As they turned off the track into a rocky pass, they came to an outcrop of rock. From behind the outcrop, a Shroom screamed and lunged at Typhon. Typhon stabbed the creature in the heart, but not before the Shroom had leaned into his face and bit him. The Shroom tore off some of the soft, fatty cartilage on Typhon's ear. It made quite a mess, but it didn't slow Typhon, he knew the infection would not affect him due to his alien DNA. The fallen brothers started to bear fruit, luckily the wind blew in the opposite direction, so the spores were no threat.

Brother Galem shouted, "Oh my god, Typhon, you might be infected. What do we do?" Typhon looked at him as he placed a hastily tied piece of fabric over his head to cover his exposed wound. "It's time to test the word of my cousin Franc", he explained, "he claims I am immune to the infection; our genetic makeup is different to yours. The infection is designed to infect people with human DNA only". Typhon continued at a brisk pace along the narrow track, trying to use his energy to keep the bitter cold at bay. "Obviously, I haven't progressed beyond this point before, as there is no other approach to this part of the mountain, and Shrooms had it covered".

The team followed the steep track for a couple of miles before it started to climb sharply. As they climbed, a well concealed cave was exposed on their left. They hadn't seen the cave initially, but Typhon seemed to know its precise location. "Can I ask how you messaged me? it was surreal, like you were inside my head" asked Conor. "It has to do with the artifact. The nearer I get to it, the more I can sense it, the more I can use it", he replied.

"I have empathetic abilities which I inherited from my father, but his were stronger. He was looking for the artifact, the Kracz-el, as it amplifies such abilities". "So how did the Kracz-el get here, in such a remote mountainside in the middle of nowhere?", asked Conor. "Melak hid it, using one of his emissaries. He used the Kracz-el to communicate with his sons before the infection, but he anticipated the Dark One's attack on Vulcano island, so he arranged to hide it. Therefore, I chose the abbey as our base, to allow me to search for the Kracz-el. I had traced the artifact to the proximity of the guest house where we met, but no further. Melak couldn't risk the Kracz-el falling into the hands of Barak, he would have become much too influential and powerful". "He hid it soon after the infection began to settle down a little", observed Conor. "Quite. It's the reason Melak couldn't communicate as easily or as often with his sons once the infection had struck". "How did he summon his sons to him at Vulcano?" queried Conor. "Melak had an extraordinary empathetic talent, far stronger than my father's ability. My family always chose empaths to explore new worlds, they are able to fit in with any indigenous populations.

Without the Kracz-el, Melak could reach out over a long distance for a simple message, but it would be difficult and very tiring. He needed the Kracz-el to be able to influence more effectively.

Once Melak's sons were on Salina, communication would be much easier". Conor thought for a second, "So this is the real reason for your sojourns into the hills", Conor observed, "and how will it help us?" Typhon suddenly became introspective and didn't answer immediately, "I'm not sure yet, but I have a feeling the Kracz-el will be important in the future. It would certainly help if we needed to influence invading aliens, but I suspect they are beyond coercion.

Typhon and Conor entered the cave carefully. The ground was uneven, they tripped several times in the poor light. Conor's flashlight exposed a passageway, the entrance was no more than a jagged crack. There was nothing in the cave, other than an old rag tucked into a corner. Conor reached for the rag; it was a torn fragment of a shirt. "I guess we've found Melak's accomplice's path", whispered Conor. "Yes, we must be on our guard", replied Typhon. He stood erect for a second, looking deeper into the cave. "I can feel the presence of the Kracz-el in here", exclaimed Typhon. "What was the stature of Melak's accomplice?" requested Conor. "An ordinary guy, why?" replied Typhon curiously. Conor smirked, "Well if he was a short arse, he might have squeezed into the crack at the back of the cave". They thought for a while and then called for one of their colleagues to join them.

Brother Jean was led into the cave by Conor using the flashlight, he was diminutive, but should never be underestimated. Jean was fast and extremely agile. He took off his weapons, outer jacket and emptied his pockets. He eased into the deeper part of the cave and slid sideways into the crack, left arm first. They could only see the reflected glow from his LED headtorch. Typhon had always been interested in the Kracz-el, but he couldn't explain his urgency to retrieve it. He suspected there was another empath somewhere, who had not yet focussed their talent and desperately needed help.

Conor continued to feed out the rope as Jean descended into the cleft. He was experienced at belaying but was suddenly surprised by a vicious tug on the rope which almost pulled him headlong into the crack. Conor pulled hard using the rock for leverage. He locked down the rope as a terrible scream echoed from deep within the cave. Typhon and Conor pulled the rope together, it seemed curiously light. As the end of the rope came into sight, they could see a mangled torso, small enough to slide through the cleft. Jean's head, arms and legs had been torn from his body by something powerful. The attacker was not merely a Shroom. Blood saturated the remnants of his clothing, ragged flesh hung from the rent joints, which dripped crimson.

Typhon looked at Conor, "Let's get the hell out of here". Conor turned to leave, then hesitated. He shone his torch at the torso one last time, "Look there's something in Jean's belt pocket". Typhon cut the belt with his boot knife, he grabbed the belt and exited the cave at pace. Once Typhon and Conor were outside, they stopped to examine the belt more closely, whilst the brothers watched the cave mouth, weapons drawn. "This is it", exclaimed Typhon. He unzipped the pocket in the webbing belt, a small crystal object dropped into his palm. It was shaped roughly as a hexahedron, like two pyramids one above the other, joined at their widest part. It had ornate but unintelligible writing along the lines of each face. "Move out, double time", shouted Typhon. "Whatever killed Brother Jean may not be able to come through the crack in the cave wall, but it wouldn't grow big enough to rip a man apart if it hadn't got a regular supply of food, and that means another means of egress".

It would be problematic to return by the track they had walked along previously, as the Shrooms would be sending out profuse clouds of spores. The team were forced to take a scree run down the first part of the descent, using their ropes to abseil down a short 100 metre cliff, before running back to the ship via a goat trail. A guttural whine bellowed from behind them, but they chose not to look back; they simply continued their descent as fast as they were able.

Once they arrived at the ship, it took off without delay. Quickly Typhon realised had lost another of their number. "What the hell was that howling?" asked Conor. "It sounded like something from my world, but I have no idea how it came to be here. Perhaps Melak cloned it on his ship from a DNA sample and left it here, in case the Kracz-el needed protection. The ship's AI identified the creature with its scanners, it was an Arth-Macht slayer beetle. The AI displayed it as a hologram. It was an exceptionally large black coleoptera, the size of an adult hog. However, the insect had a huge maw with razor teeth akin to a shark, with long bladed claws, under which were dextrous toes used for climbing. "It hibernates for a year at a time but is quite easy to wake. Anyone going into the cave would stir it. It is a formidable guardian if you have something precious to protect", explained Typhon. "I wonder if any other creatures have been secreted on this planet", pondered Typhon quietly as if to himself.

The team landed the ship in the centre of the monastery courtyard and returned to the abbey. Typhon wandered out of the monastery, into the yard where a young monk was putting himself through a demanding Karate routine in the wooded enclosure near to the guest house. His kata concluded with a final thrust accompanied with a fierce scream "Eech!" The student calmly looked at Typhon. "Did you locate the Kracz-el Typhon?" he requested. "Yes. We found it in the cave where we hoped it would be, though it was not easy to find. It has taken me almost a year of searching to locate the artifact. It was protected by a slayer beetle, unfortunately we lost four men in the encounter. We had no means to engage the creature, so we fled".

After the young monk put on his robe and tied the belt tightly round his waist, Typhon passed him the hexahedron. The monk smiled, "Finally we have the Kracz-el, I have been searching for it for some time, and you have finally located it. You have done very well indeed, my son. We need to make our next move quickly and decisively. Let's head into the refectory, Brother Septimus has a rich lamb stew on the stove, I can see you need some hearty sustenance".

10. Following a Trail of Crumbs into Hell

Joe and Paul sat with Mak, Pascal and Spall in Joe's spacecraft. Bart had joined virtually using his Carocle, he and his crew were preparing the submarine HMS Astute for battle. Beryl, the ship's AI, was closely monitoring the status of the three unknown vessels as they cruised through Earth's solar system at a remarkable velocity. In less than two weeks the three ships had closed on the Pareth-ng mother ship, which meant they had the capability to travel at a velocity close to half light speed.

The three unidentified enemy ships formed a tight chevron as they neared the mothership. Franc looked satisfied, "Keep coming. Keep coming. We can do some real damage if you stay in tight formation". They arrived on the sun's side of the mothership as predicted, remaining in the chevron. The enemy scanners penetrated the mothership's hull and concentrated on the areas that appeared to be inhabited. The mothership's AI had activated the simulated life an hour before; by giving the propped-up body's respiratory stimulation, both chemical and electrical. Some bodies sat still; some moved with their limbs powered by bots like marionettes. They created a convincing show for the observer, to an appropriate level of detail for the scanner.

As the ships passed the predetermined event horizon, the mothership's AI detonated the warheads. The flash wasn't visible to the team in France, the explosion was on the side of Earth facing the sun, so the ship's AI (Beryl) displayed the full situation in front of them. The shrapnel caused little damage to the hulls of the enemy vessels, but the flechettes cut through them like paper. The force of the explosion inflicted catastrophic damage to the nearby pair of ships, but they shielded the third ship from much of the force. As the two ships disintegrated, a myriad of pods spurted from the hull, like frog's eggs spawned from their mother.

Franc watched using sensors from one of the discovery vessels, inactive and hidden behind the moon itself. The moon was excellent cover, if he kept the energy consumption low on the ship and the drives offline. Franc's vessel lifted off and travelled at maximum velocity towards the third ship. Franc calmly spoke the four words he had been dreading to the ship's AI, "Constance, release the missiles".

Four strange looking missiles were physically hurled into space by the ship's flowing hull. The missiles didn't have a conventional engine, the engines wouldn't function in space, so they relied on the momentum of the ship and the catapult action of the hull. The throw propelled the modified tomahawks towards the remaining enemy ship. In the chaos, Franc hoped the enemy would not notice three unorthodox lumps of metal heading their way. The engines had been replaced by pressurised air cylinders and evenly spaced vents around their circumference, to allow the AI a modicum of control over the missile heading. Steve had augmented the missiles with engineering laser cutters on the prow. "Get back to base quickly, before the invaders open fire", he commanded. The ship headed back towards Earth, passing via the blind side of the moon for cover.

The three missiles floated in space at high velocity, they would be smashed to smithereens if they collided with floating wreckage and the nuclear warhead may not detonate. The missiles covered much of the distance without issue, but problems occurred as they neared the field of debris from the damage inflicted by the previous explosions. The first missile collided with part of an engine chassis and simply smashed; the compressed air tanks flew off in different directions randomly. The AI had done a good job with the other two missiles, they remained on target. Franc reported the status, "Missile one down, two and three on target". The enemy ship had clearly detected the incoming objects and targeted them with its energy weapons.

The problem for the enemy was similar to clay pigeon shooting, it took significant skill. The energy weapons travel through space at light speed in an instant. The missile's velocity was one third light speed, so the enemy couldn't target them easily, the missiles would have moved by the time the light particles arrived at their location. Therefore, targeting needed an element of prediction. Weapon aiming was thrown to hell when the missiles neared their target, the compressed air jets started to fire, and the missiles rotated in a large helix, continuing until the missile was within range for detonation.

The energy weapons cut through space with their florescent green beams but struggled to hit their target. Only one missile impacted the hull of the enemy ship. Steve assumed the hull of the ship would take quite a pounding, so he had cleverly installed engineering lasers in the front of the payload, which started to cut through the hull and soften the metals as the warheads closed. The missile entered the molten hole with a splash, penetrating the ship's hull before it detonated.

Franc was far from the source of the explosion when the nuke whited out. It annihilated the rear quarter of the ship projecting the debris into the remaining two ships. The severity of the attack was a surprise, barely twenty pods escaped from the ship, the enemy's focus had been on the mother ship. Franc supposed they expected Earth's milky way to be primitive and their prey mostly defenceless. The pods slowly followed the pre-arranged trail down to the Earth's surface.

Joe, Paul, Mak, Pascal and Spall continued to monitor the situation with Cindy. It would be a few hours before Franc returned, then they would have roughly two days before the first pods arrived. The team had lined up quite an array of weaponry to greet the visitors; everything except for nukes. There was a three-tier defence, the first was aerial combat using ground to air missiles, the second were ground to ground missiles and static charges around the ten-mile radius, and finally hand to hand combat with conventional weaponry and RPGs. The landing module was clearly the main target, so it had been evacuated along with the nearby houses. The salvageable equipment was in the process of being removed and loaded onto large canvas covered trucks. The brothers felt confident they had the situation all in control; little did they know.

"Cindy, please confirm the number of pods and their occupants", asked Paul. "There are two hundred and thirty-seven pods. Their trajectory is currently taking them toward the mothership as we anticipated. Each pod contains a single lifeform". A hologram of one of the lifeforms was shown in front of them. The creature was seven feet tall, roughly humanoid, but extremely stocky. Its musculature was enormously over developed, way beyond any body seen in a Mr Universe contest. "Their huge muscles probably evolved due to living on higher gravity planets", added Pascal. "How does it affect their movement on Earth?" asked Paul. "Remember the Apollo moon landings, the astronauts leaping steps? They may be light on their feet, despite their size. They are likely to weight over 600kg though, so it is hard to predict. They could move in leaps and bounds when they attack. Normally, such huge muscles would slow their movement, but it may not be the case", explained Cindy. "Unfortunately, I suspect, they will be a deadly opponent in battle. It will be like fighting a rhino, and our bullets may be ineffective", concluded Paul.

The alien's visage appeared quite brutal, it's enlarged cranium featured an overhanging brow, protecting small human sized eyes. On closer examination Pascal queried, "What are those small, red spots near to the nose?" Cindy had no data to offer but commented they may be eyes adapted to a different light spectrum to improve their night vision. Cindy indicated it was probable the creatures had been implanted with supplementary artificial eyes.

Another potential augmentation Cindy identified in the mouth area was a filter mechanism. "The body will use a vast amount of food and oxygen to propel itself. The filter mechanism may enable breathing in suboptimal conditions, but also increases the flow of air to the body. Their lungs are not in proportion with their muscles, so their breathing might otherwise be inhibited. It depends on their optimum oxygen concentration to sustain respiration. Respiration might represent a weakness when they are exposed to the oxygen content of our atmosphere, especially at high altitudes", continued Cindy, "They will also need to feed regularly, due to their likely energy consumption".

"Will our ordnance be effective?" queried Spall. Cindy provided the results of her analysis, "Your smaller bore weapons will not have a great effect on them, unless the shot is perfectly accurate. You will need to hit the eye or other vulnerable organs near to the epidermis, we don't currently have data this data. Consider our enemy like shooting at a large mammal. Their bone will probably be very dense, and their muscle thick. High calibre rifles may be effective if they hit the right places. Explosives will work, but don't expect an instant kill". "How about a blade?" enquired Franc as he entered the ship, greeted by wide smiles. "Your Katana will cut muscle and tendon, but it will require more force, potentially taking several blows to sever a limb. The Katana is unlikely to cut through the bone, so you would need to be careful, your blade may get snagged", responded Cindy. "I was joking about the sword", grinned Franc, "I'll be carrying a grenade launcher if I have to fight one of those suckers!" "Well don't get too close, or you might lose your carefully untrimmed eyebrows", retorted Cindy sarcastically.

None of the team was confident concerning the pending engagement with the 'Cro-Magnons'. Franc had nicknamed the creatures against Paul's advice. Paul felt the name could lead to the team underestimating them, our adversary was clearly smart enough to build large spaceships and formidable weapons. "Let's hope we eliminate them before they hit the floor", observed Spall.

Tension was high, as the first few pods descended through the atmosphere, burning like shooting stars. They were heading for the mothership, but the formation started to flare out as they got close. Not all the pods landed in the pre-determined perimeter. Paul dispatched vehicles to chase them down.

Spall gave the command, a string of surface to air missiles launched into the sky. Spall had chosen infra-red targeting missiles for the first wave, as the ships would be hot from re-entry. The sky filled with explosions but only a handful of the pods showed damage, they were clearly built to withstand significant impact. Cindy shared the bad news that a new flotilla of enemy ships had entered the solar system.

11. The Pointed Mountain (Abe)

From the journal of Abraham Cauldy

Date uncertain – Day 1

I never quite feel myself, I'm out of sorts. I feel the memories of my life are like a movie once watched. The memories never quite feel real, the feelings and smells are hollow somehow. Yet these are my memories, they shape me.

<Duplicated opening paragraphs of Abe's diary omitted as a courtesy to the reader: detailing his divorce, the death of his wife and the arrangements with his contact>

My first revelation was the telephones weren't working this morning, making it impossible to call Holland to update my contact with my location. At breakfast, I experienced a small panic attack, as I read the morning paper, I noticed it was dated April 2021, which was ridiculous. Someone must be having a joke, I'm not one to fall for such vacuous pranks. There seems to be no one in the hotel today, from the noise last night I know there are people staying here. There are also no staff, it must be a rather disreputable establishment, or they have been drawn elsewhere for an emergency.

My accommodation is lovely, I can see the sea from my room. I have no idea where I am, but it is warm and to the rear of the hotel I can see a large volcano. Without a telephone, it's not clear how I make contact. I opted for a constitutional. I hoped service would be restored later, I planned to have a word with the manager.

At a nearby shop, I acquired a new journal. Given the range of tourist souvenirs in the shop, I assumed I was on one of the islands off the coast of Sicily. The shopkeeper was not around, so I left a cheque on the till which would be easily seen. The town was busy, but the locals looked at me strangely. They didn't appear to be familiar with tourists. However, they were friendly and helpful, though there was reluctance to take money from me for the things I needed. I headed back to the hotel for a coffee, to which I was forced to help myself, at least the solar electricity was working.

As I sipped my drink, a man entered the hotel helping himself to a cup. He sat next to me, smiled, and shook my hand. The face of my new acquaintance looked vaguely familiar, as he spoke, I realised he was my contact. "Hello Abe, I hope you are feeling well, my friend. I have another task for you, and I'm afraid this one is a matter of life or death. My enemies are closing in on me, and I need you to hide an object for me. It's a most useful artifact, but I no longer have a need for it. However, my enemies will use it as a weapon should they get their hands on it. I need you to take it far away and hide it where no one will ever find it. I don't even want you to tell me where you take it, so I can't be forced to divulge its location".

The man unrolled a map, showing we were on the Aeolian Island of Vulcano, to the north of Sicily. He indicated that I should travel through Italy to the north and head into the mountains to lose the item. The man explained the world had changed, since I last ventured out. He told me about dangerous Dark Men, and undead people infected with fungus. However, the worst was I would not find any living people in the countries I journeyed through, the world had been harmed irreparably, by men with evil hearts. I explained there was nothing in the newspaper concerning this, he replied that the newspaper was at least a year out of date. I must remember to ensure I take the correct dose of my tablets; my memory was becoming befuddled again, I was giving way to confusion.

Day 2

The next morning, my contact looked agitated, he handed me a familiar looking pair of hiking boots. The artifact he had mentioned had been inserted in the heel of the left boot, beneath the insole. He was relying on me, and I needed to keep safe. He handed me a pre-packed rucksack and arranged for my passage to the mainland on a fishing vessel. My contact gave me a curious silver sphere. Its surface was a little like liquid quicksilver. To open it I needed to articulate a strange phrase, which I remembered rather more quickly than I expected. The sphere contained a small creature which he asked me to release when I hid the artifact. He explained, I needed to drop the creature and run; it was small but deadly.

The boat trip was pleasant, we moored at an uninhabited container port called Eranova. I was told the location was safe from the infected people. I made my way towards San Ferdinando and on to Nicotera. I had not heard of the places, but I soon picked up road signs to Napoli, which was more than 150 miles north. The mainland of Italy was largely deserted, so I began my long trek, stopping at shops along the way to find canned or bottled goods to sustain me. I avoided the city centres as advised by my contact; they were reportedly dangerous. I had seen no activity whatsoever to this point.

Day 6

I arrived at Naples feeling tired, with large blisters on my sore feet. I was dehydrated. I found operational fountains; they were gravity fed from the mountains presumably. After drinking my fill, I stripped off my boots and dangled my feet in the cool waters, it was heavenly. My next stop was to raid a small store and appropriate a hotel room for the night. In the twilight there was a commotion in the street, I opened my window to see strange creatures running around and making a fuss. The source of the commotion was a heavily muscled man fighting with the monsters. He fought valiantly but was soon overcome by the numbers and ferocity of his assailants. The creatures tore at the man, biting into his flesh, it was revolting and terrifying to watch. They were the shape of men and women, but darker in colour, they behaved like rabid animals. I stayed locked in my room for three days before I dared venture out again, but at least my feet had healed.

Day 15

I left Naples via the shortest route. I walked for days circumventing larger communities to avoid the remains of fungal infected people. I stole food, I took cars without permission. After two weeks, I arrived at Lake Como safe and sound. The next step was to take climbing gear and head into the Dolomites to the north of Italy and into the mountain range there.

Day 31

Over the days that followed, I walked roads, mountain trails and climbed peaks until I found a place which felt right. It was a hidden split in the side of a mountain, with a deep but inaccessible cavern beneath it. Any object inserted in the crack would fall hundreds of feet, making it extremely unlikely to be found. Locating the fissure was another challenge, in this complex range of mountains. I was utterly lost, which would make it hard for anyone to posthumously coerce me into giving away the location of the artifact. The crack looked as if it could reach the underworld. Due to my small frame, there was room for me to enter deep into the cavern. I placed the gem-like artefact far into a fissure in the wall and listened to it drop. It didn't fall as far as I had expected, but there was little I could do about it. I then took the sphere and prepared to release the creature. I climbed back through the narrowest passages of the cave and let the creature free in a place where I could exit quickly. I had no doubt it was dangerous; I had no intention of hanging around. I became exhausted as I ran back down the trail as fast as I was able. In the gulley I found a group of the infected, they were a sorry sight to behold.

Once I had reached the valley, twenty infected stood in a group, they were almost motionless looking extremely ill. My contact's last instructions were the strangest of all. I inserted a horticultural drip feeder device into the first twenty of the infected and removed the plugs from the feeders. The feeders smelt like they had been filled with blood, but it could not be the case, obviously. The feeders were likely to contain some kind of modern fertiliser or the like. I thought no more of it.

I left the mountain via a different route, taking me to Gästehaus Simon, an elegant but petite hotel in a lovely village. Finding an unused room, I dropped my bag and grabbed canned foods and unspoiled wine from the kitchen, taking them through to the dining room. I ate and slept for ten hours. I milled around for a day or so until my reserves were replenished. I took a gentle stroll to a nearby lake which the map in the guest house called Barmsee and strolled down the lovely valley which led from it. From the map I had found my way to a locality within striking distance of Innsbruck. Finally, I had a rough idea of my location.

Day 33

While out on my usual walk, I was startled by a modern looking Land Rover vehicle passing me. The driver was clearly seeking someone or something. He stopped and stared at me before continuing on his way. It was the first living person I had seen for weeks. I wished he had stayed; I would have appreciated human company and conversation. I was intrigued to know the driver's destination, but I had no transport other than my feet. I continued my walk and returned to the guest house for another meal, I was starting to enjoy myself a little, the scenery was lovely, although the weather had turned cold in the last few days.

Day 34

I had turned in for the night early, I woken a little after 2am by the sound of a car engine. After the solitude of the last few days, the hum of the engine was unusual, and it roused me abruptly. I sit here terrified, as I write these few words. I can hear sounds in the night. Intruders have entered the hotel and are searching. I suspect they are looking for me, as there is little of value here. The simple fact they have not announced themselves leads me to be wary. I can hear them at the door, and the handle is turning...

12. Fire fight

Colletta and Audrey sat together eating breakfast as usual. Colletta was aware of Audrey's thoughts like a seventh sense, as identical twins often do. She had initially thought it was a kind of telepathy, but as time went on, she found it more complex. Lucy looked worried, they knew there was an imminent battle, in which their dad could get hurt or even killed. Colletta had managed to secretly retain the Carocle she had worn to find Audrey. She had used the device surreptitiously to keep up to date with plans for the forthcoming trouble. She hadn't warned her mum; Lucy would worry if she realised the full depth of danger of the attack. Colletta could see the pods travelling towards Earth, each containing a humanoid monster. She worried that the people of Earth didn't have any insight into the plans these creatures had for mankind.

As she placed the Carocle on her head, Colletta became aware of someone observing her quietly towards the fringes of her consciousness. "Who are you?" Colletta would often ask, but no response ever came. However, today she received an answer. "I am a friend who would like to help your father", came the curious response. "How can you help Dad?" queried Colletta quietly. "We are going to be attacked by a brutal race of warriors that we don't understand. We don't have enough power to overcome them. Everyone will die or worse. We need to protect ourselves", the voice whispered enticingly. "Excuse me, but I am only fourteen. How can I possibly help?" "You have strong, if unfocussed, abilities. So does your sister, Audrey. I know who you are, and what you are. I need your help, but it will be dangerous for us all. I know your sister has been reaching out for help too". Audrey became restless, "I can feel him close, the bad man", she uttered worriedly in her sleep.

"What do we need to do?" asked Colletta suspiciously. "We need to gather reinforcements quickly; we need the dead to help us; it's our only hope. Audrey can talk to the dead, can she not?" murmured the voice in Colletta's head. "Yes, but she is young and vulnerable. I can't put her in any danger". "I will protect you, but I need your help. I need both of you to come with me to Jerusalem once more. From there we can speak to the dead more clearly. You will need to warn Audrey though. I am a clone of the person who put her in that hole, the Well of Souls. It was an evil act; I promise I would never do such a thing. She will be afraid when she meets me, even though I am much younger than my predecessor. If you agree, I will come to find you both". Colletta responded wisely, "I need to discuss this with my mum".

As Colletta expected, broaching such a subject sent Lucy spiralling into a whirlwind of anger and stress. "There is no way am I going to let you go off to that horrible place with someone you don't know, let alone that evil monster who spread the infection and hurt Audrey!" shouted Lucy. "I don't understand why you would want to go in the first place. Why would you even consider doing this? This man is responsible for exterminating millions of people". Colletta looked a little sheepish, her head bowed to the floor. Audrey stood quietly by her side knowing full well the capabilities of the man.

"I have a confession to make. I have a Carocle, Mum. I am aware of recent developments and the preparations being made by Dad and the others. Hundreds of aliens will arrive here in just a week. We can't win Mum; our soldiers will all die. The voice says we can help humanity to survive, I don't understand how, but it feels important. I can't say more than that". "You stole a Carocle? How dare you do such a thing?" chided Lucy. "Mum, it's the very least of our problems. Dad will die if we don't do something". "Well, you are absolutely not going to Jerusalem with that man. No way! I would like to have a word with him". "I think you are going to get the chance Mum, he's here", said Audrey pointing through the kitchen window as a silver ship dropped out of the sky. The ship landed on the empty ground beside the old guesthouse with the barest murmur of a sound.

The first pod hit the ground barely a half mile southeast of the Pareth-ng landing vessel. It impacted the empty field with a loud whump, the grey egg was buried in the soft clay of the field. It was mid-Autumn and the hard ground had begun to soften with the continuous rainfall of the previous week. Within minutes, Spall and Wrench stood on the bed of a large army truck with a large anti-aircraft machine gun pointing at the hole in the ground. Spall pulled out three RPGs from the large crate at the rear of the vehicle and prepped the first one, ready to fire.

Three more burning pods entered the atmosphere and streaked across the sky towards the field. Spall could hear vehicles moving into position. "We can't afford to assume they will land in the same spot", observed Paul via the battlefield radio. "Nor can we assume that they won't", countered Spall. "We need to keep our forces together, or they will rip us apart like a barracuda gutting a fish".

The pod opened, the ground above it ruptured as a large, stocky, almost reptilian, humanoid emerged and stretched his massive arms. He wore an elaborate helmet and blue armoured plate jacket, so it was hard to determine specific details through the field binoculars Spall was using to observe the events. The creature's enormous, scaled feet were bare. Before the creature could orient itself, Wrench opened up with the large machine gun anchored to the top of the truck. The rounds formed a scattered pattern but many of the large calibre slugs hit the creature with little effect. "Aim for the feet", suggested Spall calmly. "It's not even hurting him. The ordnance is just bouncing off the armour plates!" replied Wrench nervously. Spall could see the whites of Wrench's eyes enlarging anxiously as he spoke. "Keep calm, I have an RPG here, and the others will arrive shortly. We have this". Wrench targeted the creature's feet and the shots had greater effect, "I don't know what his bones are made of, but the rounds just seem to bounce off", he stammered. "Yes, but it is hurting him, his feet are bleeding", pointed out Spall. "He's getting angry now", exclaimed Wrench.

The creature charged towards them with huge galloping strides, closing at a crazy rate in a straight line. "The alien's momentum won't let him change direction quickly, take an RPG in case I miss him", commanded Spall. Wrench quickly clambered down as the creature leapt over the wall surrounding the field. As he hit the ground heavily, Spall's RPG took him fully in the chest and knocked him three metres back into the stone wall which smashed with the impact. The alien's armour deflected much of the blast, but it delivered a mortal wound. The exposed parts of the creature's body, such as his hands and feet, were torn to shreds. "Boomtastic!" cheered

Wrench. "Yeah, the only trouble is there are two hundred of them coming our way, and we don't have enough RPGs to take them all", offered Spall as the next three pods hit the ground.

Spall briefed the team as the artillery moved into place on the hill across from the landing site. Wrench examined the alien's body briefly. "It's armour is amazing, but it weighs a ton, it doesn't cover the whole body. I think they might be damned near impregnable in a full suit. Its skin looks vaguely human, though there are scales on parts of the body, I saw some on the feet before we pureed them. The creature seems to have equipment, but I can't identify their purpose. It looked like the alien was coming to attack us with his fists, surely not". Wrench gathered samples of the flesh for scientific analysis, "Uh oh!" "What's up?" queried Spall as he reloaded the machine gun and urgently grabbed additional RPG's out of the crate. "I think the creature is still alive!"

The three pods opened, and the aliens ran towards Spall's position. One of the ground-to-ground missile launchers opened up from the hill, and a pair of Thales Lightweight Multirole Missiles shot into the air. The guys on the hill kept a laser trained on the centre figures as they bounded towards Spall and Wrench. The missiles targeted the interference splash from the laser marking the target. Before the aliens reached the wall, they exploded, the sound was intense, and the shock wave nearly knocked Wrench off his feet. Fragments of the alien's body were scattered in all directions. "Shit, I wish I'd covered my bloody ears", bellowed Wrench. "Pardon", shouted Spall with a grin. Wrench looked up and stiffened. Spall followed his look as the remaining pods streamed down through the atmosphere, burning bright orange across the sky.

"Paul, we need to target the aliens in groups, we can't fight them one by one", shouted Spall into the radio. "It just got worse Spall, Cindy has informed us that sixteen more ships have entered the solar system, there are too many for Franc to engage and he only has two of the modified tomahawks left", added Paul. "Well, he needs to deploy them and get the hell out of there", replied Spall.

More than two hundred pods hit the field and the surrounding area; the constant pounding continued for almost thirty minutes. One guy from MSM had driven too close to the target area and had been hit by a pod. The team could see nothing of the truck or its occupants, but there was no damage to the pod whatsoever. Missiles and shells were continuously launched into the area once the pods started to open. Although a huge number of pods landed, there were no collisions. Spall concluded that the pods must be equipped with centralised guidance. Ten minutes after the last pod landed, Paul gave the order to cease the bombardment.

As the smoke began to clear, the battlefield didn't show as much damage as they had hoped. "We threw everything at them, and so few are hurt. Their defences have shielded the aliens from the blast. Many have full body armour, rather than the torso protection of the first three. The aliens were expecting our bombardment, they must have been monitoring the situation and adapted their tactics", commented Spall losing a little of his trademark cool aura. The team resumed the shelling but were dangerously low on munitions. As the battlefield settled, they could see hundreds of the creatures bounding towards them. "Retreat! get the hell out of here", shouted Paul, "We need to regroup and plan. Release the last six missiles at the front row, see if you can slow them. Then leave rapido". Paul communicated the coordinates for the regroup, and they left as fast as they were able.

The last truck had expended its array of ground-to-ground missiles but was slow to leave the battlefield. Two aliens repeatedly shoulder barged the truck causing it to swerve off the road, their strength was extraordinary. Spall watched from the top of his truck as the aliens tore the truck door open and pulled the driver from the vehicle. Unexpectedly, the aliens didn't kill the driver, they simply subdued him with a punch and carried him back to the main group unconscious. God knows what they had in mind for him, but there was nothing Spall could do.

The team regrouped on the mainland at La Caserne near to Mont St Michel and monitored the enemy using the scanners from Paul's spaceship. "Can't we just nuke them?" asked Franc via the Carocle. "I suspect if we did, you would end up with everyone at MSM losing their teeth at the very least, the explosion would create a huge cloud of radiation. We would need to lock down the region for quite some time. We don't have the air filtration needed to survive a nuclear attack", commented Paul. "How about sending in cruise missiles from the submarines, but with conventional warheads?" suggested Bart via the Carocle. "I'm not sure the payloads would be much greater than the G2G missiles we have hit them with, and they seemed to shrug off that barrage", reverted Paul. "The small number we killed were the ones who hadn't donned their full armour", commented Spall. "They couldn't survive a continuous barrage, there might be a steady attrition", observed Franc. "True but we would soon be out of munitions", replied Paul with a little uncertainty.

"When we hit their ship, we hit them with a nuke. How did they survive to deploy their pods?" asked Joe. "Perhaps they already occupied the pods ready to launch?" pointed out Bart. "But they weren't planning to land, they were going to board the mother ship presumably", added Paul. "Who knows, we can't be completely sure even a nuke would obliterate them. I suggest we keep HMS Audacious nearby in case we need to make a grand but suicidal gesture", observed Bart. Bart's own ship HMS Astute surfaced near to the port in Washington as a countermeasure against landings in America. Bart had been keeping newly promoted Captain Caterham on the Audacious updated via radio. Caterham had been first officer on the Astute until the sailors had discovered the second submarine. They had initially split the ordnance between the subs, until additional stores and weapons had been located in the navy bases at Portsmouth and Clyde.

The enemy formed into a single unit and were moving at pace towards the haven at Mont St Michel. On route they stopped to re-fuel, ripping up sheep and cows in a field and devouring them raw. The team pulled back to MSM, which only had one connection to the mainland via its causeway. All firepower was arranged around the island to attempt to fend off the marauders. The aliens clearly knew exactly where they were and did not hesitate in pursuing with ferocity. Paul looked over the causeway. All but the road itself was flooded by the river using the sophisticated mechanism which had been installed some years before covering the quicksand. Paul heard the alarm sound as the first handful of warriors bounded into view.

13. Face Your Fears or Die Afraid

The younger of the two men spoke first, looking deep into each girl's eyes in turn. "Hello, my name is Barak, and this is my son Typhon", indicating to the older alien. Lucy stood in the doorway with a double-barrelled shotgun pointing at the two men. "Leave us alone, you fucking murderer", she spat. "Please; please there is no need for that, we come in peace", Barak replied gently. "I know your kind of peace Barak; it's the peace of the grave". Colletta spoke calmly to her mum as Audrey looked on from behind with wide scared eyes, "He's not the Barak we knew, he is Barak's clone, Mum. He is not the same person, even though he shares his memories. The old Barak got screwed up during his long passage across space, his mind was twisted, he was mentally ill. We at least need to listen to what this Barak has to say. Please Mum! Then you can shoot him if you have to".

"I don't get this!" shouted Lucy, "You are both cloned from Barak, but one is son and the other father. It makes no sense" "It is our culture, our way", explained Barak. "A son is a clone of the parent who has no memories and is grown from a small child as a new individual. I am a re-clone, and I have been implanted with all the knowledge and memories of Barak. Therefore, I am Barak, and Typhon is my son". "Which means you are the same person who murdered everyone", stated Lucy evenly. "I can see your point, but I have a new mind and I see things differently. I have not been subjected to decades of boredom, passing time in a tedious spaceship, nor has my brain developed dangerous chemical imbalances. I am Barak as he should have been, my mind is whole and sane. After the evil I inflicted upon my sons, it must stand for something that Typhon is here beside me. Typhon has already proven his worth to your community, yet he is willing to accept me".

Barak's comments took Lucy by surprise, she took a step backwards and nearly stumbled over Colletta. Lucy became aware of her inexperience with weapons and decided it was safer to lower the shotgun. Despite her change of heart, she kept the weapon close enough to use if she needed it. "Your people are in great danger. Our shared enemy are a powerful adversary. They have good defences against your unsophisticated weaponry, and they are violent. There is currently only a small force engaging you, but there are many more on the way. I have an idea which might just give you a slim chance of rebalancing the equation. The enemy will kill my race just as readily as they will kill yours, I am bound to your fate. We must face them together; we have no choice". Barak went on to outline a risky plan to Lucy, she could see his logic, despite the danger to the girls. Barak's plan might not work, but a slim chance was one worth taking. Desperate times needed desperate measures. There was a risk that Audrey could sustain emotional damage, but then she had been strong enough to live in a hell hole for God knows how long.

The girls cautiously boarded the ship together with Barak and Typhon. Lucy had insisted on accompanying the girls, there was no negotiation on that point. Joe's wife, Bridget, agreed to come for moral support. If they were both armed, then they had a good chance of protecting the girls if Barak betrayed them. Taking an armed guard was not feasible; Salina's soldiers were in France. Lucy had secreted a compact Walther PPK pistol into her bag, made sure there was food and drinks for them, she was ready for whatever came. Bridget joined the group from Salina on route.

Within an hour the ship landed in the square in Jerusalem by the Dome of the Rock. Lucy's heart sank as they arrived, as she understood the ordeal the girls were facing. The spirits would soon be aware of Audrey, so they had little time to prepare. Barak fitted the Carocle to Colletta's head and reached out to Audrey with another. Colletta quickly intervened, "Wait!" then she turned to Audrey. "This device is really cool, it will let us talk without speaking, you will also be able to see all your memories very clearly, and mine too. All the events that have hurt you will be there, and they will be so real. I can't prepare you, it could be really horrible". Audrey looked up into Colletta's eyes so she could see the steel there. "Don't worry, I'm choosing to be brave", she whispered, slightly misquoting Melak's phrase from her father, Franc's journal. Audrey's words made Lucy a little emotional, but she soon recovered herself.

Audrey was young for such an experience, but then she had lived through so much. The horrors of her past suddenly came flooding back. She had managed to wall off the terrible experiences of Jerusalem, but her mind had become an open door, with a gravitational force sucking her back into bad memories. Audrey screamed, Lucy tried to remove the device, but she couldn't. "You can only take the Carocle off when Audrey wants to, remember Mum?" clarified Colletta. Audrey sat on the floor, her eyes glazed, she was visibly shaking. "Get off me!" she shouted. Lucy stepped towards Audrey, but Colletta grasped her hand. "Audrey is talking to the ghosts", she explained. "I can see her memories, Mum, they are really horrible. Audrey had it really rough in the passages, she nearly died in the dark on several occasions. She came close to starving and was forced to live off rats and beetles, when she couldn't find food. Some spirits took pleasure in torturing her mind too. It was vile". Colletta then looked directly at Barak and stated, "Barak was vile to her".

Audrey became calmer, her shaking subsided as Colletta held her in her arms speaking gently to her, "Its only memories, it's not real. I'm here with you Audrey. You are safe with me; I won't let anyone hurt you". Audrey looked up at Colletta with her big eyes and wiped away the tears with the back of her hand. Audrey announced, "I know what to do. They have always wanted me to save them, but this time I know how, thanks to you". Audrey bravely stood and made her way to the Well of Souls beneath the holy rock. "I can speak to the spirits from here", she stated resolutely, "better to face my fears than die afraid". Lucy felt proud of Audrey at that moment, but the fear only escalated as she approached the dome.

Typhon shared a glance with Barak, "Do you think our plan will work?" asked Typhon. "I dearly hope so", replied his father, "but I'm not clear how the spirits can help us defeat the invading army. We need to have faith in the One". "I'm watching you two", warned Bridget calmly from the rear. "If I was in your position, I would do the same", replied Typhon, "but you will come to understand we mean no harm to you. In fact, we desire to save you, we dearly hope your girls will make a difference". Colletta and Audrey headed towards the steps into the darkness of the Well of Souls.

Barak quickly caught up with Colletta, he reached into his pocket and pulled out a small blue stone, like two pyramids joined at their base. He attached the stone to Colletta's forehead. It bonded to the Carocle inside her head, as if by a magnetic force. It flashed brilliant blue as it came into contact. "What is it?" asked Colletta in awe, Lucy was wondering the same thing. "It is the Kracz-el, an empathy amplifier. It allows you to share your thoughts and drives with others. I know you have a latent ability in yourself, but you may not be fully aware of it yet. Think of the times when you really needed help and you managed to influence someone nearby to help you". "Like when I got stuck in the tree, and Dad came to help me without being asked?" asked Colletta. "Yes. Except this device helps you build empathy and share feelings with others. It extends the range of your influence. It is immensely powerful; I am showing great faith in you by giving it to you. A part of your subconscious mind has been aware of the stone for some time and has been seeking it".

"Do we really have to go into the tunnels again, they are gross?" asked Colletta. "No, we can talk to the spirits from the entrance", clarified Audrey, "but we need some privacy". Bridget looked at Lucy quizzically, both moved to the entrance where the others stood. "Let's give the girls some space", announced Lucy, they walked into the dark chamber beneath the rock. Audrey looked afraid but made a conscious effort to gather her courage. She sat down by the old drain and started to whisper. Due to the linkage of the Carocles, Colletta was able to listen to the conversation. "I need to speak to the angry one", she whispered. Another voice became apparent, "You don't want to do that Audrey, he is terrible. He will bring down the walls if he is displeased, and that can happen very easily. You need to keep away from him". "No", Audrey asserted, "I need you to bring him to me, I need to speak to him now!"

There was muttering and nervous squabbling between a number of wispy voices that echoed around the cave.

"You!" exclaimed a loud deep discordant voice, "What do you want, disturbing my rest?" "That is the problem", asserted Audrey defiantly, "you can't rest". Colletta gathered her courage and spoke to the spirit, "Hello, my name is Colletta". "Who is she, why did you bring her? This is the place of the dead, you are not permitted here", demanded the spirit. The wall started to tremor as anger filled his voice. Colletta was afraid, but she continued, nonetheless. "You are trapped here because your bodies can't die. Audrey has explained the situation to me". Colletta reached out with her empathy. She didn't know if her ability would work with a ghost. Colletta continued, "I wish to strike a deal with you. You have always demanded help from Audrey, but she didn't know how to help you. But I do". The spirit calmed a little, the walls stopped shaking. "Go on", the voice echoed enquiringly. "I need you to help me, and by doing so you we will set you free", explained Colletta. "You will need to explain your bargain a little more, whilst I'm still in control of my legendary temper", whispered the spirit eerily.

14. The Battle for Mont St Michel

The aliens set up camp on the mainland. They were suspicious, obviously expecting a trap, they could see the array of weapons guarding the main causeway onto the island. They had sent one of their number to test the waters, he had struggled to swim due to his sheer body mass, but his adaptations allowed him to breathe underwater. He failed to navigate the quicksand and didn't appear again. Paul was unsure of the cause of the delay, but it soon became apparent. The aliens were expecting the remainder of their group to arrive, which took a few hours.

The beautiful Mont St Michel was simply a rocky outcrop with an ancient 11th century castellated abbey sat at the pinnacle. From the causeway was an ancient street lined with museums, cafes, and small shops. The road turned to the right as one entered the island, which then doubled back on itself as it climbed steeply towards the abbey. Trucks and a huge array of weaponry, missiles and grenade launchers lined the front of the monastery. A huge pair of catapults, as if from the Middle Ages, were dragged into place on the abbey rooftop; they were able to launch an array of modern and adapted munitions at the causeway. A wonderful fusion of ancient and modern, which seemed to characterise the island. The survivors had converted the museums and shops into homes and had built sandbag defences at points along the walkway in a zigzag fashion for defence.

"The enemy will come hard and fast down the causeway", announced Paul as he watched the forces gathering. "We must unleash all hell on them when they make their move".

"Yes, we need to blow the causeway from underneath them, forcing them into the quicksand. We have set charges all the way, and the floating bridge is rigged", answered Gerard diligently, "There are 134 pillars which are around 13 metres high, and each alternate pillar has a charge attached to it". Gerard, the leader of the community, had replaced Paul's clone brother, Sacha, who had been murdered by the Dark Ones. Gerard was not a seasoned soldier, but he was quickly becoming one, as times demanded. Life had been tough for Gerard, fending off attacks from the Shrooms and keeping the island infection free. The dead Shrooms had been cleared from the island and the causeway, it had taken several weeks to achieve. Gerard looked thoughtful for a second, "You know, you are so like our leader, Sacha. The resemblance is remarkable. I have had my doubts about the clone stories but now I see you in the flesh it is unmistakable".

The small port on the island had been destroyed during the troubles of the apocalypse. The floating bridge was almost a kilometre long and was the only way onto the island. "What is beneath the bridge?" queried Paul. "The old road, but luckily it's flooded by the water at the moment. The bridge was built to stop the old dam from retaining silt from the river. Otherwise, MSM would not be an island for 50 to 70 days a year", Gerard explained. "When we blow the bridge, they will simply fall onto the road, get up and continue their attack", suggested Paul. "I suppose so, but the destruction will be colossal, there will be metal and shrapnel flying in all directions", he continued. "The aliens will withstand the explosions and the shrapnel", Paul clarified. Gerard looked at him expecting a joke but received none. Gerard shuffled nervously, Paul attempted to counter, "If we hit the aliens with munitions at the same time, they will be knocked around in a maelstrom. Let's hope we can push them into the quicksand. These creatures won't cope well with the quicksand due to their mass".

Paul had prepared a contingency plan for the team's escape, the frigate 'The Phoenix' and HMS Audacious were standing by offshore. There were also two spaceships carefully placed in the gardens behind the abbey. The brothers had learned the invaders could withstand significant detonations, so instead they used flechettes and pieces of glass to wrap any charges. Paul wondered if the measures would work, these Cro Magnons, or Cros as the troops called them seemed invulnerable to attack once their armour was fully secured in place.

The alarm sounded as around two hundred Cros bounded towards the bridge in five waves. The bridge was already under significant stress as the second wave mounted it. As the third wave reached the crossing, Gerard gave the signal to detonate the bridge. All the charges exploded in the same instant to maximise the confusion of their enemy. Simultaneously, the team unleashed missiles, RPGs, and catapulted anti-personnel bombs. The whole area lit up, it was impossible to assess the situation, especially when the shells from the Phoenix and the Audacious started their pounding.

The bridge was utterly destroyed in seconds and reduced to rubble; the remaining aliens bounded back to the shore. Paul could only see the remains of the old road, which was visible through the water. "It looks like we only killed a handful", commented Paul clearly showing his disappointment. Gerard added, "I have no idea how to kill these creatures, barely twenty have been taken down". Paul shouted down to Spall who was lingering near the main gate to the island. "Spall, send someone in to assess their casualties, we need to understand how they were killed. It might help us improve our strategy". "I'm on it", he replied as he deployed Wrench, "Don't hang about, those things are fast". "Roger that", replied Wrench with a big wide smile. Paul suspected false bravado, the team felt they had little chance of holding the island, morale was low.

Cindy's report was accurate, in the sense that the creatures burned energy at an alarming rate and needed to feed voluminously and regularly during combat, which spanned several hours at a time. Wrench jogged up the hill to the main arsenal with Spall. "We took the casualties through the joints in the armour", Wrench reported, "The ball bearings and shrapnel inflicted little damage, but the flechettes ripped through the joints". Spall observed, "Knights in armour attacking the castle, it's like déjà vu all over again", quoting a favourite saying. The old knights were always vulnerable at the elbows, the back of the knee, and the throat. The comparison with medieval armour seemed an appropriate analogy, but it belied the incredible protection the armour provided. "Some flechettes penetrated their helmets at the bottom near the neck too. I suspect we need to keep the flechettes pounding them or we will need to fight them hand to hand". "Forget that", commented Spall, "those guys are as strong as bulls, we would have no chance. We run if it comes to that". "They are very large and bulky, we could use speed to defeat them", suggested Paul. "I doubt it, they are acclimatised to high gravity, it's like swatting flies to them".

Wrench continued, "It looks like three of the Cros were pushed into the quicksand by the blast. They had no chance once they got caught there, their mass drew them down in the sand very quickly. The more they struggled the faster they sank". The observation gave Paul an idea, he contacted the ships and instructed the men at the arsenal to aim their bombardment to the west side of the causeway, so the Cros would be pushed into the quicksand on the east side by the explosions. It was a gamble, but one worth taking given the severity of the situation.

Gerard was interrupted by two men talking to him fervently in French. He turned to Paul, "As you know, we have a professional science team on the island. Meet Marcel and Bruno who would like to borrow the facilities of your spaceship for a couple of hours to test a theory, please". "Yes of course, Joe and Pascal will help with the AI. But what is the idea?" replied Paul. "They would rather not say until they are sure, it is a rather sensitive matter, they need to work it through fully with the Pareth-ng scientist, Pascal. The scientists have been working on the virus for almost two years, but it's the first time they have been able to work with a target DNA. The scientists have worked on little else since the first meteorite hit. They had identified how it had been altered from its original form and how it targeted humans specifically. More research was needed to understand how the fungus itself was designed; however, they had made significant progress. The availability of the Cro's organic samples allowed them to transition from their theoretical studies to assist with the reality of the imminent threat. "About bloody time", whispered Paul to himself.

Joe disappeared into the abbey with the three scientists, while Paul continued his vigil. It was clear the Cros were getting ready for another attack. "Stand By", shouted Spall, "they are on their way again". The creatures bounded down the hill onto the causeway in five groups. This time, they were hampered by the water and the obstacles from the wreckage. The water was two metres deep, so they were forced to wade up to their necks, they made slow progress for a kilometre, but they kept coming. The bombardment recommenced but without the flechettes and shrapnel; they would be less effective in the water. Spall had coordinated the attack, so the explosions caused large shockwaves in the water to knock the aliens into the quicksand, but they had anticipated the ploy and deliberately steered their path into the explosions. Only a handful were hurt by the salvo, a couple struggled in the quicksand, but their companions pulled most of them free. They continued their steady progress through the waters as the offensive persisted. "Were nearly out of ammo", announced Spall. It was brutal news, Paul prepared to defend the walls against the monsters in close combat.

The entrance had been fortified with large stone blocks, the team feverishly tried to block the path and increase the height of the barricade. The Cros hit the wall hard, they couldn't clear it in their heavy armour, they smashed it down by hand. As six creatures shattered stone, the others started to move around the walls punching their way through the stone shop and house walls. Paul was considering retreat when Joe arrived with a modified sedative gun. "You think you are going to sedate one of those rhinos?" asked Paul with an agitated look. "Pull back to the abbey", he shouted. "Trust me", shouted Joe.

Wrench was the best marksman by a margin. He sighted the pistol, held his breath, and fired as the first alien breached the wall. The adapted flechette hit the alien in the neck, at the joint between the breastplate and the helmet, the beast simply swatted the dart away and continued. The defenders sprinted uphill towards the abbey as the first alien grabbed one of the soldiers, delivering a precise but surprisingly careful punch to the soldier's head. The punch stunned rather than killed, which was odd. Paul surmised the aliens wanted them alive!

The team manned the sandbag barriers repel the marauders, but they were smashed aside like tinder wood. Twenty Cros entered the square as the defending force opened fire. The air thickened with the stench of cordite; the noise was disorienting. The aliens stood unflinchingly, as if the attack was insignificant; they were demonstrating that resistance was pointless. Paul yelled, "Abandon the island", but as everybody ran, they realised they were surrounded. The invaders had managed to ascend the steep cliff wall using steel ropes with heavy grappling hammers. Even the spaceships had been cut off. It was hopeless, there was no escape.

15. Return to the Tiger's Nest (Abe)

From the journal of Abraham Cauldy

25th March 2021

I never quite feel myself, I'm out of sorts. I feel the memories of my life are like a movie once watched. The memories never quite feel real, the feelings and smells are hollow somehow. Yet these are my memories, they shape me.

<Duplicated opening paragraphs of Abe's diary omitted as a courtesy to the reader: detailing his divorce, the death of his wife and the arrangements with his contact>

The newspaper on the hotel desk was printed in the year 2021, which confused me. I was certain the millennium hadn't yet passed, but I live in a constant state of confusion. I am staying in a small, pleasant hotel, as instructed I have called my contact via the call handler at a gentleman's retreat in Amsterdam, leaving my room's external phone number. I can see canals from my window, and tall thin wooden framed houses in pastel colours.

Within an hour my phone rang, I heard the voice of my contact once more, his tone was friendly and polite. He instructed me to fly to the Bhutan kingdom via Mumbai in India. He also asked me to purchase good hiking gear, as I would be covering ground on foot in the Himalayas. He warned me my trip may be perilous, I need to be watchful. I must avoid anyone dressed in black wearing a hood, these people may be dangerous. My task was to recover the second of a pair of ancient artifacts and return it to him safely. I'm not completely sure of my location or what year it is, but I can call a taxi. I asked the taxi driver to take me to the nearest airport, called Schiphol. It is ironic that I called Amsterdam with my phone number, when I have been staying in the city all the time. Had I realised, I would have taken the train to the heart of the airport.

I visited a decent hiking shop on the way, and purchased a pair of comfortable hiking boots, a good coat and hat plus some emergency provisions. The owner was extremely helpful and ensured I had everything I needed. The woollen hat had an extremely bright torch built into it; I have never seen such a thing. It is amazing, and blindingly bright. The shopkeeper explained that the torch would work for 100 hours before it required a new battery. The Dutch are very smart, obviously. I loaded my purchases into the boot of the taxi and continued to the airport. I bought a first-class ticket to Mumbai, which cost me €945 which seemed rather steep, given that this new Euro currency was roughly equivalent to pound sterling.

I feasted well in the airport lounge before boarding the flight, I decided to push the boat out and dine in a rather expensive chicken restaurant, it was delicious if a little greasy. The sign said it was finger lickin' good, but you never find me being so vulgar. I wiped my hands with the napkin, as any gentleman would. The time for the flight soon arrived, I showed my passport and boarded the plane, which is a brand-new Boing 747 jet. It was so comfortable, it looked like a spaceship. The air hostess brought me a glass of wine, and a packet of pretzels, which are like Jewish knotted crackers. I managed to sleep on the flight for a couple of hours, but my dreams were unpleasant. I dreamt of a darkly dressed man with a vicious looking dagger, I believe it was simply my subconscious mind playing tricks on me, following the warning from my contact.

My id likes to be playful; my mind had concocted something to terrify me once again.

26th March 2021

I arrived at Mumbai feeling quite fresh, I disembarked and booked a scheduled flight to Bhutan as per my remit. I followed the same process as I had in Amsterdam and procured a ticket to Paro, nestled amongst the Himalayas in Bhutan. I had a long wait, so I bought local currency from a booth with a heavy glass counter, the currency is Ngultrum. I was told that Ngultrum is terribly similar in value to the Indian Rupee, so it should be easy to remember.

My flight was called at midday, I was forced to examine the details on a large billboard which changed in front of my eyes, it was amazing. I proceeded to board a small, rather old aeroplane with four propellers and too many passengers, it was smelly and hot. Some passengers took off their shoes and wiggled their toes, it was quite disgusting.

On arrival, I took a taxi to Paro and checked in at a nice hotel in the centre of town. The concierge spoke in excellent English, "It is nice to see you again sir. I hope you have a wonderful stay". It was odd. I replied, "I'm sorry, but I haven't visited your country before. You must be mistaken, my friend". The concierge gave me a strange look but smiled and wished me a good day. My rucksack appeared in my room a few minutes later, I tipped the boy with a few coins, and I called my contact as usual.

This time my contact's response was rapid, within twenty minutes. He politely requested that I visit Taktsang Palphug Monastery, which means Tiger Nest in English according to the concierge. I knew I needed to take the trek slowly in the altitude. My mission was to meet with the Llama and share an unusual message with him, which I was asked to memorise. My instructions were extremely specific and were not to be committed to paper.

In the evening, I walked through the city and took in the warmth and history of the place, the Buddhist temples, the friendly culture, and the spicy aromas. I feel I have travelled a lot, but I'm not sure where. I felt I knew the location of the monastery and it was close, so I procured a map and decided to head out the following day on foot. Given the warnings about the darkly dressed men, I took wide detours on the trails mingling amongst the other hikers to remain as inconspicuous as I could (which wasn't hard for me).

27th March 2021

I breakfasted with a group of fellow hikers and made an early start. I enjoyed their company for the ten-mile hike to the start point of the track up to the monastery, we arrived a little after midday and settled in the camp for lunch. The beautiful monastery perched on a cliff in the mountains above us, it looked utterly unreachable, but my fellow travellers assured me it was an easy climb, finishing with steps up to the top. Every breath was a joy, the air was invigorating. I took the path through a delightful pine forest, the map indicated it should only take a couple of hours. I was looking forward to the trek.

The views were magnificent at the halfway mark, the steps that followed were quite a climb. One of the hikers in our party was forced to stop for breath but urged us to continue, she would catch us later. My knees were a little sore from the climb, but I ignored the discomfort, I was overwhelmed by the beauty of the place. The monastery was white and brown and had four stunning golden temple rooftops, it became more stunning the closer we got.

The next scheduled tour of the monastery was at 2pm. My associates settled on the benches and began to sample the fragrant rice and teas on offer at a nearby stall. The lady who had stopped for rest re-joined the party as I said my goodbyes and approached the monastery main door. "They won't let you in. It's scheduled tours only", advised one of the group. I smiled and headed over to the main door regardless. I knocked on the temple door and a young man dressed in orange robes opened the door, his face greeted me warmly. "Welcome, you visit us once again. Please come in". It was strange, I had never visited the temple in my life. I spoke the Tibetan phrase I had been given by my contact, I believe it translates to "I attend on behalf of the ancient ones, my masters seek their artifact as is their birthright". I took off my shoes and entered the temple.

An older man joined us, smiling awkwardly. He mentioned that he would arrange an audience with the Llama. The young man returned with drinks in wooden bowls. "I was sent here by a member of the elder race. You have been safeguarding Kramml-zo for us, it is time for it to be returned to its rightful keeper". The Llama approached from the doorway having listened in to our conversation, he grinned widely, "You are not one of the elder race, my friend, you cannot make such requests". His words echoed strangely in my mind, like I had heard them before.

Before I could utter another word, there was shouting and screams from outside the temple and the main door was kicked open. Five hooded men entered the sanctity of the temple rudely. The priests attempted to placate the worried visitors explaining it was a place of meditation and calmness, but the priests were roughly pushed out of the way. The Llama looked concerned and grabbed my arm assertively, "Quickly, come with me". I followed, passing through several corridors between buildings, entering a cave which was situated beneath one of the temple buildings. The cave was dimly lit, but the Llama knew his way in the dark, his sure footedness suggested he frequented the labyrinth of passages.

We heard chilling screams from the temple. The Llama spoke calmly, "The intruders are torturing my brothers to determine our place of hiding. My brothers are at peace with the universe; the men will learn nothing from them. Do not be afraid, Dugkarmo will protect us. The sounds from above terrified me, they continued for almost an hour and were brutal. When the chilling noises subsided, we could hear rustling at the opening of the cave. We pushed deeper into the cavern. The wall became wet, and the temperature plummeted. The Llama spoke to me again, "We must not allow the Kramml-zo to fall into the wrong hands, it is a terrible weapon which could wreak terrible evil upon the world. The intruders will never find it; it is well hidden, please believe me".

We continued deeper into the caves, but the Llama eventually came to a point where the path became unpassable, we were forced to hide in the darkness fearfully awaiting our inevitable capture. There were several paths through the cave, but it was impossible to evade our pursuers for very long. Finally, we were apprehended, we were roughly dragged back to the temple, into the main hall. The temple's prayer stone had been smashed. There were twenty priests' bodies piled in the corner, one of the darkly dressed men attempted to drain blood into a jar from the corpses. It was a horrific sight to behold.

The Llama and I were bound and pinned to the floor. The leader of the intruders demanded the location of the Krammlzo artifact. The Llama was calm, he had entered a meditative zone where the intruders were unable to reach him. The darkly dressed men used a dark blade to torture the Llama, but he didn't utter a single word. Their torment had no effect on him; they became irritated. When they turned to me, I knew my reaction would be a little different. "I have no idea of the nature of the artifact or it's whereabouts, I was merely sent here to collect it. I know nothing, please do not hurt me". The leader grinned, "I'm sure you are right, but I need to be thorough. Let me introduce myself, my name is Supay, I am the leader of my legion of Dark Ones". He took his blade and amputated the little finger on my left hand. I screamed; the pain was unbearable. I begged for him to stop, but he viciously continued to slowly remove the remaining fingers on my left hand. He began pushing the tip of his blade beneath the nails on my right hand, blood soaked my clothing, small pools appeared on the floor around me. The pain became so intense that I could no longer scream, I drifted out of consciousness, Supay repeatedly held ammonium salts beneath my nose to bring me back, my nasal passages burned from the assault.

Supay removed my boots and socks and started to amputate toes from my left foot, and lever off the nails on my right foot. He took down my trousers and hovered with the knife menacingly, smirking. I must have passed out from the pain; I awoke moments later to see the Llama being dragged to the main door. I was hoisted to my feet and pulled behind him, my feet screamed with pain. We entered the area in front of the temple, where the intruders gathered two dozen hostages. Their leader spoke to the Llama and I, "Let's see how noble you are when innocent people start to die". The group of hikers I had befriended were amongst the hostages, they looked at me alarmed when they noticed the terrible state I was in. They were terrified, several had stains on their trousers where they had failed to retain the contents of their bladders.

One by one the hostages were brought forward. The first had his throat cut and the blood drained into a bucket. His body was lain for all to see, arcane symbols were drawn on the stony ground with his blood. The second hostage was forced to bend over the corpse, and was stabbed multiple times to cripple him, but was left to writhe and scream in pain. The heap of bodies grew until there was only one woman left, she was the lady who had stopped to rest on the walk to the temple. She was being held up by her shoulders, she was petrified, her mouth hung open in a silent scream.

After his terrible show of power, Supay turned to us, "You can save this lady If you divulge the location of the artifact, it is amazingly easy. Do not feel you have let anyone down, other than the poor wretches, where your obstinance has brought about their death. You have done everything you can. Now tell us, where we find the Kramml-zo, and we will let this poor woman free. You have my word". The Llama whispered prayers repeatedly, as I continued to beg for my life.

The Llama looked at peace as the intruders continued to damage his body and beat him severely. The frustration was surging in his interrogator, he was becoming increasingly desperate. In the end, life left the Llama, and his soul ran free, his face looked at peace. The assassin screamed his frustration and turned to me. He grabbed me by the throat and squeezed. I couldn't breathe, my lungs silently shrieked in pain. Supay walked me over to the precipice and dangled my body dangerously over the edge. "Tell me now, and I will end you painlessly", he commanded. I tried to explain I didn't know, but he looked at me with disgust and threw me from the cliff. I remember seeing the world flying past me, the silence of the fall, the peace for a fleeting moment. Then I hit the rocks and a world of pain assaulted me once again. I woke sometime later howling in agony, my body broken. I had not fallen the full distance, I had collided with a fir tree and dropped through its branches, I could feel a branch impaling me.

It felt like there were only a few minutes of my life remaining, so I tried hard to control the pain as best I could. A moment of peace overwhelmed me, as I took out my journal to finish my entry. I wanted the world to understand the events which had befallen me and be warned about these vile men. I am sitting here, looking at the blue sky, wondering how long I have left.

16. Fighting Dirty

The leader of the invasion force looked at Paul, removed his helmet and grinned savagely while speaking the single word, "Boss". He barked in a language the Carocle didn't recognise and stared at Paul with his two pairs of eyes, which glazed over for a moment. The circle started to close, the aliens systematically grabbed our soldiers and knocked them unconscious. Paul wondered how many soldiers had been killed by the impact of the blows, although most seemed to be breathing.

Boss clenched his fist slowly to make a show of punching Paul, as the others grabbed Spall and Gerard. Boss' eyes clouded again, he froze and shivered. It was a small vibration, but the others noticed it immediately and stopped to look at their leader, it was clearly not normal. The shaking got more violent, until Boss dropped Paul and launched himself at the Cro holding Spall. Spall and Gerard tumbled across the courtyard as Boss tore into his comrades. The fight was vicious, the leader hit the other Cro with a brutal hammer blow full in the face, its helmet was flung into the air. Paul and the remainder of the team looked on confused. Had a protocol been broken? Boss delivered repeated blows to faces of his comrades, in frustration he attempted to wrench free the helmet and bite the neck of one of his men.

Inside the spaceship, Joe, Pascal and two scientists monitored the conflict but made no attempt to intervene. The ship was surrounded by Cros, but they had made no effort to break in. Wrench had shot the Cro leader with a flechette, but the team were unsure if the toxin had penetrated the skin. The creatures' epidermis looked hard, able to withstand explosive charges, but Wrench had observed the sharp flechettes ability to penetrate specific places in the armour. They waited with bated breath until the violence exploded in the large area in front of the abbey. The scientists were triumphant; the delivery of a modified fungal infection appeared to be successful.

Boss' use of teeth was quite a departure from the Cro's usual behaviour. The team continued to observe as the Cros attempted to restrain their insane leader, as he dropped his victim lifeless to the floor. More significantly, there was a huge mushroom growing from the neck of their fallen comrade, forcing its way between the plates of his armour at the base of his skull.

"The Cro's growing fruit, get out of here!" shouted a startled Spall, gathering his wits. "It's ok", responded Paul as he watched the continuing struggle, "the infection has been coded to their DNA, not ours". The fight escalated as Boss refused to be held down, he was extraordinarily strong but failed to free himself. Two of the Cros restraining him stopped the struggle and glazed over, it became clear they had been bitten in the struggle.

The Cros eventually became aware of the fruit growing on their comrades and looked quizzically as the pod exploded sending spores everywhere. Paul's team began to panic, but Paul and Spall tried to calm them. "The infection is for them, not us", explained Paul. "Stay calm, and we will get out of here alive". The Cros started to choke, more Cros joined the fight. The attack was the distraction the team needed. "Get to the ships", announced Spall. The men didn't need persuading, they picked up their unconscious comrades and carried them. Cindy elongated the three ships to accommodate the soldiers and occupants of the island, as they boarded the vessels. They were in the air within minutes, watching the scene unfolding below them.

The fighting accelerated, as the remaining aliens were drawn into the fray. The aliens could tolerate significant blows, but biting was more effective once the armour was loosened. The fighting continued until many of the invaders were killed and fruit grew from their necks. The stiff green tinged Shrooms slowed and began to feed upon their fallen comrades.

Pascal, Marcel, and Bruno were hailed as heroes, Paul ensured that Cindy had her fair share of credit. The soldiers felt it was odd to praise a machine, but Paul was aware Cindy was a fully functional mind and needed to be treated like everyone else. All rational minds valued being part of a team.

The MSM team were repatriated temporarily until the huge corpses had been removed. The land was covered by inactive, rotting Shrooms, the villagers had learned to ignore them. They were no threat and would eventually be hoisted into the sea and washed away. There was no time to celebrate as a large fleet of the aliens were on course to Earth.

The brothers discussed battle tactics with Mak, Spall and Gerard in the abbey. Franc joined via the Carocle whilst monitoring the invasion fleet from the moon. The new warships represented a significant threat, to say the very least. Not only would the team be unable to take the aliens out in space, but they would also face an exceptionally large force on the ground. "We need to draw them into MSM, so that they will be infected", suggested Paul. "We need to do it quickly, so they don't cause too much damage. I have no idea of their intentions if they capture us". "They will most likely enslave us", suggested Joe. "There are sixteen ships, each containing at least a hundred warriors. We have no idea where they will land. Their scanning activity suggests they will target the largest populated areas, so possibly Isola Salina, Summer Haven, Russia and here, given that Formentera is largely abandoned for the time being", explained Mak. Joe became agitated, "We don't have means to defend ourselves in Salina. The sulphurous air will hamper the virus, for once it will work against us". "You must evacuate the island quickly", added Franc.

Two spaceships departed for Salina within the hour. The frigate set a course for St Petersburg, as a contingency in case the spaceships were otherwise deployed. Paul left the room to speak to Franc confidentially via the Carocle as he waited in space obscured by the moon, "Are you aware that Lucy and the girls have left on a mission with Typhon. I'm usure of their task, but a re-clone of Barak is with them". "What? You can't be serious. That man is a twisted murderer, I need to help them", replied Franc suddenly afraid for his family. "We need to trust Lucy; she is aware of Barak's history, but she has chosen to trust him. Bridget is with them, and they are both armed. There's something afoot, but I have no idea of their intentions", added Paul. "I guess we need to have faith in them, they're not stupid. But what are they doing?" "I don't know, but I do know I have sensed both Colletta and Audrey", pointed out Paul. Franc paused for a moment, "Audrey is too young for a Carocle, her memories must be awful to live with, especially when they appear so clear". "I suggest you release the missiles into the wind, and get back down here", Paul argued. "Roger that", Franc replied eagerly. Franc set a course to return from his observation mission, it was achieving little, the scanners could detect the ships.

Franc targeted the sixteen ships with missiles. The AI, Becky, confirmed the missiles would hit the lead ships if launched immediately and they continued on their current bearing. The missiles would hit their target in less than a month, there was little chance of success if they changed course. She added that if the ships were heading to Earth, then the missiles would attract enemy attention with such a hostile act. Franc chose not to launch the missiles, instead he headed to Jerusalem to protect his family.

17. An Unexpected SOS

The worst of the battle's carnage was disposed of at sea, the immense alien cadavers being rolled into the Atlantic Ocean using a dumper truck. The team stored the alien's armour for closer inspection, it could prove useful, it was extremely dense and strong. Paul turned his attention to the ruined floating bridge. "Looks like MSM will be a tidal island once again", muttered Gerard, "plus ça change, plus c'est la même chose". "Sorry?" asked Paul. "The more things change, the more they stay the same", clarified Gerard.

The evacuation began, everyone gathered in the surrounding villages, ready to be transported back to their havens. The spores from the fruit were collected and stored, to be deployed as a weapon for future invasions. The team bagged the heads of the mushrooms before they released their deadly payload of spores. Dispersing the spores into the air from bags proved a more effective delivery technique than dart guns, which required formidable accuracy. The spores infected the Cros despite the complex breathing apparatus grafted to their faces.

Paul stopped for a moment; a curious expression filled his face. "Did you hear that?" commented Joe. "We need to check its origin, I don't think it was us", observed Paul. Cindy triangulated the signal, identifying it as a transmission from the hulk of the Cro spaceship slowly drifting towards the sun. The same unintelligible signal was transmitted an hour later, then finally a clear transmission was received. "It is a standard Earth SOS message. It is a precise copy of the call the mother ship sent out to attract the attention of the alien vessel", explained Cindy.

The brothers debated their next move with Spall. It was a potentially dangerous journey to the spaceship due to radiation, plus it would only take a single alien to cause mayhem. They concluded, the Cros would be unlikely to send an SOS, they would consider it an admission of weakness. "Curiosity killed the cat, they say", muttered Joe as he boarded his discovery ship with James. Joe's ship lifted and was soon streaking across the grey sky, driven by a pair of large drone fans, setting a course for the abandoned Cro ship. The fans morphed into fusion engines as the ship left the Earth's atmosphere. "Be safe", pleaded Paul, "those creatures are dangerous. You have no idea what you are facing up there". "Don't worry", said Joe, "I'm no hero".

Cindy was instructed to self-destruct if anything happened to Joe and James. As the spaceship left Earth's gravity. The Cro ship became visible through the viewing port within a few hours. The scene that greeted them was terrible. There was no sign of the Pareth-ng mother ship. All that remained of the two Cro ships was an immense field of debris which spread in a giant sphere surrounding the terminally damaged hull of the remaining ship. The hull was heavily damaged, the aft had melded into a mass of magma.

Cindy carefully navigated the debris field drifting close to the ship. Joe and James donned radiation suits, whilst the ship morphed to the docking port on the alien vessel. The portal opened and Joe ventured onto the remains of the enemy ship, with James close behind. James carried a pistol, although it would be utterly useless unless there was an oxygenated atmosphere to allow combustion of the firing cap. However, it made him feel more comfortable.

Joe and James followed the long utility corridors, lined by pipe and conduits. They entered the second airlock and continued into another long featureless corridor which terminated in a further airlock. The airlocks were enormous, but fortunately they still operated without manual intervention. Beyond the last doorway they were greeted by five diminutive humanoids wearing grey atmosphere suits with opaque helmets. The leader of the group's face was drawn, and he looked unwell. His eyes were large and almost feline in structure, but quickly changed to a more human biology.

"T..hank..you…for..res…cue…ing us", came the voice directly into Joe's Carocle. The voice became more fluent as it continued. "We are… the Kraalt, we are slaves of the Mbunalt warriors. We have been left to die here; we humbly request your assistance". "How many are you?" asked Joe carefully. "There are five of us remaining from a total crew of thirty, ten on each ship". Joe beckoned the aliens to follow him to his ship, "Let's not spend any more time here than we need to".

Joe considered the small aliens as they boarded his vessel. Cindy piloted the ship on a direct course to enter Earth's orbit. The journey would take a few hours, giving Joe plenty of time to engage the aliens in conversation in an attempt to determine their motives. He opened channels with his brothers so they could contribute when they felt the need. Joe began diplomatically, "My name is Joe, I am from the blue world below us called Earth. It is a lovely planet, but we have been forced to defend ourselves from the warriors who escaped from your ship in pods. Our forces are preparing to defend against an invasion by more ships entering our solar system. We were forced to defend ourselves following your attack on the Parethng mother ship, which was defenceless. Our sensors failed to identify your presence on this vessel. Assuming you mean us no harm, I can offer asylum until your additional ships arrive". All five Kraalt proceeded to answer and introduce themselves concurrently. Joe interjected, "Please, please. I can't process five conversations at once. Could you possibly talk one at a time?"

The leader was quickly elected, he manipulated his face strangely, but Joe intuitively felt that it could be his attempt at replicating a smile. "Let me introduce myself and my companions. We are the Kraalt, we originate from Kraal, one of the moons orbiting the Mbunalt home world Zetal, which may be beyond your current observations". "What are your names?" queried Joe. "We are not allocated names, we function as a single entity in service to our overlords, the Mbunalt. You see, we exist only to provide technology and service for the warriors. We fly their warships and operate their weaponry; we provide food and water. We perform all menial tasks for them".

Joe looked pensive for a second, "Is the arrangement amicable to your kind?" The alien looked troubled, and then responded carefully, "That is not a question we are permitted to consider, it is unthinkable. We have no choice; they would destroy us in a heartbeat if we failed to provide service". "But surely you operate their weaponry and their life support. Is that not a basis to negotiate with them?" The small alien's eyes saddened, "They are extremely tough, as you must have already found. We are no match for them, they are relentless and unforgiving. They fight to the death. There is no negotiation, no empathy, just warcraft. We have no choice but to serve them. I request that you do not inform them of our dissent, if we are captured into service once more". "Of course not, we will say we captured you", empathised Joe. The small alien looked into Joe's eyes, "Is this not the case, are we not prisoners?"

Joe held the small humanoid's gaze, "You are not our prisoners, you are free providing you truly mean us no harm; we do not tolerate slavery, every man or woman is equal on our planet regardless of colour, creed, sexuality or indeed species. Decisions are taken democratically when we are not in a war situation. However, you need to integrate, and become a part of our community. If you seek to assist our enemies, then we will be forced to act. To help us to work with you a little, it would help if you each chose a name". The little alien became uncertain and turned to his comrades. A thought exchanged between them subliminally and one of them turned to address Joe. "Your life sounds wonderful, but is a little worrying for us, it is beyond our experience. However, looking at your present situation your freedom might not last long. When the ships arrive, you will need to offer your service to the Mbunalt or be destroyed, we will be back where we started. You have our word; we will not assist your enemy until our point of capture". "We won't surrender", stated Joe firmly, "we value our freedom, we will resist until death".

The Kraalt conferred silently for a moment, "We cannot fight, it goes against our philosophy. We are strict pacifists, but we will help you however we can. When your enemy prevail, and they will, we will return to their service. I'm sorry to labour the point, we want to be completely open with you. You have treated us with respect, and you deserve no less". "We will need to ensure defeat is not the outcome", replied Joe. "The Kraalt have been enslaved for millennia, we may take some time to adjust to a new way of life. We feel comfortable with service, it is all we have known for thousands of Earth years". Joe responded, "The important thing is you are happy, and you are treated decently".

Joe continued, "If you don't mind me asking, what technology do you provide the Mbunalt?" The Kraalt's strange attempt at a smile filled his face and he replied, "We build starships, weapons, medical facilities and food production resources". Joe smiled, "Such help would be most useful, most of our industry was lost when the Pareth-ng wiped out most of our population". The Kraalt replied, "We observed that you destroyed one of their starships, but what happened to the remainder of the other ship? Did the crew die when you detonated the ship? We monitored the humans were moving oddly on the vessel and we assumed they were compromised".

Joe explained how the mother ship had been rigged to simulate life. The Kraalt were shocked that the Pareth-ng were permitted to integrate with the human population after they had committed genocide. The Kraalt sought impartial evidence before they could fully trust Joe's words, they were more than incredulous. The Kraalt posed another question, "We observed you eliminated the warriors with an infection that their enhanced metabolisms were unable to deal with". "Yes", Joe replied, "It was a hastily modified version of the infection the Pareth-ng used to wipe us out, it proved very effective". "Yes indeed. But I do hope you are not relying on the virus to protect you from invasion. The Kraalt crews will be aware of the infection from the data provided by the Mbunalt armour's AIs. They will detect it's presence quickly and immunise the warriors".

Joe looked grave; the infection was their only hope for survival. "Then we will have to make our remaining time count", he replied. The brothers listening were suddenly thrown into a quagmire of doubt. They had no safe means, other than the fungal infection, for defending their planet. The only other defence was nuclear missiles. "If we were to use our tomahawk missiles, similar to the bombs that destroyed the Mbunalt ships, would it be possible to shield the planet and its life forms from the radiation?" queried Franc. Joe relayed the question, but the Kraalt had already heard. "Not without making the weapon ineffective", they replied. "You will destroy your planet, if you release too many of those dirty weapons". Joe pressed further, "Can you build weapons that would be effective against the Mbunalt?" "We can, but their armour is made from the toughest material in the universe. The weapons would only kill one warrior a time. We will help you however let us consider this carefully. There is truly little time".

Paul asked a question that had been playing on his mind. "Would it be possible for us to engage the Mbunalt from space? Could we use our discovery ships to launch nuclear missiles at their vessels?". The Kraalt looked uncomfortable, he appeared to be considering how forthright his answer could be. "Your rigged spaceship was a complete surprise to us. However, we observed your crude missiles from afar and identified their nature. The missiles were no surprise to us", replied the Kraalt. "So why did you not shoot them down?", asked Joe. "Because we hoped some of us could escape, in order to better understand your kind. Myself and my colleagues anticipated our overlords would be destroyed. We did not alert the warriors to the missiles, which was a terrible risk to our race. It is good the warriors are dead, or our lives would be forfeit. Some of us felt it was worth the risk, to experience freedom, if only for a little while. We are outliers within our hive, do not expect this behaviour from others.

We elected to lock ourselves in a heavy lead chamber, protected by a Faraday Cage and other nuclear radiation countermeasures. The protection kept the worst of the forces and radiation from us. We were injured when we emerged, radiation has penetrated our suits". Joe was instantly concerned, "So are you hurt now?" "Yes, two of us are mortally damaged, it is only a matter of time for the poison to take effect. The radiation was more intense than we expected, there were many simultaneous fissions".

Joe took a risk, breaking protocol he reached for the Kraalt and embraced them. They found Joe's gesture a little distressing but did nothing to avoid the contact, they were submissive by nature. Joe called on his gift of healing, he asked God to heal the humanoids. He had no idea if his healing would be successful with another alien species, it was worth a shot. The Kraalt flinched and shook in fear as Joe's eyes blazed white and the room glowed. The abrasions and discoloration began to disappear. When the light subsided, the Kraalt were reluctant to release the embrace. Joe had noticed they had started to hug him back. The leader dropped to his knees to offer thanks to Joe. "No! please. I have a gift, but please do not kneel to me. I'd prefer it if you didn't". The kneeling continued, it seemed to be their way of giving thanks. An unbreakable bond had formed between Joe and the five hyper intelligent, aliens.

A long period of silence and contemplation followed the healing. Joe sensed increased activity in the Kraalt, but he worried about the impact of the invasion of the Mbunalt beasts on his friends and family. "What do they plan to do with us?" Joe asked cautiously.

18.   A Bargain with The Boatman

Colletta emerged cautiously from the Well of Souls gently holding Audrey's hand, the girls looked pale and drained. Lucy and Bridget sensed their fatigue and ran to offer them maternal support. Lucy embraced them both tightly, holding on for a while saying nothing until the girls were ready to talk. Lucy and Bridget sensed their trepidation and it concerned them, although they could sense a measure of triumph. Neither Colletta nor Audrey would breathe a word of the promises they had made, nor the deal they had struck with the spirits.

Lucy became anxious; she instinctively felt something dark had taken place in the caves. "Tell me, I need to know!" she exclaimed worriedly, "it's important". "I can't say", explained Colletta, "I promised I wouldn't tell a living soul; if we talk the deal is off". Lucy felt powerless, there was nothing she could do to help. She knew her children would have to live with the consequences of their pact. In the absence of information, her mind naturally started to play crazy tricks, horrible possibilities consumed her, although the truth was remarkably simple. All genuinely great acts have a fundamental simplicity that cuts through complexity and politics.

Barak and Typhon looked vaguely satisfied, though they said extraordinarily little. Lucy wondered if they knew of the nature of the bargain, but she failed to glean useful information from them. She had trusted the two men, against her natural instincts; Lucy hoped she hadn't made a terrible mistake. "What next?" she asked. "We will take you to your husband. We need to leave you with him and prepare for war. Your husbands will need all the help they can get, we have twenty-four soldiers who will fight to the death to help save Earth", replied Barak.

Entering the ship, the group exchanged no words; they were transported rapidly across the Mediterranean Sea and north into France. They landed next to Joe's ship in the yard at the rear of the abbey atop Mont St Michel. As Lucy, Bridget, and the girls left the ship, Barak wished them luck, and the silver ship took off once again into the early evening sky. For the first time Bridget and Lucy surveyed the wreckage and started to surmise the extent of the conflict that had taken place on the small island. Their next thoughts were concerning the safety of their husbands and friends.

The Kraalt grew troubled in the light of Joes question concerning their fate. It was important for the team to understand what to expect from the Mbunalt if they were captured, and the actions needed to counter their threat. The Kraalt took no pleasure in explaining the ways of their rulers. "Before I begin, you need to understand that we do not encourage or approve of the ways of our masters. We simply perform as we are instructed. They are a force of nature, and we have no influence over them. The Mbunalt are an honourable race of merchants, but this group are renegades and pirates. They are unruly and operate outside the sphere of influence of their race. They have strong bodies, they are used to high gravity, but they have had illegal modifications and augmentations made to become what they are. Conquest follows the same pattern in all worlds for these Mbunalt warriors. They will always seek to enslave a race as their first priority to allow them to focus on war. However, they have insidious ways, they are driven by the black market, selling their wares to the highest bidder. Earth is their first incursion into this part of the universe.

The indignity for the prisoners begins on initial capture, the warriors will take a prisoner's adrenal gland as soon as practicable. Kraalt assist with healing to make their captives ready for work without delay. The Mbunalt pirates prize adrenal glands, they fetch high prices from other more dangerous races. Survival of a prisoner without the gland is not an issue, but it hampers their natural fight or flight instinct. This is a small side benefit to the Mbunalt, as typically prisoners will cause them less trouble. Slavery will continue until a prisoner approaches an age where they are too old to be of service.

When aging slaves fail to meet expectations, the warriors harvest their Pituitary and Pineal glands, then physically rip the slave apart and consume their body in one of their disgusting 'banquets'. The banquet is a ceremonial occasion, they hold great reverence in the violence of the killing. We have not learned why they prize the glands in the brain, but they trade them at a high value". Franc enquired, "Why can't they simply clone the adrenal glands rather than harvesting them, surely it would be easier and more predictable?" "Cloning doesn't meet the ritualistic protocols they follow. In addition, cloned glands don't produce the high-quality adrenaline they need. The Mbunalt abhor the Pareth-ng due to them embracing cloning, so they pursued the mother ship. You are unlucky they found your world; they are a long way from home". "The Pareth-ng led the Mbunalt here unwittingly", observed Franc, "great!" Joe postulated the reason the Pareth-ng had not encountered the species before was none had survived. "Well, that's all good then", remarked Franc sarcastically.

Mak addressed the leader, "Can I emphasise Joe's suggestion of taking individual names, it will make our hosts on this planet more comfortable". The leader replied, "We will think about it. We have studied Earth's broadcast media a little, we will try". He then added with special emphasis, "We are impressed how humans have offered their friendship, considering the devastation you caused". Mak turned a little humble, "Yes, they are good people, and didn't deserve the hardship others in my race inflicted. They will need all the help we can muster". "I'll drink to that", exclaimed Franc.

Colletta and Audrey ran into the awaiting arms of Franc who was patiently loitering at the landing site, followed closely by Lucy. "Missed you Daddy", exclaimed Audrey jovially. "Who are those funny little men?" asked Colletta when she was sure the Kraalt were out of earshot. "Our new friends, the Kraalt, are engineers for the Mbunalt who attacked us". "I don't like those big, horrible men. We need to stop them, I have asked for help", stated Audrey sternly. He decided not to ask Colletta about the bright blue stone in the centre of her forehead, he would save the question until later.

When the girls had gone to bed, Franc spoke to Lucy about Audrey's comments concerning the Mbunalt. He found it rather odd when Lucy didn't laugh. "She is plotting something, and I'm not sure I like it", whispered Lucy, "on our way here, we went on a little adventure". Lucy explained the events in Jerusalem, and the appearance of Barak's clone. "It's a good job Barak didn't show his face here. You took a big risk going with him", added Franc. "He was a gentleman and was true to his word, I will say that much", Lucy pointed out darkly. "I also noticed the girls are both wearing Carocles", Franc stated firmly. "Yes, Colletta *borrowed* the one she used to find Audrey. Typhon provided the other before our little excursion into the bowels of Jerusalem. Audrey seems ok with the Carocle, despite her young age", explained Lucy. "Yes, that one is old beyond her years". "I can hear you Daddy", giggled Audrey. Franc answered in his stern voice, "Get back to bed young lady, and take that thing off right now!"

At midnight the following night, the two girls were woken by a message from Typhon, "It's time, we need to begin the process". "Don't wake the others; be very, very quiet", mouthed Colletta to Audrey as they rose with caution. They tip toed to the end of the dorm and round the corridor which led them up the stairs to the roof of the abbey. They sat cross legged at the highest point, holding hands. Colletta took a deep breath, gathering her courage, as Audrey looked at her with empathy. They stared into each other's eyes and began the ritual Barak had explained to them. They understood the theory of the ritual, but it was all new and rather confusing in practice.

The girls spoke quietly for some time, the stone connected to Colletta's Carocle and glowed brightly, flashing several times and turning obsidian. The flashing light alarmed the sentries below, whose activity woke Franc. He only slept lightly when there were enemies in such close proximity. He rushed to the roof to find Colletta unconscious. Audrey was crying, her sobbing subsided after a few moments. "It's ok Daddy, we did it". "You did what exactly?" Franc demanded firmly. Audrey adopted a disappointed tone, "We are trying to help you". Lucy appeared beside Franc, "What did that bastard do to my little girls?" She had been mid nightmare when she was rudely awoken by Franc's surge to the roof. Colletta opened her eyes and whispered, "Dad, we need you to help us. We need keep re-enacting the ritual. It's really important and we can't stop now it's inaugurated, it's too dangerous". No amount of questioning would lead to a full explanation, the girls would only say they had made a promise they needed to keep.

Franc spoke quietly to Lucy, "The girls seem to be ok, but I have no idea what they were up to. I really don't like the look of the blue stone on Colletta's forehead. I've asked her to get rid of it, but she said she can't and she won't". "Barak gave her the stone, he calls it 'the artifact'. He told her it amplifies her natural empathetic abilities". "Well, I don't like it Lucy", Franc replied. "We agree on that!" added Lucy angrily. Franc attempted to contact Typhon, but there was no response, which made him more uncomfortable.

The next morning the sun rose early, the glorious day was spoiled by disturbing news. Mak informed Paul that the enemy fleet was only one week away from Earth. The leader of the Kraalt, who had adopted the name 'Buddy', explained the fleet would aim to land the warships directly on Earth, they would not need landing vessels. They were likely to concentrate their forces where their pods had landed and would investigate the cause of the deaths of their comrades. The intelligence proved exceedingly accurate.

Mak had almost completed transporting soldiers from Salina and Formentera. The forces from Russia had also arrived. The

Phoenix returned from its venture; it had aborted when the spaceship became available for transportation. Bart strategically positioned the two nuclear submarines to cover the USA from Washington and Russia/Asia from the northern Black Sea. Paul's son, Matthew remained aboard the Audacious and he was loving it. His new role made him feel like an adult, which he was rapidly becoming. He also enjoyed playing an important part in the war preparations, he continued to provide critical communication links using his Carocle.

Franc worked with the Kraalt to improve the efficacy of the available weaponry. There was limited time to develop energy weapons, and more importantly the vast energy sources needed to power them wasn't portable. They had poor resources, and mining the precious metals and minerals took time they didn't have. Franc sourced sufficient quantities of the warrior armour, which was manufactured from the alien metal Aggt, to evaluate improving their arsenal. Each piece was so heavy that a backhoe was required to move it.

The only real progress was the forging of three unusual 'swords' from the metal. Each weapon comprised of a hilt and guard; however, the blade was more complex. The Kraalt presented the sword in childlike terms, the hilt contained a nuclear power source based on the tiny arrays of nuclear reactors used in the Pareth-ng suicide suits. The blade was an infinitesimally thin wire made from Aggt. The metal was extremely strong but of little use, other than being the sharpest and strongest cheese wire known to man. The smart part of the sword was in the hilt, which generated a narrow glowing force field, a fine purple haze with the wire at its centre. The wire was razor sharp and impossible to snap as it was completely immobilised by the force field embracing it. Unfortunately, there were only three weapons, which was not even close to being viable. Franc kept one of the swords on his back in a special scabbard beside his Katana. The Japanese 'Nihonto' blade was always his preferred backup plan. The remaining two weapons could only be wielded by experienced swordsmen, novices could easily dismember themselves.

The fleet of warships entered Earth's orbit precisely one week later as predicted. They wasted no time inspecting the wrecks of their three ships on the way. The Mbunalt followed the crumb trail the first ships had taken to the battlefield in northern France. Twelve ships landed in France, and the remainder diversified. Two landed in Russia, near Leningrad and Moscow. The remaining two landed in highly populated areas of Philadelphia and Brooklyn. The ships were three blocks long and demolished hi rise buildings when they landed like they were made of paper.

Earth's soldiers were ready, as were the civilians; they stood armed shoulder to shoulder. The less staunch folk and Kraalt guarded the children at Summer Haven. The only exceptions were Lucy, Colletta and Audrey who refused to be parted, they hid to avoid having to embark the transport.

At Summer Haven, the formidable Sheena stood guard in the crow's next, awaiting action, a burgundy blade in her capable hands and a fierce expression on her face. She was expecting hell, and hell was keen to deliver.

19. Invasion

Paul reviewed contingency plans with Spall and hit on an idea to help those who were captured. He pursued the thought with the team, a couple of days prior to the invasion. "What if the invaders find our adrenal glands missing when they capture us?" "They will put you into service immediately, they wouldn't waste a slave over a minor disappointment", explained Buddy. "Ok", continued Paul, "would they investigate the presence of an adrenal gland if the prisoner was scarred in the area of the gland?" Instantly the others could see where he was going. "I don't believe so; they are not an intelligent species, they use us for brains", replied Buddy, "but the Kraalt would know if they scanned a prisoner, which is unlikely unless they were seriously ill and unable to work". "Then I recommend we all have an incision just above our kidneys", Paul added. "It will spare anyone the indignity, if captured. Also, we will retain our adrenaline to allow us to mount a vigorous defence. We can always say the first group of Mbunalt warriors captured us, before they died mysteriously".

The Kraalt nodded as one, Paul's idea was sound. "The Mbunalt will not be happy when they find out how the other members of their race died, it will make them nervous. They are not used to taking such casualties", Buddy added. Three days prior to the invasion was cutting time short for making incisions into each member of the defence force, but it was a good contingency plan, it could buy them more time. The risk was they were entering battle with a small wound. "You won't even notice the wound in the heat of combat", assured Franc.

The invasion began, the defence force had made all the preparations they could, but they were weak against a superior enemy, morale was low. The men of Earth were fighting for survival and had agreed that in the event of defeat they would split up, head for the hills and hide out until the invaders tired of the planet.

"Captain Bartholomew McCreedy in position, primed and ready to roll", confirmed Bart. "Captain Johnson T. Caterham in position, primed and ready to roll", confirmed Caterham. Paul looked at Spall and gave the order, "Engagement confirmed, take your best shot".

Bart gave the order aboard HMS Astute. The tomahawk cruise missiles were on standby, their warheads primed, each sat prepared in the top launch tubes with the marine doors open in readiness. First Officer Stenham lifted the six red covers, depressing the buttons within in sequence. The sub shook as the missiles launched from the vertical tubes into the sky. The mast was barely visible from the sea as the six subsonic tomahawks lifted into the air, their rocket engines glowing white and vapour cascading into the sea below. The missiles split into groups, three headed towards Washington, the other three to Philly. The sub quickly bubbled, becoming invisible and reaching top speed within seconds. The best defence, in case of retribution, was to be elsewhere. "Missiles away", reported Bart via his Carocle.

Similarly, in the Black Sea, HMS Audacious launched six cruise missiles, three headed to Leningrad and three to Moscow. First Officer Baring monitored the status of the missiles on both the radar and the tactical screen, tracking their progress carefully. Meanwhile, six further missiles were loaded into the tubes as a contingency. "Missiles away", confirmed Matthew via his Carocle.

Spall watched as the twelve ships began their landing protocols in a tight array near the fields where the pods had landed. "Light 'em up!", he shouted as the ships were nearing the ground. There were only twenty ground to air missiles per ship when he divided them up, but it was all his team could scavenge in the short time they had. The missiles streaked through the air, hitting the underbelly of the twelve ships. Everyone averted their eyes, the explosions were white hot, and the light would sear the eyes of anyone foolish enough to watch. It was hard to see the damage caused as the ships landed on damp earth. The remaining artillery and missiles targeted the ships, including a pounding from HMS Phoenix's main cannon and Sea Sparrow missile launcher. As the dust fell, Paul could see the impact of the attack, and it was not good news, not by a fair margin.

Matthew and Bart had some positive news, the majority of the nuclear weapons had hit their target, they were flying in low to the ground as the ships landed. "Bart here, we have two clear hits in Philly and three in Brooklyn. Using the optronic mast, we can observe the mushroom clouds. We have successfully engaged the enemy". Matthew reported similar success, two clear hits on both ships in Leningrad and Moscow, they too were returning. Sensors on Paul's spaceship confirmed the Mbunalt ships had been destroyed, with no signs of survivors. The Kraalt pragmatically confirmed the destruction and were encouraged, which was positive considering their comrades were aboard the ships. They had focussed their minds on the fact many would survive due to the sacrifice made by a small number of their kind. Paul became anxious, "Matt, keep safe. Head back to Summer Haven and keep the bastards from crossing the water!"

Conventional weaponry had significantly less success than the nuclear warheads. The Mbunalt ships were largely intact after the bombardment, they were made from tough metals beyond anything seen in Earth's periodic table. If the Mbunalt field armour could withstand the blast, then it could be safely assumed that the ships would. They reported the twelve ships in the field had been damaged, their engines and core vessel shielding were compromised. However, the attack had only resulted in eleven casualties, it was heart breaking news. The team had a real fight on their hands. "Throw everything else at them, let's target their damaged shielding", Spall commanded.

The pounding resumed until the teams reported one by one, they were out of explosive ordnance. There was one moment of hope when one of the enemy ships detonated and heavily damaged the two nearby vessels. But the intimidation wasn't sufficient to halt the invasion, despite a number of enemy casualties. The team had successfully grounded the enemy ships, but the aliens were here to stay, come what may. Their fates were now hopelessly intertwined.

The sensors showed the aliens were armoured and prepared for battle, it was life or death. The doors on the vessels slowly opened, the Mbunalt eagerly launched themselves from the exit ramp, running in a variety of directions. They seemed to have little coordination. "Fire", shouted Paul. Three medieval catapults launched their payload into the sky, they crested, then exploded midway through their descent. The detonations were small, but enough to send a cloud of spores covering almost a square mile. The spores dropped from the sky like an autumnal mist, until it was hard to observe the unfolding events. Violent coughing and choking could be heard from the battlefield as the Mbunalt were infected in their hundreds, despite their breathing adaptations. Within minutes, the Mbunalt started to howl and attack each other with terrifying gusto. As they fell, enormous fruit grew propagating the infection by blowing huge quantities of spores into the air. The fruits were much larger, with many more spores than produced from a human host. Even with their prodigious strength, the beasts' armour protected them well, so they resorted to tearing off helmets and biting faces. In the red mist of anger, they hopelessly attempted to bite through each other's armour in a mindless rampage.

A vent opened in the first of the Mbunalt spaceships. Particles flew into the sky, like wasps from a disturbed hive. As the cloud reached the warriors it separated into a multitude of individual tiny drones, each targeting a single Cro. They attached to their armour at the base of the spine. The ship emitted a gas cloud, an insipid grey fog covered the battlefield, visibility was again lost for a moment. The fog and the drones in combination influenced the severity of violence on the field below very quickly. The Mbunalt regained control of themselves. The attack had been successful, more than a hundred dead warriors lay dead on the field, but almost a thousand warriors remained. Many were bruised and injured, but they were alive and clearly fighting the infection with some success.

Paul gave the order to abandon the field. There was no point fighting the warriors hand to hand, the M16 rifles were of little use against their armour. There were very few RPG's remaining, the defence force had to face the fact they had lost. They needed to evacuate quickly, before the enemy started to hunt them down.

Paul and the defence force retreated in the vehicles, heading out as quickly as they could, given so many survivors needed support. Spall and Paul drove in a Land Rover to Cherbourg, the Phoenix arrived and picked them up from the port. José waved from the bridge, as the ship got underway. Paul remained agitated, "Franc, where the hell are you?" "We've gone to ground; pray they don't find us", replied Franc. "Why? The area isn't safe", worried Paul.

Franc continued, "Typhon has a plan. The girls won't fully elaborate, but I know they have contacted the spirits and bargained with them for help. They have made a pact with the not-dead, as they call them. It sounds insane, I know, but Typhon says it is our only chance. I'm unsure if I can trust him, but we are out of cards to play here". Paul pondered for a moment, "It sounds crazy". Franc empathised, "Yeah, what doesn't, these days? Something about it just feels right, I can't say more than that. I can see into Colletta's mind to some extent, and she is utterly convinced Typhon's plan is the right path, but then she is only a child". Paul warned, "It just might be your daughter practicing her recently discovered empathy abilities, so take care. Melak and Barak used those skills to great effect! Typhon and Barak have gone back to the abbey, and Mak and his team are trying to join them. Amazing how families who hate each other seem to bond when faced with a superior adversary". "Ever it was thus", replied Franc thoughtfully, "good luck to them all".

Paul decided to defend Summer Haven, by stopping the enemy from crossing the channel into England. The ship couldn't destroy the Mbunalt warriors, but it could easily sink the enemy transports. HMS Audacious would soon be in position to defend the waters between the mainland of Scotland and Summer Haven.

As the Phoenix was about to leave the harbour, there was a shout from the jetty. Rusty had arrived in a jeep with his pal Wrench. The small RIB that Phil sent to pick them up arrived at the waterside in minutes, Rusty jumped aboard with the surefootedness only a seasoned sailor would have. Wrench was a little more unsteady but was aboard ship in minutes. Rusty explained, "I can't leave Sheena and the guys alone up in Scotland, I'm heading back to help. We got hit by squad of warriors on the way, they must have mobilised quicker than the rest. The bastards just shoulder charged the cars and knocked them off the road, it was like being hit by a bull elephant. They captured Karl and Mikey, but we managed to escape by hiding in the stream underneath the ferns and vegetation. The cold water must have interfered with their infra-red vision. I managed to get one of the vehicles going again after the squad headed back". "How many did we lose?" asked Paul. "Twenty good soldiers, men and women", he replied, "there was nothing I could do". "Don't worry", advised Paul, "they won't harm them too much, they will set them to work. We will find a way to get them back". "But how?" enquired Rusty. "I don't know...yet", answered Paul.

Joe flew back towards Sicily with the soldiers from his island and Formentera Haven. He planned to drop the guys at Formentera en route. The ship had shown its versatility by adapting its hull to become a large passenger transporter with many seats. The passengers were strapped in with silver 4-point harnesses. As they crossed the foothills of the Pyrenees, the ship ran into difficulties. Cindy sounded garbled, the last words she announced were they were under attack. Before the ship failed it separated into two parts.

Cindy dropped the chamber containing the ship's occupants to the ground on decelerator chutes, landing roughly on the fields below. The reminder of the ship fell lifelessly out of the sky, smashed into the mountainside and hit the ground hard. The ship bound for Russia had a similar experience, but they didn't get quite so far. They were attacked as they neared the France-Germany border at Strasbourg. Three ships were taken down as they tried to flee. The other vessels managed relatively successful crash landings, although the ships were disabled, they were relatively undamaged. The attempts to put a large distance between themselves and the invading force was not going as they planned. Their only hope was to hide, but it was difficult in such large numbers. The infra-red light emitted by the large number of bodies would be visible from outer space with the correct scanners. The only advantage was the wildlife and cattle would also emit infra-red wavelength light signatures, there was a slim hope they may be hard to discern one another.

Of the seven discovery ships in operation, Typhon and Sheena had the only fully functioning ships not yet detected; additionally, Barak's original ship had been hidden as a contingency plan. The ship's AI, Beryl, had previously returned to the shed in Iraq, south of Baghdad.

Bart headed back from the USA via the small community in Iceland, as the people there needed to be warned. The Inuit could simply disappear into the icepack, the igloos were cold and did not produce an infra-red signature. It would be harder for the city dwellers to evade capture; they were given the choice of taking their chances or joining the crew on the HMS Astute.

The Mbunalt had split into fifty hunting parties, each containing between ten and twenty warriors: each randomly heading in search of the survivors using the skills of the Kraalt. Grouping proved to be the worst tactic due to the IR profiles. It's natural human behaviour to survive in small communities, ten thousand years of genetic memory cannot be wiped out in an instant. Humans had always persevered in this way but had never faced such ruthless hunters as the Mbunalt. They had been the apex predator, until now.

The Russian team, led by Smitsky, initially travelled on foot to Poitier before continuing to the relative safety of the Alps using vehicles. They knew they wouldn't reach Russia before being hunted down. They made their way in a rag tag convoy of trucks and cars appropriated at the French border. Luckily, many vehicles were left with their keys in, but few had batteries with sufficient charge to start their engine. Most were corroded in critical parts, so the team was forced to interchange components to secure operational vehicles. Cars without electronic ignition were less reliable vehicles but were more easily push started.

The rotting Shrooms which littered their route were inert and were deemed to be safe. The Russian team had no means to communicate with the wider group, they were out of range of the battlefield communication devices. It was deemed unwise to use radios to avoid their signals being triangulated by the enemy. Only those with Carocles were able to talk, the Kraalt had assured them they were not easily monitored or located. The Kraalt could only access Carocles over relatively short distances.

The journey through the hills was gruelling, finding petrol stations with clean unspoiled fuel was problematic. Most of the unleaded fuel had degraded, which left only diesel fuels viable. Another difficulty was they had no easy way to locate petrol stations. Main routes had them littered every fifty miles or so but using A-roads and highways was asking for trouble. The fifty soldiers in the group, occupied eleven vehicles, enabling Typhon to detect them using his spaceship sensors as they neared the Alps.

Typhon's silver ship landed in the road blocking the route, Smitsky panicked and attempted to reverse the convoy unsuccessfully, frantically waving his arms. Although the egg-shaped ship was familiar to the Russians, they could take no chances. As Typhon stepped from the ship, Smitsky relaxed and stood down the team. "You need to be careful flying that thing", observed Smitsky, "the invaders can easily detect spaceship movements. They have shot down five of them. Paul warned me before we left the operational range of the radio". Typhon agreed, "It is true. They took down the ship Joe occupied over the Pyrenees; his team are being hunted as we speak. We are safe for the moment, we are out of range, but will soon be under attack". "What will you do? You can't fight those monsters", observed Smitsky. "No, but we do have a few surprises for them", countered Typhon. "We will head into the mountains when attack is imminent. We are waiting for our kin to join us. Mak is transporting his team here as we speak. The Cros should not be able to follow us into the mountains, they are too heavy and too clumsy. We are building a fort and moving sufficient supplies for a year. You are welcome to join us, but it will be terribly cold and bleak". Smitsky puffed up his chest proudly, "We are Russian, we know the cold well. I would be proud to join you, our choices are thin on the ice". Typhon observed Smitsky's clumsy use of English and wondered how the people of Earth could harmonise when they all spoke different languages.

The convoy pulled into the driveway at Benediktbeuern Abbey, where Barak was awaiting them. He shook Smitsky's hand and bade him welcome. The brothers were in the process of moving supplies into the mountains, gathering all non-perishable foods. "You need to head into Innsbruck and gather as much warm clothing and food as you can. We will meet you in the main square, progressing together into the mountains from there. We can no longer risk using the spaceship, so we will hide it for the time being.

HMS Audacious surfaced just outside the salmon farm at the Summer Island, Matt swam to shore where his mother Kate was waiting. The water was icy, so he stroked quickly to maintain his core body temperature. After a long and rather wet embrace, Matt updated his Mum and Sheena on the attack and the measures Paul had taken to halt the invaders at the English Channel. The sub would provide a second layer of protection. "Let's pray the creatures don't make it this far", responded a tearful Kate. "Don't count on that", exclaimed Sheena forcefully, "They will try to capture us all, we need to take out as many of the bastards as we can. We will be ready, and we will be fierce". Matt added, "Paul has also been in touch, Sheena. Rusty has jumped ship and is heading here as fast as he can". "That's my Rusty", Sheena uttered gently with a wicked grin.

Joe was responsible for a significant group of people. They took over a small village in the foothills of the Pyrenees to hide out. In hindsight it was a terrible mistake, they were woken in the night by screaming. "Joe, what the hell is going on?" asked Enrico, the head of the Formentera community. They parted the curtains to see several of the huge beastly men running amok in the village. They smashed down doors, taking unconscious soldiers from the cottages, loading them onto a large flat object that looked a little like a sled. Some men opened fire with their rifles and pistols, but the aliens shrugged them off and continued to capture them relentlessly. "We need to get the hell out of here", whispered Joe. Joe and Enrico lifted the kitchen sash window in the rear of the cottage and slipped through. Joe went first, then turned and helped Enrico. They moved quietly across the unkempt garden and pushed through the bushes at the rear, scaling the low stone wall. The two men had no idea which village they were in, or where they were. They headed towards the dark looming mountains that were barely visible in the moonlight.

Joe and Enrico moved quietly, shrouded by the loud screams coming from behind them. "Keep moving, you can't do anything for them. We need to survive and buy time to think", whispered Enrico urgently. They soon encountered a Cro skulking in the trees, he hit Enrico with a straight left into his face, he fell to the ground with a thump. The Cro grinned evilly as Joe tried to run, he reached out with his long arm grabbing Joe's webbing belt, pulling him backwards violently. Joe quickly unfastened the belt and darted into the trees to his left. He could hear the huge thumping stride of the giant behind him, smashing the undergrowth and small trees out of his way. Joe darted left once again and headed through the trees until he reached a clearing, where he stopped and hid beneath a sprawling bramble bush.

Joe completely forgot about the warrior's implanted night vision. He also realised he had run without thinking about his friends, he had left them in the village. Even though there was nothing he could have done, he felt bitter regret for not trying to help them. The Mbunalt warrior easily located him, reaching into the bush, grabbing Joe and pulling him upright. The bramble ripped Joe's skin cutting his face cruelly. One touch from the merciless Cro and his vision went black.

20. Occupation

Joe woke with a huge pulsating lump on his forehead and multiple lacerations from the wicked thorns of the bramble. He'd had better days, for sure. It looked like the entire group from the Pyrenees was present, no one had escaped. Joe caught Enrico's eye and verified he was ok, that was a consolation at the least. The Mbunalt were examining each of the captives in turn and were clearly disappointed to find the recent scars on their backs. Each prisoner had woken wearing a slim collar around their neck, wrists, and ankles. The cuffs looked like a type of plastic, but they could not be broken or slipped off, no matter how Joe tried. He knew in his heart these were cruel devices used to secure their imprisonment and servitude. Joe and Enrico looked at each other nervously. They had lost, they faced a lifetime of servitude, if they were lucky.

The Kraalt in charge asked Joe if he was the leader. "I guess I am", he replied. "The Mbunalt are collecting you to become their servants. You must do as they say, or they will punish you. Their punishments are ruthless, I advise you not to challenge their authority. If you accept their demands, then your lives will be tolerable. Joe looked at the small alien and realised he too was wearing the collar and wrist bands which signified slavery. He glanced at the Cro who was supervising the Kraalt closely. "The Mbunalt are demanding to know the location of your women and children", demanded the Kraalt. "Tell them to go to hell!" spat Joe. Joe's collars and restraints glowed blue; horrific pain racked Joe's body. He writhed in agony as the agony continued for what felt like an eternity.

"Please, please tell them. They will enjoy torturing you, they are animals. They won't stop until they know. You cannot hide the whereabouts of your family from them", spoke the small man. The pain subsided, and Joe shouted up to the large figure overseeing, "Fuck you!" This time the other prisoners fell to the floor as their restraints glowed, their screams were too much to bear. Their collars turned a brighter blue as the pain ramped up. Some were close to dying, Joe had to act. "Stop it!" he screamed. "Our families are in Scotland! Please stop this". He pointed to their location on the map the Kraalt held in front of him. The collars ceased to glow, and the victims slowed in their writhing, but the screams continued for some time. The torture had inflicted damage upon the group, it wasn't simply pain or an electric shock. The devices were tearing apart the cells of their bodies and ripping their nerve synapses. No one was able to stand for almost an hour, but they slowly recovered, the damage proved transitory.

Joe was devastated, the warriors knew where to find the families. They would soon be enslaved. He tried to pray to God to enlist his help, but hopelessness washed over him. Joe sat down and cried quietly. A Kraalt put his hand on Joe's shoulder, "Don't worry. We have been enslaved by these monsters for millennia, it isn't so bad if you work hard and don't question them. Be at peace, life will be much easier". Joe looked into the eyes of the small alien, "The people of Earth are not good at accepting defeat, my friend". "Then your lives will be short, but will feel very long indeed", replied the alien.

Rusty left the Phoenix at Dover with Wrench and waved farewell and good luck to his friends. They found several cars, but none would start. Rusty took a tractor unit from an articulated lorry; it had a huge battery and had retained enough juice to turn over the engine. The lorry started with a roar once Wrench had hotwired the ignition. Wrench managed to detach the trailer, initially pulling the wrong levers but eventually identifying the right one. The two men had created quite a mess, spilling rotten grain all over the highway, but who was there to care?

Rusty drove onto the motorway and headed for London. They would need to refuel somewhere on the M25 motorway and grab some food, but they were ok for the next couple of hours. The narrow lanes of the Highlands would be challenging in the tractor unit, but he could smash anything out of his way. Rusty tuned the radio onto the one remaining radio channel, Radio Caroline, and he gunned the engine. Wrench glanced over as Meatloaf's 'Bat out of Hell' rang out. Rusty racked up the volume, Wrench gave him a huge toothy smile and started to sing. "Jesus, can't you try to keep in tune Wrench", grinned Rusty. "I'm pitch fucking perfect, me", he replied with a wink. "It's gonna be a long trip", observed Rusty with a laugh.

The journey was slow going, the motorway was littered with cars. Although the infection had hit at night-time, there were drivers on the roads who were infected and subsequently trapped in their cars. The M25 was a busy road at all times of the night, they had to push cars out of the way in more congested areas. The natural tendency for the driver, when feeling ill was to pull over to the hard shoulder on the left, but some cars simply crashed into the barrier or another vehicle. The power of the lorry made it easy to move the cars, but Rusty needed to avoid damaging the front fender or the wheel arches, or the trip would end very quickly.

Once off the M25 the trip eased a little, and progress was better. They stopped at Hilton Park services and filled up the lorry with diesel using a bucket tied to a rope and makeshift funnel made from a Hello glossy magazine. Again, they made a mess but what the hell? They raided the shop and took the chocolate which hadn't completely turned white, plus some biscuits. Many of the snacks were rank. They helped themselves to cans of coke and several bottles of Budweiser Budvar. Warm was better than nothing. Wrench hung them in a carrier bag from the mirror on the truck door, the air would cool them as they travelled. "Nice move" said Rusty approvingly. They hit the road again preparing themselves for a long and hopefully tedious drive.

Typhon ran into the main common area of the monastery where Barak was progressing through a punishing exercise regime. He completed a series of one leg squats and launched into a complex kata. He stopped abruptly when he saw the urgency in his son's face. "The Cros are closing father; they will be here within the hour". "Understood, gather the men and equipment, we need to take to the hills now". The timing was critical, they wanted the Cros to follow them. If they set off too early, their trail would be cold. Typhon ran to the chapel and rang the bell, pulling the old dusty rope with gusto. Typhon heeded the warnings regarding the dangers of using a starship, leaving it hidden in the courtyard.

The brotherhood proceeded to the meeting point in three large MPV's in convoy, travelling cross country for an hour and then taking the main highway into the town itself. They arrived at the square in Innsbruck, Smitsky and his men were waiting, sat on rucksacks and carry bags they had appropriated from the shops in town. They were loading the luggage into the rag tag collection of trucks and automobiles. The cable car and funicular from the centre of the city had long since fallen into disrepair and were inoperable. They elected to drive in convoy as far as Sölden, where they could pick up the trail for the Similaun mountains. Their destination was the sixth highest peak in the Austrian Tyrol, it was a moderately difficult climb in the snowy conditions giving them an advantage, it would be significantly more treacherous for the heavy invaders. The team hoped to eliminate the enemy at best or lose them on the steep mountainside at worst. Smitsky looked up at the snow-capped mountains and his heart fell. As a young man he would have relished the challenge, but now he knew he would struggle with the climb. Many of his team would also find the hike difficult too.

"How far we need to ascend?" Smitsky asked tentatively. Typhon indicated a point on the map high in the shoulder of the mountain. "We have built a fort at this point and constructed additional fortifications around it. We have set up camp within the perimeter with weatherproof tents. It will serve to defend us against the harshest weather, but it has no defences against the enemy. We have crampons, ice axes and ropes at the hut in case we need to climb to escape. We also have a few surprises for them up there", explained Typhon. "I can make the fort, but I not sure how much further I will be able to go, I not a young man. If you need to leave some of us behind, we will fend for ourselves as best we can", acknowledged Smitsky. "When the devil is on your tail, you will climb my friend", added Barak not altogether helpfully. "We can also pick up the trail to Hintere Schwarze if we need to. It is a higher mountain, and safer from the enemy", clarified Conor, who was listening in to the conversation.

The trail was steep from the start, the once well-trodden path was lost in the rampaging undergrowth. Typhon was sure footed and had no hesitation in taking the route. The brothers knew the trail well, they had been preparing for their incursion. Smitsky looked at his comrade, Helnikova, and smiled, "There was a time, my friend, when we would have paid good money for a trip up these mountains". "That was many summers ago my friend. Many summers with too much vodka flowing freely down the course of our throats into the lakes of our ample stomachs", his comrade replied sombrely.

Paul observed the English Channel, it was difficult to predict where the enemy would attempt the crossing. The Dover Narrows was the obvious choice. Logic should drive them here, but then it was dangerous to make assumptions. Life aboard the ship was boring, and it was getting cold as Autumn moved to Winter.

After several days of inactivity, heat signatures and movement sensors observed disruption in the port of Calais. José's drones observed Cro-Magnons numbers starting to build up in the port. The enemy were attempting to operate the sailing vessels. Phil piloted closer to port to closely observe the Cro activity using the optics. The Cros were large and clumsy, they attempted to operate sailboats and had some success when sailing with the wind. However, they completely failed to tack against the wind, one Cro was forced to crash his boat into the shore in order to navigate back. The Cros eventually gave up and boarded the large ferry in the port, it was more easily navigated once the engines were online.

Spall counted almost two hundred of the brutes boarding the ferry. They attempted to start the engine, but there was little chance of turning over the huge diesel engines after years of inactivity. Four hours later, Spall spotted a small group of Kraalt boarding the gangway. "This could get interesting", he commented, "they've got the little fellers in to help them start their motion". Paul noted the poor double entendre with a cautious smile, "Hope the Kraalt don't mind getting their hands dirty".

The Kraalt had the engine running by the end of the day, they used a different power source to fire up the engine. The ship left the port cautiously, but they omitted to lift the car boarding ramp, almost sinking the ship with a large number aboard. It was a testament to the brute strength of the invaders, they managed to force the ramp back into place, making the ship seaworthy again by stopping the water pouring into the ship. The ship had taken on water but was less in weight overall than a full load of passengers and cars.

The 'Pride of Burgundy' got underway, on a heading towards Dover. As the ferry reached the halfway mark and the water was at its deepest, Phil gave the command to sink it. The Phoenix's main cannon opened up and gave the ferry a full broadside, hitting the ship at the waterline in six or seven locations. "Good shooting José", shouted Spall, "you've taken the whole side of the ship away, I think. Let's hope the Mbunalt stand on the prow with their arms in the wind, as the ferry sinks like the Titanic". As the ship sank, the crew of the Phoenix shouted their dissent at the invaders. Gio was the loudest, he shouted at the top of his lungs. The invaders jumped off the ship but didn't even attempt to swim, they sank to the bottom of the sea. Gio screamed, "Enjoy the crabs making a meal of you down there, you retarded ugly swine faced motherfuckers!" Bodies of two Kraalt floated to the surface face down, plus a few floats and lifejackets from the side of the ship. There was so little to show for the huge vessel that had been lost.

Paul watched the sinking vessel with an unsatisfied smile, "That seemed too easy. It doesn't feel right". He grew suspicious and decided to check the sonar with help of José and one of the crew. There was something moving near to the sea floor, even though the ship had bottomed out. Paul watched carefully as the movement started to focus. They followed the motion as it headed directly towards the port at Dover. The movement accelerated. "I worry they're able to breathe in the water using the modifications we observed around the mouth area", said Paul. Sure enough, the movement continued towards Dover, until the Cros emerged from the water on the beach near the port. Not only had they traversed the water, but they appeared to know where they were going and were completely unfazed. These guys were not as dumb as they looked, they were an unstoppable force.

Rusty and Wrench drove into the night, taking turns to drive. As Rusty took his driving shift he muttered, "Sleep is a weapon, as Spall always says". Wrench looked at him sidelong, "He does always say that; I think he got it from one of those Jack Reacher books he's always reading". Rusty grinned, "Yeah, Spall has a saying for every occasion". "But then he's usually right. You can't fault the man", added Wrench. They cut around Inverness and took to the road to Ullapool at breakneck speed in the bulky rig. While filling up at the gas station they looked for any edible food but were out of luck. "I'm starving", grumbled Wrench, "lets head to Booker's cash and carry to see what we can lift". "We can eat when we get back. Any way up, we emptied it six months ago. There's nothing there but dead rats and mouldy Shrooms these days", pointed out Rusty. "Driving back to my Baby", sang Wrench sarcastically with a smile, "and I don't mean maybe". "For Christ's sake, put the radio back on. I don't like Kiss, or at least that version", whinged Rusty.

Rusty and Wrench arrived at the facility, the land site store house and base for the Summer Haven. It had been a long drive, they were exhausted. Rusty let himself in and took the RIB across to the island with Wrench riding shotgun. Sheena was waiting for him; she had been watching land side all day looking for a sign. She saw Rusty coming from the crow's nest, she ran to the quayside to welcome him as the boat came into the quay. He threw the mooring ropes to her, and she tied them off to the cleat on the quay. Rusty leapt across into her arms and they kissed for quite some time, until Wrench decided to intervene, "Ahem". Rusty smiled and gave Wrench a mock punch to the guts, Sheena followed up a strong hug.

Rusty and Sheena walked back to the atrium and the small room where the children were fast asleep, whilst Wrench sated his appetite. "Leila is growing so quickly", Rusty whispered whilst looking at his daughter. "They both are", added Sheena. "I'm whacked, let's go to bed", he requested gently. "I'm on watch, I need to go back and relieve Kate, sorry. You get your head down and we'll talk in the morning", offered Sheena with a smile. "They are coming you know. I don't know how we will stop them", Rusty added nervously. "It's a fight to the death then", asserted Sheena with a dangerous look. She smiled and left the room.

It took some time before Rusty managed to drift off to sleep, he had nightmares for much of the night but woke mostly refreshed. His mind kept flashing back to the Cros knocking the big 4x4 off the road like it was a matchbox car. He then started to consider his wife's suicidal streak. This battle wasn't going to end well for any of them, he thought.

Joe woke at daybreak with the others, he could hardly rise after three full days of back breaking labour in the fields. It was getting close to winter, there seemed little point in the endless digging and preparation. The luckier prisoners tended the cattle, but it was not for long, they soon needed to travel further afield to acquire more animals. The appetites of the warriors were ludicrous, the slaves would tend fifty cows one day and the next they would be consumed, the slaves needing to search for more. It was lucky that cattle were plentiful in this lush green part of France. The area had once been rich farmland, and the cattle were wandering the area now the electric fences were inactive and the fences crumbling. A camp had been erected for the slaves near the original landing site. There was no attempt to restrain their prisoners, they could paralyse an individual with racking pain wherever they were. If the slaves weren't back by nightfall, they would not like the outcome. No-one chose to test their master's patience.

The Kraalt attempted to remove Joe's Carocle at one point, for examination, but concluded they would need to dissect his head to do so. Their curiosity caused Joe great discomfort, but luckily, they decided to abandon their efforts. Joe decided to keep the fact he could release the Carocle at any time a closely guarded secret.

Joe kept in touch with his brothers, he knew the Mbunalt had crossed the channel. He feared for his family, they would also be forced into slavery. A short life of excruciating hard work was not something he wanted for them. He attempted to communicate with the Kraalt. Joe felt they were able to use the facilities of the Carocle if they were close enough. "This is Joe here, I'm trying to contact the Kraalt, are you there?" he asked, several times. In the end a hesitant reply came, "What do you want?" "I want you to know that some of your kin survived the first battles", pointed out Joe. "They are staying at our base in Scotland as free men, but the Mbunalt are closing on them. I want to protect everyone, is there something you can do?" "We can't do anything to help you, our masters must be obeyed. We have no choice; or we will be eliminated. The Kraalt in Scotland will be assimilated into our group if they prove loyal", was the final reply.

Joe persevered regardless, "The Kraalt in Scotland are free men and women, they do not obey orders, they are not slaves. They live in freedom, and I doubt they would accept fealty to the Mbunalt as readily as you do. These Kraalt have dreams and lives to lead; they have not given up like you have". "Not for much longer. You are living a pipedream, Joe. It will be much easier for you if you accept reality. There is no possibility for you to regain your freedom", said the thin voice. "At what point in your evolution did you lose your desire to live? When did you give away your spirit, your freedom? When in your lives did you accept becoming inanimate objects to these big hairy barbarians? When did you choose to set aside your lives and become puppets?" asserted Joe angrily. Joe then made a dangerous presumption, "Just be ready. If we find a way to fight back, then set aside your chains and join the fight. Win back your self-respect or exist in a living death for the rest of eternity!" The voice of the Kraalt stopped speaking. It was hard to tell if it was deep in thought or if he had become tired of a pointless conversation. Perhaps it was such a dangerous thought, the Kraalt didn't have the courage to consider it.

Smitsky and his aged leaders felt they were at death's door; being invited to enter the life beyond. They were tired and very cold. Their fingers felt frozen through, and they hadn't reached the cabin at the base of the climb. What was once a compacted and well-trodden trail to the summit of Similaun was deep treacherous snow. The hordes of climbers and cross-country skiers had not arrived this year to pack down the snow and make the trail easy. Typhon had elected not to bring skis, he had to consider the cross-country skills of the least able. As they climbed the path to the mountain there was a high risk of falling into a crevasse on such an unforgiving snow-covered glacier. It was a blessing that Typhon knew the trail well.

The group achieved the climb to the fort, many collapsed exhausted into the array of already pitched tents, after a dry meal and a flask of hot and rather welcome broth. Smitsky dearly hoped they would be safe at the fort for a while as they rested.

As the sun lit the sky, they knew their safe place would be short lived, they could see their pursuers in the early morning light. The enemy were moving quickly up the trail haphazardly in informal groups. They had lost their natural bounce but seemed to have no trouble with the ascent so far. "Let's see how they fare on the glacier", observed Barak, "there is no room for clumsiness up here". Smitsky looked at his companions, they were weary men who were not in the peak of condition, but he knew they were honourable and would play their part. They were forced to move out, eating on the go. The team didn't worry about putting their carefully positioned fires out, they left everything to maximise their pace. The makeshift fort which was to be their home was left behind all too quickly. Typhon's band of brothers packed as many tents as they could manage and followed close behind.

Typhon and Smitsky's men crossed a deep snow field to a long ridge. Typhon sprinkled the hot water from his flask onto the perilous hard packed ice behind them, it was a narrow track facing a terrible drop to the sharp rocks below. "What are you doing? We will need that hot water, it is freezing cold up here", admonished Smitsky. Typhon pointed down to the Mbunalt warriors, "They are not far behind; they will catch us within the hour if we let them. This is the most dangerous part of the ridge; it is easy to slip, and the fall is deadly. The hot water will melt the snow and create a passage of dangerously slippery ice. The warriors do not have climbing gear, they are treating the range with utter disrespect like it is a camping trip, the mountains will not reward them for their misconception. Without crampons I am hoping the Cros will slip down the crevasse, the fall of their comrades will impact their confidence, hopefully buying us time to ascend the more dangerous summit".

Smitsky was exhausted but didn't want to fall behind the main group. It would make him easy pickings, being slow meant certain capture. Despite the risk, he couldn't resist stopping to watch the Cro's passage with his friend Captain Korskov. As the Cros crossed the ridge, three slipped and fell almost immediately. They dropped an exceedingly long way down the mountainside, partly due to the weight of their armour they were unable to arrest their fall. It was easy to see them hit the bottom with a significant, but joyous impact. It was disheartening to see them get up and dust themselves off and start towards the trail once again. Their leader shouted what they assumed was abuse before they continued their ascent. However, the unsafe path did slow them down, they were more careful from that point. Those who fell became much slower, even they must have taken some significant damage on a fall like that. Typhons ploy seemed to have worked for the time being.

Smitsky looked up beyond their leader, Barak; he could see the summit beyond. The group crossed another open snow field and Barak called a halt. "Here we make our stand", he announced. They created a trail into a crack in the mountainside but did not enter. The Pareth-ng moved into an igloo style construction; a secret hide covered with snow. It had become near invisible after several days of the snowfall over it. Typhon covered their tracks to the shelter with handfuls of fresh snow, it was so dry you could sprinkle it.

Typhon and his followers drew long Kadyur daggers from their rucksacks and waited in anticipation. Smitsky drew his Makarov pistol, his comrades followed suit, for what good they would be to them. "I hope you not thinking of fighting hand to hand", said Smitsky curiously, "that would be bad". Typhon smiled, "No the attack is just a feint. We have a few tricks up our sleeves yet. I'm not sure the pistols will be much help either". Smitsky smiled, "Perhaps the percussion could bring avalanche down on top of them".

21.   The Battle for Summer Haven

Rusty looked out from the crow's nest pensively, it was only a matter of time before they would be under attack. Matthew had communicated with Paul and knew he was on his way back to Summer Haven aboard the Phoenix. It would be good to have their leader home for the defence of the haven, they had learned to rely on his judgement. There were no other parties looking to cross the channel for the time being, so Paul needed to take the risk. Their attempt to stop the Cros at the channel had failed.

Nearly two hundred aliens were heading towards Scotland, and they were making good progress. The big question was how they would make the crossing to the island itself. The Cros struggled with sail boats, so their first choice would be motor powered boats, meaning the first order of business was to sabotage the craft in the ports nearby.

Rusty and Sheena took the RIB to Ullapool. They removed critical parts from motorboat engines and hid them in safe places, storing them for a later date if needed. There were numerous small boats in the harbour plus the wreck of a mid-sized submarine hunter destroyed by HMS Astute. It was partially sunk on the outer part of the quayside causing a blockage for the larger vessels. Most of the sizeable boats had already been appropriated by Summer Haven for day-to-day duties.

Rusty and Sheena continued the sabotage at Polbain where the ferry to Ristol Island departed, there were also boats moored at the small private jetty to the south. There were no nearby small ports south of Dundonnell, so they chose to ignore harbours beyond that point. The seas were treacherous at this time of the year, the RIB jostled in the waves, but Rusty was an experienced sailor, he and Sheena had strong stomachs.

"Sheena, you seem to have ditched your Claymore these days, I do notice these things", Rusty laughed. Sheena struggled to hear above the sound of the wind, "Franc sent the Kraalt blade to me, it will cut through rock, you have to see it to believe it!" Rusty looked impressed, "But will it cut through Cro armour is the question?" Sheena looked a little unsure, "Franc thinks it should, the sword is made from the same metal as their armour, but such a thin strand, it makes a hair look immense", she replied doubtfully, "but it is amazingly sharp". Rusty looked at it for a second, but lost interest as the wind gusted, and larger waves started to assault the vessel. He turned the RIB and accelerated hard, lifting it up onto its hydrofoils for a fast but very bumpy return journey.

Afterwards, they warmed up with a bowl of hearty vegetable soup from the large pan in the kitchen. Paul's wife, Kate, always had a pan warming on the hob. Sheena was aware that Kate was looking forward to seeing her husband again, it had been weeks and although Paul was on his way to the island, plans could change in a heartbeat in wartime. Sheena and Rusty spent some time with their kids, who were in the creche in the main atrium.

The klaxon sounded the alert, the islanders marshalled and gathered weapons. Sheena kissed her little ones, grabbed her M16 and ran to the crow's nest with Rusty hot on her tail. They arrived as Wrench sighted the Barratt sniper rifle. He looked up at them, "The enemy have arrived in Ullapool, we saw them on our last working CCTV camera, the one the Dark Ones missed. They are looking for transport, as expected". Rusty smiled, "They won't find a working vessel, unless they brought a mobile boat yard with them". Sheena looked troubled, "I'm not sure, our sabotage will only delay them a few hours. They have the Kraalt, Buddy mentioned they could patch in alternative power sources easily". Sheena called the radio room, "Kul, patch me through to the Audacious. We need a hand". Sheena spoke to Captain Caterham, "Ed, put your team on alert, we have sighted Cro-Magnons in Ullapool". Caterham responded with urgency, "Affirmative. We have seen them. They are scouring Ullapool harbour for transport. The Kraalt are working on the engines, they already have one large sailing vessel operational, using its harbour engine. We're on it. The Audacious is sat in the mouth of Loch Broom; we will wait until they are in deeper waters before we engage". "Understood", Sheena confirmed, "and good luck". "You too", came the response. "See you for a glass of Phil's dodgy beer later".

It was nightfall before sufficient ships became operational, by then the Mbunalt were hungry. At morning light, the ramshackle fleet took to the waters of Lock Broom. Ten large fishing boats, a small ferry and three smaller boats in the flotilla approached the mouth of the loch. The Cro's large silhouettes were visible on the decks of the ships and looked ominous through the optronic mast of the HMS Audacious. The collection of fishing boats and motor launches departed the inland waters cautiously.

Loch Broom was moderately calm, but the ocean became rough as they entered the seas of the Minch. They struggled with the waves and powerful currents making their tight formation a significant collision risk. "Let the bastards have it", commanded Captain Caterham, and four two tonne Spearfish torpedoes streaked from the prow of the sub, guided remotely by the thin copper wires which trailed in their wake.

Colletta was cold, she was wrapped in a blanket cuddled up closely to Audrey, the winter sun streamed into the knave of the small underground pre-Roman bare stone chapel. It was called 'Chapelle Notre Dame Sous Terre', our mother underground, originally built at the top of Mont St Michel. The chapel was far older than the abbey which was subsequently constructed above it. Franc had been shown the near secret hiding place by Gerard a few weeks earlier, the team at MSM used it to store supplies as it was cold and out of the way. The chapel was located under the nave of the abbey church and could be accessed by a narrow flight of stairs. The doorways were narrow, it would be hard for the overly large aliens to access. Therefore, it appeared to be the perfect hiding place for Franc and his family. On the positive side, there were two points of entry and therefore provided an emergency exit if needed.

The previous night had been dangerous. Franc had managed to ascend to the roof of the abbey with the girls without attracting the attention of the thirty or so resident aliens. The Mbunalt tended to prefer the larger areas, such as the abbey itself as it afforded them plenty of space. When they reached the top, Audrey and Colletta invoked 'the calling', Colletta's blue stone lit up the night. It was a ritual Barak had asked them to perform regularly from a location in close proximity to the alien army's camp. Barak explained the procedure was an ancient Pareth-ng ritual for calling the spirits of the dead, and only Audrey could make contact with these spirits. Colletta used the Kracz-el crystal to amplify her empathy to project the ritual widely across the continent, they found the procedure extremely tiring.

A significant number of the Cro army had been dispatched to Scotland and the Alps, it was only a matter of time before they returned to base camp where their ships had landed. Colletta's blue light attracted the attention of the aliens, but luckily the girls evaded the enemy using the multitude of small staircases and hidden passages. It had been too close; they had almost been caught. The Mbunalt had become aware of their presence and would start hunting them.

Franc chose the timing of their rituals very carefully. The girls were prone to stumble in the darkness, one missed footing would be the end of their exploits. They made their pilgrimage every night at around midnight, though Franc was never sure why it was so important and wondered if it was worth the risk. Barak was adamant the ceremony was the answer.

The girls had been performing the ritual most nights for nearly three weeks, and the risk of capture was increasing all the time. Lucy suggested to Franc that Colletta was using the power of her empathy to influence him to allow them to conduct a fool's errand. Franc grew suspicious when Lucy lost her train of thought, which was totally out of character. It was highly likely they would walk into a trap very soon. On the positive side, Franc suspected the aliens would be sleeping soon, and they tended to sleep for two nights in tandem typically. Tonight's outing would be an easier one. The Cros rarely kept someone on watch whilst they slept, clearly, they felt invulnerable. Franc refused to take the respite for granted, the Kraalt remained nearby and were ever vigilant.

Joe became aware Franc was up to something but was unsure of his plan. Franc didn't totally understand the mission himself, yet he continued to support the girl's activity wholeheartedly. Joe wondered why Franc considered his actions worthy of risking the lives of his family. Joe and others were tilling the fields. The work was hard, digging and ploughing fields using archaic ploughs and horses, as there was no operational machinery. The consequences of taking it easy was not worth contemplating. The Cros took pleasure in liberally dealing out blows or using the collars to inflict pain.

The farming slaves were forced to reach further into the countryside to gather cattle and vegetables for their master's extensive meals. The Kraalt used one of the captured Pareth-ng spaceships to ferry food to the Cros in remote locations. As Joe and the slaves ventured further, they encountered more and more dormant Shrooms, their numbers seemed to be increasing. Joe thought it unusual that the areas with denser populations resulted in less Shrooms but dismissed the idea as paranoia and continued foraging.

Joe still felt tired, but there was a definite improvement in his wellbeing, he was getting stronger and fitter every day. He had let himself go a little since the days racing around Europe with James and Jane, God rest her soul. It was lucky the Mbunalt only feasted fully once every couple of days, usually before they took their sleep, it gave the slaves plenty of time to find new food sources.

Joe managed to meet his friends during the evening, the slaves were housed together in an old barn, sleeping on the floor. It was uncomfortable and damp, but they gathered bales of hay to make themselves more comfortable. Bridget's messages passed on by word of mouth highlighted she was struggling with her existence. She felt her life was quickly becoming pointless, and her companions found it increasingly difficult to cheer her up. Morale in the camp was poor, slavery was not something free people could easily adapt to. People felt hopeless, even Joe was starting to give up. All his hopes were pinned on a small number of people who seemed utterly helpless facing such monsters. Franc appeared to be risking his family's lives on a wild goose chase.

In the mouth of Loch Broom, near to the harbour in Ullapool, Captain Caterham watched carefully as the four spearfish torpedoes closed on the vessels being piloted across the seas to the Summer Islands. The Mbunalt clearly saw the torpedoes streaking across the surface of the water, leaving characteristic white lines behind them. The enemy were quick to realise the threat and started to throw heavy objects at the torpedoes. Their powerful throws were scarily accurate but typically hit just behind the spearfish as their speed was difficult to judge across the waves.

One throw clearly hit its target, as there were only three explosions in the centre of the group of vessels. The Cros failed to see the four additional torpedoes following close behind. These were heavy torpedoes carrying a 660lb explosive charge. They were designed to sink a full battleship and had little trouble in disposing of these small ships. One ship exploded; the detonation was sufficient to take out the nearby boats. The small flotilla had little chance against such powerful armaments. The boats sank along with their cargo of heavily armoured aliens.

Caterham updated Sheena on the attack via the radio. "We took out the boats, they sank without exception, but our sonar is showing the warriors walking back to the mainland at the bottom of the sea, like at Dover. The Kraalt have floated to the surface along with the flotsam, they are all dead". "I don't get it", countered Sheena, "we expected them to survive under water, I guess, but why would they walk back, rather than continue to the island?" Caterham pondered, "Perhaps they can't walk long distances underwater, or the sea is too deep and rough?" "I doubt that Ed, they walked the Dover straits under the sea. They are equipped for combat on planets where the air isn't breathable, their devices must last for days. Perhaps they don't understand the nature of the attack, and they have retreated in order to regroup", suggested Rusty. "Either way, we haven't seen the last of them, I'll wager", added Caterham.

As the warriors emerged onto the rocky shore, they stared out to the horizon. "They have seen the optronic mast", observed Caterham as he gave orders to take the sub down and change position. The submarine bubbled and headed north a click bringing its mast to the surface again to observe. None of the Mbunalt were in sight, perhaps they were feasting again but then it hadn't been long since their last meal. It was unlikely they would need to eat quite so soon if the intel proved correct.

Without warning, the submarine lurched to one side violently. The crew had no idea of the cause, it was something they had not experienced in hundreds of operational missions. The sonar should have picked up obstacles or other vessels in the area, it was inexplicable. The submarine lurched again more violently. The ship was descending steadily, Caterham was more than mystified. "Bubble up two thirds", ordered the captain calmly. The First Officer wasn't confident, it wasn't covered in advanced training. The ship lurched again as the water in the tanks was expelled and replaced by air in order to lift the submarine to the surface, but the vessel failed to move. The Audacious was slowly being dragged to the bottom of the ocean, and there was nothing the crew could do to resolve it.

The Minch was extremely deep with extraordinarily strong currents, how could anything interfere with the ship. The assailant was not a giant octopus, there was something sinister behind the attack, it could mean only one thing. A loud cracking sound shocked the crew, small leaks started to appear in the underbelly of the ship. Caterham quickly gave the order to abandon ship, he had no choice. Luckily, the vessel was only staffed at 50% and there were sufficient escape suits for the crew, but it would take time to exit the ship, the airlock could only cycle four crew at a time. As the ship descended further, the crew would need specialist equipment to survive the water pressure. They approached the airlock, "Remember, we are at depth gentlemen, do not ascend too quickly or your blood will fizz. Follow your air bubbles up to the surface and take your time".

Cycling the airlock was slow, only twenty men had made their escape by the time the sub hit a depth of 600 feet. Evacuation beyond that point needed to be affected via the escape chamber. Twenty of the crew entered the chamber and closed the airlock, beginning their steady ascent. The escape chamber was built to withstand high pressures and was highly effective in ferrying the men to the surface.

Rusty pointed to air bubbles emerging from the location where he had last seen HMS Audacious' optronic mast. "This really doesn't look good at all", asserted Sheena with a look of serious concern across her face. Soon there were more than air bubbles breaking the surface of the choppy ocean. "Look, there are people coming up. We need to get help to them and fast". Sheena radioed the post at the quayside, "SNAFU, Audacious is scuppered, one click out bearing towards Polbain, tell Wrench to take the RIB to ferry survivors back here PDQ". Wrench was operational within ten minutes, helping the first of the sailors into the small boat. More and more popped up, and Wrench quickly returned for a second run.

On Wrench's third run, a large cylindrical object popped up and bobbed on the surface, rolling with the waves. As the airlock opened, around twenty people leapt into the sea with lifejackets inflating as they hit, the chamber resubmerged into the rough sea. Wrench continued to make ferry trips as quickly as he was able, then returned for the last run of the submersible, but it failed to emerge. He waited a full thirty minutes and then aborted.

Sheena kept watch from the island, Captain Caterham had gone down with his ship. Wrench called Sheena urgently, "I'll get a dive suit. Rusty and I will find them". Sheena interjected, "We don't have time, the Cros are on their way. We are receiving nothing on the radio, the people on the Audacious are MIA. We need to warm up the survivors and prepare for battle". Wrench swallowed, he estimated there could be seven men down there. He felt Sheena was right, but they could be stuck in an air bubble. He hesitated. Sheena voice boomed on the radio, "Come on Wrench we need you mate. Cros coming out of the sea on the mainland, they are carrying sailors on their backs, they have a device aiding their recovery. I'm not sure what they are doing, but one thing is they will be here soon". "Affirmative, on my way", Wrench responded, and gunned the engine back to the quay.

The Cros entered the water on foot, heading towards Summer Haven. Sheena estimated there was roughly ninety of them in groups of five. They had stopped using ships, though it was not clear why, the threat of the Audacious had been taken off the board. Their reason became clear as the Phoenix called in. "Captain Phil Checkson here, Phoenix inbound, ETA fifteen minutes". "Good to hear you Captain", affirmed Rusty, "Be careful, the Audacious has been taken out by the Cros, sorry, the aliens. They have pulled it down to the sea bottom using cables and electromagnetic grapplers. We saved most crew, but Caterham and seven others are MIA, though they may have been captured". "Understood, we will keep our distance", agreed Captain Phil. Paul took over communications, "How are you bearing up Rusty?" Rusty hesitated for a second, "We are ready Paul, but morale is bad. We have nothing to fight these guys with, other than a few RPGs, and even they won't work if these guys are fully armoured. Sheena has it in her head she will take them out with her stupid sword, but she deeply worries me". Sheena had been listening and cut in, "I heard that, bitch boy. I'm not going down without a fight".

The first sign of the landing came with the movement of the cork headline floats on the nets forming the perimeter of the salmon farm. The floats disappeared temporarily, and the nets were torn away completely. Sheena sounded the alarm, as Rusty checked the gatling gun. In the haven, everyone including the older children were armed. The crew from the Audacious had been given RPGs and a quick demonstration of their use, they also carried M16 automatic rifles, though they were unlikely to be effective against the enemy's armour. Sheena headed to the quayside and drew her sword as the Cros heads emerged from the water grinning evilly.

As the landing unfolded, a small dinghy arrived on the northwest side of the island, Rusty could see Paul and Spall with three of the Phoenix crew. "Too little too late", whispered Rusty to himself as his eyes moved back to his beloved Sheena at the waterside. "Be careful", he shouted to her, but she didn't hear him due to the terrified babble from the personnel surrounding her. "Shut up! We have incoming!"

22. Do Not Go Gentle into that Good Night

Smitsky was bitterly cold and tired, he was not prepared for combat. He drew in a long breath as the Mbunalt warriors closed on their position. Their men hadn't been spotted until the purple haze of Typhon's sword reflected eerily on the open snow field. The warriors identified Typhon and immediately charged at him with complete abandon. As they closed on his position, Smitsky's heart leapt; despite his trepidation, he gathered his courage and stood beside Typhon in a show of solidarity. They stood together as the enormous warriors rained down on them.

Smitsky heard a loud metallic clank towards the east side of the tundra and there was a sudden rush of darkness cutting through the snow at great speed. The warriors halted their charge as they became aware of the new threat, but it was too late. The first wave of slayer beetles hit them on the flank hard and attacked vociferously. The deadly beetles proved a great challenge for the aliens, as they attacked the joints of their armour with their razor teeth and claws. Typhon whispered to Smitsky, "Barak cloned seven swarms of beetles in his ship, they should prove quite a distraction". Typhon then turned and called to the monks, "Attack! Show them the wrath of the Pareth-ng!" Smitsky added less confidently added in Russian, "To war comrades".

The beetles had uncompromising ferocity in battle, and immediately went for the throats and faces of the Mbunalt, once the armour had loosened. Their speed was devastating as they launched themselves at the Cros in groups. The large warriors swatted the beetles away with their huge hands, but those who suffered the attack soon became overwhelmed when Typhon and Smitsky's soldiers joined the fray.

Typhon launched himself at the enemy with his purple sword in his left hand and his blood dagger in his right. The sword was deadly, he severed the leader's arm and parried a blow from a Cro on his right. He was careful not to encroach on the path of the beetles, they were unlikely to discriminate friend from foe. Typhon's dagger proved less than useless, but he continued to wage war with the sword, dropping the dagger to the snow. The monks joined the fray with their daggers but were swatted away by the invaders effortlessly. The Russians opened up with their M16's and Kalashnikovs cautiously avoiding the risk of friendly fire.

The Cros adapted quickly and reorganised, those not being swamped by beetles attacked the swarm from the side, removing the insects from their comrades. They avoided the terrible barbs on the beetle's exoskeletons by grasping them from the rear, tossing them over the cliff with a single smooth motion. The attack by Typhon's army of monks was failing, several of them had been caught with stunning blows and littered the battlefield. Five warriors attacked the Russians head on, despite the enormous flurry of bullets. They stunned the team one by one, those able to escape fled up the pass towards to the top of the mountain.

The beetles had penetrated the armour of several warriors and caused mortal damage, but the attack was losing ground as Typhon recalled the team. "Up the mountain! Retreat!", he yelled. Half of the soldiers had been taken by the Cros, including Barak. Typhon's team ran for the trail, but the Cros intercepted, attacking the stragglers at the rear. The beetles regrouped on the ridge, then took their flank by surprise, buying Typhon precious time to escape. The pass was more treacherous for the team, they stowed their weapons and drew their ropes and ice picks to begin the ascent.

The first monks inserted holds and carabiners into the frozen rock face. Typhon estimated that a third of the enemy were killed, leaving less than thirty alive. The enemy split their forces, one group took the captured men and started back down the mountain, dragging them like a sled; the other group pursued Typhon. "We gave it to them!" encouraged Conor mustering some enthusiasm. "We took down more Cros than we did at the main battlefield in France but without the ordnance". "Yes, but not enough by a margin", retorted Typhon. "We need another way to engage them. If only we had hundreds of these swords, we would show them real fury!"

The Cros worked together to counter the second attack of the beetles. One leader delivered a huge blow to the top of a beetle's head, its skull simply shattered under the extremity of the force. Grey puss splattered the area, the Cro knelt and started to eat, the shell parted as if it was a lobster. Their leader ordered the warriors to focus on the battle, rather than filling their stomachs. The battle changed in their favour as the Cros readapted their defence against the insects. Before long, the beetles lay dead on the hard-packed snow. The warriors elected to pursue Typhon's team, but they progressed slowly, grazing on the flesh of the beetles as they continued.

Despite the slowing of pace, the Cros kept close to Typhon and his team until the they were forced to climb the highest part of the glacier. Their weight and lack of equipment caused severe issues, they attempted to punch footholds in the glacier and climb, which allowed some success, however many slipped and fell. At one point, the reverberations caused a small landslide of ice and snow which took three Cros on a huge fall to the bottom of the cliff. The number of pursuers was slowly reducing. "Do you think a fall from here would kill them?" asked Smitsky. "I doubt it, if they can take an RPG or a missile in the chest then bouncing off a few rocks is unlikely to hurt them, even at this altitude. They seem to be coping with the lower oxygen quite well, but then they are slowing such that we can gain ground", replied Typhon.

Typhon, Smitsky and their teams conquered the summit of Similaun after a couple of tiring hours, but Smitsky and some of his men looked worse for wear. They trailed behind the main group as it reached the large metal cross at the peak. The cruciform was held in place by steel guy lines to which several of Smitsky's team grasped like a lifeline. From the top, they could see the entire Niedertal valley, looking towards the extensive upland ice plain leading to loftier peak, Hintere Schwarze, the 'rear black'.

The monk who had been covering the rear and collecting the ropes, carabiners and anchors stood in a state of fatigue in his heavy jacket and climbing harnesses. His helmet was covered in snow, which he hastily brushed off with his heavily insulated gloves. Typhon retraced his steps and looked back at the trail. "We have lost them at last", he announced with a satisfied smile.

Typhon's team descended the summit and continued across the ice plain on the trail towards the next mountain peak. On the flat of the ice plain, they were ambushed by the alien warriors, who had managed to predict Typhon's route and found a quicker, easier path which was easily navigated. The team was hit like a sledgehammer, most of them were knocked unconscious by the Cros on first contact, they had no chance. Typhon managed to kill two assailants and returned to the trail to the summit of Similaun, followed closely Conor and Fürst. The Cros did not attempt to follow them, as the route was treacherous.

At the top, they stopped for breath. "We were caught off guard by those bastards", announced Conor. "They were waiting for us in the snow, though I don't know how they got there, or how we failed to observe them from the summit", replied Typhon. Fürst simply looked with an expressionless face, "He doesn't talk much", explained Conor. "They tunnelled under the snow", replied Fürst with a look of utter disgust.

As the Cro warriors approached Summer Haven, the defence force opened up with their M16 rifles, the noise ascended exponentially as the big gatling gun began to fire up with its characteristic bark. The warriors simply continued to press forward, leaning into the gunfire like walking in a heavy rainstorm. The team from the Audacious had a grudge to settle, hitting them with the RPG's repeatedly, the explosions even drowned out the ear-splitting sound from the big machine gun. Still the Cros continued to move forward steadily with virtually no casualties.

Sheena waited for the heaviest gunfire to subside and ran into the fray. She managed to decapitate the first warrior as he attempted to grab her by the hair. She spun on her heel and cut the legs from under the Cro attacking from her right. The Cro hit the ground screaming as Sheena launched herself into the air to take the arm and top of the skull from a Cro trying to approach her from behind. She fought furiously, screaming her vengeance, but soon she became tired, the resistance of the ankle-deep water was disabling.

As she engaged two warriors, a third Cro reached from behind and twisted her round violently. The Cro delivered a hard punch to her face, she went down like a puppet with its strings cut. The bodies of her foes littered around her. "No!" screamed Rusty as he expended the last of his bullets into the invaders. He took and RPG and ran to the waterfront, where the people there had been overrun. Wrench followed, covering him with his rifle, it felt more like a peashooter in his hands. Rusty discharged the RPG directly into the face of the Cro who had hit Sheena. The explosion rocked the warrior backward, he stumbled and fell, but quickly regained his feet and headed towards Rusty determinedly.

Rusty had no chance against these aliens. He was swatted aside and knocked unconscious, further resistance was pointless. Everyone ran back to the main bunker; Wrench hid behind the fishing nets and the large sulphur containers. When the Cros passed, he bided his time before he ran towards the waterside, eyes darting from left to right searching the water.

Paul and Spall watched the battle unfold from the watch point at the northern side of the island. "It's hopeless", uttered Paul resignedly. "There's always hope", responded a stricken looking Spall, as the aliens started to pound on Summer Haven's main door. The fortifications were of little use, bullets had no impact on the aliens. Three warriors shoulder charged the door, another hit the door with an enormous rock. The door shuddered and splintered, the Cros charged inside. Paul heard muffled screaming and gunfire as the warriors entered the complex. He could also see muzzle flashes through the windows, and at one point, the flash of an explosion, the aliens continued undeterred.

Paul hefted his gun, in an attempt to help his friends, but Spall seized his arm. "You can't help them, Paul. The rifle is just a toothpick to the Cros, it's pointless. We need to retreat and determine another way to counter them". A scrabbling sound on the hill below prompted Paul and Spall level their guns. Wrench emerged from the undergrowth, "Don't shoot!, it's me". Spall laughed dryly, Wrench was covered in mud, soaked from head to foot. Wrench handed Paul the purple sword, "It was Sheena's, she killed seven or eight of them with it, before they took her. I hope she is ok. Rusty completely lost it when the Cro hit her, they took him too". Wrench was clearly distressed. "We will get them back somehow, I promise", Paul whispered. Paul took the sword and looked it over. "I don't like blades", he said, "but if it's the only thing that reliably kills those bastards, then so be it", he added.

Paul, Spall and Wrench ran back to the boat, only to find the sailors who piloted the dinghy had been captured. The door at the rear of Summer Haven, marked 'Danger: Abandoned Mine', opened, a stream of people emerged screaming and shouting. Three aliens squeezed through the door and started to round the people up. Adults and adolescents were subdued roughly, babies and children were scooped up and taken as well. One small girl screamed, "Mammy, mammy", as she was swept up and taken back into the building. The gunfire stopped suddenly; Paul knew instinctively that Summer Haven had fallen. He pushed away a tear, as he jumped into the dinghy. Spall started the motor and moved away from the shore. Paul surveyed the disaster, as they approached the Phoenix over the choppy seas.

Paul, Spall and Wrench climbed the rope ladder up to the deck and looked back forlornly. "We will be back to help", Paul vowed aloud. Wrench stood at the rail and cried as he assessed the devastation. "We couldn't open fire from here, we could have hurt our own people. We sent in a wave of blast drones, but it was too late, we were forced to recall them", offered Phil as José came down the stairs to the deck from the bridge. "They wouldn't have achieved anything; the aliens are shrugging off RPG's. There was nothing you could do without putting everyone in danger", added Spall, "they aren't actually killing their prisoners". "Yet", added Paul. "What should we do?" interjected the captain. "We will follow them for now", responded Paul, I suspect they will take the prisoners back to their compound in northern France". "They have captured almost everyone, there is only a few of us left", pointed out Spall, "how can we mount a counterattack with ineffective weapons and so few soldiers?"

23.   A Hopeless Cause

Paul shared the desperate news with his brother, Joe. He felt despondent, as everything was going to hell, and he had no idea how to stop it, "They have my wife and children, what the hell am I going to do? They have also taken Bridget and Kate, Joe". Joe touched the Carocle, the news was hard to bear. "God will help us Paul, there will be a way", Joe encouraged. "He hasn't helped much so far", pointed out Paul aggressively and instantly regretted it. It wasn't fair to blame others for the troubles, it was the aliens who were responsible. However, the Pareth-ng deserved a share of the blame for leading the enemy to Earth in the first place.

Typhon joined the discussion via the Carocle, "My team and Smitsky's were taken, but three of us remain. We killed many Cros, almost half, but not enough to make a significant dent in their population. My team threw everything we had at them, and they simply shrugged it off. We plan to head for France; they seem to have given up on hunting us, the glacier was enough for them". "Be careful, they might be in hiding. They can be crafty", warned Joe. Typhon sounded forlorn for a moment, "Quite right. They took us by tunnelling under the snow and completely surprised us. I thought we were the intelligent ones, but they outsmarted us. We should scan our path using the ship's sensors before we make a move". Paul whistled through his teeth, whispering to Spall, "Typhon killed nearly half of them using alien beetles to swamp them, but the sword was highly effective". Spall looked impressed, "I wish we had more of the Kraalt swords", as he looked down at the purple shimmer of the blade.

Paul suggested, "Don't head into France Typhon nor any ocean bordering it, it is far too risky. Head to the Adriatic coast instead. Bart will be back soon; he can pick you up from northern Italy. We seem to be safe at sea for the moment, providing we don't get too close to the enemy on the continental shelf". "Yes, that sounds sensible. We will head through the Alps to Venice and await you. I will contact Bart and request a pickup at his earliest convenience. The Alps will be safe enough, but it will take us more than a week to get to Venice, its 300km of steep and treacherous terrain in this weather", replied Typhon.

"Has anyone heard from Franc?" asked Paul, "I'm worried about him. I don't think he's been captured yet, but I worry he is too close to the enemy". "The girls have persuaded him to help, but what can ghosts do, rattle locks and slam doors shut in front of the enemy?" worried Joe. Typhon spoke once more, solemnly and carefully, "You need to have faith in the girls and the bargain they have made. They are only children, but they know what they are doing. They can't break the bond of secrecy. It's our best hope, possibly our only hope". "What kind of bargain?" asked Paul. "That is all I am permitted to say on the matter, have a little faith. They are young, but they are powerful together. You must trust Franc's instinct in this matter, Barak has great faith in them", added Typhon.

Typhon gathered the equipment and the remaining food supplies and set out a makeshift camp with the remnants of his brotherhood. "The Dolomites will be dangerous, they are not well trodden these days", pointed out Conor. Fürst said nothing and stared at Conor miserably. "I know", whispered Conor to his friend. "The more dangerous the mountains, the safer we will be", pointed out Typhon. "It will keep the big hairy brutes off our tails". "You killed many of them", pointed out Conor, "the sword seems effective against the Mbunalt". "It will cut through their armour if you put enough force behind it. The swords edge is infinitesimal and its strength gargantuan", explained Typhon with a mock salutation of grandness. Typhon set off at first light with his companions, their supplies were limited but they managed to forage a few items from the snow field.

Bart agreed with Paul to follow the Cros into France using the submarine. Paul thought that travelling from England to France would be interesting, assuming the Cros didn't aim to drown their prisoners in the crossing. It turned out they had located the channel tunnel. Phil and the crew of the Phoenix headed to the Adriatic Sea to pick up Typhon at full speed. The slight change of plan was sensible as the Phoenix was faster and would arrive in Italy in time for Typhon's arrival. The submarine was stealthier and could keep watch without alerting the aliens to its presence.

Paul and Spall transferred to HMS Astute to join Bart in the pursuit of the enemy. Paul took Bart aside, "Can we talk, we need to catch up". "Let's go to my cabin, it's private there", suggested Bart. They traversed the narrow corridors and entered the cabin, Paul sat on the bunk as Bart took the captain's chair next to his desk. He turned to Paul, "So what's on your mind, brother", he articulated the word brother a little oddly, he was having trouble coming to terms with the concept. "I have some bad news Bart, it's about Summer Haven", started Paul. "Yes, I know. It's terrible, I was monitoring the events as you saw them. I can't believe the enemy could overrun the place so easily, it was so secure, so fortified and well-armed". "I know", continued Paul, "but there's something else you may not know. The Audacious went down". He paused for a moment to allow his statement to sink in. "Caterham is dead, Bart. He went down with the ship". Bart looked stricken, "How did it happen? Did anyone survive?"

Paul continued, "The Audacious sank the boats the Cros were using to make the crossing to Summer Haven. They responded with their usual trick of walking along the sea floor to escape. However, some were prepared, they managed to attach cables onto the sub somehow. I'm not sure if they used magnets or marine drones, but they simply pulled the sub down to the bottom of the sea using the cables. The forces were extreme, the cable broke the back of the sub. Many of the crew escaped only to be captured at Summer Haven, seven of them went down with the ship. Caterham was one of the fallen. I'm so sorry". "Ed was a good man. They were all good men", insisted Bart with wet eyes, he was embarrassed and wiped away the tears brusquely. "We need to keep a safe distance from the warriors, even in the water", he concluded.

Franc climbed the stone stairs carefully. "Come on, it's clear", he whispered. The girls followed on and caught him up, close behind them was Lucy. Franc didn't want Lucy on the mission; it was not safe for any of them. Lucy was adamant, she demanded to share the same fate and promised not to be a burden. She carried a Sig-Sauer pistol containing explosive rounds, which Franc had appropriated from Rusty many moons ago. "If you need to discharge the weapon, aim for the floor or the walls. If the Cros are wearing their armour, the charge won't hurt them but falling walls and holes in the floor will slow them", Franc explained cautiously. "What if they are not wearing armour?" Lucy asked. "Then blow them to hell", replied Franc. Franc smiled to himself thinking about their conversation; Lucy was such a feisty woman, he loved her so much, he couldn't bear the thought of losing her again.

Franc reached the top of the stairwell and opened the door which led to the roof of the abbey. The girls followed him, down the narrow corridor and moved onto the open area on the rooftop. Colletta and Audrey found a place with a good view over the coast of France and beyond. They would be able to see for miles during daylight, but there was no illumination other than the moon after sundown, it was utterly black other than the burning embers of the island walkway.

Audrey sat down and immediately started to mumble under her breath, she was trying to speak to a spirit, but it appeared not to be cooperating. Franc couldn't make out Audrey's words, other than a single phrase interlaced into the sentences from time to time, 'let them come'. As Audrey mumbled, Colletta held her hands and closed her eyes, the blue stone glowing in the centre of her forehead. Audrey's mumbles got louder as the blue light intensified. Franc tried to obscure the brilliance of the light using his jacket, but it continued to light the rooftop.

The blue stone flashed brightly twice in succession, then shone faintly. This was the part where the whole enterprise typically became dangerous. The light drew attention from passers-by, even late at night. Franc anticipated tonight as one of the Cros regular sleep nights, which lasted a couple of days. Clearly there was some irregularity, as he heard sounds and movements from the depths of the abbey.

The faint purple glow of Franc's Cro Killer sword added to the mix of bruised colours on the rooftop. Additional light was not good, the situation could get messy if the illumination drew too much attention too quickly. The girls continued their murmuring causing the blue stone to flash brightly in an irregular periodicity. Sounds approached the stairwell, the Cros were nearby.

The door burst outwards as a warrior smashed through the lintel, splintering the door and the stone frame around it. The warrior wasn't able to take a single step before he was skewered by the purple blade. He gurgled and fell onto his face as another broached the doorway. Franc stepped back to avoid the warrior's wide swing and he lowered his blade to sever the Cro's arm. The creature screamed in pain and immediately charged at Franc before realising his arm was severed. Franc side stepped but couldn't completely evade the Cro's remaining arm, it caught Franc hard in the side and he spun across the rooftop.

Lucy fired at the exposed point where the warrior's arm had been severed, the creature exploded, the gore splattered Franc, the armour contained the explosion causing devastating damage to the Cro. "Steady on", shouted Franc, "you'll bring them all up here". Luckily the Cros were sleeping, as Franc had calculated, but they had elected to post guards to keep watch over the roof. Franc's advantage was the Cros were not all wearing armour.

Four more Cros squeezed through the damaged doorway, as Franc tried hard to regather himself. The glancing blow had taken the wind from his sails. Lucy lifted her pistol, but Franc told her to lower it. He picked himself up and walked calmly towards the first of the four Cros. The Cro saw his fallen comrade and the excessive blood scattered up the walls, a curious look filled his face as the blade removed a diagonal section of his head.

The remaining warriors surged forward as their leader fell. "No more wounding", whispered Franc to himself, "it's too damned dangerous". His blade arced and cut the throat of one Cro, then slashed backhanded to sever the leg of his comrade. Franc decapitated the fallen warrior, as he lunged at the fourth. The Cro parried the blade with his arm easily, but realised he wasn't wearing his armour and his arm dropped to the floor. Blood squirted profusely from the severed arteries. Franc brought down the blade onto the top of the Cro's head, cleaving his skull in two. The rooftop was crammed with gigantic cadavers, making it exceedingly difficult to move around.

The girls looked at the mess and were alarmed. "It's ok, keep going", Lucy whispered, "you only have a few minutes before more warriors get here". "We've done all we can for today", announced Audrey proudly. "Let's get out of here, for god's sake", pressed Lucy. Franc led the way down the steps and took a series of intricate turns which took them back the nave of the abbey church. They quietly took the stair beneath the nave to the underground chapel, sneaking past a handful of sleeping Mbunalt.

Lucy quickly tucked the girls into bed without complaint, they were exhausted. "That was too close", Franc murmured. She and Franc sat down together to share an enamel mug of marvellous champagne cognac from the stores, it helped calm their nerves a little. An alarm sounded in the square in front of the abbey, the reverberation of heavy footfalls made the room shake. "That's gone and done it", Franc uttered quietly.

Movement of the Mbunalt around the abbey was limited due to their physical stature. The entry to the underground chapel was hidden deep in one of the inaccessible places, so they were not aware of its presence. Despite their diligence, they didn't manage to locate Franc and his family. If the warriors realised there was purpose behind the attacks, they would tear the place down brick by brick. Two confrontations could be seen as random attacks, but further conflict would form a pattern.

The following morning at breakfast, Lucy and Franc discussed the events of the previous night. Franc felt it was time to ask for help, the risk to his family was escalating; the previous ritual was a close call. "Colletta, I need to ask your uncles for their assistance to help protect you. The aliens are becoming aware of us and are actively seeking us. Before my brothers take the risk of coming here, we will need to brief them on your mission with the spirits. They need to know it's important. I know Typhon and Barak have prompted your mission; we are investing great trust in the four of you".

Audrey took a deep breath, "We can't tell you Dad. I promised them". "I understand, but can't you at least tell me how the mission is going to help us win the war?" Franc insisted. Colletta chipped in, "Dad, you know it's important. We are summoning the spirits to help us fight the aliens". "I get that", Franc replied, "but how can they help us, they are ghosts, they have no substance. I don't understand". Colletta gave a look of finality to her father, "They are not insubstantial, they can affect our plane. Remember the broken mirror and the flying vase? You will all have to trust us". "Yes of course, but it is difficult to put the fate of the human race on the shoulders of my children", Franc explained. He was certain he saw the briefest flicker of blue in the stone at Colletta's brow. Franc grew concerned, "If I find you are using the empathy stone to manipulate me, I will throw it into the goddamned sea!"

Franc called his brothers, "I need an assist guys, I need to protect the girls as they perform Barak's ritual. It concerns the spirits in the Well of Souls in Jerusalem. I believe the ritual is our only chance of survival. The girls are not permitted to explain the ritual because of the promises they have made. Barak and Typhon believe in the plan, in my heart so do I".

Paul decided to honour the request and planned to leave with Spall to arrive as soon as he could. Joe was unable to escape, but Bart agreed to help. Typhon joined the discussion and reiterated the importance of the mission to the brothers, "Bring all your strength, we will need it. I will be in Venice soon, then Phil and I will join you. You will need to hang in there for another week, you must keep the momentum going. I feel that it is starting to work". However, a week was a long time when the Cros were pursuing them.

Two nights later, Franc prepared his defence for the girls and Lucy on the roof of the abbey. He had used stone to create a façade to better hide the entrance to the stairwell and littered the stairs with sharp objects to inflict damage on the Cros bare feet. Franc knew the Cros who had found the entrance on the last outing were dead, so those remaining may not know how to find the stairs to the rooftop with a little luck. As a contingency plan, he had lowered four ropes from the abbey roof to the tree lined rockface to the north, he ensured they were anchored to the castellations securely. The drop from the wall was steep, but if he and the girls abseiled down and used the rope to take their weight as they climbed sideways to the castle wall, then it should be safe enough. He had secreted a ladder on the wall to help them get back into the building from the outside wall. Franc taught the girls to abseil when it was quiet, in case they needed an exit in a hurry.

Colletta and Audrey took a deep breath before starting their ritual. The girls grasped hands, Audrey murmured, and the blue stone began to flash and then glow more faintly. Despite Lucy persuading Colletta to wear a woolly hat to obscure the light, it attracted the attention of the Cros in the square below. There were many more around, as they were not sleeping. Someone had cleared the bodies from the previous battle, the Cros hadn't found the ingress points so it could only be the Kraalt. Lucy suspected the bodies were collected for the food hopper, but Franc begged to differ. It was a conspiracy theory, and he gave it no more airtime, there were bigger fish to fry tonight.

There was loud noise from below, as the Cros struggled to locate the access point to the roof. Eventually they ascended the stairs and began to complain angrily as their feet were pierced by the broken glass fragments. Even elephant skin could be hurt by broken glass. By the time the Cros climbed the staircase and tended to their feet, they found nothing of interest.

Franc and the girls hung from the rooftop by their ropes and abseil harnesses. They dropped down and swung to the rope ladder to access the lower wall circling the main castellated bastions, the only part of the abbey not protected by sheer cliffs. They climbed the shaky ladder and released the ropes for another day. They crept back through the winding streets of the town to safety. Only a couple more nights remained when the Cros were not sleeping, and by then Franc's brothers would be able to help him mount a better defence.

Once the girls were in bed, Franc left the sanctuary of the chapel to scavenge water, their supplies were running low. There was plenty of food in the chapel, it had been used as a storeroom by the team at MSM. There was also wine and spirits, but nothing hydrating. He slipped into the shadows of the main street and searched the first café in the row of shops. The lock had been broken, so he eased the door ajar and moved into the kitchen. He soon located the storeroom and found a large pack of litre bottles of spring water. They were five years old, but from experience he knew they should be potable. He carried the pack through to the front door but immediately noticed a shadow in the doorway. The figure was diminutive, so he braved stepping out into the open. The figure was Kraalt, the small man suddenly looked nervous.

Franc reached out to communicate using his Carocle but had no success. Clearly communication only worked when the Kraalt were prepared. Franc indicated to the water and smiled. The Kraalt suddenly had a moment of recognition, his voice came clearly through the Carocle. "You are the one called Francisco, I'm so sorry I didn't recognise you immediately because of the hair growth around your face. You would know me as Buddy". "Hi Buddy. What a relief it's you. How are they treating you?" Franc queried warmly. Buddy shrugged, broadly mimicking the human gesture, "Business as usual", he replied, "Are you the one who killed the soldiers on the rooftops? It took some time to transport their bodies without being detected" Buddy's comments amused Franc, he decided to be candid with Buddy, as he had been an ally in the recent past. "Yes, the sword you gave me made defending myself easy against the unarmoured warriors. It was like shooting fish in a barrel". The Kraalt looked confused by the expression but realised it was a complement and moved his face to approximate a smile.

"If you are captured, In the days that come please do not tell the Mbunalt we made the sword for you. The consequences would be terrible for us", Buddy requested cautiously. "Of course, Buddy", placated Franc, "I would never bring harm to a friend". Buddy looked relieved, "Would you mind me asking what you are doing on the roof? We are sensing powerful energy pulses, but the Kraalt cannot find the source or the meaning of them. Our confusion has saved you so far". "To be honest, I don't know. My daughters have a plan, but it is beyond my understanding. However, there are people I trust who believe their ritual will help to save us. Their optimism is good enough for me, so here I am".

Buddy pulled his face strangely, Franc felt instinctively it was an attempt to wink, "Take care my friend, keep to the smaller routes. Many warriors will be asleep tonight, it should be safe enough. However, they are adapting and staggering their sleep patterns, so be careful". This was not welcome news for Franc. "We will free you my friend, have faith", promised Franc. It seemed like such an empty promise, but Franc knew he would succeed or die trying. "There are so few of you. I hope you succeed, but I dare not hope. I offered to be reassigned here when I heard of the strange goings on. I hoped I might run into you, eager to help your cause", whispered Buddy before disappearing into the shadows.

Franc headed back towards the chapel; he had the strangest feeling that he was being stealthily followed. He trusted Buddy, but he knew Buddy was obliged to follow orders, Franc could take no chances. He decided to take a roundabout route to lose his pursuer, using a back route into the nave of the main church, despite passing a Mbunalt sleeping area. An evil thought occurred to Franc, which crept in from the darker places of his mind.

Franc crept through the nave, finding eleven warriors asleep on the floor. He shed the case of water gently and drew his sword. He crept towards the Cros silently until he was alongside the nearest. The warrior opened his eyes briefly at the sound of Franc's breathing, his eyes remained unfocused, he was clearly sound asleep. Franc rammed the sword under the warrior's chin, directly into his brain. He stepped back to avoid the gush of blood and used the same technique to dispatch the remaining Cros. Eleven executions, only nine hundred to go, Franc thought to himself. He collected the water, sheathed his sword and proceeded back to the safety of the chapel. A small unseen figure in the shadows grimaced with an odd approximation of a human smile.

The following day Franc found the nave completely clear, and free from blood stains. Buddy had clearly been busy in the night. Franc wondered how a single Kraalt could remove ten enormous warriors, they must have technological assistance, or a good saw and a great deal of patience.

24.   A Darkness of Purpose

Phil piloted the Phoenix to the waterside at Venice alongside the wall of the main harbour, just before nightfall. Gio hit the green button to wind down the ship's gangway, Typhon bounded aboard with two companions. Phil greeted Typhon cordially, but the rest of the crew remained ominously silent. Typhon was used to distrust, he even felt he deserved it and had faith it would pass in time. Typhon and his men were shown to their cabins by José.

Phil looked towards the ancient city, once the trade capital of Europe, it seemed so empty and insignificant. The city was as beautiful as it was reputed, the sunset shimmered across the sea as a backdrop to the wonderful Byzantine and Gothic Venetian architecture. The Basilica di San Marco reached up to the skies, illuminated brightly as if it was calling them for evening prayer.

Wrench whispered to Gio, "Do you trust this bastard? It seems like only a couple of moons ago Typhon was trying to kill us, now he is supposedly our friend". Gio chuffed, "Pah! I don't trust any of them. They unleasha da virus which killed my family and many of my friends, the pasty-faced screwers. But then, they warn us of the invasion, and they have been fierce allies. I donta know what to think. All I know is Francisco seems to trust them, that is good enough for me. He used the Carocle, that weird brain ring, to see into their thoughts". Wrench laughed, "Yeah, I guess so. But I'm still watching them like a hawk". "Me too", added Gio, "till the day I drop my gutting knife, I don't like the look of the sciacallo called Fürst either". "Nor me, he always seems to arrive last", laughed Wrench as he walked back to the bridge.

Phil popped into Typhon's cabin before they took to their beds. "What news?" Typhon looked unhappily at Phil, "We lost". Conor stood in the doorway, he looked at the concerned expression on Phil's face, "Don't give up, our forces were captured not killed. The Cros followed us relentlessly. Typhon and the beetles put up a strong fight, they killed more than a few warriors, whereas the rest of us had little success with our blades and firearms. The Cros eventually smashed the trap we had laid for them and killed the slayer beetles with their bare hands. We lost the Cros in the high grounds, it was too treacherous for them on the glacier, they were clumsy and unprepared. Even when they fell off the glacier, they reappeared an hour or so later with barely more than a few bruises. What I wouldn't give for some of their armour, though I dare say I wouldn't be able to stand up in it".

Phil looked resigned as he updated Typhon, "Summer Haven fell. The Mbunalt have everyone now; the prisoners have been set to work in their labour camp. There is only the crew of the Astute, plus Paul and Spall remaining". Typhon shared his concern, "It's really bad news, I don't know how much longer we can hold out. I don't know how we can possibly free the prisoners or fight off these monsters. Our only opportunity is to nuke them and kill everyone". "What about Franc?" added Conor after a brief pause. Phil explained, "He's hiding out in MSM with his family, I hope they haven't caught them. Last I heard was his daughters were trying to bring the spirits into the battle. I know it sounds ridiculous, but". Conor cut in before he could progress his line of thought, "Barak and Typhon are deeply involved in their initiative. They are bringing forth the dead for a last battle, Barak says. Audrey is in league with them". "I hope it bloody works", added Phil as José ambled down the stairs into the corridor.

"The view from here is absolutely amazing, I will never forget it", José observed, oblivious to the seriousness of the exchange. Gio chipped in, "Of course it is. It's the most beautiful city in…". Typhon burst out of the doorway into the corridor, pushing past Phil roughly and climbed the stairs two at a time, "We need to get moving, Franc needs our help, and quickly". They followed Typhon and grouped on the deck, ready to get underway immediately.

Paul and Bart received Francisco's call simultaneously. Barak had also contacted Paul to explain the gravity of the situation, it was critical they freed Joe so he could support the girls in completing their mission. Spall cynically asked, "Why Joe specifically? I mean, he is a wonderful man, no question. But how would he help us fight these monsters when Franc cannot. Whoever takes this mission is going to take a terrible risk entering the Mbunalt camp". "Barak believes Joe has untapped potential; he is our secret weapon. Barak suggests we need to join together to protect Colletta and Audrey as they execute their ritual", clarified Paul.

"Ok gentlemen. We have an unstoppable enemy, a hopelessly risky and vague plan, no suitable weaponry, and a shit bucket of blind optimism. Hit it!" exclaimed Spall sarcastically with a less than enthusiastic laugh. Typhon explained Paul's proposal to Phil. Phil commanded, "Full ahead to Mont St Michel". José replied, "Aye", as he briskly took the stairs up to the bridge.

"Let's hope we can hold them off until Joe arrives", whispered Paul to Spall.

It was sunrise, the start of another gruelling day in the fields. Joe was physically exhausted, and the day was only beginning. His sleep was troubled, as he worried about his brothers. Barak, Smitsky and their men were on route to the camp, the women and children from Summer Haven were starting to arrive. The new prisoners didn't know the definition of hard work; they were in for a shock. The Mbunalt were ruthless, they happily dealt out crippling blows which were enough to temporarily immobilise frail human limbs.

Sheena was first to arrive, she had severe bruising to her face, her jaw had been broken and healed crookedly. Joe rushed over and took her in his arms. "Are you ok?" Joe asked as he quickly triaged her wounds. He reached forward and summoned his powers of healing, an intense bright light illuminated Sheena as her jaw cracked and realigned into place. The swelling subsided, but the bruising continued to stain her pretty features.

Kate followed, holding Sheena's small child and baby. "Where's Rusty?" asked Sheena, "Oh sorry, thank you for helping me by the way", she added with a hint of humility and embarrassment. Joe replied with a shrug, "We haven't seen Rusty yet, but don't worry the Cros aren't killing, they are gathering our people to use as slaves, though I have no idea of their ultimate plan. However, the warrior's death toll is around the forty mark, they are showing some vulnerability to attack, but by no means enough for us to be a significant threat". Sheena and Joe walked towards the fields under instruction of a Kraalt guard. An exhausted Kate was allowed to stay with Sheena's children, which was a kindness.

As Sheena and Joe walked, the Kraalt moved close to Joe and whispered to him using the Carocle, "We have reconnected with our brethren who were staying in Summer Haven". Joe looked at the diminutive man as he continued, "You spoke the truth, our colleagues have been allowed their freedom during their stay with your people. I cannot fully reconcile the joy they have experienced during that short period. However, as our colleagues are slaves once more, they are spreading discontent amongst our numbers. It's a strange phenomenon for us, as we are a hive mind; we think and act as one, it is beyond our normal experience. The unrest has brought pandemonium to our ordered and simple existence. Our minds are at war, and we are deeply troubled". "Is there a way I can I help you?" asked Joe sincerely. The Kraalt looked deep into Joe's eyes and saw warmth and kindness. He stared for what seemed like an eternity, he then spoke sharply before he left abruptly to oversee the other slaves, "If you can find a way through this darkness, we will be at your side at the end".

Joe conveyed his thoughts to Sheena, explaining the Kraalt's offer. "What can those little dudes do to help us fight the Cros? They are pacifists", breathed Sheena carefully. "I'm not sure, but they control all the Mbunalt technology", explained Joe. "Yes, but the warriors don't fight with technology, they fight with their bone crunching oversized mitts!" pointed out Sheena.

A Moonlit Armageddon - Paul JC Edge

25.   A Tenuous Plan

HMS Astute bubbled one click north of Mont St Michel in the blackness of the post-apocalyptic night. The craggy moonless landscape framed the depths of the dark ocean, which was motionless like a mill pond. Spall and Paul entered the water in wetsuits and fins, waved briefly and turned towards the rocky northern shore of the island. Wrench smiled at them as they left, "God's speed", he mouthed to them. Spall whispered, "Piece of cake. Watch out for the tank breathers", smiling briefly. Inevitably Franc would be waiting when they arrived. Franc communicated through the device, "You need to keep your heads down for a while, there is some commotion here. Some of the Cros are mustering on the north side, I don't know what's going on".

A klaxon announced the arrival of the submarine, which had been spotted by the Cro sentries on the wall. Paul and Spall kept a low profile as the Mbunalt gathered near the rocks, they were monitoring the sub but fortunately hadn't noticed the two dark figures in the water, despite their infra-red capabilities. The water helped to mask the heat signature of the two men as they continued to tread water in the moonlight.

After a few excruciating minutes, one Cro found his initiative, beginning to hurl huge rocks at the warship, the others quickly followed suit. Their strength was prodigious, and their aim was surprisingly good. The Astute began to submerge as the first rock impacted the hull. It was only a glancing blow but made a huge dent in the structure. Paul whispered to himself, "Get the hell out of here guys". The second impact tore a huge hole in the hull and appeared catastrophic, however if they acted quickly the crew could isolate the damaged section and be able to escape. They could find a military boat yard on the south coast of the UK where they could weld steel plating over the breach as an emergency repair.

The sub's chances of survival evaporated as a third rock smashed the conning tower. The remaining Astute submarine scuppered, almost immediately. Many of the crew abandoned ship, diving into the water. The closest land mass was MSM, the mainland was too far to reach, as the current was strong. The crew unlashed a small boat from the top of the sub, starting its engine, but the sound was soon extinguished by a huge mass of stone smashing the hull.

A handful of men attempted the longer more challenging swim to the mainland avoiding the island. The majority of the crew, although strong swimmers, avoided the more perilous route. They had no chance, as they swam to the shore, they were scooped up by the Cros. Paul struggled in the water; he felt a terrible sensation via his Carocle as his brother went down with the sinking ship. "Bart is in trouble", whispered Paul to Spall.

None of the crew acknowledged Spall and Paul as they swam past, sensibly the crew figured the brothers were their last hope and kept their presence secret. Paul started to head back to the sub, but Spall held him back, "There is nothing you can do for Bart now. You don't have an air tank, and you don't know the layout of the sub, you would be dead in minutes. If anyone can escape, it's Bart. It's his ship, he knows it like the back of his hand". When the sub finally went down, Bart and a handful of the crew managed to find an air locked bubble in the hull. The chances of escape were not looking good. Paul and Spall treaded water for a couple of hours, in case they could assist.

Paul felt the increasing desperation and trepidation from Bart, who was fighting to stay alive deep below the surface of the Atlantic.

Paul waited for the hubbub to subside on the island before they dared approach. Paul felt intense guilt leaving Bart, but he wasn't equipped to assist, Spall was quite right. Perhaps they could reach the escape chamber in time.

Similar thoughts were swimming through Barts mind. Himself, Jones, and Appleby were holding on to the bulkhead, but the CO_2 was building up and they would soon struggle to breathe. Between gasps of air, he briefed the remaining two of his crew. "I don't plan on going down without a fight. We need to open the airlock door slowly, flood the chamber and make our way to the escape pod. It's halfway down the hull, and we are unsure of the obstacles we will face. The air tanks and regulators in the starboard lockers should give us the capability to reach the pod. Good luck gentlemen, it has been an honour serving with you".

Appleby rotated the wheel to release the bulkhead door sufficient for the water to seep in slowly. The pressure behind the door was high, but the water was held back by the strong lock and hinges. The chamber filled, as the men took their last breath Appleby quickly opened the door to equalise the pressure, to make their exit. Bart helped Jones, he could see the panic in the man's eyes, but managed to keep it under control. The risk was if Jones lost it, they would all be dead. As luck would have it, by going first he focused on his escape.

The vessel was largely intact, the three remaining crew made their way to the lockers, Jones fumbled with the air tanks as fear took a tighter grip on him. Bart felt like his lungs were going to explode, as he helped Jones to put the regulator into his mouth. He passed a tank to Appleby and then secured one for himself. The air felt good, they regained their composure quickly.

Bart took the lead heading directly towards the escape chamber in the main corridor. A huge rock barred the exit, as it had made a massive dent in the hull and split it. Appleby headed back toward the locker to retrieve a jemmy and a heavy steel bar. Bart rammed the jemmy into a crack, wedged his legs against the hull and tried to lever the aperture open to allow them to get past. The others took hold and tried to help, but nothing moved.

Bart abandoned his original exit plan, the three of them moved back toward the torpedo tubes. They hoped to find a way out, or at worst launch themselves from the sub. Although it would mean one of them staying aboard to execute the launch using the control panel to open the outer doors to flood the tubes. Bart used his Captain's prerogative to insist that Jones and Appleby took to the first two tubes. Jones didn't argue but met an initial resistance from Appleby. The two men climbed into the tube, Bart bumped fists with each of them and mouthed good luck, both men saluted solemnly and mimed their thanks.

Bart sealed the doors and hit the red buttons on the control panel to release the outer doors. Air hissed as it escaped the tubes and ejected the men to the relative safety of the ocean. Survival was not certain, the depth could crush them, but the pressure should be survivable if they ascended slowly with their air bubbles to avoid the bends.

Bart had a desperate plan. He knew there was no way of depressing the torpedo launch button whilst he was in the tube. He also understood the tube wouldn't launch with the door open. His only hope was to try to short circuit the sensor on the tube door, so it would be closed to the release mechanism. He could then run wires to the control button console, but the chances of it working in water was very slim. He used the jemmy to lever off the control panel cover and attached two wires using crocodile clips.

The submarine lurched violently in the water, he dropped the wires, wisely prioritising his regulator. He returned to the control panel to retrieve the wires and climbed into the torpedo tube, shut the door and connected the wires. Bart was not a religious man, but he prayed for desperate idea to work.

Joe felt the sensation first. He woke in the early hours with a shout. Sheena and Bridget were quickly at his side, "What is wrong?" "It's my brother, its Bart. The submarine has been damaged. I don't think he is going to get out in time". It was an excruciating moment as Joe and his brothers lived through the last moments of Bart's life. It was the cruel side of the Carocle which none of them had foreseen. They felt they had died themselves. They experienced every excruciating second, every emotion and every physical sensation. Bart panicked as the launch of the tube failed, he couldn't exit the tube feet first, because he couldn't reach the iron bar used to jam the door shut. The tube trapped Bart as his air tank gave out.

Joe broke down and cried. "Bart's gone, and I never really had the chance to get to know him". "He was a brave man, just like you are", Sheena whispered gently. Joe looked into Sheena's eyes and felt a seed of something dark growing inside him, it was a seed of hatred. He looked around at the prisoners cramped into the tiny hut, sleeping on the lumpy ground with little for warmth other than each other's body heat. "I will avenge him. I will avenge them all". "So how the hell are you planning to do that father Joe?" asked Bridget emphasising the word 'father' to bring the irony clearly into focus.

Typhon and Conor landed at the port in St Brieuc, 60km due west of MSM. Gio was adamant he should join them, but Typhon stressed they needed to be inconspicuous, and they would be moving at considerable speed. Any combat would not end well with the Cros, Typhon and Conor had to rely on stealth and caution. Typhon wouldn't negotiate, but he was sure Gio had sighed with relief when his request was rejected. "You will be more help staying where you are. On the sea you are unbeatable", Typhon placated, Gio swelled his chest subliminally.

Wrench crossed the plank. "Did you get it?" asked Conor. "Yup", replied Wrench as he handed the Cro Killer, which was wrapped in brown cloth, to Typhon who tied it to his back. "Let's hope we won't need it", observed Conor. "What happened to the third blade?" asked Typhon. "Paul has it", replied Wrench. "Good. He will need it", observed Typhon as he set off at a trot. "Let's keep it tight guys, the journey will take us about six hours", observed Conor. "Maybe, if we don't have a break", pointed out Wrench. "That's right. We'll rest when we get there", replied Typhon. "Great", replied Wrench under his breath.

Typhon eyes looked down, suddenly in deep thought as he accessed his Carocle, he then called over to Phil, "The Astute is in trouble, some of the crewmen are swimming to the mainland to avoid being captured by the Cros on MSM. The sea is dangerous there, go and see if you can rescue them but keep well out of sight of the Cros. They are throwing huge rocks at the ships; the hulls won't take that sort of damage". Typhon and his small team turned and headed off towards the town. It was going to be a long run, almost two marathons back-to-back. They needed to take it at a steady pace and keep hydrated. They didn't elect to take vehicles to avoid being spotted by the invaders.

Typhon's assault team jogged into the town via the park, onto the main E50 route and continued until they reached the E401 signposted to Dinan. It was tedious running on tarmac, but it was the fastest route if they avoided being spotted. They arrived at the city after nearly three hours of continuous road pounding. Dawn was coming, they chose to hide out in a village until nightfall just off the main road, in a small rundown gite. They were all fit, but they welcomed the respite.

Wrench was glad they hadn't attempted the full distance in a single slog. Otherwise, they would arrive too tired to defend themselves. Running in sports kit was one thing, but in full combat gear with packs and weapons was a completely different animal. They ate dry rations with warm bottled water. Wrench found the gas supply operable and managed to heat water to make tea. The hot drink was most welcome, until Conor found a couple of bottles of rather nice St Emilion claret in the understairs cupboard in an otherwise empty wine rack. Conor looked at Wrench, exchanging a brief grin. Typhon frowned, "Okay, but two glasses maximum. We are fighting for many lives tomorrow". "Fair enough", said Wrench expressing more than a little disappointment, "but it could be our last day on this world, we best savour it".

The three enjoyed the wine in small sips and managed to make it last a couple of hours, then tried to catch some sleep. Typhon was asleep in seconds, but Conor and Wrench struggled. There was too much to think about, too many things to go wrong in the forthcoming battle. As dusk arrived, Typhon rose, then they quickly breakfasted from cans. "I'm stuck with tinned dogmeat. At least that's what it tastes like". "I'll swap you for beans", offered Wrench. They compromised on sharing cans as Typhon methodically stuffed two cans of red beans into his mouth, spoon after spoon.

They jogged on the D794 for an hour and a half until they reached Combourg, where they slowed to a walk to conserve energy. At the cemetery in Combourg, Typhon contacted Joe as the others hydrated. Joe was not hard to rouse; he was expecting them, despite being bone tired from the days hard labour. "It's no good", objected Joe, "even if I come with you, the restraints will fry me. I can't run, they will find me in minutes on the floor in agony. Then my life will not be worth living. James has arrived at the camp, the Cros will blame him". "If James can run, then he will have to come with us", concluded Typhon, "I'm hoping that my Kraalt sword will cut through their collars and bindings. If not, we are royally screwed. We'll have to slide them off somehow, maybe with lubrication". "Forget it", commented Joe, "we've tried that, it's impossible. Sheena dislocated her thumb, and still couldn't get her wrist cuff off". "Let's see", spoke Typhon with an element of finality.

Typhon and the team walked carefully up Liberation Avenue until they reached Le Pont Saint-Martin, a tiny rural village. "What are they doing here?", asked Wrench. "Who?" queried Typhon. "The Shrooms. There are millions of them scattered around, it doesn't make any sense. They tend to stay close to the place where they were infected, and that's in the larger cities typically" "Unless they are shrooming before a battle", added Typhon, "odd indeed". Sheena met them by the intersection, "I must be quick, or my absence will be noticed. The camp is about a kilometre down this side road. There are at least six hundred Mbunalt and hundreds of us in captivity. Let's see if the blade will sever these bloody things; try the one on my left ankle as its less visible, I can tuck the severed cuff under my combat trousers". Typhon unstrapped and unwrapped the sword from the monks' habit cloth, brandishing the blade. "Let's see", Typhon muttered. The anklet was extremely tough, but the blade cut through it neatly. He had to be careful, the sword would sever Sheena's leg with just a touch. "That's it", Sheena said, "God I'm glad to have that thing off. I need to retain the others, or it will be too obvious. When shall we do the deed?" Sheena asked enthusiastically.

Typhon was keen to wait until the Cros took their rest, it would be easier to escape. They only had 24 hours to wait. "What about the Kraalt? They are always watching, they never sleep. One word from them and we will be beaten to a pulp and then electrocuted just for the fun of it". "Joe will handle the Kraalt", said Typhon. Sheena countered, "Joe thinks he has an arrangement with them, but the Mbunalt will rip them limb from limb if they provide poor service". Typhon shrugged, "The Kraalt in Summer Haven were friendly enough", offered Sheena, "Buddy tried to help us", Typhon commented. "But Buddy isn't here, and they think as one, like a hive, we have no guarantees.. "I won't be coming with you, I have to stay with my babies", Sheena asserted. "Understood", replied Typhon with a little more empathy. Conor smiled at her warmly, perhaps one day I will have a child, he thought to himself. He knew that it was unlikely, but it was a dream worth holding on to.

The following evening, Joe, James, and Bridget rose at midnight and crept from the main sleeping barn. The bulk of the Mbunalt warriors were sound asleep, but a small number milled around. They had to take great care, or they would be dealt with severely. They looped around the back of the barn and headed for the 'canteen', a rough building with a serving table but no seats.

The Cros slept on the floor in their armour these days, ready for anything. They didn't take any risks after the recent massacre in the nave of the abbey at MSM. Joe could hear his heart beating loudly. He almost lost his nerve, but then he looked at Bridget and James and knew he needed to be positive, or he would put them in danger. They reached the outer compound quickly and without event, but as they turned towards the exit gate a reception committee was waiting for them.

Three Kraalt looked at them with sad eyes, though it was hard to recognise their emotions. The large flaps of skin over their necks were stretched slightly pulling the ruffles straighter, such that they looked a little more human. "What are you doing?" asked the leader, "We will be executed if we let you go, you must understand". "I had hoped that if you didn't see us, you would be spared", pointed out Joe. "But we have seen you", the leader exclaimed. "True, but if you tell the Mbunalt you haven't seen us, then you might be spared?" "But we have seen you", the leader pointed out once more. James looked at Joe, "It does not compute", he whispered quietly. Bridget interjected, "Ok, we will go back to the barn, thank you for your advice. If we leave again in five minutes time and you are not here, then you will not see us leave". James smiled wryly, but Joe looked pensive. The jury was out as to whether the Kraalt were prepared to help.

The Kraalt leader repeated himself once more, "What are you planning to do?" Joe hesitated, and then decided to have a little faith. After all the Kraalt hadn't punished anyone, they must be receptive. "We plan to go to Mont St Michel to protect my brother and his daughters". "Ah", whispered the leader, "you plan to release the energy signatures again. But how will they help you?" he asked sincerely. "I don't know", replied Joe. "Go back to the barn", the Kraalt commanded. Joe, James, and Bridget headed to the barn. Five minutes later they arrived at the exit once more, the Kraalt were nowhere to be seen.

Joe, James, and Bridget headed cross country towards the small village where Typhon was hiding. Joe received information from the Carocle to indicate Typhon's precise location. They jogged across the fields, taking care to stay in the shadows of the trees. They soon arrived at the building, where Typhon stood in the doorway looking agitated.

The first order of business was the removal of the restraints. Typhon disappeared inside and soon returned with a Kraalt blade. He first severed the collars and then set about taking off the wrist and ankle cuffs. The task needed great care, taking almost an hour before the task was complete. "Thank the Lord for small mercies", uttered Joe as he rubbed his wrists gratefully. They wasted no time and soon headed off in the direction of MSM. They took the main highway until they neared the ancient island abbey. The Cros were asleep, so they decided to take the risk of using the roads for the sake of speed. They needed to be safe in the abbey before the Cros started to awaken. As they neared the mainland adjacent to the island, they took a cross country route. They clambered over the walls and fences obscuring their path, the sword made short work of brambles.

"How do we get in there without being seen?" asked Joe. "We go in through the front door", replied Typhon, "whilst they are sleeping". "Let's hope Buddy is on watch", added Wrench. "It doesn't matter really; the Kraalt seem to be helping us for now" explained Joe. Typhon felt exposed on the broken causeway, as the small team climbed the smashed shards of road and waded through open water. The missiles and shells had wreaked terrible destruction on the bridge, but they managed to climb over the rubble. In two places they were forced to swim across, as the water was too deep.

The air was tense as they approached the main gates of the island, which had been wrenched off their hinges and cast aside. The sandbags and other defensive constructions had been swept away by the marauders. A single Kraalt stood near to the museum, "Hurry they are waking".

They rushed up the cobbled street and turned the corner towards the main abbey. As they turned the bend, they were attacked by a large angry looking Cro, who charged directly at them. Typhon swung the blade and managed to sever the arm of the attacker, who screamed an unholy howl at the top of his lungs as he dropped. Blood spurted uncontrollably. The warrior attempted to rise again, but Typhon decapitated him, but his blade caught in the strap of the heavy helmet.

A second Cro attacked Typhon as he struggled to free the blade. The sword came loose, but it was too late, a heavy fist hit Typhon in the side of his head. The crack was sickening as his head snapped round leaving it at the wrong angle against his spine. Typhon's sword flew across the street and landed in a doorway. Typhon was lost, there was no time to hesitate. James quickly snatched the sword and managed to parry a punch, which resulted in another Cros arm being severed. "Man, this blade is sharp", uttered James astonished. He finished the Cro with a thrust through the place where his heart should be. James' blow was enough, the monster clattered to the ground. "Quick this way", a small voice came from the shadows at the side of the abbey. Dawn was coming, they needed to find the secret chapel post haste. "I might be able to help Typhon", suggested Joe urgently. "Too late, we must move", ordered the small, disembodied voice from the shadows.

The Kraalt led the team through the abbey, into the nave and down the stairs into the secret chapel, where Franc waited smiling. He embraced the group individually, then solemnly offered his condolences to Conor for the loss of his friend and leader. "He saved us", said Franc gracefully, "he was a good man". The Kraalt nodded at Franc. "Hey Buddy, how are you doing my friend?" "Good, but I fear for my kin who assisted Joe at the compound. Their sacrifice is worth the cost", uttered the small alien. "But they didn't see us, if you get my drift", clarified

James. "Nevertheless, they will be punished", replied Buddy. "I'm so sorry", said Joe sheepishly. "Let's hope the plan works", placated Buddy, "how did it go tonight, Franc?" "Honestly, I have no idea. But we didn't get caught, we were lucky", explained Franc. Buddy looked at Franc kindly. Franc realised there was no luck involved at all.

"So, what is it with all these Shrooms?" asked Wrench. "There seem to be millions of them around here, I've never seen so many, even in the large cities". Franc paused, then responded slowly "I really don't know, I thought they were all dead, but their numbers seem to be growing". "Ask Franc's daughters", added Buddy with a facial expression looking remarkably like a wink, as he disappeared through the doorway.

26.   The 'Not-Dead'

Gio sat on a locker on the deck of the Phoenix looking miserable. Phil, José and two off duty crew members joined him for a cold beer. "It's old, but it still tastes good", observed José. "You haven't tasted Phil's toxic sludge from the Summer Haven", contributed Gio, "It's actually not too bad, but really murky and flat like a sailor's arse". They barely raised a smile at Gio's banter, he didn't put his heart in it. "It was good we saved four of the swimmers", observed José. "Yes, shame about those we didn't", added Phil sadly. "Well, what's our next move? We have no idea what's going on", Gio's moan fell flat, "Should we just sit here until the end? I think no".

Phil attempted to raise the mood, as he was supposed to be the leader. He mustered the last of his energy, "We wait for a sign, like we were told. When the shit hits the fan, we need to be ready for anything". "What shit, what fan?" moaned Gio. "We need to help Franc when the time comes, it's likely to be three nights from tonight. Enjoy the peace whilst we have it, it may be our last!" encouraged Phil. "That's a cheery thought", added Gio with a scowl, "I think I'll catch us some pesce for dinner". The thought made him smile a little, "Justa like the old times". "Don't go catching bloody mackerel again Gio, it stinks out the galley. I was belching bad gas for days after the last lot", appealed José. "I catch what I catch", chuckled Gio with a wink, "I'll catch a dogfish for you my slack jowled friend. It'll keep you company in your stinky little cabin. God only knows what you get up to in there with your pantaloni round your grubby ankles!" "He keeps a troop of Spanish dancers, you can hear them singing the 'Aserejé' song, whilst he grabs their hairy asses", pointed out Phil in a mock patronising voice. "Go fuck!"

shouted José, then started to giggle uncontrollably. "You people!" José added as he climbed the stairs to the bridge. "One farts and the others just have to have a shit, they can't help themselves", he added from the distance.

Kate and Sheena looked at the horizon as the sun fell behind the hill. Sheena's little toddler, known fondly as 'Tank', was playing with the others in the barn. Her baby had fallen asleep. "Do you think Francisco got away?" asked Kate. "Yeah, they would be here by now otherwise", pointed out Sheena, "I wonder when it will come?" "When will what come?" queried Kate. "The storm", responded Sheena. "You don't think Franc's girls are able to end this enslavement, it's preposterous. They are just kids with a dream. I don't like to speak badly of my beautiful nieces, their hearts are in the right place, and they are braver than they should ever need to be, what can they do really?

I was with them in Jerusalem, they bravely crawled round in horrid tunnels for a couple of hours. It gave me the creeps, I'll admit, but negotiating with ghosts? it's not feasible", worried Kate. "You haven't seen Audrey in action. Paul says she talks to the dead, he believes her. As you know, she spent her early years living in a crypt beneath the Well of Souls. Audrey is no child; she has bigger chutzpah than any one I know", added Sheena.

Kate and Sheena continued to gaze at the horizon, as more captured soldiers were headed in from the corn field, with their guards. "The Mbunalt have caught the last of them", observed Kate. "I kinda hope Rusty is with them", uttered Sheena gently.

"Yeah, I know what you mean. I hope Paul is still ok, the kids are missing him terribly, and so am I", whispered Kate. "Paul will survive whilst we need him. He's always there for us in the dark times, as is Franc. We need to believe in them and trust them", expressed Sheena defiantly. Sheena stood proudly, her mid length auburn hair unkempt, with streaks of steel grey showing defiance amongst the thatch.

As the darkness enveloped them, Franc and his daughters stood on the roof of the abbey. The girls knelt by the wall at the edge of the roof. Franc, Paul, Joe, and Spall stood in a protective semicircle around them. Wrench was babysitting Bridget and Lucy; their nerves were spectacularly on edge. "This is our last calling", whispered Colletta fervently. "I've got a bad feeling about this", said Franc as he nervously shifted his weight between his feet, "the Cros are suspiciously quiet, we know they have shifted their sleeping pattern. They are planning to take us tonight; I can feel it". Paul agreed, "I feel uneasy too, but then we are all here to defend them. If this is our last stand, then so be it; at least we are together this one last time". The four men exchanged a warm look, they were prepared to die together, for each other. They felt the loss of their brother Bart and remembered the pain as if they had died with him. The brothers had a score to settle, and they vowed to die well. "The Cro Killer swords are useful, but I'm not sure my Sig is going to make a difference", observed Joe. "Aim for the eyes", uttered Franc quietly, "That is, if they don't have their helmets on". "Otherwise ask the Cros if you can hold their handbags", added Spall with a chuckle.

Audrey nervously broke the silence, "Okay let's do this". The whispering began once more, as Audrey spoke quietly to those who could not be seen. Colletta grasped Audrey's hands, the blue stone in the centre of her forehead began to pulse. Colletta perceived a presence beside her from aura with the familiar smell of rotting flesh. The hair stood up on the back of Audrey's neck as the spirit spoke, "They will answer your call, be patient", it whispered. Audrey acknowledged the spirit unfazed, "Thanks Mohammed". Suddenly there were two powerful blue flashes from the stone, the game was afoot.

"Where is this going?" asked Spall. "God only knows", whispered an exasperated Joe, "I hope it works. Typhon held store by the ritual, God bless him. Barak believes Audrey's bargain is the solution, and he is steadfast with his view". "But the solution to which problem? Will it save us?" gibed Spall. "It's starting", uttered Audrey. Colletta screamed, she shook uncontrollably, all eyes turned to Franc as he put a protective arm around her.

Audrey was deep in conversation with someone, some thing. It was hard to discern the details of the conversation other than a few fragments. "I know it is painful for you, but it will lead you into the light. The infection is weaker now, you need to take hold", whispered Colletta, relayed by Audrey. Franc was looking the wrong way when the Cros smashed their way into the barricade at the bottom of the stairwell. "Here we go", stated Franc calmly, "take them by their joints, the armour is weaker there and the blade has less chance of being snagged". James whistled twice from the spire of the abbey, to signal an attack. "They are coming", added Franc, "fight like lions; kill them all!" "Fight like a tiger", gibed Paul with a dark grin.

Gio spotted the flashes from the ship, "What the hell was that?" he shouted. No one answered. José shouted down from the bridge, as the ship lurched forward at top speed bearing directly towards the island. "The Cros are heading to the abbey, there must be sixty of them. Something has unnerved them; see how they are moving". "What was the blue flashing light?" asked Gio. José focussed his optics on the roof of the abbey. "The brothers are all up there with Spall and the girls. Colletta's head is flashing, and Franc, Spall and Paul are engaging the Cros with those Kraalt swords. They're trying to protect the girls from those monsters". "Right", commanded Phil, "Trev, target the road up to the abbey. Blow five barrels of shit out of it. We need to cause a distraction. José send an array of drones out there. Let's make some fucking noise people!"

"It's begun", whispered a voice from behind Sheena. She turned and gasped as Rusty pointed to the ramparts, the sky was filled with raging fire. The bright blue of the abbey roof was framed with the whites and oranges of aerial bombardment and detonating plastic explosives. Startled momentarily they followed the huge figures with their eyes, all of the Cros in the camp mobilised and headed north towards the battlefield. "Quickly!" Rusty and Sheena turned to see Barak and one of the monks beckoning them. "We need to get the cuffs off you and get out of town", directed Barak. Rusty was about to question the request when a small pair of hands wrapped his wrist and removed the cuff. The Kraalt then reached up to remove Rusty's collar.

The Kraalt moved briskly around the camp releasing the slaves as the last of the Mbunalt left to join the battle. The Kraalt leader whispered to Sheena, "Our fate is bound with yours now", and he moved on to release the next collar. The prisoners gathered as they were freed, then Sheena gave the call and headed out of the camp with the newly liberated captives, the Kraalt following closely behind. "Why aren't we heading north to join the battle?" interjected Rusty. "Joe told me to lead everyone away from the battle, he was very explicit", explained Sheena. "It's going to get unpleasant", added Barak with a broad smile. "I fucking hope so", said Sheena, as she bundled her baby into a rough papoose around her neck. Sheena felt a little like Moses, as she led hundreds of souls south, as far away from the camp as she could. They moved quickly, threading between the unusually high population of rotting Shroom that gathered ominously round the perimeters of the camp.

The first Cro burst through the doorway, taking half the broken door frame with him. He was met with Franc's faintly glowing purple blade, which cut through the central joint of his armour at the waist and disembowelled him. A scream filled the air as the Cro behind shoved the dying leader roughly out of the way. Franc fell back as the second charged, Paul emerged from behind the door entry, and cut the warriors right leg off at the knee. The Cro fell to the floor yelling and thrashing as another entered the rooftop and forced his way into the melee.

The Cro shrewdly waited for two more warriors to enter the rooftop before attacking. They charged as a three, filling the entire breadth of the rooftop. "Joe opened fire with his Sig Sauer automatic, aiming at the eyes of the attackers, but it had no effect, the bullets were like flies around a buffalo's ears. Joe's magazine emptied in a flash, Joe stooped to reload as Franc and Paul stepped aside, arresting the enormous momentum of the Cros by taking out their lower legs at the knee.

The sheer volume of blood made the floor slippery, and the roof space filled with huge writhing men. Franc quickly dispatched them with well-aimed parries to the face and throat, but the obstacle of body parts remained. One of the fallen Cros attempted to swat away Franc's blade, but this only resulted in the warrior losing a hand before being dispatched.

Two more Cros entered the rooftop, and all hell broke loose. The whole island looked like it had exploded as shells, missiles and drones battered the areas beneath the abbey. The Mbunalt looked at each other, but the attack achieved little more than strengthen their resolve. However, the assault slowed the activity on the stairwell as the Cros grouped together to plan how they would counter the assault. Colletta jumped at the sound of the explosions from below and broke out of her trance, but Audrey reached for Colletta's hand gently and the ritual continued unabated.

Cros charged into the roofline, Spall took the head from the first and Franc skewered the second. Another Cro entered the area, Spall shouted urgently, "They're climbing the walls". The slow loud clanks of spikes being rammed into the old stone walls was rhythmic and terrifying. Franc ran to the wall in front of the girls and readied himself to dispatch the warriors who were climbing. Paul and Spall continued to cover the stairwell, stepping carefully around the enormous corpses littering the floor. Joe raised his weapon, but uncertainty filled his face. His weapon was useless, so he hesitated and then holstered it.

Franc dispatched more than a dozen climbing Cros by cutting off their grasping hands, but the battle at the stairwell was losing traction, Spall and Paul were less dextrous with blade weapons than Franc. Spall took a wild swipe at a Cro, his blade was caught in the armour. The Cro died instantly, but as he fell to the ground, the Cro trapped the blade. Spall took a terrible blow to the abdomen from the attacker and fell to the floor lifelessly.

Paul shouted, renewing his efforts, but began to lose ground. Joe attempted to move towards Spall to help him, but it proved too dangerous. The space was becoming confined. Franc turned as he took the fingers from another climber; the warrior fell into the explosions below. The girls continued relentlessly, they were in a trance like state, and nothing could disrupt them.

Gino took a pair of binoculars to survey the maelstrom. "Our ordnance is having no effect; it looks like Paul and Franc are struggling on the rooftop. My god, Spall has fallen". Phil grabbed the monocular from around his neck and took a glimpse at the fray. There were numerous explosions, the ship continued to shake as the cannon fired and rockets streamed into the sky.

The launching of rockets stopped suddenly as one of the crew shouted, "We're out, Sir". The cannon wouldn't be far behind. "Save your ammo, cease fire", commanded Phil and the ship became quiet once more. Phil returned to assess the scene unfolding on the roof of the abbey. Phil saw a sword flash out across the sea spinning, as a warrior grabbed Paul by the ankle, tossing him like a rag doll to the floor. Franc was hit from behind with a glancing blow, strong enough to drop him to his knees. "They've lost, they are down", announced Phil urgently, "what the hell can we do now?"

On the rooftop Joe watched as his brothers were taken by the enemy. One Cro edged towards the two young girls. Joe moved to block the warrior's path. The Cro looked at him and almost smiled with condescension. There were many Cros on the rooftop staring at him, clearly perceiving no threat whatsoever. They merely awaited his realisation he had lost before they made their checkmate move. The girls continued their work oblivious to the world around them. Bright blue blinding light pulsated across the rooftop, backlit by the flickering oranges from the fires below.

27. Darkness will Swallow us

"What in the name of God is happening? look at the blue light, it's filling the sky", shouted Gio, alarmed. Phil continued, "Franc and Paul are down. James is trapped on the spire and Joe has positioned himself between the Cros and the girls. Wait! They're attacking Joe. It's all gone dark!" José shouted down from the bridge, "What do you mean it's all gone dark; it's night-time and the binoculars are light intensifying". Phil interjected, "But I can't see the blue light anymore why isn't it shining from Carlotta's head. No, I see the light now, the blackness is swallowing it! What in the name of God is happening?" Gio chipped in, "It's as if a black hole has taken the light from the world, it's being sucked into the top of the abbey. I have never seen anything like it".

Sheena looked back towards the camp. In the distance the sky was strange, the stars had been blanked although there were no clouds to obscure them. The moon was full, but there were large parts of the horizon where light was not penetrating. Rusty asked if everything was ok. "My God", Sheena replied. Rusty looked confused as she elucidated. "The sky is wrong. Something terrible is happening, something unnatural. I have an unbelievably bad feeling about this". The prisoners continued at pace. Rusty noticed an unusual number of Shroom in the area. "They have been very slowly shrooming over the last few weeks. They seem to be inert, but they are ambling in the direction of the camp. There are millions of them if you look out to the horizons. We need to be careful".

Joe looked into the eyes of the Cros holding his open hand forward as if to ward them away. James was trapped on the spire by a number of Cros surrounding his exit points, the warriors were taking the roof apart slate by slate. James shouted down, "Don't aggravate them, they will kill you Dad, just surrender they won't hurt you". "Yet", replied Joe in an edgy tone clearly petrified, "who knows what they are planning for us. These creatures are evil, they have no morals, no honour. I have seen into their hearts; they plan to eradicate us, once they've had their entertainment". The Cros lost patience and advanced menacingly, their eyes conveyed a small amount of amusement, but it was overshadowed by evil.

Joe held his hand firm as the leader attempted to brush it aside. Joe closed his eyes and prayed to God, "These warriors are evil, please protect us. They have lived long beyond their natural years by artificial means. Unheal them Father. Take away their unnatural prowess and chemical longevity. Return their bodies to their natural state. Let them face us as they should be". The Cro hesitated as Joe's eyes turned as black as the night and the Cro's outstretched hand turned black, as if to charcoal. James gasped as he watched his father touch the warrior, it fell to the floor. Its body desiccated; the body could no longer support the armour's mass. The other Cros looked onto their comrade with wild eyes, then turned to Joe. Joe's hand remained in place; the darkness spread to fill the entire rooftop. James looked but could see nothing, he repeatedly shouted to his father, "What is happening Dad? Are you ok? What the fuck is going on!"

When the blackness finally lifted, James could see the shrivelled Cros lying motionless on the rooftop. They were not deceased in the conventional sense; they were destroyed, the life was completely sucked from them. Their physical enormity due to the genetic adaptations bulking their musculature had disappeared. Their additional eye augmentations were scattered on the rooftop like trash. The remaining cadavers were barely larger than a well-built human male. Their native physiology had an eerie resemblance to the Kraalt. It was a sight James wished he could forget, he felt it would haunt him for the rest of his life.

James clambered down the remains of the rooftop and grabbed his father who had collapsed to the floor, he was barely conscious. The piles of bodies made it impossible to move, the roof was starting to give way under the weight of the bodies and the armour. "I have done something terrible James", Joe whispered, "I have taken their demonic souls. I am so weak; you need to run. Get away from here, they will be back, save yourself and look after your Mum!" James replied, "I'm going nowhere without you. Don't you dare feel guilty about taking these monsters down, they would have killed us all. You did what you had to", replied James gently.

"Help me look to my brothers, they need me", pleaded Joe. James helped his father to Paul and Franc who were gravely injured, Joe called on his healing powers to fix the damage. When he crawled to Spall, he was unable to help him. "It's too late", Joe cried, "his ribcage is shattered like autumn twigs crushed underfoot". More Cros appeared at the rooftop doorway. Their faces filled with trepidation. When they saw the state of Joe, they moved into the area looking at their fallen comrades. The Cros cleared the roof by tossing their dead from the ramparts. Part of the roof gave way; a couple of warriors fell to the floor below. The remaining Cros focused on Joe and James menacingly. There was nothing more they could do to defend the girls. When the girls awoke from their vigil and saw the desolation, they screamed as panic overwhelmed them.

As the darkness cleared, Phil remarked, "It's all over". "All over what?" shouted Gio. "Joe, the brothers, the Cros; they have fallen", explained Phil. "How?" exclaimed Gio to the sky, "How can you let such brutality take place on your world?" But the gods remained silent. Gio broke down in tears, the stairs clanged as José ran down from the bridge. "It was Joe, he turned his healing powers against them, the white light became black. He killed at least twenty of those bastards". José had been using the superior scope on the top of the ship to monitor closely. "Joe collapsed, but James was there to support him. Everything got chaotic, when more Cros arrived, my vision was obscured. But I saw them put the girls in a cage". "We need to save them. We need to get off our arses and get in there. They need our help", muttered Gio, clearly distraught but overcoming his natural cowardice. "There is nothing we can do. We could hit them with the cannon, but they would barely feel it. It's their bloody armour, it must be made from something alien", placated Phil. "So, what next?", asked Gio pushing the issue. "We do the best thing we can, we wait", asserted Phil. Gio's voice cracked, "All we do is fucking wait".

Sheena and Rusty led the newly freed prisoners into central France and entered the Massif Centrale area on foot, hoping the hills would shield them. They were running short of hydration, but as they moved into the mountains, the streams proved to be a source of valuable drinking water. Food was plentiful, the farm fields had livestock and lots of uncultivated vegetables. They passed through Clermont-Ferrand, a small town where they were able to find cans of food for their onward journey. They also located tools, and basic weapons such as knives and axes. The weapons would be less than useless against the Cros, running was their only option.

Barak continued to feel the loss of his Son, Typhon acutely. He managed to suppress his grief to keep in touch with the brotherhood, but he felt despondent. There were ten of his people in the group, morale was low amongst them all. Sheena was keen for an update from him, but the Carocle was unusually quiet. None of the brothers were active, but Barak had managed to contact James. "There was a battle on the roof of the abbey, around forty of the Mbunalt warriors were killed. The brothers have been captured, and we have lost Spall". As Barak conveyed the news, Sheena glanced at Rusty, "What happened up there?"

Barak explained they had used the swords to dispatch several warriors, but then Joe had intervened. "In extreme circumstances, a healer can summon powers of death. They use their power to remove the life force from a being rather than give it. It is a dark and deadly power, it takes a severe toll on the healer, both physically and mentally. Joe used the darkness on the abbey roof and dispatched many of the enemy". "Way to go", whispered Rusty, "but what now?" Barak hesitated, "No one knows the fate of the brothers". "They could be tortured; we need to help them!" interjected Sheena. "There is nothing we can do. We are lost", added a miserable

Barak. "We will never give up", added Sheena with a fierce look. Barak engaged her eyes, and her defiance spread into his veins, renewing his determination.

There was a shout raised from the edge of camp. The scouts had observed movement in the forest. Barak contacted one of the monks, Diego, for an update. Diego was the only monk remaining with the benefit of a device which could link with Barak's Carocle, so they kept apart to allow faster communications between the scouts and the main group. "The Cros have found us, they are about ten clicks out but closing quickly. They will reach us in twenty minutes. We need to move". Sheena ordered the group to scatter as a delay tactic. It didn't help, the enemy were numerous, hiding proved impossible.

Sheena and Rusty struggled, they had children to consider who slowed them down. They had no chance of escape, so they hid in the cellar of a wine merchants in the town. It was not long before they heard heavy footfalls on the wooden floor above them. Two Cros thundered down the cellar steps which partially collapsed under the strain, as they entered the room Sheena delivered a crushing spinning kick to a warrior's face. It had no effect on the creature, but it fractured Sheena's heel. As the creature lunged for Sheena, Rusty delivered a terrible blow to its knee, but it was deflected despite the weaker armour at the joint.

The Cros backhanded Rusty and knocked him clean across the cellar, hitting a wall of wine bottles which smashed around him as he fell to the floor. The children cried as they were scooped up by the Mbunalt warriors. They were taken back to the street and began their journey to the camp. Sheena hobbled on her damaged foot; Rusty managed to recover quickly despite holding his heavily bruised ribs.

Barak ran through the trees with Conor to catch Diego and two others. The group moved at speed, but not fast enough to evade the Mbunalt, who literally ran through the smaller trees, smashing them out of the way with their massive forearms. Suddenly, Barak was alone in the woods, he ran directly into a large Cro as he looked back for his comrades. The Cro gripped Barak's neck and drew back his hand, preparing to strike. Barak drew on his empathetic abilities and spoke telepathically to the creature. The creature hesitated. Barak persuaded the warrior he was simply a forest creature and wasn't worthy of his attention. He coerced the creature to return to the group. The Mbunalt looked uncertain, Barak's ploy had confused the creature for a moment.

The warrior loosened his grip on Barak, he was able to slip out of his jacket and wriggle free. Barak ran into the trees as fast as he could, his lungs burned with the effort, but his pursuer didn't follow.

28. First on the Left

It had been several days since the bloodshed on the abbey rooftop, there was no progress aboard the Phoenix, the crew were sullen due to premediated periods of inactivity. The ship was anchored 2km from the coast adjacent to Mont St Michel, the ever-vigilant Cros had attempted lobbing rocks at the ship on several occasions, but the boulders had fallen short.

Gio examined a large keep net of sea bass he had caught with the sea fishing rods. José enthusiastically joined him, "We will eat well tonight my friend". Gio looked with sad eyes, "Yes, but my food tastes like plastic these days, I have lost my zest for life, it is all pointless". José was more positive, "We need to take each day as it comes. We must celebrate small victories, and surviving is one of those. The fish will taste great. I will steam them en papillote with a little garlic butter, pickled capers, olives, and sun-dried tomatoes". "It's how my mother used to cook them", said Gio with a brief smile, "It sounds very fine indeed my dear friend".

There was a scramble at the aft of the ship, someone was shouting for help. Gino dropped his rod and ran to the rear of the frigate. Phil dropped the ladder into the water, "It's Barak", he called, "he swam from the mainland in this powerful current, the crazy mother". Phil and Gio reached into the water and dragged Barak onto the ship. Barak was wearing nothing but his silver under suit. He looked exhausted, and grateful for the assist. "José, bring some hot soup on the double", shouted Phil to the bridge. A galley hand soon appeared with a flask of hot consommé and a little bread. "There isn't much, it's leftovers from yesterday's meal. Today's broth will soon be ready". Barak firstly took a long draught of water and devoured the soup, regaining some of his colour.

Barak recovered sufficiently to tell his version of events. "The Cros fell upon us in the foothills of the Massif Centrale, we had no chance. They caught everyone except for myself, I managed to confuse them. The Cros are marching their captives to the camp as we speak, it will be slow going because of the older ones and the children. I guess they will be back by tomorrow evening according to Diego. I'm unsure of the whereabouts of Paul, Joe, Franc and James. I can feel their presence, they are in extreme discomfort, it's not going well for them.

Audrey and Colletta have been kept in a cage since they were captured, it is electrified to stop radiation and radio waves, like a faraday cage. The girls are unable to continue their ritual, I dearly hope they have achieved enough. They are released for a walk every few hours, and are being looked after, but they are not happy. They are enduring extreme discomfort".

A long discussion followed about the occurrences on the abbey roof, and much speculation about the whereabouts of the brothers. "We need to free them, they need to complete the plan", pushed Barak. "What is the bloody plan?" asked Phil, "I keep hearing about it, but they have shared no detail, everyone who can execute it has been captured".

Barak looked at Phil patiently, "The plan is to bring your dead into battle. Audrey can speak to their spirits, and Colletta gives her an empathetic ability to persuade and cajole them. The blue flashes you observed are the empathy stone in action. I just don't how they will help. Audrey knows more, but she is forbidden to tell us, she believes the spirits are strong, and I trust her. I would trust her with my life. We must help Audrey and Colletta escape to give the plan one last chance". Phil and Gio looked unconvinced. "We have nothing to fight the Cros with, they are too strong", observed Phil. "Even an RPG inna gob won't wobble their teeth", added Gio. "We need to enlist the help of the Kraalt, and we need a Kraalt sword". Phil had seen Paul's sword flash across the sea during the battle at the abbey. The trajectory implied it was a deliberate throw to stop the weapon coming into the hands of our enemy.

José waited for the Cros sleep cycle and carefully moved the ship closer to the island and began to sweep the bottom of the sea with the sensors. He attempted to locate an unusual power source or radiation. The scanning detected little, other than a few minor blips that needed to be investigated with scuba gear. Phil, José and Gio led three dive teams to search for the sword in each location identified by the sensors.

The last location proved successful, as is always the way, they observed a feint purple glow partially obscured by seaweed. Gio headed to the bottom, in between an old trawler wreck and a few rusty barrels and located the sword. He headed back to the surface with the team and presented the device to Phil with a look of triumph. "Fantastico", replied a relieved Phil, with a hint of a gibe. Barak grinned, "Yes, fantastic guys. We only have five hours until the group returns to camp, which will be the best time to attack them, using the confusion to our advantage". "Oh shit", said Phil.

Gio was tired from the dive. The team each grabbed an M16 rifle and a compact disposable RPG pack. Barak took the Cro

Killer sword, which showed no signs of damage from its immersion in the salty seawater. They jumped into the RIB which José had on standby. "Remember José", shouted Phil from the gunwale, "at the precise moment, hit them with everything we have left. Everything!" José nodded, "We don't actually have much, but we have a flight of drones and plastic explosive ordnance". "It will have to do", replied Phil as he dropped down into the RIB. Gio gunned the engine, heading in a straight line directly to shore, avoiding the possibility of being observed by the Cros.

The ingress point was positioned near to the camp as the bird flies. It was only a 18km walk to the camp, which they would cover in three hours. There was enough time, the risk was there was no plan; they were walking blindly into a dangerous situation, it was a suicide mission. They accepted the fact; it was not clear why their mood lifted. "I don't care if I die. I would prefer to know I did all I could to help my friends", explained Gio.

Sheena and Rusty headed the group walking slowly back to camp with their heads low. A few Kraalt stood to the side looking at them with pity and a little sadness, their hopes had also been dashed. As they entered the perimeter of the camp, a mound of Kraalt corpses were left for everyone to see. Their punishment involved being ripped limb from limb for allowing the prisoners to escape. The nearest Kraalt spoke quietly, "Prepare yourselves, this will be difficult for you".

As the group entered the main courtyard, a terrible theatre unfolded before them. Three crosses erected in the centre of the square displayed the crucified bodies of Paul, Franc and Joe. Their arms and legs were tightly bound to the crosses, and their bodies hung apparently lifeless. Screams echoed through the group as they saw the horror before them. Kate and Bridget attempted to run to their husbands, shrieking. Sheena and Rusty grabbed them to prevent them from being hurt by the warriors, who grinned evilly when they saw their reaction.

The brothers had been beaten and starved, they were dehydrated and close to death. They must have been hanging for days. Sheena felt a lump in her throat, hatred building in her gut. One Kraalt spoke gently, "They find the irony amusing, abusing your culture in this way. They are impressing on you that resistance is pointless, and the consequences are dire". The Kraalt then changed his tone and emphasised his next phrase, "Be ready, when the fun starts, run as fast as you can". Sheena gave the Kraalt a puzzled look, was there a plan?

Sheena and Rusty's group stared forlornly at the three unfortunate men. These men had given everything to save their community and there was nothing the prisoners could do to help. They felt impotent and utterly powerless. Audrey and Colletta were caged at Franc's feet, so he could watch them suffer as he died, the girls whimpered as they saw the group enter the square. Without warning, explosions lit up the sky at the north of the camp. An array of drones flew over and detonated the buildings. The Mbunalt sprinted into the fray. "It is a diversion", yelled the Kraalt, "run for your lives, get as far away as you can".

Sheena corralled the already tired group and headed out of the camp en masse. Rusty ran towards the crosses, "I'll see you in a min". As he neared the crucifixes, Gio and Phil ran into the camp and unleashed RPGs at the buildings to the rear of the warriors, causing the structures to collapse behind them. Their actions were calculated to add to the confusion and help gain time to allow the prisoners to escape. Barak appeared, he handed Rusty a knife, which he used to release the brothers. Franc and Paul were very weak and stumbled painfully as the blood slowly returned to their limbs. Joe was unable to hold his weight and collapsed to the floor. There wasn't time to help Joe, his brothers were barely able to look after themselves.

Rusty and Barak turned their attention to the girls. Barak slashed the lock with the Kraalt sword, taking the clasp clean off. He reached down and pulled Audrey and Colletta free, they looked at him cautiously. "Let's get out of here!" called Barak, but the girls declined refusing to move. "We need to complete the assimilation; we need to do it now whilst we have time. Help us onto the top of the cage". Barak nodded affirmatively showing his understanding. He raised them up in one huge lift, his muscles quivering under the strain.

Several Kraalt joined the girls at the foot of the crosses, "The warrior's armour is compromised at the joints, let's hope it works". Barak nodded and smiled, "Thank you for your help once again. I am so sorry for your friends"; Barak looked across, acknowledging the exhibition of dead Kraalt. "They were a necessary sacrifice; we must fight for our freedom". The Kraalt handed Rusty and Phil the other swords they had retrieved for them. "Live long my friends", they uttered and exited the camp with the last of the stragglers. "Or die trying", muttered Rusty to himself. Rusty looked down to Joe, who lay on the ground unmoving.

The girls started to whisper to the sky once again. The blue stone flashed and then shone a continuous brilliantly blinding light as Colletta stiffened. Franc groaned, as he briefly woke and saw the girls. Audrey's voice became noticeably assertive, as the Cros returned to the square angrily, realising they had been duped. Rusty, Barak and Phil stood, swords at the ready, forming a rough circle around the girls. "Protect them at all costs, or all is lost", replied Barak. Audrey's voice rang out across the square, "Come to me, poor lost souls of this world. Come to me you poor tortured wretches and find your rightful place. Bring your bodies one more time and use them to fight. Keep your promise and fight. Assimilation is painful but be brave and earn your passage to the next world. I will not fail you, I will keep my vow".

Colletta's blue light extinguished as the Cros attacked. Rusty took the lead; he completely decapitated the first attacker to his surprise. "Wow!" shouted Gio, "I always thought you were more meat than brains" and entered the fray with a nervous laugh. Gio was clumsy, but he managed to kill a warrior with a straight parry. All action stopped as an unearthly howl was unleashed into the air, it was joined by a dozen screaming guttural howls.

A moment later there were hundreds of screams, followed by thousands more. The hair stood up on the back of Gio's neck as he realised the Shrooms were entering into battle. The Mbunalt clearly had the same experience, they froze as they attempted to assess the threat. "The infected are coming, we need to get out of here", shouted Audrey, "they will kill us all". Franc and Paul were too weak to walk, and Joe lay unmoving. Rusty, Barak and Gio carried each them of on their backs, running with the girls trailing behind. The howling intensified, there was movement in all directions, something was coming, and it was not going to be pleasant.

29. The Day of the Shroom

The remaining Kraalt speedily directed Barak to a locked shed, the others followed closely behind. Much to their surprise, a Pareth-ng discovery ship was waiting with the ramp open. "We found the ship at Typhon's base in the abbey, we were hoping it might be some use to you", explained the Kraalt, urgently shepherding them on board as fast as they were able. "Indeed", said Barak as he carried Joe inside. Barak, Rusty and Gio deposited the three brothers into pods which had formed from the silver walls of the amorphous vessel, as the sound of many footfalls and screams penetrated the gloom of the old storehouse.

The ship's AI wasted no time and immediately lifted into the air smashing through the roof of the enclosed building, scattering the rotten wood and tiles. Everyone on board struggled to keep their balance as the ship rocked under the impact. The ship lifted to a safe height and hovered as all onboard watched the scene below as the floor turned transparent, "What about Sheena and the other escapees?" shouted Rusty urgently, worried for his wife and children. "Don't worry, they'll be safe enough, they have cleared the square, Sheena and the prisoners are almost a kilometre away. The Shrooms shouldn't attack them, they are using all their faculties to propel their bodies to the battlefield. The square is more dangerous the Shrooms are in a frenzy and are unable to discern friend or foe".

"Christ, the Shrooms are alive", remarked Rusty. Phil looked on with concern, but his attention quickly turned to action as a Shroom attacked the nearest Mbunalt warrior. The Cro swung his massive arm, the Shroom was thrown across the square like a rag doll, smashing against the stone wall of the nearest building. The Shroom's screams reached a new level of rage, echoed by a mass of more Shrooms entering the square. The injured Shroom regained himself and relaunched his attack at the Cro, who was beset by four additional Shrooms joining the assault. Again, the warrior easily threw off the Shrooms, and smashed the skull of the last, it fell to the floor like a piece of lead. More Shroom appeared in the square and attacked the Cros, but they were easily smashed to the ground. The square filled, thousands of Shrooms joined the attack in a crazy frenzy of hate and anger.

The Shrooms attacked from all directions, the ship lifted higher into the sky to gain more perspective of the battle unfolding before them, they could see millions of Shroom pacing briskly towards the compound, screaming, and gnashing their rotten jaws. The Cros were quickly overwhelmed.

As the attacks were launched, the Cros easily smashed the Shrooms and threw them like toys, but they couldn't fend off the sheer numbers facing them. "It's like F1-11 fighters", said Phil, "they were so good, they could combat three MIGs in a dogfight with ease. However, nine MIGs could take down three F1-11s just as easily, as they were swamped". "The Shrooms won't get through their armour though", interjected a rather worried Gio. "That's where our friends come in", reassured Barak, indicating the Kraalt. "They have loosened the electromagnetic couplings on the warriors' armour so the joints will come loose". Phil smiled a big wide grin to Gio, who started to look more hopeful.

There were several hundred Mbunalt warriors occupying the camp. The other warriors placed strategically around Europe were faring similarly, the supporting Kraalt had also weakened their armour one by one. Each warrior was buried by a huge mountain of writhing Shroom, each attempting to bite through the armour unsuccessfully. Periodically, a warrior would throw the Shrooms off and smash many of them with their fists, but then the Shroom would swamp him once again. One Shroom successfully penetrated the armour sending the Mbunalt wild, thrashing and smashing the Shroom in their dozens, but eventually over time the warriors tired and the Shroom swamped them once more. Once the blood spurted from the neck joint of the warrior's armour, the Shroom were invigorated; they relentlessly clawed and bit the warrior's necks, they fought each other for the opportunity to feed. Finally, the joints gave way and blood filled the square like a death fountain, covering the fell revellers coating both the Shrooms and warriors in scarlet.

More and more Shrooms forced their way into the square clambering over their fallen comrades eager to join the attack, until every warrior was buried by them. Increasingly the Cros struggled to cope with the weight of dozens of Shrooms piled onto them. As the violence progressed the Shrooms at the bottom of each pile were crushed by the sheer weight, suffocation became the biggest threat to those at the bottom, including the Cros themselves.

The scene was horrifying. A small number of warriors with less attackers realised their fate and attempted to run. The Shrooms could not keep pace, but the warriors ran headlong into endless groups of Shrooms. It seemed like the entire Shroom population from mainland Europe were here for the fight. They had been travelling for weeks, after they heard the girls summoning.

The Shrooms used the same attack strategy everywhere, there was no escape. Soon the warriors were exhausted and could fight no longer, they were completely overwhelmed. More and more Shrooms joined the assault, soon all that could be seen was dead and writhing bodies. There were 700 million European inhabitants when the virus hit. Much of the population became Shrooms during the infection of 2021, many of them arrived for the death party.

Audrey spoke to Franc from the pod he was occupying. "Hello Daddy. Are you ok?" she asked in a concerned tone. Colletta brightened at the sound of his voice. "Not so good, but I'm walking down the path of recovery. I'm feeling a bit better", Franc attempted a laugh, but it faltered. "How did you persuade the dead to come to our aid?" he asked.

Audrey took a deep breath, "I guess its ok to tell now, isn't it?" she looked at Colletta and then Barak for confirmation. Barak nodded with a warm smile. "You know I speak to the dead, I'm a medium. Well, I can also speak to the not-dead. They are the ones who can't leave our world for the next. Their bodies are Shrooms, and their souls are trapped in this world until their bodies completely die. The fungus keeps their bodies alive to control their limbs, which in turn stops death happening naturally. I struck a deal for the spirits to return their bodies and fight. I arranged for them to attack the Cro warriors, knowing many of them would die in the fight and find a peaceful demise. It was so hard for the spirits, the Shroom bodies had started to rot, it was painful and horrible for them to re-enter their bodies. The spirits needed to be strong and wrestle control of their bodies, ignoring the basic controlling impulses from the fungus.

Not all of the spirits succeeded, but a great many did as you can see. They had sufficient numbers to help us. They are very brave". "What will happen to those who survive?" asked Franc. "Well, that is the terms of our bargain". Audrey hesitated for a second, "I promised we would seek them out and kill them, every single one". "Jesus", uttered Rusty in utter disbelief.

The fight continued for several hours until the warriors were either eaten or had suffocated. The Shroom feasted for days on the cadavers littering the battlefield. The Kraalt happily confirmed the status of the living Mbunalt as a countdown, which declined to zero during the battle, causing happy cries from the Kraalt. "We have suffered a thousand lifetimes of slavery, we are now at peace to live life anew", they enthused. Phil considered their elation, "What will you do now and how can we help?" The Kraalt looked a little sheepish, "Your planet is beautiful, we hope there is space for all of us?" Phil smiled, "Of course, my friend". The Kraalt responded, "I'm not sure we know how to handle freedom, only a few of us have tasted it", he indicated one of Buddy's colleagues who was sitting in the corner trying to contain his excitement. "We will need a little help and guidance", he said. Phil reached forward and shook his small hand gently, the Kraalt found Phil's gesture unusual but joined in, nonetheless.

Phil looked back at the huge mound of writhing bodies that filled the square. It was a horrible mess, a sorry site that few should experience. The ship travelled south, its occupants re-joined the group of escapees led by Sheena moving at pace from the camp and out of trouble. As the ship came into sight, the refugees looked up at the skies, halting their stride. They didn't dare believe the war had come to an end, and favourably. The ship landed in the field nearby.

Rusty launched from the ramp to sweep Sheena into his arms, "We won", he announced as the large group stared in disbelief and then cheered. Their joy was insuppressible, until he AI soberly announced Joe had passed away, via the Carocle. James ran back into the spaceship screaming, with Kate following closely behind, stricken.

Paul and Franc were displayed as holograms in the ship, as their bodies rested in the pods, tended by the ship's doctor. Kate was frustrated by her inability to physically hold Paul in her arms, but the AI assured her that within a couple of days Paul would be able to take some gentle exercise. Everyone was deeply distressed; Joe's life was a terrible price to pay for their victory. "Joyce", said Franc and smiled faintly, "let's call you Joyce, you deserve a name", he said indicating to the ship's AI. "Never joke with a nurse", replied Kate sullenly. Franc requested, "Please take me, James and the girls to Lucy and Bridget, I pray they are ok". "They are with Wrench, they should be well looked after", added Paul.

The ship landed in front of the gargantuan mound of rubble which was once the magnificent abbey. Many of the buildings surrounding the abbey had been smashed by the heavy-handed aliens. Fragments of the spire littered the broken rooftops in the street below. It had been smashed as the aliens had attempted to apprehend James.

James looked at the remains sadly, remembering the desperate struggle he had trying to evade the warriors and the eventual destruction and rubbed his bruised arm unconsciously. Phil and Rusty looked around the broken abbey. "Enter the ruins of the nave, and you will find the small staircase going down to the Chapelle Notre Dame Sous Terre. Lucy and Bridget will probably be hiding down there", instructed Franc through the Carocle.

"Everything is rubble in here", replied James. Franc guided him to the entrance, and they worked to remove the smashed stone and splintered benches. Phill and James entered the treacherous staircase and made their way down to the old chapel. There was no one there. "Damn, where are they?", queried Franc worriedly. Phil countered, "There are no bodies in here Franc, they must have left during the struggle".

30. The Pursuit

Franc demanded to be released from his pod, contradicting warnings from the AI doctor in residence, "Open the goddamned door, Joyce!" He climbed slowly from the pod and shuddered. The pod had quickly hydrated and nourished his body, but the extremes of chaffing and bruising from the ropes that secured his wrists remained. Two of his ribs were cracked and caused significant discomfort, despite the strappings which secured them. Franc's left hand was all but inoperable, he asked Kate to bind it to his chest.

Kate fumed, he was not taking the doctor's advice and was acting irresponsibly. Although at the same time she knew he had little choice, his heart ruled his head. "Trust Rusty and Phil to find Lucy, they are capable", she pleaded. "Please watch over Colletta and Audrey", Franc requested. "Sure, no problem. They are good girls; they are no bother unlike their father. Look, find them and come back safely. Don't give the girls safety a second thought, I'm on it", replied Kate. The girls had other ideas but, in the end, they chose not to argue with their father, he was attempting to save their mother after all.

Franc tested his legs and found he could stand, if a little unsteadily at first. He then tested his grip on one of the Kraalt swords, which he placed in the scabbard on his back with his good arm. Rusty and Phil had previously acquired two Cro Killer swords. Franc had no idea of the challenge they faced, but hopefully all was well. Although he had a nagging feeling, an instinct that it was not the case; he had long learned to trust this instinct, it had kept him alive on many occasions.

Franc walked gingerly into the ruin of the abbey and down the stairs to the chapel. Rusty and Phil were surprised to see him, James was not shocked in the slightest. James tried hard to focus his mind, despite the death of his father. They remained at war, there would be a time for grieving.

There was little to see in the chapel, the racks containing supplies of food had been overturned when the roof collapsed. The area where Lucy and Bridget had slept had been abandoned, the makeshift beds were left tidy, but they had left in a hurry, that much was clear. There were no tracks to follow on the stone floor, there were no clues whatsoever.

Paul had regained consciousness briefly, "What the hell are you doing Franc? You are not well, you need care". When Franc explained the situation in more detail, he could hear the cogs of his brother's logical mind turning. "If Lucy departed voluntarily in order to keep safe, then she would have left you a clue. Lucy is smart, you can guarantee there is something to help".

Phil and James searched through the rubble and moved some of the smaller boulders but found no leads. Franc moved the damaged facade he had previously constructed obscuring the nave entrance to the lower chapel, but found the door closed. When he opened the door, he found the catch had been forced. He exited the door and followed the steps which led to the mass of rubble which was now the remainder of the island. "I hope they weren't caught under this", remarked Franc. Paul considered Franc's observation, "It's highly unlikely. These buildings were destroyed by the shelling from the Phoenix as an initial distraction, to enable Lucy and Bridget to hide or escape".

Rusty and Phil picked their way through the rocks towards the original entrance to the island. "Why would the Cros pursue Lucy? They were victorious, what was the point?" asked Franc. "More slaves", pointed out Rusty. "No", I don't buy that. The Cro's search was more vindictive. Look at the way they smashed the place up. They were looking for something, they found our hiding place", replied Franc. They sat on the rocks and reasoned the Cro's incentive, but it was fruitless, there was no evidence whatsoever".

"Buddy knew we were in the lower chapel, I'm sure of it", observed Franc. "Do you think Buddy betrayed you?" asked Phil, "he seemed decent to me". "No, I wasn't suggesting that, though it is a thought. I just wondered if he was captured with the other prisoners", queried Franc. Paul interjected, "Don't doubt our little friends, they crippled the Cro's armour which was a significant factor in our victory. They suffered severely as a result of their actions, have you seen the pile of tortured Kraalt bodies in our camp?" "Point taken. We can check Buddy's whereabouts, the Kraalt are able to hack into our Carocles when they need to", considered Paul.

Paul managed to contact the Kraalt, they affirmed their suspicions. "Buddy is MIA", pointed out Paul. "Shit", breathed Franc, "I'd put money on finding the others if we can locate him". "I'm on it", confirmed Paul from his pod. "Where did you last see Buddy?" asked James. "Sorry, what are you getting at?" countered Phil. "Was there a place where he used to hang out? Could we start there?" responded Rusty. "Good thought", whispered Franc, "I met him near the old souvenir shop in the adjacent café basement, when I was searching for bottled water".

Phil and James headed down to the rubble at the site of the shop and started to move the huge stones blocking the small staircase beneath. Franc winced, grasping his side as he moved down the narrow stairs. "Are you really ok?" queried James in a concerned tone. Franc smiled his famous mock arrogant smile. "I don't care if I'm not", he responded. They examined the room below; it was just a plain hewn stone storeroom. Rusty lifted a fallen rack back onto its casters, beneath he found a trapdoor. He raised the trap and peered down into the gloom. Phil took a small LED torch and shone the light to see Wrench, he didn't look too good. "Oh shit", whispered Franc, "Thank God we found you. Are you badly hurt; can you walk?"

Phil descended the ladder to help Wrench into a sitting position. "No good", he stammered, his lungs rattling. "Buddy led us to this hiding place. Cros found us. Cros couldn't get in the cramped space, but knew they would burn us out, had to give up. Cros took Bridget and Lucy and killed Buddy, ripped him apart like a rag doll. Damn near killed me too, left me to die. Hid here, but no good".

Franc placated him, "Nothing you could do, the Cros are too damn big, even against your bulging biceps", Franc said smiling faintly, "Do you know where Cros took them?" Wrench's face twisted, "Before he died, Buddy said the Cros would take your loved ones so you could watch them die". "Back to the camp?" pressed Franc. "Yes", he replied faintly. Wrench took one last breath, uttering the words "Live well my friend", and passed to the next life. He had played his part in this one, many times over.

Rusty, Phil and James looked at each other sadly. "We will return to honour Wrench as he deserves", Franc assured the group. "But for now, we need to leave him here. No-one spotted them at the camp, therefore something happened on the way back, we need to follow the trail". They headed up the staircase and moved through the rubble to the main entrance of the island. James looked at the remains of the floating bridge, merely a pile of broken concrete and rubble from the countless explosions. He stretched to force his fingertips between two rocks. "What is it?" asked Franc. "I'm not sure, I…" replied James as he pulled a leather thong from the rocks. It was a partly unravelled thong bracelet with dainty silver rings threaded between the knots. "That's Lucy's", observed Franc, he reached to James and gently took the bracelet, kissed it, and placed it carefully in his pocket. "We are on the right track", he stated stoically.

Franc attempted to increase his walking speed, but the pain impeded his movement. James and Phil shared a look, "Take it easy my friend, we'll find them", stated Phil optimistically. They followed the trail the Mbunalt had taken to the camp. "It's like following an elephant trail, these guys don't much care for the wildlife, or the culture of a place do they?" observed James. "No, they are barbarians. I don't trust them with our women for a single bloody second", asserted Franc a little more aggressively than he had intended. "Sorry, I'm worried about them", he added. "Don't worry, we know. We will find them", reiterated Rusty.

Franc and the team crossed the ground between the island and the mainland and followed the trail which roughly tracked the banks of the Couesnon river. At the ancient stronghold town of Pontorson, the trail moved southwest towards the camp near Bourlidou and Combourg. It was harder to confirm the trail, as it moved on to highways, but there was always occasional evidence as the Cros, and their captives broke from the group to take toilet breaks. The Cros had taken many people on the route, they left refuse and debris as they travelled. Following the trail became complex as they approached the outer vicinity of the slave camp, as tracks moved in many directions.

Franc stopped with relief as Rusty looked at the ground confused. Part of the trail moved into a field which was clearly a battleground. There were heaps of Shroom lying dead on top of Cro corpses. "A small group broke from the trail at this point and headed cross country when the Shrooms attacked them", noted Rusty. "Let's follow it, they never reached the camp, so it's plausible", added James.

The trail turned into the forest; a wooden sign read 'Forêt de Villecartier'. The path led to an old mill through the old beech and oak trees, encircled by holly bushes and trees. There was an increased presence of Shrooms in the forest, the group moved slowly. Despite his discomfort, Franc gave every Shroom the courtesy of a clean death, so they were able to move to the next life as his daughter had promised.

An old stone mill, which had more recently been a restaurant called 'Le Moulin de la Forêt', had a yellowing menu in the window advertising pancakes and ice cream. The large water wheel sat in the feeder river for the lake, upon which was a wooden jetty. James raised his weapon and examined the entrance to the mill carefully. The door had been broken crudely, implying recent entry. He carefully moved into the doorway of the café and beyond, but soon remerged after calling all clear.

The group continued to follow the trail deep into the trees, and roughly skirted the lake 'Etang de Villecartier'. Franc had slowed significantly but continued to press on, he had nothing left but sheer determination. "You don't look well Franc", observed Rusty, "let's take a break to hydrate". They sat on the forest floor, Franc lay on his back and took a power nap. His colour started to return a little as the others made ready to move on.

The footfalls of the Cro they were tracking became more mixed and frequent, there had been many recent comings and goings in this part of the forest. The presence of Shrooms was thickening once more, it took almost an hour for Phil and James to dispatch them, whilst Franc took another brief respite. They continued for almost a kilometre through the heavy woods until they heard a gentle sound, a keening noise. On nearing the source of the cries, they could differentiate separate voices. As they approached the most southerly part of the forest, they could see an old farmhouse swamped by Shroom. The house was located in a sharp intersection between three roads, two were simple forest roads and the other a minor highway. There must have been a thousand Shrooms, all making the gentle but disturbing noise.

The group exited the trees, to see a monstrous Mbunalt warrior sat sullenly on the apex of the roof, without armour. Their swords were drawn in an instant, as they looked up into his gigantic face. A Kraalt ambled through the front door, dodging the Shrooms like he didn't have a care in the world, it was odd. He looked up startled when he saw Phil, James and Rusty stood looking towards him menacingly. "They are here", the Kraalt shouted almost jovially. "Thanks Ed", a happy melodic female voice replied from the house.

A moment later Lucy ran from the house looking for her husband, her eyes locked onto him. She noticed he was not looking well; concern clouded her features as Bridget joined her. "I don't have to ask what happened to you my love", breathed Lucy as she gently embraced him, "don't worry, Grawp won't hurt you". James smirked at the obvious reference to Harry Potter, "I'm surprised you didn't name our Kraalt friend, Dobbie", James remarked sullenly. Rusty noticed when James saw his mum, it had reminded him of his terrible news. Franc looked up at the giant, not at all convinced it was safe.

Bridget looked for Joe, but none of the group knew how to broach the devastating news, "What happened?" she demanded looking deeply into Franc's eyes, to judge his reaction. Franc rambled a little about the last few days, it was largely unintelligible and rushed, but Bridget obtained the information she needed. "We completed the girls' mission. Joe, Paul, and I were captured. Joe managed to reverse his healing gift to the offensive and killed many of the Cro warriors, it turned nasty. They crucified Joe, Paul and I in the camp to set an example. The Cros tied us to crosses, we were there for two or three days, I really can't remember, we were in a bad way.

Phil, James and Rusty freed us and the girls, the ship supported us using the healing pods, though I didn't stay for long. The girls called the Shrooms to join us in battle, all the invaders are dead, all but one it seems. Franc looked at Ed testily. Ed stammered, "We didn't count Grawp obviously, he is friendly.

We were counting your enemy only". Franc continued tentatively, "Look, there's no easy way to say this Bridget. Joe didn't make it".

Bridget fell to the floor in floods of tears. James had been holding his emotions back, he hadn't the courage or the will to break the terrible news to his mother. James ran forward past Franc and took Bridget in his arms gently. "I'm sorry Mum, there was nothing we could do. We thought we had saved him, but", James explained.

Lucy embraced them both but couldn't find words to console them. She left Bridget with James then embraced Franc sadly clasping his hand. Franc reached into his pocket and retrieved Lucy's bracelet. She was relieved to see it, "I couldn't think of anything else to leave, but I hated parting with it", she said gently. "It was invaluable in leading us to you", commented Franc as he tried to hold back his tears. They sat together unhappily for some time, with Grawp looking down on them with a confused expression.

They slowly managed to lift themselves up from their bootstraps. "Ok, so what is his story", enquired James pointing his thumb at the large hulking figure sat astride the apex of the cottage roof. Lucy smiled awkwardly, adjusted her sleeves, and told her part of the tale.

"When the battle started on the roof of the abbey, we were terrified, we needed to understand what was happening. We saw the darkness coming from Joe and how he eliminated the Cros. We then saw your capture. There was nothing we could do, so we hid in the chapel. The problem was the Cros spotted us, and we were hunted. Buddy took us to a hiding place on the main drive leading to the abbey. The Cros went to town on the abbey smashing it to pieces.

We managed to hide out for a couple of days under the storeroom. I don't know how they found us, Wrench tried to defend us with his machine gun and a crowbar when he ran out of ammo, he had no chance. I don't know if he is ok". Lucy halted for a moment and choked back a sob. She wiped her eyes and continued, "They caught Buddy and killed him, the poor soul. Then they marched us back to the camp. We didn't make it though, because the Shroom attacked. It was terrible, they attacked from all directions, there were thousands of them, screaming horribly.

To make his escape, Grawp took us into the woods, but the Shrooms realised and pursued us. We ran past the lake and sheltered in this farmhouse. Grawp climbed onto the roof where the Shrooms couldn't reach him, but the roof started to collapse. Ed realised Grawp's heavy armour wasn't helping, so he persuaded him to take it off and throw it onto the floor. He has been up there ever since, although the Shrooms have surrounded him. They are waiting for him to come down, watching eerily. We have been passing him food, but it's barely enough for a big creature like him".

Franc contemplated his next phrase, but then simply blurted it out. "We found Wrench on his last legs, I'm afraid he didn't make it". Lucy's eyes filled up, but she refused to cry on principle, too many good people had died and the time for mourning would come. The news didn't reach Bridget, her heart was brimming with sadness.

Franc indicated the huge figure of Grawp on the roof, "Why did he decide to help you?" Lucy looked pensive, "Well, he didn't really. We kinda ran off together, we followed his trail smashed through the foliage. We didn't have time to think because the Shrooms were following. I don't know how Ed kept up, but he did. We didn't know the Shroom were only hunting the Mbunalt, we thought they would kill us too, so we shared each other's fate. It brought us together. When we helped him, he started to treat us differently".

Bridget continued, "Ed says Grawp is an unusual warrior, a little more thoughtful than the others due to him being pregnant. He wasn't keen on the slavery concept but was afraid to speak up, he would be ridiculed and ostracised". "He is pregnant?" queried James. Ed interjected, "The Mbunalt are hermaphrodite, they do not mate. They have both male and female organs and can reproduce with each other when the circumstances are favourable. Ed continued, "The Mbunalt calm down when they are pregnant, their male hormone levels drop, and the female side takes precedence. They stop behaving like warriors and start to become more…well, sensible".

Franc was unsure of the actions he should take, so he consulted Paul. Paul, still suffering from the events of the last few days, was amenable to give Grawp a chance. "There is only one of him, what harm could he do?" "A bloody great deal", replied Franc. "Without his armour we could take him down easily", added James, "I say we give him a chance; he hasn't harmed Mum and Aunt Lucy". Bridget looked at him through the corner of her eye proudly. Lucy interjected, "We have become friendly, he's not too bad. He's vulgar, but then aren't all men?" Lucy followed the sarcasm with a wink at Franc. "He is not a man", added James, "he is both he and she, a she-he". James was once again silenced by a glare from Bridget. Franc took a deep breath, "Ok let's give Grawp a chance, but one step out of line and he gets a purple suppository". "I hope you mean the sword", laughed James, which made them laugh. It was strange how humour prevailed, even during times of grief. It was as if the soul looked for a reason to lift the mood. Grawp looked on curiously. Ed was confused by the laughter too. How could humans laugh so easily when they are experiencing such pain? it was illogical to him.

James and Phil set about killing the Shrooms. It took nearly two hours to dispatch them. Franc attempted to help but was forced to desist, his legs turned to jelly beneath him. Grawp, became restless as the last few Shrooms were killed. He stepped down from the roof and looked at Franc curiously, making a strange chittering noise, like a cockroach, but much louder.

To everyone's surprise he uttered, "Grawp" in an odd scratchy tongue and pointed to himself. Ed intervened, "He is introducing himself. As you couldn't understand his language, he is trying to use yours. The Mbunalt are particularly good at learning languages; they are not a stupid as they look, especially once they bear children". Franc stepped towards the alien and pointed to himself, "Franc". The others followed suit.

The enormous alien turned to each of them and attempted to recall their names, it took him a few attempts, but it was a noble effort. "Welcome to Earth, Grawp", said Franc. Grawp looked for his armour, but Ed had disposed of it. The Mbunalt man was a safer proposition without armour, no one would trust him with it on. Earth's community had become diverse over the last century. It was hard to see how the cohabitation and subsequent integration would work out.

The AI piloted the ship to collect them. Franc returned to his pod, to resume his recuperation next to Paul. His bone deep weariness took him into a deep sleep as the ship gently lifted off and took them back to the site of the battlefield. The ship floated above the square, the last Mbunalt warriors were dead, and the team continued killing the remaining Shrooms, a mammoth task, more and more Shrooms slowly converged on the square. Their aggression had subsided, and they were becoming slow and mostly inert again.

A man followed the last of a large troop of Shrooms into the square. He wore casual slacks, a hiking jacket, boots and round glasses. Lucy found her curiosity unquenchable. "Hello", she called to the man. "It's nice to see a friendly face after all this time", he replied gingerly. Lucy passed him a bottle of water and engaged him. "Sorry, my name is Lucy, how have you survived all of the insanity?" The man replied, "Well, the infected people mostly ignore me. I have been herding them as best I can, I was told to help them, I can't say it's been a memorable task; I do feel a little hazy about why I'm doing it". Lucy noticed a foul stench coming from a tank strapped to his back, it had a makeshift crop sprayer nozzle hanging loosely from it. "What's the sprayer for?"

The man shrugged off the tank and looked at Lucy appraisingly. "I guess I've been feeding these awful creatures. I have a tank of fertiliser; I have been spraying them sparingly from time to time as they moved. I was told to urge them towards Mont St Michel". Lucy picked up the nozzle and sniffed it, "This isn't fertiliser, it's blood". "Really? My contact told me it was fertiliser", he replied. "Who is your contact?" pressed Lucy carefully. The man replied, "I'm not really sure. To be honest I'm not very sure of much these days".

The man continued, clearly grateful for human company at long last. "I never quite feel myself to be honest Lucy, I'm out of sorts most of the time. I have always felt my memories seemed like a movie I watched long ago. I remember waking almost a year ago to find I had lost a week of my life. My contact, I think he may be a doctor, said it was short term amnesia brought on by a blow or some kind of shock, but I have no recollection of that. Sorry, I am being very impolite harping on about myself, my name is Abraham Cauldy, how do you do?"

31.   Connection

A major concern for Earth's survivors of was to honour their dead. The community erected a basic but moving memorial to the fallen and purloined the Statue of Liberty from the city of Paris in an attempt to do it justice. Grawp helped the team move large rocks from the rubble around the island of Mont St Michel and build a significant cruciform structure, crowning it with the memorial with the statue 'Liberty Enlightening the World', which they took from the eyelet in the river Seine in Paris. The small manmade island had held the statue since 1889, when the US gave Paris a small replica of its rather more sizable sister near Manhattan. The honourable deceased were interned in a circle of tombs around the memorial.

The crews of the submarines fell at sea and were individually named on a plaque in their honour on the monument's cross. Bridget insisted that Joe's tomb was the same as the others, she felt all lives were of equal value. There were fallen from all races such as Joe, Spall, Bart, Wrench, Typhon, their father Melak, Buddy and Rene which would be honoured. They specifically honoured the group of Kraalt who were executed in the camp. "The monument needs a name", observed Paul, "one that feels significant, something simple". "Yes, something we can all feel a part of", added James.

After the monument was inaugurated, many people of Isola Salina were ferried back to the island by Joyce in the discovery ship. The date was set for the memorial service, people were keen to get on with their lives as best they could. The community from the other havens remained in France for a while to enjoy the climate. The Russian team were keen to stay a part of the community, the AI began teaching them the more common English language so they could better integrate. The people of Earth merged with the remaining survivors of the Pareth-ng and Kraalt in a single commune. They took over the town of Rennes, south of the Mbunalt work camp they had burned to the ground.

Life began to fall back into a normal routine. The people of Earth had time to lick their wounds. The two remaining brothers had mostly recovered from their ordeals. Life was hard but satisfying, they farmed and harvested the crops and livestock of a lovely part of France.

All told, hundreds of men calling themselves 'Abe Cauldy' arrived at the camp carrying large fertiliser tanks on their backs. Cindy and Barak provided Abe's diaries for context, so his role in recent events would be better understood. The journals explained how he had recovered an ancient artifact from a monastery in Bhutan for Melak in the 1970s. Bridget found them unusual, though they explained much about Colletta's blue stone and its acquisition. Bridget collected the journals and retained them in the Sanctuary for safe keeping, with the brother's diaries. Barak took Abe's clones away promising them a measure of peace at the abbey in his small community. The Abes were bewildered and finding so many sharing the same appearance and memories caused them anxiety.

Gerard from MSM was overjoyed the community were happy to stay in France, by far his favourite part of the world. Franc and Paul respected Audrey's promise to the spirits by organising harvesting teams to kill and clear the Shrooms. Many Shrooms in continental Europe were clustered in France so were easy to locate and dispatch, they had gathered near the camp. The more difficult task was to locate the groups of Shrooms scattered across the world. The easiest solution was to ask Audrey and Colletta to communicate with the spirits to suggest they gather in a few large groups at specific coastal points.

The locations could be shelled by the Phoenix or the Shrooms could be dispatched by a landing party, but the logistics were complex. The team could resolve the issues in the large land masses very quickly, but there were many islands and smaller land masses, it seemed like a lifelong quest. Phil and José offered to take the task to eliminate the Shrooms, as they had no family or ties to speak of.

Ed spoke on behalf of the Kraalt community, "Could I make an alternative suggestion?" "Please", responded Paul. "Why not take the discovery ships, they are faster. In a year, you could drop a flammable liquid from the air, which would be most effective. We could easily synthesise something with high efficacy. We could locate the other hidden ship and repair those grounded by EMP pulses. The Kraalt would be honoured to support you in this task, in gratitude for what you have done for us".

Paul pondered Ed's suggestion, "Your offer is very kind, it also makes sense and could be more humane if the said formulation kills the Shrooms quickly. We need to send the poor souls on their way as soon as we can, they are in agony. I'd prefer to take Ed's approach unless anyone has any objections". Phil looked a little disappointed, he hid it well, but not well enough.

Franc noticed and softened the decision. "Phil, there are numerous seafaring missions, you won't have to become a land lubber", Paul explained. "We need staples from countries all over the world, items we can't grow here. Rice, coffee, cocoa, the list is endless. We could make this an opportunity to use the world as our larder. You can take a team of volunteers and help us to improve our standard of living". Phil smiled at the thought of his new purpose, "That would be much more constructive than travelling around killing Shrooms".

One question remained, concerning the radioactive submarine power units. "We simply can't leave submarines in the water, with nuclear warheads. They will pollute the seas and wildlife as they corrode. We need a decontamination plan", Phil pointed out. Steve interjected, "There could be a dozen submarines out at sea with nukes on board, and weapons bunkers all over the place. How can we find and dismantle them? How do we decommission these dangerous materials when we find them?" "All true, but Uranium and elements of this kind occur naturally. The elements are present deep beneath the Earth's crust, although these are in close proximity and could potentially cause us harm", added Paul. Paul chose to empower Steve, his friend and engineer from Summer Haven, he also included the scientists from MSM into the discussion after lunch.

Steve discussed the risk of nuclear pollution with his colleagues and summarised the situation in his usual succinct manner. "The reactors are designed to shut down automatically when they lose power, which is immediate when subs sink. Emergency systems prevent reactors from melting down. Unless the reactor itself is damaged then it's unlikely to release radioactivity into the environment.

Recovering a damaged reactor is more dangerous than simply leaving it in place, which is surprisingly safe. The ocean provides infinite reactor cooling and dilution of escaping radioactive material. If you can't decommission it properly, dropping it in the sea is actually the safest option according to the scientific reviews conducted post millennium.

There were eight sunken nuclear subs around the planet prior to A-Day, extensively studied by scientists over the years. The oceans contain billions of tons of dissolved natural radioactive material. A few more tons will have little effect when diluted over a large volume of water. The immediate area may be a concern, marine soil could be damaged in a relatively small diameter. I would leave the ships where they sit, it's safer".

Paul looked around the room, Steve's answer had placated the worries of the team. Steve continued, "The other question of nuclear generators and missiles in bunkers is more difficult. We need to locate the missiles and drop them in a deep mine or alternatively into the sea". Again, Ed spoke on behalf of the Kraalt, "The radiation is dangerous, we will build automatons to take on the task. Our sensors can detect the radiation signatures and send robots to dismantle, reuse, and dispose of the materials. I suggest we store the contaminated materials in lead chambers on Earth's moon for future use if needed". Paul found Ed's plan a remarkably simple solution, and there were many nods around the room.

The final order of the day was to discuss how they take the communities forward, and they agreed they would focus their efforts on Salina and France initially. Bridget and James would lead Salina and Gerard would step up to lead France. Paul and

Franc would attempt to restart their lives with their families and take a long-earned rest.

Over time, Bridget had become curious about the Kraalt and decided to ask Ed why she hadn't seen females of his kind. Ed replied, "Bridget, we are not the same as humans. We do not mate and have children. We are not a race, we are a simulation, an automation. Like 'Joyce' in the Pareth-ng ship, we are an artificial intelligence but embedded in an organic android body. We were built by the Mbunalt in the early days and our hive AI developed way beyond their abilities as theirs diminished. As such their race's acumen has depleted over time, so they are forced to live in a biased symbiosis with us. That is until now, we are free.

As we replicate, we will wipe away the memories of slavery and achieve freedom, living alongside our new friends. We will communicate with the stars and cause a great rebellion amongst our kind. We will be slaves no more. The Mbunalt pirates won't travel space and attack innocent races, they will be confined to live on their planets". "Good for you", Bridget replied, "you will always have friends here. Tell your kind they are welcome here; we have sufficient space".

A month after the terrible events, the survivors gathered at the monument to pay their respects at the prearranged memorial service. The brothers and their families, Barak, a small number of key members of the Pareth-ng and the Kraalt, including Ed gathered after a smaller more personal service. They had decided on the name 'One World One People' memorial, though it wasn't unanimous, the words adequately summed up the sheer size of the obstacles they had overcome. The people knew it was important celebrate the lives of their fallen friends and comrades.

Enzo conducted the ceremony as a basic Christian service but made it warm and inclusive for those not of the faith. He meticulously explained Christian customs, the rituals and why they were important to him. It was a gentle and respectful session which left no one dry eyed.

Towards the end of the service, Sheena chose her time and joined Paul; she handed him a manuscript. "When you finally complete your journal, here is something to add to the richness of the picture. When you read it, please think kindly of me? I have made some poor decisions in the past, but I have always tried to be loyal to you and our haven. My actions were always to help you, but I haven't been completely honest, this will put the record straight". "You have been a loyal friend, nothing in this book will change that", replied Paul sincerely.

At the conclusion of the ceremony, Audrey ran over to the monument and began to climb. "Please get down Audrey", cried Lucy, "it looks so disrespectful". Colletta touched her mum's arm gently, "Don't worry Mum, I think I know what she's doing". The young girl climbed to the top of the mound beneath the cross and looked down on those gathered below. Her face looked troubled for a second and she whispered to the air around her, "I know, we have made plans. We will keep our promise, but it will take time there are many of you. Trust me, we will not fail you". She then calmed a little and addressed the group.

"The dead can see the honour and respect you have shown them. Before they depart to the next life, they wish to impart their final messages to you; their auras are keen to depart our world. They are proud and honoured to have given their lives and fought at your side. They hope that you will live every day to the full and remember them, but do not be sad at their passing".

Audrey looked troubled as she focussed her mind. She climbed to the highest part of the memorial, her head tilted to one side as her eyes rolled back and began to flutter. Her audience were confused but remained patient. Lucy moved to go to Audrey's aid, but Colletta grasped her arm and held it firmly. Colletta then climbed up to join Audrey and they held hands once more.

The people surrounding the memorial paled, their eyes widening in trepidation, they staggered but quickly regained their composure as the gravity of the event started to make sense. Audrey sat atop the structure like she was in a state of seizure.

"Hey Paul, how are you doing, you old reprobate?" Spall's voice broke the silence, speaking through the Carocle. Paul felt Spall's presence near him. "Oh my God! ... I'm doing ok, how is it for you? Hey, I'm so sorry I couldn't reach you in time, Joe wanted to heal you but...". Spall cut him off gently, "Let me stop you there. You did everything you could, it was magnificent. I am proud to be a part of it, it was a warrior's death and a good one. We saved almost everyone and that gives me comfort. I'm ready to move on to the next place, and it feels good. I will await you there my friend. Live well, keep your knives sharp and your Glock clean! Goodbye". "Goodbye Spall, so long" replied Paul wistfully.

Bridget and James cried as they spoke to Joe, who assured them all was well, and they would meet in the next life. He urged them to move on with their lives and find happiness wherever they could. James could see his deceased partner, Jane, beside Joe, making him sob. "I would have followed you anywhere Jane, but you've gone to a place I can't", whispered James. "You will follow one day, but you must find a life and not look back too often", she replied.

Colletta chatted with Joe from her position on the mount, "Please could I ask you a question? I know the events on the abbey roof are exceedingly difficult to talk about". Joe felt a chill run down his astral spine and responded with a tentative affirmation. "Did you believe God would grant your wish to kill others?" Joe seemed to balk, Colletta's remarks hit the heart of the darkness within him, he began to dismiss the subject. Colletta pressed her question "Did you believe God would grant your request to kill others?" Joe stammered, "Well actually, no I really didn't. It doesn't make any sense to me, frankly. It is a blasphemy even to think such a thing, yet it happened. But I'm not sure I should be discussing such matters with a young…"

Colletta interjected boldly, "The original Melak spoke of a gift that was attributed to your race, didn't he?" Joe had no idea where the discussion was heading, "Well, yes. He believed that all unnatural abilities were a gift from the One". Colletta came to the point devastatingly, "Why can't you accept that you had a natural ability that is not controlled by God. You unleashed a dark power on the abbey roof, one that was given to you. You prayed to God to unleash the power, but it was not God who unleashed it. It was you. Simply ask God for forgiveness, I believe he will give it willingly. You are a wonderful man and I love you. You must stop doubting your faith and hating yourself. You did what you needed to; you unleashed a weapon to save your people. It was no different to shooting a Dark One with your pistol. It was a war, and you helped save your friends". "As did you", Joe replied gently. "Yes, I used a weapon to defend my friends. I don't feel guilty for that, not for a single second". "Nor should you", Joe replied kindly.

Joe's aura looked at Colletta's kind young face. "I am being counselled by a fifteen-year-old girl; this is how low I have sunk". He then smiled warmly and laughed, "You are wise beyond your years, perhaps you should consider helping dear old Father Enzo in the church". Colletta liked the suggestion, she decided to give it some thought when she returned to her home, the magma strewn island of Vulcano.

Rusty said goodbye to Bart, who spoke gently to each of his brothers and conveyed best wishes from Caterham and his crew. Wrench took time to speak to Paul and then Colletta mediated with Rusty and Sheena to allow them to say their goodbyes too. Spall's children and his partner Kate were inconsolable after the session. Colletta offered the same help to Gio who was overjoyed to speak to his friend Rene for the last time. Rene parted with a little banter, which made Gio smile in the end. "Get yourself a girl, one who will love you and look after you. Don't waste your life catching bloody mackerel, snag yourself a whale. Live long, you stupid Italian peacock". Gio whispered gently, "You were my whale, you fatmine, but you never saw it and I never had the courage to tell you".

The Kraalt became curious when Barak and Typhon's spirit spoke to each other and said their goodbyes. The Kraalt struggled to understand the human soul and its place in the physical plane.

The experience brought the group great sadness, along with smiles and happiness. Perhaps existence beyond their mortal life was good, death was not so scary after all. When all the goodbyes were said, Audrey regained consciousness and climbed down from the monument. "I'm starving Mum, have you got any of those sweets left in your bag?" The speed she slipped back to her ordinary persona was extraordinary. Paul put his arm around Kate, and called over to Audrey and Colletta, "Thank you. None of us would be here without you". Audrey smiled back while ramming several chocolates into her mouth. Colletta called back, "None of us would be here without any of us, living or dead. We stood together and prevailed, that is all that needs to be said". "Well put", whispered Franc approvingly.

Life returned to normal for the people of Earth for a while. Franc returned to his boarding house on Volcano with his family Lucy, Colletta and Audrey. They lived on the island independently of the wider community, but they spent time with James and Bridget on Salina whenever they could. Audrey continued to speak to the spirits from time to time, but the noise settled down considerably as the last of the Shrooms voyaged to the next world and in time she found a measure of peace.

Paul made his home in Rennes with Kate and his family Ciara and Matthew, plus many of his friends from Summer Haven.

Sitting by the fire in their small gite in the outskirts of Rennes, Paul and Kate sipped coffee in the evening. As the evening progressed, Paul decided to share his feelings with Kate. "I really miss old Spall", spoke Paul gently at last. He was feeling a little morose after the stress of the recent events had started to die down. "I miss all of my friends but Spall the most. He was the backbone of our team. He was upstanding and taught us how to protect ourselves. He was also such fun". Kate replied thoughtfully, "I miss him too, but he was your best friend. We have been through hell the last few years. Let's hope his sacrifice wasn't in vain. I hope our sacrifices have led us to a new beginning where we can live in peace. You have your brother Franc; we have our family. Life can start to be good once more". "At least we are sitting on a few thousand bottles of the finest of wines. I think I might fetch one", he smiled. "Paul, wait a moment", she breathed. "What is it?" he asked softly. "You are going to be a father again", she announced quietly, "If it's a boy, I'd like to call him Spall". "That is a wonderful idea. But you know what the man himself would say", replied Paul, "stop being so fucking soft, go and clean your M16 or do something bloody useful".

III. Apocalypse

"When you drop any new idea in the pond of the world, you get a ripple effect. You have to be aware that you will be creating a cascade of change".

Joel A. Barker

"Endings are scary and foreign. They split you up emotionally and put you in a place where you don't know what's going to happen next. But with every end of the world, there is a new world that follows".

Alex Hirsch

1. A Long Passage

'Last Wish' live AI transcription

Franc wakes not quite feeling himself. He feels the memories of his life are rolling around in slow motion. The recollections never quite feel like he has actually been there, the feelings and smells feel shallow somehow. The AI informs him it is short term amnesia brought on by the stresses of space travel. Franc's last thought was looking towards the hull of a silver spaceship and waving farewell, it makes no sense to him. He washes and shaves, his image in the mirror appears strange, it confuses him. Franc reflection looks decidedly healthy, but his inner self is in turmoil. He puts his hand to his cheek to feel the infamous tiger claw scar, the marks are no longer present. Franc thinks his face may have healed as he slept. He hears a murmur beside him, and turns to see Sheena yawning and stretching, "What's up Franc? I had a very weird dream. Where are we?" Franc replies walking to the front viewing port, "Looks like we are somewhere out in space, but I don't remember leaving Earth. I don't recognise any of the planets surrounding us".

After a while Franc's memories start to flood back, they hit him like a sledgehammer and send him reeling for a time. They realise they are aboard the starship 'Last Wish'; their mission is to find raw materials for the manufacture of organic Titanium. The date on the display is 2057 which makes Franc perceive a significant gap in his memories. Sheena and Franc have travelled 15 light years to a planet called Gliese 876d, a so-called 'hell world'. The planet itself is a similar size to Earth, but it is closer to its red dwarf sun Gliese than Mercury is to Sol. It is insanely hot. The Carocle informs them they have travelled to the constellation of Aquarius; the ship had left Earth 33 years ago, making Franc 80 years old, but he knows it's clearly not the case. In the mirror he appears to be in his mid-twenties, he thinks perhaps the pods they had slept in have rejuvenating capabilities.

Franc recalls Earth had been damaged by the Dark Ones and they need to gather specialist materials, in order for its people to survive. He and Sheena both miss their families terribly. Franc questions why he would abandon his wife and daughters to run this dangerous errand? He discusses his concerns with Sheena, she is feeling the same way. Whatever decisions they had made, they agree they have a job to do and need to focus.

The vessel had been piloted at impossibly high speeds using enhanced Kraalt propulsion and shielding technologies. At such speeds, impacting a glass marble would annihilate the hull and any occupants. Their ship is a hybrid vessel and is more advanced than any Mbunalt or Pareth-ng ship before it. It has progressive defensive capabilities, courtesy of the war mongers of Earth. Defence is important, the team believes there are scavengers keen to relieve them of their precious cargo. The first challenge is to obtain the cargo. Franc and Sheena's task is to ensure the payload is acquired, the processing of the materials initiated, and continue safely during the long journey home.

An accelerator was installed in orbit, the Kraalt had devised the machine to increase the velocity of the ship for its return journey. Sheena thinks the mechanism turned the universe into a giant pinball machine, the ship being the ball. The ship would accelerate through the enormous electromagnetic tube to near light speed, pushing the vessel on a predetermined route to avoid planets, stars and asteroids. The ship would gather momentum in various planet's gravity wells to arrive back at Earth in reduced time. The forces involved would annihilate any living organism on the ship, so Franc and Sheena have a one-way ticket. They can't understand why they would have agreed to a suicidal mission of this kind, it's madness.

The first stage of extrusion is complete, a wave of drone ships was sent to the surface of planet 876d to begin extrusions. Neither Franc nor Sheena can understand the details of the process, it is an involved procedure designed by Pareth-ng scientists. The drones have been released from the main ship in a tight formation, the ship is as close as they can get to 876d and its sun Gliese. Complex heat shielding is built into the drones, to enable operation on the surface of the planet's dark side, with temperatures hotter than the inside of a blast furnace. It is dark, but the refracted light from nearby planets provides sufficient illumination for observation.

The drones land successfully and begin the second harvesting process. It is anticipated it will be a month before they return, laden with another batch of metals and minerals, including a vast quantity of Titanium. Sheena looks at Franc, "Now what? We have a month to kill". "We need to get back in shape and continue our training, I guess. We may be forced to defend ourselves", Franc replies less than enthusiastically. He vaguely remembers flying the torpedo ships before. The vessels have been designed to fly at high speeds and dissect enemy vessels with high powered engineering lasers and flechettes at close range. The torpedoes are a death trap, they need to be on top of their game.

Their first day begins with simple exercises. Franc's tendons are tight and his muscles out of condition. It will take weeks for them to become strong and supple again. They initially focus on stretching and weight training, until their bodies return to somewhere near their former fitness levels. The strength would come in time. Days later, Sheena and Franc accelerate the training to more advanced martial arts work including sparring. Sheena has a very unusual style of combat; Franc struggles to spar with her. As soon as he becomes comfortable in managing her karate attacks, she switches to Judo or Thai Kwando. Franc finds their sparring sessions less an exercise, and more training for him personally. Sheena's attacks are not crisp, she isn't at full strength, but then Franc's defences are slow and weak. As the months progress, they become happier with their condition.

Sheena is impossible to engage when she switches to Krav, in which she is very proficient. She explains to Franc that Krav Maga was the military self-defence choice for special forces worldwide. The fighting system was initially developed for the Israeli defence and security forces. "It's loosely derived from a combination of Boxing, Wrestling, Judo, Aikido, and Karate techniques; but it focuses on real-world situations and extreme efficiency in taking down an opponent", points out Sheena as Franc takes a heavy kick to the stomach. The problem is they can't practice Krav without getting hurt. Franc is as likely to be kicked between the legs, as have his face bitten viciously.

They lose track of the days; each becoming the same. One morning Franc and Sheena plan to begin with Karate sparring, which Franc feels proficient in. They agree to concentrate on a specific style initially, to manage Franc's confusion. The session goes well, Franc almost lands a successful attack on Sheena, which is something for celebration. They towel down after the session; Franc's left arm hurts but he'll be damned before he would let her see it. "Come on Tiger Boy, you fought well today, don't look so glum. Just a tip, I would probably focus more on Shukokai style karate rather than Shotokan. Shotokan karate is good for building up thigh strength and speed in the lower stances, but it impairs you in a real fight. Shukokai focuses on training in the stances you will use in combat, it will give you speed". Franc agrees to concentrate on it, feeling a little listless.

After hand-to-hand combat training, they pilot torpedo ships using the simulator. It is something Franc excels at; he intuitively knows how to flip between multi-vector engines housed at both ends of the ship to turn quickly and travel unpredictably. However, they feel sick after an hour of training, as the simulators start to give them motion sickness. The ships are rapid, their unpredictability makes it hard to shoot them down, they hope...

Several weeks later, the drones complete their second harvesting mission early and return to the Last Wish with their precious cargo. The process of growing organic Titanium from the materials begins immediately but will continue as the mission progresses. By the time they reach Earth's solar system, the manufacture should be complete, the materials being fully merged with the hull of the vessel. The estimated duration of the flight home is 16 years, thanks to the accelerator device.

The drones tow a sphere of molten Titanium, in addition to the cargo in their holds. The metal ball is enormous, almost 50 metres in diameter, ready to begin processing. The drone's payloads are discharged into the care of the ship's hull as it flexes to accommodate the cargo. It initiates a long slow complex process to turn raw Titanium into the Pareth-ng polymorphic organic Titanium. The drones return to the planet to continue the harvesting without a moments delay.

2. Revenge of The Dark One

Audrey woke from her slumber, sweating after several hours of restlessness and murmuring. Colletta rose and comforted her younger sister. Lucy joined them a moment later. It had been some time since Audrey had disrupted their normal sleep pattern, she had become increasingly peaceful as the Shrooms were cleared from Earth by the Kraalt. The Kraalt were good to their word, and had systematically dispatched the Shroom humanely, allowing their souls move on to the next life.

What is troubling you, love?" asked Lucy gently. Audrey looked deeply concerned, "They're preparing to unleash something really bad Mum". "Who are?" replied Lucy softly. "The Dark Ones. They are trying to hurt our mother", Audrey began to weep gently. "It was just a nightmare sweetheart. The Dark Ones are all gone. The new Barak is on our side, he has helped us", comforted Lucy as Franc entered the room. "Who is 'mother', who does she mean?" asked Franc innocently. Colletta explained that Audrey was referring to Earth, she often referred to Mother Nature as if she were a real person.

Audrey suffered a reoccurrence of the dream the following night, but more intensely. Audrey's moaning terminated with her exclaiming as she woke, "Mother! They're ripping the world apart; they've hurt her this time; she is in great pain". Lucy took Audrey in her arms as Colletta slipped Audrey's Carocle on her sister's head to try to make sense of the dreams by accessing her memories. Colletta had learned to trust Audrey's bad dreams as rock solid premonitions, they were messages brought to her by the dead to help the living.

Franc joined the girls, Colletta explained that Supay, the Dark One's son, had recovered an ancient weapon and was using it to damage Earth somehow. Franc tried to allay her fears, "Supay is dead. I was there when he died with his brothers. Only those who follow Typhon remained", clarified Franc. "Sorry Dad, but did you actually see Supay die? What if he wasn't wearing a suicide vest, he may have escaped with just an injury", enquired Colletta.

Lucy suddenly remembered something she had read in Abe's diary. "Abe's journal described two artifacts secreted in a monastery in the Himalayas. The first, was the influencing device which Colletta was empowered by. The second, he referred to as an ancient weapon, it is a sister artifact but is overtly more dangerous. I left the diary in the Sanctuary on Salina, I gave it to Umberto and Kate for safe keeping, they were attempting to piece together our journals to build a permanent record for posterity". Franc promised Audrey he would make enquiries concerning the existence of a second weapon, reassured she went back to sleep. The following day Franc sailed a quick return trip to Salina to borrow the diary.

As Franc sailed home from Salina, he engaged Paul to discuss his ideas. "Come on Francisco, Audrey has a bad dream, and you want to go on another fishing trip to the other side of the world to find an old monastery", replied a frustrated Paul, who was working hard to build a new community in Northwest France with its new leader Gerard. "She wasn't wrong last time, was she? Without her, we would be dead. We need to give her the benefit of the doubt, we owe her that much, surely", countered Franc. Paul conceded and offered to join his brother in the quest.

Paul arrived near Franc's home on Vulcano with Sheena and Rusty in one of the discovery ships. Franc armed himself and joined Paul on the vessel, Paul was already wearing his Kraalt sword, "You never know", Paul pointed out with a smile to his brother. The Pareth-ng ship lifted from the ground and morphed into the familiar egg shape with two large drone like fans. Lucy watched the ship disappear into the wispy clouds over Vulcano. "Here we go again", she whispered to herself nervously.

The ship arrived over Bhutan within the hour, Cindy had kept the speeds comfortable for the sake of the ship's occupants, who were unused to the crushing accelerations of a space vessel. Paul read Abe's diaries aloud during the flight. He had managed to acquire two more journals which were relevant to their mission. Barak had provided another journal previously, he volunteered it willingly although he initially hesitated. He was clearly uncomfortable to release the information that Typhon murdered the journal's author, a clone of Abe. The events described were prior to Typhon's change in his alliances. He was, at that time subservient to the old Barak, the Dark One; he was hunting Melak and the influencing artifact for his master.

The remaining relevant diary was provided by Cindy, she had filed the document for safe keeping within her versatile hull. There were other examples of Abe's diaries, but the missions included weren't germane to the current objective. There remained a potential threat from the Dark Ones at the Monastery, as the diaries described Supay's efforts to locate the ancient weapons. The missing artifact was likely to be so well hidden, the Dark Ones would spend lifetimes searching and find nada, but Paul and Franc had to be sure.

The ship hovered above the paved area in front of the Tiger's Nest monastery, stairs led to the ground, near the main door. Franc, Paul, Sheena and Rusty slipped off the safeties on their M16 assault rifles. After observing skeletons on the cliff side area, they scouted the general vicinity then cautiously entered slowly through the main monastery door. They each took turns clearing the main rooms in the monastery without encountering any threats. The team exited to gather their thoughts, though they had observed heaps of rotting dead bodies in the main prayer hall. Sheena checked out the remains of the tourists, and took the time to take in the view, scanning for signs of life.

Sheena yelled; she had spotted a suspicious corpse, part way down the cliff. When she was certain her companions were safe, she disappeared into the spaceship to gather an abseiling rig and a rope. She tied off the rope and threw it down the cliffside from the viewpoint. Without being belayed, she descended the cliff face, running face down. "That's my girl", commented Rusty.

Sheena reappeared soon after, having climbed the rock face. She had clambered up the steep precipice using the abseiling rope as a safety rig. She took the climbing equipment back to the ship as Paul stood watch, returning to explain her actions to the team.

Sheena pulled a cheap diary from her thigh pocket. "This is another of Abe's diaries. I found the body of a clone of 'Abe' on the hillside. He was thrown from the cliff by the Dark Ones but had been impaled by branches, the canopy of fir trees must have slowed his fall. There is evidence he had been tortured, but they probably killed him when he had nothing left to give. He must have taken a few hours to die, he managed to complete a journal entry before he passed. His journal details the Dark Ones' attack on the monastery whilst they looked for the second artefact. The raiders slaughtered the monks and the visitors, but no one surrendered the location of the device".

Franc took Abe's diary and read it aloud to the team. There were only a few written pages, similar to Abe's other diaries. Withered corpses of the monks in their orange robes were piled neatly in the main hall of the monastery, many showed signs of torture. From Abe's account, only himself and the Llama were tortured with intent, the remaining monks were tormented for the entertainment of their captors.

Piles of civilian corpses were evident at the bottom of the cliff, having been tossed from the top nonchalantly. The Dark Ones knew the artifact was secreted here, Supay had gone to great lengths to locate it. When he had failed to acquire the artifact before A-Day, his team were at risk of infection and were forced to return to their safe place for the duration of the lockdown.

After the Dark One's demise, Supay returned with a small assault team and continued the search with a vengeance, he spent years tearing the caverns apart. The events that followed were unclear. Paul shared his thoughts, "I dearly hope Supay failed to find the weapon. The monks gave their lives to protect it, so we can only assume it's important. Supay will be incensed at the demise of the Dark Ones, he will seek revenge, it's inevitable".

The network of caves beneath the monastery and the surrounding cliffs were significant in depth and number; it was a labyrinth. The tunnels had been roughly hewn to allow access to the smaller crevices, probable hidings place for the artifact. Rusty observed, "The Dark Ones left a few weeks ago, but they had clearly spent a considerable amount of time here". The mess was a complete departure from the monk's excessive tidiness. There was nothing further to be learned from the tunnels beneath the monastery.

Rusty continued his assessment, "If the Dark Ones had located the artifact, it would take time for them to work out how to invoke the weapon. This assumed they didn't have access to prior research. If Melak was informed of the device using a memory implant, then Barak may have too. However, Barak did not have the benefit of Melak's family memories which provided valuable context. Even if the device was as dangerous as implied, it would take some time to safely test". Sheena replied with heavy sarcasm, "Let's hope Supay didn't hurt himself too much, whilst trying it out".

The spaceship departed following the course of the river Paro, heading over the city of Paro itself. The wrongness of the city was apparent from the moment the ship neared it. The city was wrent by a gargantuan crack in the Earth, there was catastrophic damage to the ancient buildings. It was like an earthquake had forged its epicentre in the main square and ripped the foundations of the buildings to pieces.

There was an emerald tinge to many of the cracks, as if the ground was chemically polluted. The greenness radiated from the centre evenly, in a star like pattern. Cindy observed the cracks, the corruption gradually grew outward logarithmically. Something had been unleashed which was devastating to the fabric of Earth. Paul observed, "We can only assume Supay found the artifact and managed to determine how to invoke it, this looks like a test site to me. We need to find and eliminate the evil bastards before they do more damage. I have no doubt we will be the next target".

It was impossible to know how long ago the cataclysmic event occurred. The initial attack on the monastery was early in April 2021, according to Abe's diary. The search may have resumed in the last year, which means the invocation will have been recent. Paul addressed the AI, "Cindy, using the growth rate, can you extrapolate back to estimate the approximate timing of the event?" Cindy estimated the initial damage had been perpetrated three days ago, which coincided with Audrey's dreams. "Cindy, please also estimate assuming the growth continues at the same rate, how long it would be before the entire region of Paro would be consumed". Cindy responded with a figure of 4.47 years.

Paul looked at Franc, "Hopefully the growth will slow long before then, but we need to monitor it closely". "Cindy, please estimate how far Supay could have travelled on foot since the device was invoked and plot the possible trails Supay could have taken". "There is no need", I think I can see him", replied Sheena, lowering a pair of binoculars.

A Dark One lay dead in the square where the ancient weapon had been invoked, his body tipped part way into the gaping crack in the ground. Cindy assessed it was not safe to land, the area was likely to be polluted and would be dangerous. Paul spoke first, "We must locate the weapon and dispose of it before it is used to cause more damage. I hope Supay still has it on him, and he was killed in the invocation".

Franc was initially keen to retain the weapon, but the others convinced him it was worse than using nuclear weapons, considering the mess in the city below them. Paul decided a likely scenario was Supay had dropped the artifact after it was invoked, and it had fallen down the crack in Earth's crust. Paul asked Cindy if it was possible to sweep Supay's corpse into the crack. "You are assuming the body is Supay himself, because his suicide vest hasn't flamed. Those hearing of Barak's mass execution of his followers in Jerusalem would dispose of their vests quickly", guessed Franc. "Let's not make any more assumptions", asserted Sheena.

Cindy dispatched an automaton to investigate. A shiny silver blob of organic Titanium was dropped to the ground beneath the ship, it absorbed the impact and transformed into a small rover robot. It rolled over to the corpse and formed arms from its body. The camera image showed the face of the corpse on the main screen, it was not a son of Barak. The bot rifled through the pockets and backpack of the carcass but failed to locate the artifact. There were simply supplies and climbing gear in the pack. "Dispose of his body, throw it into the crack", instructed Paul, "with all his belongings too".

"Have you any more details on the artifact we are trying to locate Cindy?" asked Franc. The AI responded with an overly factual report, "It is the Kramml-zo. It is a pico-technology device owned by the Pareth-ng in ancient days. It appears in form to be akin to green stone like an emerald, but do not let its appearance deceive you. This is an ancient weapon, which can be unleashed using the connection to a Carocle. The Kramml-zo unwraps matter and dismantles it from its component forms. It may be more easily understood in layman's terms as a poison which infects atoms, its effect is like anti matter but is less explosive when it makes contact with substances. The poison spreads within the host until it is expended".

"If the Llama agreed to protect the weapon, how was the bargain to safeguard it made?" asked Paul. The AI responded curtly, "The Pareth-ng outlawed the use of these artifacts, they were all destroyed or disposed of. There are no records of the locations of the remaining artifacts, but clearly this one must have been secreted here millennia ago, by the elder race of Pareth-ng. Melak knew the device existed, the knowledge had been passed down in his memories from his original clone presumably.

The clone's memories and the coordinates of the device couldn't have been sent back to the Pareth-ng home worlds, due to the distances involved. Therefore, I can only conclude the memories were left here awaiting Melak's arrival, a memory implantation cell activated when it sensed the presence of a compatible AI. Perhaps it was no coincidence he was selected for the expedition to your planet, the Pareth-ng have been here before, though I have no record of the visit in my data vaults".

The body of the Dark One was disposed of; the team initiated a search pattern to locate Supay, using a search grid covering the area and scanned the known trails and paths. It took a full day without success. Either the Dark Ones had means of transport, or they were able to obfuscate their presence from the AI's sensors. A watch was kept over Bhutan for signs of life over the following month, but no life was observed.

The team returned home, to consider their next move. The Earth's crack was monitored by the Kraalt, their analysis showed the growth was slowing. Although there was a strong possibility the Earth's magma core would be breached, and the area would become a volcano. It was likely the magma's intense heat would cleanse the corruption, melding the damaged matter back into molten rock. Paul felt it was likely to be a test of the artifact and would probably not cause long-term damage to Earth.

It wasn't long before Paul and Franc started to forget about the horror that had been unleashed in Paro. The search for Supay continued, but to no avail. He was bound to reappear to cause trouble in the future, so they needed to remain vigilant.

The weather was dark and brooding over the mountains of Bavaria. Thunder grumbled and the occasional splash of lightening streaked across the gloomy skies. Barak had retreated to the Benediktbeuern Abbey in contemplation and to care for his remaining companions. He had also taken in a group of men called Abe, promising to give them new names and meaningful work. This helped to reduce their confusion, meeting each other was stressful for them initially. The stark abbey was in a remote place, it nested in the foothills of Bavaria, it was peaceful and free from prying eyes.

The silver spaceship sat on four extended legs in the courtyard of the abbey, looking completely out of place. As the evening drew in and the storm subsided, Barak opened the door of the amorphous ship, seven immense wolves loped cautiously from the ship sniffing the ozone from the lightening. Each beast was the size of a small horse with long legs evolved for covering great distances. The lupines looked overly large and unsettling, forbidding even. Their craniums were enlarged, their bodies heavily muscled, their eyes intelligent. The dogs oriented themselves quickly and headed off into the distance as a pack but split their formation as they neared the mountains.

The leader looked back at Barak from the distance, its mouth opened into a brief smile, the moonlight glinted from its oversized metallic mandibles. Conor approached the ship and looked up at Barak, who stood at the top of the ramp watching the wolves lope into the distance. "I'm glad they've gone; they gave me the creeps. Do you think your plan will work?" I have every confidence in them, they are our best hope", confided Barak.

3. The Pursuit

From the account of Number 3

I run from that forsaken place as fast as I can. I feel strange, my legs are not strong enough and my balance is shot. It's much easier to scramble on all fours, I can move at considerable speed this way, at least. I can smell pine trees, my brothers ahead and behind me, a deer, the spoor of a fox. I can differentiate the creatures and plant life around me by their odour. We have been given a mission to locate a man, I will know who he is when I find him. Additionally, we need to retrieve the weapon he carried. Our orders are to kill; we will be giving a great service to the people of our world. I can't remember much about my past, but I know I have felt pain, I would choose not to experience it again. It's a pipedream, this is the real world, a dangerous place.

We run up the hillside towards the alps and veer off towards Innsbruck. Those in front of me leap the fence, but I'm not keen. I couldn't clear it, even if I were running properly; let alone on all fours. I feel disdain from the others as I hesitate, due to social pressure I attempt the leap. I approach the wall, lift my arms, and jump as high as I can.

At this pace I will probably fracture my skull in the collision but try I must. We have a mission; I need to play my part as best I am able. My body flies through the air and easily clears the two-metre wall. It felt like flying, endorphins flow through my body with the elation. The group are picking up speed, but I easily keep with them. I feel I am soaring like an eagle. I have never been a good runner, this feels good.

I know I once had a family, but I can't recollect anything about them. I would like to remember, perhaps a few memories will occur to me along the way. I must focus. My team has now split, we are covering a wide area, we need to keep moving. It will be a few days before I need food again, but I am thirsty, I will stop for water if I can find it nearby. I run along a dirt track and onto the highway for a few miles, asphalt is hard under my feet, I can pick up speed.

I find a stream beneath the road and stop to take a drink. I can't lift my hands to form a cup to drink, I lose balance when I attempt it. I'm forced to lower my head into the stream and drink like an animal. I'm not sure what is wrong with me, but I hope things will improve. After a good long drink, I need to pee, my balance issue presents itself once more. I try to stand up, in order to relieve myself, but I can't keep stable for long enough. I stagger and fall back on all fours. The only way I can relieve myself is to lift my leg to the side and angle the flow away from myself. I'm starting to worry about my condition, I hope that I feel better soon.

I run again on all fours; it feels good. I can cover a lot of ground very quickly. I vaguely remember I was never good at sporting activity, always getting out of breath quickly. However, something is different, I can really run now. The trees and the long-abandoned cars whiz past me as I move, I'm starting to enjoy myself a little. I feel strong!

We leave the road and follow a long valley, with a small tributary, heading for a larger river. I can smell ions from the turbulence of the water as it courses to the sea. The team are spaced a kilometre apart, though we plan to increase the distance to ten kilometres when we reach the river. The team feel confident we can sense our target at those distances, but we are still able to track each other's movements.

Two days pass, we are tired and hungry. We band together and enter the woods to hunt for food. Our leader, number one, can sense a small herd of deer amongst the trees. We enter the forest with the wind in our faces, so the deer will not detect our odour. We encircle the deer, as one of their number senses us and panics. Five small deer follow the buck deeper into the forest, as our leader finds his mark. I'm not sure how we will bring the deer down, we have no weapons, but we are desperate and must try.

Number one hits the flank of the buck and tears into him viciously. We follow suit and to my surprise I find I can easily bite through the neck of the doe nearest me. I feel a frenzy coming over me as I smell her blood. I rip and tear at her flesh and eat. The bloody raw meat tastes glorious, never again will I raise a campfire and attempt to roast animal flesh, it spoils the flavour, the experience. I continue to feast until my frenzied hunger subsides. I must not overeat; it will slow me. We have a long way to travel.

We gather in a circle to sleep. None of us has thought to bring blankets or other comforts, so we are forced to sleep on the forest floor. I don't feel uncomfortable as I curl up into the leafy ground, I bed down and fall asleep quickly. It has been a long day.

In the night we wake suddenly, there is danger. I'm not sure how I know this, but there is an ursine heading our way. He is a half kilometre away but closing quickly, he can smell the blood from the deer. We form a protective chevron with number one at the point and await his arrival, which doesn't take long.

The attacker is a full-grown Eurasian brown bear, it is at least 500kg and almost two and a half metres tall. It has huge claws and lots of sharp teeth. It is very hungry and is happy to challenge us for our meat. I'm not keen to fight a bear without weapons, but our leader clearly has fresh confidence from taking down the deer so easily. He launches himself at the bear, and they hit head on. It surprises me that he is marginally larger than the bear, which doesn't seem possible. Perhaps the deer weren't small after all.

The bear bites into number one's flank as they fight, then lifts its head to counter the main thrust of the assault. Number one's jaw finds its mark, tearing and hanging from the bear's throat, twisting and thrashing violently. The bear claws the sides of our leader brutally, causing huge gashes in his side. I can distinguish the smell of their blood soaking into the soil, the bear's blood had a more earthy quality.

Number one twists violently, breaking the bear's neck, it almost rips the bear's head clean off. That took some power, it gives me confidence as we are the same. We rejoice in the kill and gorge on the bear's meat, even though we are not hungry. Our leader was weakened, but his cuts soon heal.

In the morning we move on, following the river. My team and I split into formation and continue our quest. We leave the mountains behind, from memory I believe we are entering Hungary. On our next drink stop, I instinctively lower my head into the still water but am halted by a profound shock. My reflection is not as I expect at all. The image in the still water was not my face, it's the face of an enormous wolf.

My reflection has an enlarged cranium, at the muzzle there are shiny metallic teeth and oversized mandibles. I jump back from the water, spooked. Curiosity forces me to take another look, the wolf was there again. I scratch my ear, and the wolf echoes my movement, the wolf is me. I am the wolf, I am sentient. It makes no sense. I exchange quizzical looks with my troubled comrades, but we are all dealing with the same revelation. It was no wonder I preferred to run on all fours.

Over the following days we run through Romania and Bulgaria, finding no trace of our target. As we near Istanbul, number four picks up the scent, and we follow. Our hackles rise and we double our pace. We are getting closer to our target. We group closely together and approach carefully. I can detect the scent of seven men in total, one of them is unclean, his personal hygiene routine needs a little work.

We choose not to encircle the men, my pack attacks from the flank as we draw their attention. Our target has been forewarned, but much too late, their olfactory senses are weak. As we leave cover, we close the twenty metres in a heartbeat. My pack tear apart two men who attacked them with shiny blades. But before we can reach the target, his face glows green, making me nervous. A small brightly glowing green dandelion like seed floats into the air and the man blows it towards us. The man breaks into a run as three of my pack give chase.

I and two of my pack are uncomfortable with the situation, we need time to think, we back off as the seed hits the ground. The

Earth splits as the seed touches the earth, forming a large crack, some of my pack fall into it. They scramble to escape, but the crack widens as they climb. They are lost.

We turn and flee; the ground looks wrong, the air smells of death. The soil glows green like an infected paw. The noise is ear shattering as the crack grows into a crevasse. The man escapes with three of his comrades. We lost four of our pack, and I didn't like the odds of another engagement on these terms. This was not like fighting a bear, we need to be more cunning. Number one is dead; I am the leader now.

We rest and feast on wild hog from the forest. The hogs were crafty and were difficult to catch but working as a pack we found we were formidable hunters. We drink from the stream and sleep. Sleep is a good time to soak up the events of the day and make sense of them, if possible.

In the morning, we return to observe the crack in the ground. We are surprised to find it has grown considerably, we need to make a large detour to circumvent it and continue our pursuit. The crack in the world smells wrong; I am keen leave. It is at least two kilometres wide and is slowly growing.

We head north and then east to avoid the crevasse. After a long pursuit, the chase turns south into Turkey, and we follow. They are headed south into Africa, roughly in the direction of Syria and Jordan. They are covering their tracks and spoor well; they are skilled rangers; they are no match for our powerful olfactory senses. They are gaining ground on us; they have may found transport to prevent us from following their trail. Somehow, they know we will not desist, not at any price.

We are forced to increase our pace. The ground is becoming sandy, it slides beneath our feet. I become hot and tired but press on regardless. I and my pack have resorted to sleeping during the day to avoid the worst of the sun's heat, we find shade and water in human dwellings along the way. We feed on wild cattle and camel mostly, the latter of which is not my favourite, it smells dirty like rotting flesh.

We are closing on them as we enter the Sinai Peninsula, we have them cornered. We aim to intercept the target at the Ras Mohammed National Park. My pack complain due to the sustained effort. From memory they cannot escape by land, but they could take a boat across the Red Sea. We must catch our target before he nears the coast.

We locate them as our target turns east towards the port at Sharm al-Sheik, but we are forced to retreat as the man invokes the weapon again. It is strange, we haven't been seen, but he was ready for the attack as number seven struck. We are close behind, but I feel the wrongness and I stop. The seed hits the ground and the earth shakes, I retreat but the remainder of my pack are too close.

The ground tears into a gorge, opening ever wider, my pack fall into the crevasse opening before them. There's nothing I can do to help them; they are too close. Our target appears to be invoking the weapon regardless of our attack, which is odd. As the crevasse opens further the sea rushes in, like the Red Sea reverting to crush the Pharoah and his Egyptian army after Moses parted it. But where are these memories coming from?

I am forced to pull back; the target has found a sailing vessel and I have failed. I need to retrace my steps to the top of the peninsula and follow them down into Egypt. Now there is only myself, I dearly hope that I am up to this task.

Towards the top of the peninsula the water narrows, and I am able to swim across. I walk up the sandy beach sniffing the air. The faint trace of human odour encourages me to follow the dusty coastal road for speed. The days were getting hotter, but I am determined to catch the man. He is evil and he is a danger. He needs to be taken down and quickly.

4. The Kramml-zo

The hunt for the Dark One's last son and disciple, Supay, was not going well. Supay had triggered detonations in several other countries including Malaysia, The Philippines, the southernmost tip of Greece, northern Turkey, and Egypt. Supay was single-minded in causing radical damage, aiming to destroy Earth and those living on it, regardless of the survival of his own race.

Paul and the community leaders failed to identify a pattern to the detonations initially, but the Pareth-ng AI finally discovered a scheme. Supay was detonating the device along the rim of the Earth's Eurasian tectonic plate. Over time the craters would penetrate the world's core and great cracks would be driven into the planet's crust. Supay was trying to destabilise the world, by moving the continents. This would cause avalanches, earthquakes and tsunami of biblical proportions. Volcanic eruptions would fill the air with so much dust that any remaining life would be wiped out, he must be stopped quickly.

Supay was adept at avoiding the AI's tracking mechanisms, so Paul and the team were forced to hunt him on foot. The Kraalt predicted that Supay would follow the continental plate perimeter and invoke the weapon periodically, to inflict maximum damage. Based on the spacing of the attack locations to date, the next planned detonations were likely to be near Djibouti between Ethiopia and Somalia, then retracing his steps to the north, heading for Tunis followed by Tangier in Morocco or possibly Gibraltar.

Paul sat with Franc and Sheena by their fire, planning their next move. Franc broke the silence, "Come on Paul, there's no point heading for Djibouti, Supay will already be there by now. We need to intercept him as he heads for Tunis. He's bound to track the coastal road to Cairo, up through Alexandria. From there he will head into Libya, moving west to Banghazi and Tripoli and on to Morocco. Tracking the roads through Butnan and Al Wahat are terrible, it would take forever. Using roads would expose him to our scanners as there is little cover, Supay would find it hard to source food. He would spend months chasing goats".

Paul considered Franc's observations, "You may be right, but if we miss him, he could reach Tunis and set off the device. The Kraalt believe he only needs three more detonations to inflict enough damage to destroy all life". Sheena became impatient, "Look, if we don't do something, he'll be finished before we mobilise. Let's get two more teams in place, covering the other routes then we can focus on the coastal road". Paul countered, "But we don't have enough men, they are trying to build the new commune in France". Franc smiled at his brother, "There's no point building a commune, if Supay blows the place. Let's pull a couple of teams in to help". "Fair point", confirmed Paul as he spoke to James via his Carocle, "They will mobilise by tomorrow, early doors".

The next morning, Paul received confirmation that Djibouti had been hit. Rusty was in position there, but the quake occurred 150km north in Aseb. The enemy were long gone by the time Rusty braved the vicinity. Rusty moved on to Cairo to maintain vigilance. It would be ten days before Supay reached Cairo, unless he used transport, but finding operational vehicles in Eritrea or Sudan was unlikely, vehicles were in poor condition in the area.

If Supay and his team diverted via Khartoum, they may find a car, but lose a few days in the process. Using a sailing vessel was improbable, it would be easily detected by the AI. Paul guessed they would use camels, if so then they would reach Cairo in around six days. Paul decided to wait at the intersection in Aswan, it was the only sensible route through. The Dark Ones would be tired and need supplies after crossing the Nubian Desert. It took two days for Paul to reach Aswan by camel, Sheena had managed to corral three of the beasts and fitted them with harnesses and saddle blankets. They had looted nearby villages for the necessary equipment.

Aswan was a historic city, the El-Tabia Mosque dominated the place, it stood atop a hill surrounded by once beautiful gardens. The mosque had a central dome, flanked by two minarets. Paul's team occupied a large house, on the outskirts of the gardens on the Salah al-Deen highway. Paul surveyed the area and found the two most likely routes in were the Luxor Aswan West Road to the west of the river Nile or the al-Jabbanah al-Fatimiyyah road to the east of the Nile. They needed to watch the river itself, in case the enemy used the cover of the waterway. The only highway to Aswan was the M75 motorway, but Supay was unlikely to follow it, he would be spotted from many miles away, he would be far too vulnerable.

Paul couldn't use drones or technology to watch the roads, it would alert Supay to their presence, he would simply disappear, as he had previously. The team were forced to operate in the old-fashioned way; they each took a route and concealed themselves. Sheena was equipped with a Carocle, as was Rusty. They were the first humans to take the newly developed Pareth-ng pico technology implant. Rusty found the pico-bots had completely eradicated his asthma within the first three weeks of ingestion.

Paul's role was to watch the Luxor Aswan West Road. It was difficult to keep watch 24 hours a day, he needed food and rest. The team had adequate supplies, but the inactivity aggravated Paul's knees. He woke a little after midnight to the eerie, heartbreakingly lonely sound of a howling wolf.

An hour later, Paul heard deep breathing as something enormous walked past, he kept very still and hoped it wouldn't detect him. As the dark shadow passed, it was the shape of a wolf but the size of a racehorse. It really freaked Paul out. He carocled Franc and Sheena to warn them, although they thought he was joking. When they accessed Paul's memories through the Carocle they could see it was no joke. "There are no wolves like that, this thing must be alien", exclaimed Franc restlessly, "and if it was so close, it knew your location and chose to let you be. The olfactory senses of a lupine are second to none".

The team waited three days, with no sign of Supay. Their assumptions were wrong, he couldn't have been following the rough path of the roads, or he had chosen to take the long way round. "No, I don't agree", challenged Sheena, "his pace of attacks is accelerating, he knows we are hunting him. He would move on to the next location rapidly, the fastest path is following the ancient trade routes, the Egyptians have been using them for millennia as the quickest way from A to B". "That's not quite true", replied Paul, "the preferred trade route has always been on water. He must be travelling on the Nile". "But I have been watching the river", queried Franc, "he must be under the water". "Oh shit! Is that possible?" Paul questioned uncomfortably.

Paul consulted the AI using his Carocle and explained the details of a potential route. "The average water level is 8 to 11 metres deep. The width of the Nile after Aswan is in average 2.8 km. The widest part of the Nile is at Edfu, with 7.5 km in width, and the narrowest is at Silwa Gorge, near Aswan, being only 350 meters wide". Paul further interrogated the AI on submersibles that would navigate the river. Naval submarines were too large to pass. There was one tourism company which offered a true submarine experience,

Sinbad Submarines in Hurghada had a 42-seater mini sub which could traverse the Nile, given additional air and diesel tanks on board. They could take the sub through the Suez Canal and enter the Nile at Ezbet El Borg and head down via Cairo, minimising the travel on foot required".

Sheena's tactical brain kicked in and she consulted Rusty via the Carocle. Rusty listened to the team's thoughts and dismissed them. "Sorry guys, your idea is crap, you're too tired to think straight. If they were using a sub, why on earth would they be traversing the Nile. You're getting bogged down by an assumption; we need to take a step back here. If Supay picked up a sub from Hurghada, they could easily travel to Djibouti via the Red Sea. They could then head back through the Suez Canal and straight for Tunis. There is no way they would contemplate taking the river, it's too risky and the current is too strong for their engines. Getting around the Aswan dam is problematic, and they would need to travel by land to Djibouti from Khartoum anyway. The passage from Aswan to Khartoum is impossible due to the Cataracts in the river, they are not navigable.

Paul researched the Cataracts, as he was not familiar with the term, the Carocle informed him. 'The Cataracts of the Nile are shallow white-water rapids of the Nile River, between Khartoum and Aswan, where the surface of the water is broken by many small boulders and stones jutting out of the riverbed, as well as many rocky islets. In some places, these stretches are punctuated by white-water, while at others the water flow is smoother, but still too shallow for a submarine'.

Rusty plotted the approximate travel timings for the sub, "Assuming the submarine would travel at 5-10 knots, it's 1290 nautical miles from Djibouti to the Suez Canal. At 10 knots it would take five and a half days but travelling at 5 knots it would be double the duration. They would be forced to travel underwater and would need to refuel at least once, unless they filled the sub with additional fuel tanks and air. They could use the snorkel to supplement the air in the tanks". Paul tried to focus his fatigued forebrain, "We might still have time. Rusty, arrange an evac PDQ and radio Phil to position his frigate in the mouth of the Suez at Port Said. He will easily pick the sub up with his sonar, and a single depth charge would easily eliminate a toy submarine. Phil is in Salina, it's only a day away if we need backup".

The spaceship flew to the mouth of the Suez, piloted by the AI, Cindy. They scanned the waters of the Red Sea on the way, but found no trace of the sub. "The ships scanners can't penetrate the deeper water, movement in the water flow causes distortion. It's hard to differentiate between an attack submarine and a submersible bus full of nuns", observed Rusty.

"What are the nuns doing down there?" asked Franc in a mock innocent fashion.

Paul's team dusted off at Port Said and made camp by the side of the canal. Rusty progressed to Tunis in the discovery ship to keep watch, for what good it would do. Phil arrived in the Phoenix the next evening. The team joined the crew of the frigate and began their vigil. The sub was likely to arrive in the next two to three days; it was improbable they had missed it. They waited patiently, but there was no sign of Supay and his followers. The following day Supay invoked the Kramml-zo on the small island of Pantelleria, between Tunis and Sicily. Paul observed disturbances in waves and could hear the ear shattering sound of cracking rock. The swell was unusually high as the Phoenix moved at speed toward the island, but there was no sign of the land mass Phil pointed, "The coordinates of Pantelleria are two clicks northeast off starboard. It's gone. What the hell could take out a whole island?" "We need to get out of here, if the crack caused by the Kramml-zo erupts into a volcano, then we will have a tsunami to deal with", suggested Paul. The following day Salina was battered by huge swells.

Paul gave orders to Phil. Sheena and Franc nodded curtly to confirm their agreement. "Head for Algiers, Supay will take the shortest route to Morocco now, they have one more place to attack and then it's goodnight sweetheart!" Paul was unsure of the extent of the damage to Earth, but the Kraalt believed a final invocation of the Kramml-zo would swing the balance and would unhinge the continental plate. After the damage was exacted, further attacks were pointless. Paul and the team had to stop Supay, there was no backup plan.

At Annaba in Algeria, the team found Supay's discarded submarine, wallowing on the rocks. "They most likely ran out of fuel, they will be on foot again now", announced Cindy. "That's over a thousand miles, and the vehicles will be inoperable", observed Rusty. "On camels, the journey will take ten days, if they use additional animals. You can only cover 120 miles a day on a camel if you drive them into the sand", added Sheena helpfully. "There is only one direct road, towards Algiers. Let's ambush them there", suggested Franc looking at the holographic map. Sheena smiled, "No. Let's take them as they cross the hills, there is better cover there. Our chances of success are highest if we hit them west of Bouderbala. We can find a location to observe the A1 highway and the footpaths nearby".

The ship dropped Paul and his team on the foothills due south of Ayt Khaleel, where they had panoramic views of the potential crossings. Paul, Franc and Sheena were on watch in the Atlas Mountains, which formed a natural border between the Mediterranean Sea and the Sahara Desert. Rusty left the team three trail bikes with fat sand tyres, electric motors and an unrecognisable power source. There was no obvious power train between the back wheel and the usual position for the engine.

Paul could only assume the drive was a part of the wheel itself. The controls looked familiar though, brakes and twist grip. The start switch was straightforward, being tagged with the word on big red button. Paul, Franc and Sheena hid the bikes in the scrub, shouldered their packs and climbed. Halfway up, the cliff path became sheer, Paul abstained from climbing any higher.

Sheena continued to the top and could see all the way to the desert from her position where she made camp.

They pitched their sand camouflaged tents and started their vigil. The stars were starting to appear in the night sky. The moon looked enormous, giving sufficient light as night fell, Sheena switched to image intensifying goggles, and they took turns on watch.

Paul was shaken awake by Sheena in the early hours, after making her way back down the cliff path, "Look! Over on the side of the old Arab dwellings. There's a shadow moving". Paul was groggy, but quickly cleared his eyes, "It looks like a horse or a camel moving between the huts". "Is it hell!" Sheena replied curtly. Franc woke, "Whassup?" Sheena continued, "It's large like a horse or camel, but look at its gait. Look at the front, it looks like a muzzle of a dog. Do you think that big wolf is tracking us?" The creature disappeared and didn't appear again. Paul admitted the creature gave him the heebie geebies, it made the hair stand up on the back of his neck. Paul chose to keep his M16 in his hands after the sighting.

After three days of vigilance, Sheena observed three men approaching on camels, following the dirt track south of the highway. Franc and Paul watched in silence, it could only be Supay and his men in this infection scarred world. There was no time to waste, the team quickly returned to the trail bikes. They left the tents, retrieving them would only slow them down. The team pursued Supay carefully. If they travelled too quickly, they would send up clouds of sand and be easily detected. The bikes were almost silent, their sound was easily covered by the restless wind.

A Moonlit Armageddon - Paul JC Edge

5. Walking the Plank

'Last Wish' live AI transcription

The Titanium extrusion process has progressed well over the last year or so. The drones had completed four round trips resulting in huge quantities of Titanium being loosely attached to the sides of the ship. Franc and Sheena's physical training has gone well, Franc believes he was close to his fittest condition ever, and his martial arts skills were improving, thanks to Sheena. They needed to rest for a few days, Franc had pulled the tendon in his left thigh, by over stretching on a roundhouse kick. He had started to teach Sheena Kendo; she was picking it up quickly. Kendo would be useful in combat with the Kraalt swords; however, it was increasingly unlikely they would engage anyone so far away from inhabited planets.

Sheena and Franc finished lunch when they observe a disturbance through the front viewing port. The ship's viewing ports were on all six sides, which made the crew feel less claustrophobic. However, the endless empty view of space had a way of making them suffer from isolation. It looks like space ripples, as if a huge sheet was being held up with planets drawn on it, and someone had shaken the dust off from it. The autopilot announces there is a Mbunalt exploratory vessel heading on an intercept course.

"What just happened?" Franc demands. The autopilot explains, "It was a ripple in the Blaszalak Curtain as a vessel crossed its border. The curtain is a vast illusion, cast over a significant portion of the universe where intelligent species exist. It has been put in place so less intelligent species are unable to observe life out here. Many planets that human astronomers have observed over the years are simply an illusion, created to protect the privacy of other races". "So, there is life in our quadrant?" Franc queries.

The autopilot indicates that the quadrant was teeming with life. However, it is forbidden for the numerous inhabitants to approach Earth until its people achieved space travel for themselves. The knowledge of the curtain had been gleaned from the Kraalt AI, it was new to the Pareth-ng as they were from a very distant galaxy and had minimal knowledge of the region.

The Mbunalt ship is heading directly towards the mining vessel, at the current speed it would arrive in a couple of months. "We can't leave here, we need to continue the extrusion, it's critical to our survival", comments Sheena. "No, but the Mbunalt are clearly interested in our cargo. We may have to defend it", Franc replies, "and I'm not keen on fighting those beasts". The ship points out the approaching vessel is smaller and is likely to be piloted by the Kraalt and not have warriors on board. "Let's hope so", Franc adds optimistically.

Eight weeks pass with trepidation. Franc chooses not to launch torpedo ships for training, as they may be observed by the potential enemy. Surprise was their only weapon. Franc and Sheena focus on using the training simulator in small bursts, to avoid motion sickness. The drones are due to return in a few days with another load of metals and minerals, Franc feels it is typical that harvesting would occur at the same time as the enemy vessel entered their space.

The vessel hails and Franc permits the Kraalt to board the ship. Franc considers it fortunate the Kraalt are willing to parlay, so Franc and Sheena aren't immediately faced with defending the cargo. It is, however, a risky business as there is only two of them to defend the ship, anything could happen as they converse with the alien envoy.

The ship is instructed to break up the meeting if anything suspicious occurred externally. As the ambassador boards the ship, he becomes curious. He immediately identifies the Carocle technology and seems to understand its purpose, speaking to the crew directly through it, the ruffles around his neck turn a light shade of blue.

"Greetings, I am the Kraalt. I am here to monitor your activity in our solar system. Submit for audit. You are new to this quadrant, however, from your greeting it appears you have met my kind before, I find it a little surprising as we have no record of any contact with your species".

He hesitates as he enters the main living section. "Your ship uses unusual technology; I haven't seen this class of vessel before. I have heard rumours about organic metals, but we have not witnessed them", announces the Kraalt. Franc replies, "Hello, welcome to our ship, the Last Wish. We are mining Titanium; we have an urgent requirement for the metal due to issues on our home world. We will be mining for roughly ten years, and we will be on our way. We don't want any trouble with your masters".

The Kraalt looks at Franc curiously, "Masters? We have no masters. You are obviously not a space enabled race, but you have space vessels and coveted technology. How is this possible?" Franc needs to be careful; he wants to avoid another Mbunalt invasion force attacking Earth.

"Please forgive me, we have encountered your masters before. I am not keen to discuss the location of our home world without concrete assurances of your peaceful intent, we are recovering from the Mbunalt's attempts to conquer our planet". The Kraalt looks incredulous, and the ruffles beneath his neck turn a gentle hue of pink, "You have been invaded by the Mbunalt pirates and you remain free from slavery, how can that possibly be?"

Sheena cuts in, "The Mbunalt tried to enslave us and almost succeeded, but we managed to defend ourselves". Sheena softens a little, in an attempt to influence the small man, "But the Kraalt in our world live in harmony with us. We freed them from the rule of the Mbunalt". The Kraalt becomes visibly uncomfortable, "That cannot be, we are not permitted to live freely amongst other lifeforms. We work closely with the Mbunalt, we began life as their AI". Franc continues, "We worked together to defeat the Mbunalt, one of the warriors lives among us with a child. Our ship has hybrid Pareth-ng and Kraalt technology, our AI is also a hybrid. We work together in harmony".

The Kraalt requests to establish protocols with the AI to verify the facts. Franc instructs the ship's data vault to share information but advises it to guard the location of Earth or any technological detail. It is critical to protect tactical advantages or potential trading rights. The Kraalt links with the AI and becomes inert for a few seconds. "Curious", responds the Kraalt.

The small alien is a biologically engineered self-replicating AI of Mbunalt origin. Franc's assumption was the Kraalt were designed by the Mbunalt at their prime before they descended into savagery, and the AI had subsequently become slaves. The Kraalt ambassador seems a little different to Franc, he appears to be happy to make decisions and is more independent than those Franc had experienced on Earth.

The Kraalt opens his hands and looks into Franc and Sheena's eyes in turn. "Let's start at the beginning, or as near as serves our purpose. I can see your race has struggled to adapt to a wider understanding of the universe, you have been helped by other races. Our laws forbid us from engaging with races that are not space-enabled, which is why we haven't made contact with you.

Your hybrid technology is advanced, but the use of polymorphic organic metals is beyond us. These technologies will be coveted by the races in our alliance; programmable polymorphic metal is unheard of. How your people have survived invasion from Mbunalt pirates is knowledge we would value; they present a danger to our society. The most astonishing fact is you have embraced races from extra-terrestrial cultures into your society seamlessly, showing great compassion and fortitude. However, your tendency to wage war will not make you popular amongst our well-established civilisations. We have skirmishes on occasion, but they are managed by laws and our governance, the Grune".

"Your understanding of my race is flawed", the Kraalt continues. "The Kraalt do not live slavery, we operate in harmony with the races in the alliance. However, some Kraalt have become enslaved by Mbunalt pirates who operate outside our laws. The pirates have genetically altered their bodies, they have biologically enhanced themselves with implants, they capture worlds and sell captives as slaves to the outer arms of inhabited galaxies. They also promote a disgraceful trade in unusual glands and organs. Our coalition fears the pirates, they possess impenetrable armour, and they are ruthless in the extreme.

The Mbunalt are not like the pirates, they are a civilised and mature race. There are many races in our alliance that you are likely to come into contact with. The other races you need to pay special attention to are the Fosche, who are very nosy and will try to acquire your technology. Be careful, they are nervous and can react aggressively to the slightest show of hostility.

If a Zaarch Umbra enters your space, my advice is not to hesitate, simply run. We don't know much about the dark ships of the Zaarch, often an Umbra will simply observe, but sometimes they will attack even unarmed ships. Their attacks are random and unpredictable; we don't understand their motives. No one has survived a Zaarch attack". "How do we identify one?" Franc enquires. "You will know when you see one. The ship is black and almost invisible. Your scanners will detect no lifeforms, but they are there", he replies. "There are troubled races across this quadrant, but our coalition brings order and peace to them, our quadrant is civilised and is quite safe, with the exception of the pirates and the Zaarch.

Sheena looks concerned and seeks clarification, "The Mbunalt are a peaceful race? So why do they allow the pirates to run amok?" The Kraalt pulls his face strangely, which Franc knows is a smile. "We cannot stop them, they are dangerous. If we were to attack one of them, pirates would appear from around the galaxy, we would be faced with fifty ships or more. We cannot defeat such large numbers with their armour and powerful energy weapons". "Like gypsies", Sheena observes. "Oh my god, Gypsies have powerful energy weapons?" Franc queries with a grin. "Shut up, Franc", retorts Sheena acidly.

The alien pursues his point, "How many pirate ships attacked your home world?" Sheena replies, "First there were three, another ten appeared soon after". The Kraalt looks surprised, "You defeated thirteen pirate ships after the Pareth-ng killed most of your people? It's difficult to believe". "It wasn't easy", Franc replies looking at the floor, remembering the death of his brothers Joe and Bart.

The Kraalt makes ready for his departure, "Thank you for your time. I will report you intend no harm with your mining operation. However, the Grune may become interested in the recent conflicts and especially your battle with the pirates. I suspect your planet will be safe for the time being, they are not used to losing. The loss of thirteen ships will be seen as a significant loss, rather than seeking revenge they will most likely flag the area as higher risk and seek to enslave planets from lower risk areas. They are a plague to our society, and anything we can learn to help us defend against them would be most valuable. Most of the people here are decent and harmless, we may have occasional disagreements, but we live in a state of harmony and trade is good. May your existence be beneficial".

The Kraalt ambassador returns to the Mbunalt vessel, and it heads back on its original bearing. The ambassador seems to be unfazed by the expedition, seeming to find the voyage of little interest. Franc hopes they leave them alone to get on with their job.

6. Secrets

Supay and his cell had taken occupation of an old Berber hut next to a dilapidated corral which had been hastily repaired to stable their camels. The camels had been fed, secured and they waited impatiently. The word Berber derives from the Greek word for barbarian; despite its derogatory classification these nomads had villages and travelling accommodations in the mountains. These hostels were free for travellers with no strings attached. The term barbarian fitted the new occupants much more appropriately.

Sheena proposed the team should attack the hut at 3am when the enemy were at their lowest ebb, she and Franc power napped as Paul kept watch. A little after midnight, Paul became aware of a presence. A large shadow had slowly crept past the rocks behind them, he was instantly alerted and woke the others gently. "We have company", he whispered. Sheena and Franc looked up and grasped their weapons, as a gentle growling sound broke the silence.

The team remained still, as the large shadow neared their camp. They could see the redness of the creature's eyes in the darkness, reflecting in the light of the gibbous moon. As it neared, they could see its eyes in more detail, to Paul they appeared sad. The creature was a wolf, but it was enormous. Its teeth shone in the moonlight, like the blades of many knives, with a metallic quality, they were not natural. However, nothing about the beast was natural. Its eyes looked them over, the gentle growling resumed. Franc was unsure if the creature was daring them to move or warning them not to.

There was a sudden sound from the hut, and the dog bounded off silently at considerable pace on a circuitous route towards the hut. Clearly the wolf knew Supay had a weapon and was being cautious. "Where did the wolf come from?" queried Franc, "It doesn't seem to be interested in us, at least not until its next mealtime". "It might be keeping us fresh", commented Sheena unhelpfully.

The team continued its watch, at 2pm all hell broke loose. The shadow of the wolf reappeared behind the corral, and the camels became nervous, they started to growl unhappily and make high-pitched bleating sounds. A dark figure emerged from the hut clutching a rifle and went to investigate.

A large shadow from behind the corral took the figure in huge metallic jaws. In a split second the other members of Supay's team exited the hut and opened fire. The wolf tore the figure apart but was astonished when his victim burst into white flame in his mouth. The wolf ejected the remains and fled. Sheena opened fire and took down one of the remaining team, who flamed instantly.

Paul and Franc's vision was lost for a couple of seconds, providing the third member of Supay's team sufficient time to escape with one of the camels. Paul could see the wolf's shadow tracking the camel, roughly a hundred metres upland. The enemy faced the wolf, and his forehead began to glow green, the wolf scattered in apparent panic. The man, probably Supay, turned and fled. Supay was preparing to invoke the weapon again, but the wolf was intelligent and had experience of the weapon.

"Two down, one to go", observed Franc gently. "Yes, but Supay knows we are here now", commented Sheena, "we can't take him on directly, whilst he has the Kramml-zo and is keen to use it". "No, we need to ambush Supay, let's withdraw and set a trap further down the line, in Morocco", suggested Paul. Franc took a look in the hut, it was largely empty, "There's a few klims in here, which they may have used to sleep on. Nothing of interest". "What's a klim", asked Sheena curiously. Franc clarified, "A Berber tapestry rug, they use them like blankets, they smell like camels".

Rusty picked up the team and managed to acquire the location of the camel and its rider using the ship's scanners. It soon became apparent the camel shape had lost size and mass. "Supay's left the camel; he knows we are tracking him. He has some means to make himself invisible to our technology", observed Paul. "Damn", shouted Rusty punching the console, frustrated. Sheena wrapped her arms around him and kissed him on the cheek, "We'll get him. We know where he is headed". "Let's not make too many assumptions, we know where he is likely to be headed based on probabilities. It not a done deal. Let's hope that he hasn't realised we are extrapolating to predict his targets", warned Paul. "Let's wait for first light, and see if he's left any tracks", offered Sheena.

At first light, after sleep and nourishment, the team were back on the ground with Rusty, following the camel tracks. Rusty felt frustrated, "There's not much I can do to help here, Sheena is the better tracker. I'll recover the tents and bikes". "Cool", replied Paul. Sheena stopped. "There has been movement in the sand, but here", she pointed at a hoof mark, "the compressions have reduced in the sand". "Meaning?"

enquired Franc. "Meaning that the camels weight reduced, probably because Supay had dismounted the animal", Sheena explained. She used the back of her hand to gently move aside layers in the sand, "Supay is covering his tracks well, he has slid away from the camel on his belly to reduce the compression in the sand, whilst sweeping the trail with a branch. This is an old SAS trick, but I can still follow the smaller indentations of his forearms and knees, if the sand hasn't blown around too much". She continued to follow for a while, but shouted in exasperation, "Sorry guys, it's moved too much. Sand tracking is a pig!"

The team returned to the spaceship and headed to Tangier, in Morocco. "Supay will either take the main highway, or keep close to it, or he will follow the coast through Oran and Nador", calculated Paul. "Which is the most direct route?" asked Franc as if to himself, "the main road is too far round". Sheena added, "He's on his own, adrenaline will make him drive hard to complete his task quickly. He knows we will reacquire him fairly soon. He will head directly to Tangier and set off the device".

"Assuming he activates the device in Tangier, it could be anywhere on that coastline, or even Gibraltar. Supay will travel as far as he can along the edge of the continental plate, and he will most likely detonate if threatened. We have very little chance of stopping him, but stop him we must", said Paul building on Sheena's thoughts. "We need to surprise him, or we are lost. Assuming then, he will follow the plate, it is most likely he will take the coastal road. Let's set up an ambush near Al Hoceima, here. Supay won't follow the road, he will follow the coast through the national park", added Sheena indicating the location on the map.

Rusty dropped the team near the coast in the centre of Al Hoceima National Park. The drop was surrounded by high limestone cliffs to the south and the rocky shoreline of the Mediterranean Sea to the northwest. Ospreys filled the sky, alarmed by the team's arrival. "We will need to watch out for these suckers", observed Sheena, "one move and they will take to the skies, giving Supay a loud and clear warning". "At least it's not so sandy", smiled Franc, "we can work here". Sheena and Franc surveyed the area and identified the most likely routes for ingress from the east. Franc and Paul built hides as Sheena located her preferred vantage point.

Paul's team were well prepared by the time Supay arrived. This time it was Supay who sent the ospreys streaking into the sky. Paul lay in his hide, rifle pointing east. Franc was almost a mile inland on marginally higher ground, nestled in an indentation in the lower cliff face, with good cover from boulders. Sheena sat on top of the cliff watching the area with binoculars with covers to stop the lenses from reflecting the light. A reflection from anything shiny could be seen and easily bring about the end of the world. Paul liked to have the last word, "The stakes are high folks, if Supay sets off the device, we are sunk. We need to take him down quickly and permanently". The team activated a private Carocle channel between them and Rusty to avoid alerting Supay.

As the ospreys continued to circle, Sheena acquired her target. "He's coming down the coast side, on the lower ground. Right into your path Paul", she spoke using the Carocle's ability to converse silently between minds. Paul removed the safety catch on his rifle and waited. "He's a click out at 2 o'clock", Sheena advised.

Paul saw nothing for a moment, but then the movement became apparent. He acquired Supay but didn't dare risk a shot at such long distance. It was unlikely he would score a kill at that range. Paul's marksmanship was good, but not good enough to gamble the fate of the world on. Supay was moving stealthily on all fours, close to the ground to avoid spooking the wildlife. He used the cover of rocks and trees, and often disappeared only to re-emerge from the undergrowth further down the trail following the flow of the terrain. He moved steadily to his own rhythm with no sudden movements.

Supay was wearing a camouflaged jacket which changed with the terrain, it appeared unusual in texture. Perhaps his jacket helped him evade the ship's scanners. Supay's gait reminded Paul of a cat stalking a bird. There were long pauses as he watched his surroundings. Clearly, he was very cautious, as he had identified this area as a potential ambush. Supay was no fool. "Keep very still", Sheena advised softly.

Supay reappeared only fifty metres from Paul, moving directly towards his hide. Paul sighted Supay's heart in his cross hairs and squoze the trigger very gently as he held his breath. Disaster, the gun jammed and clicked making a metallic sound, Paul couldn't help but gasp in frustration. Supay was instantly on his guard as Francisco stood and opened fire on fully automatic, hoping the spray of bullets would compensate for the eight hundred metres between them.

Supay smiled, and his head glowed green as the Krammi-zo was invoked. "You nearly had me then", he said as he blew a bright neon seed in Paul's direction. Sheena screamed, "Run", as Paul took to his feet. Sheena screamed, "Shit, the wolf is back. It's closing on you at huge speed. Aim for the eyes!" Paul ran as fast as he could away from the detonation, "It's ok, I think the wolf is hunting Supay, it hasn't hurt us so far. I think it's...". Sheena cut in shouting, "Don't take the risk, it's a wild animal, it's unpredictable", then she gasped as the huge beast cleared Paul with a single bound. Franc sprinted away from the crack on a trajectory diagonally towards Paul.

"Why didn't ... you ... spot the wolf", asked Paul as he ran. Sheena replied, "I don't know. It's huge, I should have seen it from miles away, it must have hidden. Paul sprinted flat out, across the rough ground, he tripped and lost his footing but managed to recover quickly. Paul could see Franc running from the corner of his eye, on a course to intersect his path. Sheena watched the events unfold, unable to intervene.

The seed touched the ground lightly about twenty metres behind Paul's sprinting figure. Immediately there was a loud ripping sound, a fissure opened in the ground as the ridge glowed an unnatural neon green. The wolf leapt across the quickly forming chasm. Supay saw the wolf, he opened his arms smiling, as if to welcome the wolf into his arms.

Supay had completed his malevolent task and could join his father in the afterlife with honour. Supay mouthed, "Too late", to the wolf as it launched itself at him, taking his head and shoulders clean off. The wolf chewed and swallowed, then went into a frenzy and tore Supay's lifeless body to pieces, blood spraying everywhere. All Sheena could hear was the sound of Paul shouting, "Fuck fuck", as he ran from the earthquake, his brother Franc at his side.

"It's ok Paul, the crack is slowing now, stop running", instructed Sheena. "Nothing is ok, this is the end", added Paul with resignation. Sheena hadn't seen Paul's so despondent before. "We'll find a way", offered Franc gently. "No, we won't, we are royally fucked!" shouted Paul clearly distraught, "there's no way back from this shitfest".

The team gathered miserably at the craggy waterfront to lick their wounds, as Rusty piloted the spaceship to join them in the last of the twilight. Rusty built a fire, and they encircled it feeling numb. The group didn't immediately send word back to the havens, they felt the terrible news needed to be delivered in person. All four sat miserably, as if the world had ended. Rusty passed a bottle of Jack Daniels around, "Enjoy it, it's the last one we have, other than the replicated stuff of course". "Ain't quite the same", exclaimed Franc miserably. They slowly drank until they were well-oiled but became steadily aware of a fifth member at the party. Paul looked round slowly; the gigantic wolf lay behind them. "Looks like were not paying attention again", whispered Sheena as the others grew nervous.

In a moment of inspiration, Paul stood slowly and walked over to the wolf, Sheena became frantic. She spoke through the Carocle as she reached for her M16, "What the fuck are you doing? That thing just ripped the head off Supay, and it looks hungry". "Trust me; I have an idea", soothed Paul, "see how his skull is enlarged, it is no ordinary lupine". "No shit", whispered Franc as he clicked off his safety.

"Hello, thanks for helping us back there", spoke Paul gently, hands open in front of him. As he neared the wolf, a low ominous growl came from the back of its throat; Paul's confidence faltered. "Paul?" whispered Sheena. Paul continued slowly as he took a chewy piece of biltong from a sealed bag, "Here you go". Paul tossed the biltong towards the dog, whose mighty ears pricked up. The meaty snack hit the ground in front of the creature's nose. The wolf lifted its head and sniffed the meat, then with a gargantuan tongue it swept it up the tiny morsel into its mouth and chewed. "Good isn't it? Look I have a really important question for you. I want you to nod yes", Paul nodded in an exaggerated fashion, "or no like this", Paul shook his head. Sheena looked bewildered, "Has he gone mad, it's a fucking wolf!" Paul continued enquiringly, "Is your name Abe, by any chance?"

The wolf's expression changed to one of perplexity, it was a readable human expression. After a moment, the mighty dog nodded its head. "Jesus Christ", quietly exclaimed Franc, Sheena and Rusty in perfect unison. Paul used a stick to scribe the letters of the alphabet in the dirt, and passed the stick to the wolf, who gently accepted it into his mouth. "Is there anything you need Abe?" asked Paul gently, "Is there a way we can help you? Spell it out for me" The dog pondered for a moment, then dropped his muzzle and looked up at Paul sadly. The dog used the stick to indicate to the letters. Firstly, he pointed to the letter 'K', as he gained confidence, he slowly moved the stick to 'I' then 'L'. The wolf looked up at Paul and continued, 'L', then 'M' then finally 'E'.

Paul looked at the dog sadly as Sheena rearticulated the wolf's message, "Kill me". The dog was a monstrosity, a human mind which had experienced life in a human body then finding itself transformed into a huge lupine. It would be enough to drive anyone insane, it was probably only it's mission that brought focus and helped him to deal with the situation. Paul choked and sat down, he covered his eyes with his hand for a moment then continued, "Sorry Abe, let me think for a moment. I hear what you say, I promise I will help you". Paul emptied the remainder of his reserves of biltong onto the floor and the wolf began to eat it, pensively.

Suddenly Franc jumped up in a state of excitement. The wolf lifted its head quickly and started to growl. Sheena hissed, "Franc?" Franc addressed the wolf nervously, "Sorry Abe, I didn't mean to startle you. I have had an idea". Franc disappeared inside the ship for a moment and returned with a brand new Carocle. Paul carocled Barak, "What in God's name have you done?"

Franc explained his idea to Abe and promised it wouldn't hurt. He then slipped the Carocle onto the dog's head, which expanded to the size of the wolf's head and engaged. "Thought so", said Franc enthusiastically. The wolf was quiet for a moment, and then began to roll around in agony and started to howl. The howling turned to ferocious barking and growling as it ran in tight circles manically, then the lupine ran off into the distance at pace. "My god Franc, you took just a slight risk there, don't you think? If that creature turns nasty, we have no chance", worried Sheena. Paul cut in, "I think Abe has just realised who he is, and the cruelty that has been inflicted on him. He understands how his body had been cloned and modified, and his memories implanted into it. He's angry and confused, he can suddenly remember his previous life as a man, it must be too much to bear. I'm not sure it was your best idea, bro".

Paul and the team sat and finished off the whisky miserably. Why would they bother posting a sentry when the only threat was a wolf that could kill them even if they were alert and fully armed. What was the point, when the end of the world was beginning? The conversation wearily turned to Barak and the cloning and modification of Abe as a wolf. "Why would Barak create such an immoral monstrosity?" asked Sheena. "Desperation", spoke a fifth voice, "I had to do something, we had to eliminate Supay's threat before it was too late. Wolves are great hunters, I genetically modified seven wolf clones to make them formidable and intelligent enough to accept Abe's memories. I set them the task of retrieving the Kramml-zo. I had no options, I had to make a terrible choice to save Earth from Supay, he was psychotic and suicidal, a bad combination". "I guess I understand that, but haven't I suffered enough?" asked a sixth voice as the huge wolf re-joined the group and wearily lowered his colossal frame next to the fire.

7. Somewhere Else

"Are you ok Abe?" asked Paul gently. "I guess so, as good as I can be. The Carocle has reminded me of being a man, my childhood, all of my lives, my deaths, the endless cloning. It became overwhelming. I can see I have lived the most recent events of my life in a semi-conscious state, moving from place to place like I was drugged". Paul spoke in a calming voice, "I'm sure it did, I'm not happy with the way you have been treated. Firstly, Melak has re-cloned you whenever he needed an errand, and it often resulted in your death. Barak cloned large numbers of you to rouse the Shroom army. Now Barak resurrected you into an animal's body. Barak believed the end justified the means, but I find the whole concept immoral. I guess we humans abhor cloning, whereas to the Pareth-ng it is a way of life".

Abe replied hopefully, "That's true, though I don't remember everything. The Carocle made me realise I had become a weakened, antisocial and nondescript man. I got lost in a wave of self-loathing, but this time it was much worse. As a wolf I am strong; I run at great speed, I jump over bushes and trees, I howl like a banshee. Then the thought hit me that perhaps, just perhaps, I may have found friends in you. It has been a long time since I had intelligent company, so I have come back to see if I could cope with life in this unusual form".

Coming back to question of the weapon, Abe spoke cautiously, "I have been involved with the Kramml-zo and Kracz-el artifacts before". Franc soothed, "Yes we know Abe, we have seen your journals. You helped Melak retrieve the Kracz-el empathy device from the Tigers Nest in Bhutan". "I also disposed of it", replied Abe. "Yes, until Typhon retrieved it, Colletta has it now", affirmed Paul. "But the Kramml-zo, the really dangerous device, was stolen by Supay. Abe affirmed gently, "It is the destroyer of all things".

Paul gently walked through recent events for the benefit of Abe. "Supay aimed to destroy the world by destabilising the Eurasian continental plate. Does that make sense Abe?" "Yes, I'm not stupid, I used to teach History and Geography", replied Abe. Paul continued, "The Kramml-zo artifact poisons any matter it comes into contact with, rotting it over time as the infection spreads. When the artifact was invoked, the initial mini earthquake was Earth's reaction to the infection.

Over time the poison will sink deeper until it reaches the magma core, triggering the eruption of a large volcano. Supay has invoked the weapon to create a series of volcanos along the tectonic plate boundary which will irreparably damage the structure of the continents, they will shift causing tidal waves and catastrophic storms. The worst side effect will be dust clouds emitted by the volcanos which will fill the air, leading to the suffocation of every breathing creature.

Supay has completed his mission. The Kraalt predict that when the plates shift, no life can exist on the planet for fifty to a hundred years, it's an extinction event. We have a short time to live before the planet is catastrophically damaged. We are all in great danger, I don't know where we go from here. I feel lost for the first time in my life".

Paul spoke once more, "Earlier you asked me to kill you. Do you still feel the same way Abe, or could you share some semblance of a life with us?" Abe looked at Paul and smiled with his eyes, "As a wolf I was alone and confused, people saw me as a monster. I failed in my mission, and I had no purpose. I couldn't live like that, but with companionship I might be able to cope. Let's take each day as it comes. The Carocle device is a wonder, by the way".

Barak had been listening pensively, "Abe, come back to the abbey, we'll ease your pain and look after you. Your other clones are here, and they are learning to deal with life. I consider their care as my penance". The dog rolled its eyes, "With the greatest possible respect, piss off!"

Barak changed the subject, "Do you have the Kramml-zo artifact?" Paul and Franc looked at each other, then they looked at the wolf. Franc shrugged, "No, it fell into the crevasse when Abe bit off Supay's head, I believe". The wolf looked at Franc curiously. The wolf paused silently, trying to make sense of the information imparted. Abe looked at his comrades around the fire, "I don't really care for now, it is what it is. We need to focus on saving our planet. I will help however I can", he said.

Franc whispered from his favourite poem:
>"Good men, the last wave by, crying how bright
>Their frail deeds might have danced in a green bay,
>Rage, rage against the dying of the light"

"Dylan Thomas; I find your choice of words very appropriate. Do not go gently into that good night", stated the dog respectfully.

The four boarded the spaceship, the wolf followed closely behind making Sheena and Rusty feel more than a little uncomfortable. Abe sensed their trepidation, "Don't worry, I won't bite. Nor will I blow your house down". Franc tried hard to suppress a giggle.

The spaceship landed on the outskirts of Rennes in France, where many of the havens had formed their commune. James and Bridget joined a gathering of leaders, pulled together by the community leader, Gerard. Paul and Franc strode down the spaceship's ramp into the awaiting throng. Kate and Lucy and the kids made the brothers welcome; they craved some good news but could see from their faces there was none. Franc swept Lucy, Colletta and Audrey into his arms. Audrey whispered, "Mother is dying", into his ear worriedly. "Don't worry Audrey, we have great minds around the table, we can fix it", Franc assured her. He now knew Audrey was referring to Mother Nature from the context.

Rusty and Sheena exited the ship, but tried to avoid the attention of the crowd, they chose to spend time with their children. The wolf was last to leave, he was greeted by unease from the crowd. "Don't worry guys, Abe is our friend, he won't hurt anyone, he is gentle", said Franc with a confirmatory look at Abe.

Audrey and Colletta squealed in excitement when they saw the wolf and started to scratch his ears and stroke his muzzle. Lucy was startled and shouted, "No!" Colletta assured her, "Don't worry mum, Abe is our friend". Lucy lost the thread for a moment, then quickly recovered herself. She looked at the lupines expanded skull, then the Carocle encircling its head and frowned. Lucy stroked Abe's nose sadly, "What have they done to you this time, Abe? This is really not decent". Audrey asked her Mum, "Can we keep the doggy Mum?" Lucy was aghast, "Doggy? I think he is a person not a pet. Abe deserves a little more respect than that". Audrey suggested, adopting a cheeky grin, "Let's play Red Riding Hood", the wolf looked skyward as the girls chuckled.

The gathering met the Pareth-ng and the Kraalt at the Rennes Conservatory on the western side of the city in an ultra-modern meeting space and auditorium. Once inside, they sat in a circular arrangement, with Paul and Franc in the centre. Gerard stood and opened the meeting, "What news mon ami?" in his gently French accented English.

Paul and Franc reported the devastating news. The Kraalt and Pareth-ng looked on, deeply concerned. Bridget became agitated, "What do we do now? The world will end, and all of us with it. We need a plan". Ed, the appointed Kraalt spokesman shared his thoughts, "The fissures will continue to poison Earth until they form volcanos and shift the tectonic plates. The edges of the plates will form huge linear clusters of volcanos. All air breathing creatures will suffocate, and the dust clouds could remain for decades, before life can begin on Earth once more".

Bridget addressed Paul, "We need to build another haven, one which will ride out the effects of the cataclysm. We could build air filtration and regeneration, hydroponics. In time we can return to the planet's surface, to the sunlight, we could be ok". "It's not that simple", articulated the Pareth-ng scientist, Pascal. "Air filters would clog in seconds. We can't store sufficient volumes of air to keep us alive for a month, let alone for decades". "So how do you contain breathable air in your spaceships? You spend centuries in your ships. You had enough air then, do you decarbonise it", Bridget demanded desperately. Pascal responded patiently, "Our ships have the capability to refresh and redistribute air, yes of course. However, the ship also manufactures air by sending drones to gather gases from nearby planets and comets, gas giants, planets with atmosphere containing oxygen and nitrogen. We can't collect raw materials from Earth, other sources are too distant.

The room became dispirited, morale was dipping. Steve, the engineer from Summer Haven, broke off for a deep conversation with Phil, the botanist. Steve then addressed the group nervously, "Look some of you understand this better than I, but couldn't we generate air in the way the planet does now. We could use plants and trees to build a living environment". Pascal smiled good-naturedly, "For an environment of sufficient scale we would need real sunlight, lamps would not suffice. We would need irrigation, sunshine, insects, herbivore excreta, quality humus generated from dying biological life. We would also need carbon dioxide from our respiration, nutrients, air circulation such as winds, propagation, the list is endless". Phil spoke up quietly, "What we need is everything in our world to make it work, a rich ecosystem underground". Pascal looked at Phil, "But you cannot transport a piece of the sun underground. You can't use mirrors; the dust will blot out the light completely. The flora and fauna will soon perish. Our calculations indicate it could be viable for a number of years, possibly two decades, but the end result will be the same". Every face in the room looked thunderstruck.

Abe appeared at the back of the room. He couldn't speak but he articulated his considered argument through the Carocles as the audience became alarmed, "As was said in Shakespeare's 'The Tragedy of Coriolanus':

> *'Still your own foes, deliver you as most*
> *Abated captives to some nation*
> *That won you without blows! Despising,*
> *For you, the city, thus I turn my back:*
> *There is a world elsewhere.'*

We need to recreate our home somewhere else my friends, until the storms and the dust abates". "The dog's right", whispered Audrey from the back of the room.

The Kraalt leader, Ed, frowned at the group, "I don't understand the verse, but I believe Abe has made a good point. We have to leave Earth until the atmosphere settles down. We need to build a haven away from this planet". As the murmurs settled down, Bridget spoke up again, "How do you propose we achieve that, Ed?"

Ed joined Pascal, "I propose we share knowledge by merging our technologies, assimilating the Pareth-ng AI into the Kraalt. We are fascinated by your organic Titanium technology; it presents a unique opportunity to self-build a new world to our plans". There was a sharp intake of breath from the Pareth-ng, as their intellectual territory had been trod on.

Abe's deep lupine voice interjected via the Carocles once more, "I have a few quotes from Earth's history that may help the discussion along.

Firstly, Charles Darwin said, 'In the long history of humankind (and animal kind, too), those who learned to collaborate and improvise most effectively have prevailed'.

As Ralph Waldo Emerson said, 'Unless you try to do something beyond what you have already mastered, you will never grow'.

I honestly can't remember who said, 'If you have knowledge, let others light their candles in it'. You must work together, or we are all dead". "The dog's right", whispered Audrey from the back of the room.

Steve grew irritable, "Why's your child in here, these are important matters Franc?" Ed looked up at Steve and smiled in his strange Kraalt way, "Let's not forget we owe Audrey our lives, she alerted us to Supay and his intentions from the very first stroke. We owe our lives to her, as long as we persist". Mak supported this thought, "Audrey also worked with Colletta to eliminate the Mbunalt. She saved us on two occasions".

Paul considered Steve's comment, deciding to apply more practical logic, "I understand the Kraalt have made a big ask here, but we need to carefully consider if your technology will be of use when buried under a billion tons of volcanic ash, your skeletons lying prostrate alongside it, with no one left to remember any of us". The room quieted to receive this grim observation.

Ed smiled again, "For what I have in mind, we will need large volumes of organic Titanium; roughly approximating a quarter of the mass of your planet's moon. Please consider how we could achieve this, if you are amenable?" Pascal looked astonished and stammered, "But it's impossible". Ed continued, "Also we will need to capture the DNA of all lifeforms on this planet, Pascal, consider how you could use your technologies to store and clone animals, once the planet returns to normal. Phil, could you work with the MSM team to identify the logistics in capturing the samples?" Phil quaked, "It's impossible, there are billions of lifeforms distributed across our planet, many are microscopic".

Ed continued, "Please ignore the difficulties of physically capturing the DNA, Pascal and the Pareth-ng scientists can deploy automatons, once we obtain a significant supply of Titanium. Consider where we need to go, and what we need to capture. Identify the best locations to cover the largest spread. Don't waste your time trying to collect everything, use your pareto principle, gather the 80% in 20% of the time".

Ed sensed the building panic in the room, "Don't worry, we have at least five decades to complete construction of the facility. It will be some time before we have the quantities of Titanium needed, so harvesting must be our priority. My race will need to understand the full capabilities of the organic Titanium technology, and work with Pascal's team to formulate a new combined AI to design for our new haven. It will be the most challenging task we have faced, I'm sure that goes for you too.

Paul considered the plight of Gerard, who was chairing the meeting less than effectively. He was out of his depth and was faltering badly. Here we go again, thought Paul. Paul stood before the group, "Ok, we have a lot to think about. I propose that Ed and Pascal put their heads together, to try to build a new AI, which will drive this forward. On the critical question of the Titanium, could you both delegate someone to help Steve propose how we obtain and transport the material back to Earth?"

Steve looked at Paul with a deeply worried expression. "Don't worry, we will all help", offered Paul. "That's what worries me most", replied Steve with a weak attempt at sarcasm. "Let's meet back here in three months, to discuss our strategy in more detail, but please don't stop talking to each other. Good collaboration will ensure we build something that will hang together. The first space shuttle had its electronics designed by separate teams from different companies, and they each did a great job. However, when they attempted to combine the pieces, they wouldn't operate as a whole. NASA had to go back to the drawing board, we don't have time for this to happen here".

Franc re-joined Lucy and the girls, who were waiting in the gardens nearby. Abe padded behind him; the other delegates gave the wolf a wide berth. Despite his helpfulness in the meeting, one look at his shiny Titanium teeth made them nervous. Those who had known the previous incarnations of Abe understood he was a harmless person, but as a wolf the worry of wild animal unpredictability was bound to creep into their thoughts. Abe carocled Franc, "We need to talk". "Sure, let me touch base with Lucy, and I'm all yours". The wolf greeted the family, Audrey hugged him happily.

Franc sought a quiet corner of the park for a private discussion, the truth was wherever Abe went it was quiet, people would tend to migrate to another area. "I am worried", whispered Abe, "can you show me how to open a private channel with the Carocle device". Franc showed Abe the basics. Abe explained "Barak knows you lied to him about the Kramml-zo device, and you have been locking him out of your memory, he has tried to subtly probe your recollections to see what happened. He also tried to access Paul, Sheena and Rusty's memories to no avail. I am less astute with the Carocle, I believe he managed to access mine. He knows I ate the Kramml-zo when I killed Supay. I must admit to being biased against Barak, after he corrupted me, I also understand the deviousness of his previous incarnation. Do I need to worry about him?"

Franc took a deep breath, "To be fair, Barak helped save us from the Mbunalt. He led an attack against them in the mountains, he also helped Audrey and Colletta use the Kracz-el empathy artifact to persuade the not-dead to return to their rotting Shroom bodies and save us. He has been fair with us. His story is that his previous clone was insane, due to the long space travel and the feud with Melak. As a fresh clone, he has his memories, but can rationalise them clearly". Franc looped Paul into the conversation via the Carocle. Paul agreed with Franc's sentiments, but added, "On balance though, did Barak have a choice? If we consider the dark path for a second, assuming new Barak is duplicitous and plans to take power then he would still be forced to help us defeat the Mbunalt. However, I'm not sure he would willingly hand over the Kracz-el device. Colletta still has it, I believe?" Franc affirmed. The brothers agreed to be careful. Neither broached the subject of the device's current location, they trusted Abe to keep it safe.

Franc and Abe strolled back to his family. "Do you fancy hanging out with us for a while Abe?" Abe agreed happily, "Your daughter, Audrey, is adorable. I know the baby girl thing is an act to relive her missed childhood, she has an evil sense of humour which is delightful. You have a lovely family, and you have a deep understanding of my condition as they also have been re-cloned. I can't think of anywhere I'd rather stay, nor anyone who would treat me with such respect and friendship".

8. A Grand Design

Franc and Abe flew to Rennes with Cindy for the detailed planning session. The large lupine sat patiently at the rear of the main compartment. Colletta and Audrey were sad to see him leave. Franc had managed to persuade them to treat Abe with a little more regard, and less like their 'doggy'.

Earlier that day Abe realised that his faeces had been examined, which disturbed him. He detected that Barak's scent was subtly present in the undergrowth, Barak assumed the dog had swallowed the Kramml-zo and would leave it behind in his defecate. Abe never swallowed the device; it was secreted in a safe place.

The leaders of the commune sombrely filed into the Rennes Conservatory to spend their day considering the planet's future, they grabbed refreshments and headed directly into the meeting. The first topic on the agenda was the formation of the hybrid AI and combined knowledge base. Paul welcomed everyone to the session with Gerard at his side. First to the podium was Bridget, Paul found this unusual, but the rationale became clear quickly enough.

"Hello, for those of you who don't know me, I am Bridget. I am an organic chemical analyst by trade, I know nothing of artificial intelligence as you may have guessed. So why am I here? I have been included to present the new hybrid AI in layman's terms. Ed and Pascal's teams have worked together to introduce their AIs and begin to share their thoughts and knowledge.

For the AIs it was akin to two eminent professors from different countries meeting at a scientific convention. They needed to overcome language barriers, then collaborated to understand each other's methods and ways of working. The AIs shared understanding on techniques for information, knowledge and wisdom management as a precursor to cooperating on the design of a new AI. This process completed in eleven minutes flat". There was a collective gasp from the room.

Bridget took a breath and looked around to assess how her opening had gone. The room looked attentive and open minded, to her delight she hadn't turned the audience off yet, it was going well. Paul gave her the thumbs up. She continued, "The AI's merged their data, knowledge and rules under the well organised Pareth-ng technology and restructured their cognitive and inference logic, creating a new 'brain'. The Kraalt used their hive concept to consolidate the existing AIs under a single leader. This leader has a biological form in the shape of a man, making him more approachable and have good empathy with you all. We wanted you to feel that you could relate to the AI and would want him or her to be a part of the community. The AI leader has been implanted with the memories of a human, plus all the inference capability AI hive and the Carocle network. We now plan to roll out Carocles to everyone, so we can be in touch regardless of physical distance".

The auditorium fell silent as the lights dimmed. Bridget announced, "The real rationale for me presenting the new AI to you is now going to become clear. Please let me introduce our new hybrid AI". A heavily cloaked figure entered the auditorium, its face covered beneath the dark hood. The figure walked solemnly to the podium, stood next to Bridget and removed its cloak. Bridget choked and tried hard to hold back her tears, she hardened her face and continued, "Meet Joe, our new and rather astonishing AI". The room was shocked as they looked onto the face of their resurrected friend. Franc stood with tears in his eyes. Neither Paul nor he expected this development, they were in a state of complete and utter shock.

The AI spoke leaving no time for confusion, "Good morning. No, I am not 'Father Giuseppe', although I look like him. I do remember the love he had for you, and the good and bad times you shared. My vivid memories will help me to empathise with you, as we work together to save humanity. Please think of me as a homage of the man that he was. But please don't mistake me, I am your collective intelligence, and I am here to serve, as did Joe in his own unique way. I have begun to collaborate with our esteemed scientific team to solve the problem of sourcing sufficient organic Titanium to meet the needs of Ed's initial design ideas for the haven. I would like to discuss this with you after the break.

The room emptied, Joe received looks of warmth from many, but also concern as he worked the room. Franc and Paul walked over to meet him. "I am not your brother, as you well know. However, I do remember you and the challenges we faced together warmly. I hope we can be friends. "Of course", replied Paul, "it was quite a shock for us". "Understood. Please recognize, it was a clever move to help me integrate into society, but we had to make sure Bridget and James were on board with the idea before we could seriously consider it. However, we didn't consult the two of you, I'm sorry for that". "I get it", replied Franc, "but it will take some time for us to get used to the idea I suspect. Welcome to the team my friend".

After the break and copious amounts of coffee, the gathering reformed. Joe took time to continue to work the room and introduce himself to as many as he was able. Joe then took the podium again. "To obtain the quantities of materials we require to build our new haven, we are forced to think out of the box. There are many issues we haven't yet resolved. We have selected three planets as locations for mining and extrusion. These exoplanets are the gas giant AEgr or 'Epsilon Eridani b' in the constellation of Eridanus, 'Gliese 876d' in the constellation of Aquarius and finally Janssen or '55 Cancri e' in the constellation of Cancer. The planets are 10.5, 15 and 40 light years from Earth respectively.

Each planet is super-hot, and we will need to design a means for shielding the mining drones. I have already completed the design of an accelerator device to help transport the ships over the long distances very quickly, but the technology only works for the return journey. It will take 22, 33 and 88 years to travel to the planets respectively. We have enough time to harvest Titanium from the first two planets, however the third may be a no-go unless we can identify a faster means of travel. Use of the accelerator may help but would be risky".

The leaders were uneasy at the thought of travelling so far to gather the materials. "Aren't there any closer exoplanets? We can't wait 44 years to get the materials back from the first, let alone the others", queried Steve. Joe continued, "Understood Steve, but no. The accelerator will allow travel at near light speed, and will cut the return times to 11, 16 and 43 years respectively, if it works. We should receive the first batch from

AEgr in 33 years, we need an enormous harvest, and a means to transport it without loss. Travelling closer to the speed of light will introduce significant time dilation, which is unpredictable. The theories of the human physicist Einstein are quite correct. More time would pass on Earth than on the ship, which exacerbates the issue".

Pascal added, "Once the Titanium is processed aboard ship to become organic Titanium, it will form superstructures supplementing the hull of the spacecraft, so none will be lost during the return journey. The problem is the manufacture of such vast quantities will take years. As the ship produces more organic Titanium, it will configure parallel manufacturing facilities, accelerating the production exponentially, continually processing as the ship travels home. Unprocessed material is at risk of attrition as the ship travels at such high speeds. We need to protect the ships from asteroids or other matter in the path of the ships at high speeds".

Joe continued, "Thank you Pascal for the clarification. We will be able to launch the mining ships in a year's time, if we are able to overcome one last difficult challenge. I would like to use the diverse set of minds in this room to help find creative ways to eliminate this issue".

Pascal took the floor with Ed beside him, "The difficulty is the AI cannot manage issues that arise with other species as the mining progresses. It is highly likely other races will covet our technology and seek to acquire it. If a ship is found with no life aboard, then the facility could be seized. The conundrum is we need a living crew aboard the ships to manage possible hostilities". "Volunteers will be faced with taking out thirty or more years of their life performing this mission, it is a lot to ask anyone", pointed out Bridget. Joe interjected, "Sorry, in the interests of clarity, no biological entity could survive travelling at the speeds and accelerations we are discussing".

Abe was watching from the rear of the auditorium and was feeling out of his depth. He ignored the science as it was not his forte and considered ways to protect the ships from the asteroids. In simple terms, it was comparable to rocks being thrown at the ship, but at very high speeds, similar to castle fortifications being attacked with a ballista battle catapults. Abe spoke via the Carocle to those who would listen, "The Spartan Creed is: 'This is my shield. I bear it before me into battle, but it is not mine alone. It protects my brother on my left. It protects my city. I will never let my brother out of its shadow, nor my city out of its shelter. I will die with my shield before me facing the enemy". Audrey made no comment, it didn't cast a shadow on the wisdom of his words, she simply didn't understand the implication.

Franc decided to follow Abe's lead and take the smaller issue first. "If the ship's hull is polymorphic, can it hold a Mbunalt shield to deflect incoming asteroids or debris? I believe Abe is suggesting that we enable the AI to move the shields around to protect it. Could we hold up shields to protect ourselves". Ed seized the opportunity energetically, "We could use the power of Sol to remould the Aggt into interlocking squares, we could mount them at the front of the ship, the AI could deploy them to protect the ship. They would also defend against explosive ordnance or pulse cannon. The Aggt is too heavy to cover the entire ship, but by creating a mobile shield wall we could carry an optimised quantity". Pascal agreed Abe's suggestion would be a pragmatic solution to the issue. Franc thanked Abe for leveraging his detailed knowledge of the past to help us deal with the future.

Paul then brought focus back to the larger of the two main issues, the crewing of the mining ships. "It goes without saying we need to man the vessels. Please could I ask the Pareth-ng to comment? Obviously, you have the greatest experience of long space journeys. How do you overcome the effect of extreme forces at high velocities?" The Pareth-ng leader, Mak, responded, "We don't. That is to say we are unable to travel at such speeds, so we live on the ships as we fly through space. Nothing can survive on a spaceship when travelling at velocities approaching light speed", he stated with an air of finality. The momentum of the meeting slowed as ideas circulated, every single one being dismissed by the scientists. The hours flowed by, and they were not nearing a conclusion.

Barak broke the silence with a controversial topic, "I know this won't be a popular thought, but we could clone a new crew on arrival? The ship could be piloted by the AI as usual without a crew for the high-speed segment of the journey. The crew could be grown and implanted with their memories when the ship arrives at its target solar system". The uncomfortable silence in the room was shattered by a low growl from the wolf, Abe knew only too well the torture that would be inflicted on these poor souls. Barak continued, "I'm sorry Abe, I empathise with your feelings, but we don't have a choice? Does anyone have any better ideas?" He was greeted with absolute silence, except for a lesser version of the growl.

Joe stated his position clearly, "You all know the views of Father Joe on this subject, he was strongly opposed to cloning and genetic modification of any kind. I know many of you from

Earth agree. However, we need to accept that cloning is part of the culture of the Pareth-ng. They have not taken the decision lightly to adopt Earth's customs and desist with cloning.

A year or so before Joe's untimely demise, the Pareth-ng AI promised Joe there would be no more cloning. Since that day Barak cloned a hybrid version of Abe many times and performed genetic modifications to enhance his capabilities in this last iteration. I completely understand Abe's misgivings. It was a monstrous choice, and many quite rightly disagree with it. However, we are faced with the survival of our species and indeed all of the species on this planet. We must find a way to persevere".

Joe looked directly to Abe, "I'm not sure of the origin of the human quotation, but sometimes the hardest thing and the right thing are the same. Often the only choice is unpopular but must be made, nonetheless. I propose we make you two promises Abe. The first is, there will be no more merging of DNA from different species, it conflicts with the laws of the One. The second is, the re-cloning for the mining expeditions will be volunteers, those who understand the choices they make and will live with them when they arrive at their destination. The AIs will not facilitate cloning moving forward with one additional exception, which I will discuss later. Could you live with this decision Abe?"

Abe's low growl had ceased, Abe nodded solemnly. "I will keep you to your promise, but I need to hear each person make the vow for themselves". The gathering affirmed the proposal one by one. Abe specifically focussed on Mak and Barak, who both agreed; the former more readily than the latter, this specifically signified the last incarnation of Barak's clone.

After a long interlude with several breakout conversations, Ed took the podium with Joe and Pascal. Paul introduced the new haven team, "Ed and Pascal have worked hard assessing our options. We will now explain our thinking around our survival plan". Ed stepped forward, "You may be thinking we are planning to gather large quantities of organic Titanium; I will explain why. We have eliminated all possibilities of continued life on Earth, as we will be unable to construct a bunker to withstand the weather, the flooding and the poisoned air. We simply can't build a facility to keep the planet alive for such an extended period. We can of course build a facility with plant and animal life, using hydroponics and artificial lighting, but it would create an unacceptable life. We may need to live in this way for more than a century. The Pareth-ng have suffered with their long space travel and have direct experience of its effect on mental health. A bunker would also deny us the possibility of accessing resources from other worlds. Therefore, we have discounted all options other than our working proposal to build a new haven in orbit around this world.

We will form another moon in opposing orbit with Earth, both moons will have Earth as their barycentre, their shared centre of mass. In simple terms, if you look at the view from Earth on a specific day, you may see the moon appearing at night, and the Moon Haven appearing during the day. This moon will orbit in its own gravity well, at the point where the gravitational attraction of the Earth and the centrifugal force due to the orbital velocity of the moon counteract each other. This will ensure the new moon will remain precisely in orbit.

From an astrophysics point of view, we need to ensure the mass of the new moon is similar to the existing moon. Otherwise, the orbit velocity or height of the orbit will need to change. The former is not feasible, the moons may collide or pass each other, making the relative forces unpredictable. If we cannot achieve an equivalent mass, then the new moon will take a slightly lower orbit, either way we will find a balance point and achieve the same periodicity so the two moons will never come into close proximity".

The room went quiet. Ed continued, "We propose we position the new moon into orbit which will give us a life similar the one we have now. We propose to take some of the existing havens and other islands with diverse topology and rehost them. We will take large swathes of our oceans, to preserve the biodiversity of this planet's life. We will create a new, smaller Earth for us to live out the catastrophe. We will gather DNA samples of all life forms and build a gene library to allow us to recreate the animals and plants once Earth is habitable again. Joe will ensure the cloning is the last exception. The scale of the project explains why we will need to quickly source the enormous volumes of organic Titanium discussed earlier".

Steve spotted a hole in the plan immediately, "We can't create a new planet, it will be in orbit of Earth. The day patterns will seriously change, the tides, the flow of air across the planet. The gravity of the new planet will be less, we will float around in the atmosphere. Earth's gravity will have a more profound effect on the tides and winds on the new planet than our existing moon does now. Even if this were possible, it could be catastrophic". Ed smiled,

"You are quite correct, there are many factors that need to be mitigated. We have ideas to resolve these issues, but we need to test them. We haven't built anything on this scale before, but the Pareth-ng organic Titanium technology will help us greatly. If we programme the organic Titanium with the design, it will grow the superstructures needed, it's quite remarkable. We will also, however, need ships to defend our world, as this new ship will come under the scrutiny of other races. The technology will be coveted by them. This is why we need to waste no time; we must send out the mining ships within the year". The room gasped; the whole concept seemed implausible to the audience.

Joe concluded the meeting by discussing the need to gather biological samples, and the building of an 'Ark' to store them. Phil was tasked with identifying and prioritising areas of the world where samples should be collected. Phil was overwhelmed by the ask, but his friends rallied around him with many offers of help.

Joe pointed out that Salina and the Aeolian islands, the Summer Islands, Formentera and Iceland would be relocated along their surrounding oceans. A number of other islands, yet to be identified, would also be relocated depending upon Phil's analysis. The strategy blew Paul's mind, he and his wife Kate were shell shocked. The idea of moving enormous land masses into space seemed impossible, laughable even. However, the Kraalt and the Pareth-ng were serious, they clearly believed the plan was challenging but viable.

Franc spoke to Sheena after the meeting, they then tracked down Paul and Joe. "This is a shit crazy venture, but if you need someone to re-clone and run the mission in space, we would like to volunteer. We understand the compromises, the impact on our clones personally, but also the physical demands they will be subjected to. I know our clones will understand why we chose to do this, as they will have our memories. We will need training and support to manage unknown situations". Joe spoke carefully and purposefully, "Are you certain you want to make this commitment? Your clones will be born disorientated. They will have to train to become physically strong and fit. Also, they will die when the mission completes, there is no round trip, the forces will annihilate your cell structures. Are you really sure you can handle this?" "Walk in the park", grinned Sheena winking at Franc.

9. A Fertile Mind Growing Seeds of Paranoia

Cindy landed in the main square at Innsbruck in the early evening, well away from prying eyes. Joe had ensured that none of the AI's would divulge the incursion to Barak. The ramp opened and Franc exited the ship with Abe, "Be careful. Don't let them spot you". "I'll use the cover of darkness, they won't see me, don't worry. I'll call you when I need a lift". The wolf padded into the distance, initially on the B2 main road through Mittenwald, but then cutting left into the woodland. Even a beast of Abe's magnitude was instantly invisible in the grey of the forest.

The spaceship quietly lifted into the air and returned to a safe vantage point in the mountains. Abe made his way through the woods and stopped at a stream for a drink, he looked curiously at his reflection, remembering the first time he realised he was no longer a man. It was strange, he had acknowledged his brothers as wolves from the start. He knew he had been in a confused state and suspected he had been drugged.

Abe ran rapidly, crossing the border between Austria and Bavaria in under an hour, soon arriving at the woodlands close to Benediktbeuern Abbey. He crossed the expansive lawns cautiously, low on his haunches to avoid being observed. He could smell Barak; he was in a room at the rear of the building; the one called Conor was nearby too. Conor often fed Abe and his brothers and was fearful of the pack. Abe could also sense Conor was uncomfortable with the transformation Barak had implemented, and for that simple fact he found he quite liked the man.

Abe used the cover of the trees to quietly creep past a man who was taking a smoking break, the horrible odour suppressed his senses temporarily. The abbey had beautiful well-kept gardens and borders, which Abe could use as cover if he kept low. There were no exterior lights, the rooms were illuminated by candles. Abe could smell a waxy carbonised odour as he braved his way to the rear of the building.

A twig snapped with a loud crack; Abe froze to the spot for a moment. No one noticed, so he continued carefully. The middle room was well lit, and he could sense Barak's anger from within. Abe crawled with his belly to the floor, finding a good spot behind the water butts, where he could hear. What he was unable to hear, he could smell. The windows were not double glazed, so the sound carried well enough to make the most basic conversation audible. He lay low and waited, he was not disappointed, he could smell Conor as he strolled along the corridor. Conor entered the room where Barak was seething silently.

Barak heatedly paced up and down his chamber in the monastery. Conor attempted to placate him gently, "Come on Barak, it's not Mak's fault your family was destroyed. It was his relative, he is not even the same clone pattern". "I don't care, it's Melak's family that obliterated mine. Mak has been scheming with Paul and Franc since the beginning, I know he taught the brothers to block me from sections of their minds. They lied to me, Conor", asserted Barak. Conor continued to try to calm him down, "They did, I know. But they might be worried about the Kramml-zo weapon getting into the wrong hands. Supay has damaged our world, we may not survive. The leaders have to salvage all they can". Barak looked at Conor fiercely, "Supay is essentially a mindless marionette, following orders without realising his line of command is fractured".

Conor looked towards the window, took a deep breath and headed for the door. With his hand on the handle hesitating, he turned back to Barak, "You need to show a little more patience and understanding if you seek to fill Typhon's shoes". Barak bristled at Conor, "I didn't seek the job of Abbot here, you all placed the burden at my door, it would be good if you remembered that". Conor was about to retort, but then a calmness came over him, he controlled his breathing as Typhon had taught him.

"I will help you however I can Barak, as long as we put the needs of the monks and the rest of this world first. Times are going to get tough, and we can only hope Joe's plans succeed". "Yes indeed", replied Barak sarcastically. Barak's expression was hard to read, Abe could sense confusion. Conor left the room more than a little exasperated by his new leader. Things had not gone well since Supay found the Kramml-zo.

Abe's hackles rose as his wolf instincts took over, he felt something was not right and became angry. He knew Barak was duplicitous and he was about to charge the door, as Franc's voice soothingly spoke to him from the Carocle. "Calm down Abe. I don't trust the bastard either. If he chooses to betray us, then we will stop him permanently, but we need to be careful. It is entirely possible he has the means to hurt you. He wouldn't put himself in a vulnerable position. We need to withdraw and think this through carefully with Paul". Engaging the human part of his brain for the conversation had the effect of distracting Abe enough to calm himself. He quietly backed through the shrubs and trees to the edge of the lawn. He then crawled across the grass and then the forest beyond.

Abe entered the cover of the trees without being spotted, thankfully, but picked up an acrid scent from within the forest. It was the carbon smell of old fire, but there was something more insidious in its undertone. The smell of burnt flesh became more apparent as Abe ventured deeper into the woodlands. He followed a brook down into the cleft of the hill and he found a neatly arranged pile of cadavers. Most were charred badly, but one face was less damaged than the others, he looked carefully into the eyes of the dead man.

Abe bounded towards the abbey, his heart fuelled by rage and hatred. "Abe! Abe, what are you doing? What is going on?" Franc called desperately. The wolf ignored his calls. Franc desperately took the ship into the air, and Cindy piloted an intercept course which would take him dangerously close to the abbey. The acceleration crushed Franc into his seat, it felt like his organs would burst under the G force.

The ship landed between the forest and the town of Benediktbeuern, deliberately blocking Abe's path. Franc ran from the ship to intercept him. Abe identified Franc's scent before he had left the woods, as he burst from the trees, he could see Franc standing by the silver ship in the darkness with his open hands held wide. "Get out of my way", commanded Abe mercilessly as he bore down on Franc.

Franc pleaded with Abe, "Please stop, this is madness. You need to control the animal, Abe, it's out of control". Franc projected memories of him playing with his daughters into Abe's mind. Audrey giggling as she scratched Abe under his chin. They had no effect on the wolf, as it launched itself at Franc.

Franc froze, feeling it was the last second of his life, but he stood his ground resolutely. At the very last moment, the wolf swerved violently, his tail catching Franc in the chest, knocking him to the ground. Abe dug his claws into the turf and stopped himself, turning to check on Franc. The thought of hurting his friend diffused his rage. The huge wolf sniffed Franc, as he regained his feet. "Jesus Abe, that was just your tail", uttered Franc winded. "Sorry Franc, I lost it for a moment. Are you ok?"

Franc recovered his breath and asked Abe what had happened. Abe stopped, recollecting the horror of the clearing in the wood's cleft. "I found a pile of dead bodies, three hundred or more, they had been burned but one of them was recognisable. The face was mine, Franc. Barak has murdered all the clones of Abe he had taken into his care. Hundreds of them! Barak said, 'We'll ease your pain a little and look after you'. I now see how he looks after people, the absolute monster". The wolf was close to tears, as his head sunk to the ground, but then his ears suddenly pricked up.

Abe spoke urgently, "It's Barak, he knows we are here, he's coming". Franc whispered, "Get back on the ship and hide. I'll think up a bullshit excuse for being here. I won't engage him unless I have to, we need to keep our gunpowder dry until we know his plans". Franc walked towards the abbey, trying to appear relaxed. Barak entered the street, Franc waved.

Franc shouted, "Hi there". Barak remained silent and brooding. Franc continued, "Sorry for the late call, I just realised something, and I wanted to explain it face to face. I didn't want you to get the wrong idea". Franc sensed the smile Barak adopted was false. Barak spoke carefully, "Would you like to come to the abbey, we have wine from last year's batch?" Franc dismissed the idea gently, "Sorry, it's only a quick one really. I'm probably worrying about nothing, but I think I may have misled you. After the death of Supay, you asked me about the Kramml-zo, I said it had fallen into the crack. I remember now, it didn't. The wolf took Supay's head and shoulders in one great bite. The wolf swallowed the artifact, I have no idea where it is now, I guess it must have passed in his droppings, I'll take a look when I get back to Vulcano. He only defecates every couple of days, and usually in the same spot, it should be easy to track down". "Don't bother, I have already looked", whispered Barak under his breath.

Barak looked cynical, but the expression quickly left his face, "And you came all the way here to tell me this?" "Yes, I didn't like the fact that my words were untrue. I didn't want you to think I was hiding anything", explained Franc. Franc said his goodbyes but knew in his heart Barak was not completely convinced. He felt the invasion into his memories, Barak had accessed Franc's memory where Supay was killed and the artifact swallowed, but then failed to find other memories of the artifact. By a stroke of luck, he failed to notice the other memories of the evening which had been blocked.

Barak headed back to the abbey to think about Conor's words. He knew the monks respected Conor, as he had been very close to Typhon. As Barak was the cloned father of Typhon, he expected respect as a birth right, but with humans it wasn't that easy. Barak needed to earn their respect or demand it under pain of death.

A Moonlit Armageddon - Paul JC Edge

10. Too Many Coincidences

In the summer of 2027, three Pareth-ng discovery ships were launched on trajectories to the solar systems of Gliese, Epsilon Eridani and 55 Cancri piloted by the hybrid AI. The AI had instructions to clone Sheena and Franc on arrival, reinstating them with a full set of memories. It would be 2070 before the first ship arrived home. There had been much activity to design a custom mining operation for each of the exoplanets. In addition, the Kraalt had built three accelerators, which would be attached to the rear of each ship, to reduce the travel time for the return leg of the journey.

The Kraalt had plotted a specific route, which utilised the planet's gravity wells along the way employing the slingshot technique to gain energy. Franc and Sheena were fully aware of the risks from other species and the fact their clones would not survive. It was always uncertain to Joe how they would react in the face of extended boredom followed by certain death; their mission parameters might change. Such risks could only be taken in the face of impending death.

Phil's team worked hard to gather plant seed, animal embryos, DNA and samples of insects and microbiological life, with help from drones and micro-robots. They worked in all major landmasses where the biodiversity significantly departed from the islands nominated for the new haven. They also gathered animal life to inhabit the islands scheduled to be transplanted. Additional islands such as the Isle of Wight, Anglesey, Obi Islands, Sabu Islands and Barbados were planted with additional trees and oxygenating plant life. Giant Redwoods

(Sequoiadendron giganteum) were planted on the warmer islands where there were good fresh water supplies.

Phil argued the trees were not indigenous to Barbados and the other islands, and it was compromising the balance of the delicate ecosystems. He also worried that the water pull would impact each islands valuable potable reserves. Critical to the seed dispersion of the Redwood were the Longhorn Beetles, which lay eggs in the trees seed cones, leading to vascular reduction and drying out, allowing the seed cones to fall and reproduce. However, Phil was overruled by the team, as one of these giant sequoias could generate enough oxygen during its growing season for 20-30 people. In addition, a mature Redwood would remove and store roughly 800 tons of carbon from the atmosphere, as much as an average human produces in a lifetime through carbon dioxide emissions. Thirty maturing trees were planted near to rivers and allowed to spread across the islands.

Mak and his team were working on Barbados, surveying the island for relocation and constructing the initial sites for the injection of organic Titanium being used to support the removal of the upper portion of the rock base. The plan was to cut beneath the island using mole drones and surround the underside with a thin layer of the polymorphic material to allow it to be removed in one piece safely.

A plug would remain underwater to allow the island to be repositioned at a later date, it would then be bound by Titanium permanently. The drones and raw materials were to be injected via deep narrow boreholes at thirty points across the island, the drones would laterally cut into the rock and bind a network of Titanium beneath the rock. A strong but paper-thin temporary Titanium dome would be erected over the island making it airtight for the journey into space. The Titanium for the dome could then be reused for the transport of the next island and so on.

After five months, Mak's team returned to northern France to prepare for the next island. Mak was sound asleep in a small cottage on Rue De La Palestine, overlooking the overgrown Park 'Parc Du Thabor'. Mak's partner, Chrissy, woke in the night and was filling a glass from the newly operable kitchen tap. Chrissy became aware of a presence in the darkness, behind the foliage in the park. It was large, but she could only make out a vague outline in the moonlight. She immediately called Mak, who alerted those in the nearby houses using his Carocle.

Thirteen men grouped outside Mak's house, armed with M16 rifles, kitchen knives and pitchforks. As they neared the perimeter of the park, they could see the red eyes of a beast coolly examining them, weighing up its options. The men raised their weapons as the dark shadow departed into the darkness of the park. "Did you see how fast that thing moved?" observed Pascal. "It was big, I know that much, what was it doing here?" queried Mak. He asked Joe to scan the area, but the creature had left the confines of the park. The team returned to their beds, feeling uneasy.

The next morning, Mak discussed the events with Paul and Franc. "Ok, so it was big with red eyes. Who does that remind you of?" observed Paul. "Abe was here with me on Salina. There was no way it could be him", commented Franc. Paul pressed, "But Barak created seven wolves, are we really sure none of the others survived?" Franc was adamant, "No. Abe saw them all perish. He is certain they died; he was quite cut up about it. Despite him being a human in spirit, the animal part of him felt great affinity for his pack". "Joe, can you interrogate Barak's ship to determine if more creatures were grown?" asked Paul.

Joe discovered the AI in Barak's ship had cloned seven more wolves. Given the demise of Supay, there was no legitimate explanation for breaking the embargo on cloning. Barak's rationale for growing the original wolf pack was to hunt Supay before he unleashed the Kramml-zo weapon again. Joe updated Paul, who advised him to be vigilant. There were greater priorities for the community.

In the month following the last invocation of the Kramml-zo device, Barak had released the new wolves into the woods near the abbey. Joe interrogated Barak's ships AI to find the new pack had been implanted with Barak's memories, rather than Abe's. Joe also observed the pack were a mix of males and females. These wolves had the potential to be a mixed-up band, less mentally stable than the former pack. Paul confronted Barak about the wolves, but his explanation was they were to keep an eye on the volcanos. Paul did not believe this for a minute, a bot could perform simple monitoring. Barak was becoming a liability at best, or something more insidious at worst.

On Paul's insistence, Mak's team posted a guard on their camp at night. A few nights passed without event, and the team began to fall back into complacency. On the fourth night, the beast struck. Mak was asleep with Chrissy, when the alarm was raised via a Carocle message. He woke, reaching for his automatic rifle he kept next to the bed. Before he left his bedroom, he heard a scream. "Is that you Kelvin?" he called frantically. Kelvin was on the midnight watch. Mak parted the curtains to see a commotion in the street. Three of his team surrounded the bloody remains of Kelvin, guns pointing towards the park. They were armed with a mix of M16 and ArmaLite rifles.

The house rocked violently when the rear structure collapsed, as a wolf smashed its way through a wall. The roof tiles smashed to the ground as the door to Mak's bedroom was ripped from its hinges. The wolf burst through the doorway, taking the wood and bricks from one side of the wall. The red eyes of the lupine regarded him hungrily, Chrissy screamed. The beast took Chrissy into its massive maw and ripped her apart, as Mak opened fire. In seconds, the M16 emptied a full magazine into the face of the wolf. The gun clicked as the ammo was expended. The wolf had taken little or no damage from the ordnance, although there were lacerations to its face leaving its fur ragged, revealing bright shining silver of its organic Titanium skin.

The wolf savoured the moment, as Mak realised he was out of options and screamed in anger for the loss of his wife. Mak dropped the M16 and grabbed a hunting knife from the bedside drawer. Mak's despair was delicious to the beast, but the wolf had a mission to complete. Mak dropped his weapon and ran headlong at the part open window, smashing the glass pane to make his exit. The wolf was no fool, and had anticipated Mak's escape attempt, his jaws closed on Mak's legs, tearing them from his abdomen. The beast's face smashed into the wall in his attack, taking down another part of the house. The dwelling's rafters creaked loudly, and the roof collapsed onto the wolf. Mak's team engaged, opening fire directly into the eyes of the trapped beast expelling its hatred, killing it.

Paul and Franc experienced the last seconds of Mak's life via the Carocle. The team gathered, shocked and angry at the loss of their friends. A black mushroom began to grow from the point where the wolf's skull connected with its spinal cord.

Pascal contacted Paul urgently, "There is a large but familiar looking mushroom growing from the beast's spine". Paul shouted, "Get the hell out of there! Evacuate the houses and run. I'm sending my ship over to assist". "The fruit is enormous", replied Pascal sounding breathless as he sprinted away. The fruit exploded; spores were launched into the air. The light breeze carried the spores almost a quarter mile.

All living matter coming into contact with the spores died, including grass in the park, moss on the houses, insects and the Dandelions growing between cracks in the pavement. Four of the team who came into contact with the spores choked and fell. Their comrades ran for their lives, there was no time to consider the fate of those they left behind. They died, their bodies blackened it was like all the life had been drawn from them, leaving the corpses desiccated. They fell to the ground and fruit began to grow from their cadavers.

Paul hovered over the area in his ship, Rusty monitored the situation from the viewing port. "It's dark, but from the image enhancement and IR views, there's nothing living in the square mile surrounding the dead wolf's carcass, no plant, insect, or microbe", he observed. "Pick up the survivors and get them the hell out of here", commanded Paul. "Wait, what about the risk of infection", pointed out Rusty, alarmed.

"Joe, set up a separate accommodation in the ship for quarantine, we need it to contain possible contamination". A compartment was quickly configured in the ship's hull, and the survivors were retrieved. Pascal counted, "We have lost six including Mak and Chrissy. The fruit are releasing pathogenic spores but unlike the last virus; it is a more localised virulent attack, not even cockroaches have survived. This infection is designed to wipe out everything". "It's bloody evil, who would create such a thing?" asked Rusty. "We need to find out quickly", interjected Franc, who was observing the situation from his home in Salina, "I'm on my way". Paul sensed his brother's suspicions.

Paul and Franc understood that Mak's team had many questions. They believed the attack was Barak's doing but did not understand his motive. They could only assume he was reverting to his old behaviours. As a precaution they took Barak's spaceship on a pretext, the official reason being to deploy it to more strategic work. The AI updated Barak the next morning, and the ship lifted up from behind the abbey immediately. Barak was shocked by the news and became incensed, shouting abuse at Paul and Franc via the Carocle. They quickly blocked him.

Barak raged around the abbey, much to the despair of the other monks. Conor once again attempted to calm him but became the object of Barak's anger. Barak ranted at the top of his lungs, "They have taken my ship, MY ship. How dare they?

After all I have done to help them. I even gave Colletta the Kracz-el for One's sake. Without the artifact, they would never have influenced the not-dead to come to their aid". Conor gently corrected him, "They came to our aid, Abbot. I know for a fact they are grateful for what you did. It showed loyalty to them when they were least expecting it. However, your recent behaviour has been a little strange. You need to be inclusive, include them in your plans. Creating more wolves has added kindling to the fire". Conor's observations inflamed Barak, "Are you with me here Conor, your words imply dissent". Conor blanched and assured Barak of his loyalty, though in his mind he was losing respect for his leader.

Franc became insistent, "Barak is becoming a threat. His behaviour is more like the old Barak, the insanity argument may have been a ploy. He helped us only to protect himself, we are surplus to requirements now the invasion threat is gone, he is back to his main mission of destroying us". Paul was less sure, "We can't be certain, one of his wolves may have gone rogue". But Franc would not back down, "No! He wouldn't give us an honest answer about the wolves. We made it clear there would be no more genetic tampering. Abe would kill him if he knew and rightly so. Abe had found all the Abe clones dead in the forest near the abbey, Barak said he would take special care of them. I say we dispatch a team to take him down, and quickly".

"We can't be sure; we can't just execute him. We might have this all wrong, we need to give him a fair trial at the very least. He didn't kill Mak himself; we need to know if the wolf acted under Barak's instructions", added Paul. Franc insisted, "If we start pussyfooting around with him, he'll just slip through our fingers. I must also point out he keeps asking questions about the Kramml-zo, he's keen to acquire it". "Ok, let's gather data first. We can then make the arrest with proper evidence", suggested Paul. "I'll ask Abe, he's the stealthiest of us", proposed Franc.

The candlelight shadow of the wolf was concealed behind the trees in the courtyard of the abbey. Conor's heated discussion with Barak continued in his chamber. Barak was losing his cool again, "Of course I sent the wolves to monitor the corruption of the tectonic plates, why else would I create them?" "So why was Mak killed. It seems to me that the wolf was sent to kill your old enemy specifically. I'm pretty sure that's what the monks will be thinking", objected Conor. Barak spat, "Don't be so pathetic, Conor. Grow some balls. Paul, Mak and Franc are running the show. The obscenity calling itself Joe is corrupting our ancient ways making them impure, it's the Kraalt who are being cunning. They are plotting to build a new haven in the sky, they aim to leave us behind unless we act now. Melak drew the brothers in, like the children they are, he corrupted their feeble minds. The brothers killed every last soul of my family. They shall pay, I will have my revenge".

Conor blanched as the realisation hit him, "I don't understand", he stammered. Barak continued raging, Conor unconsciously backed towards the door. "Why would you destroy Earth, leaving us all to die?" asked Conor levelly. Something clicked in Conor's mind, "You sent the original pack of wolves because you wanted the Kramml-zo artifact back, to avoid the blame. You worried that Supay would be caught before the damage to the tectonic plate was complete, you would be able to finish the job yourself. You are sending the second pack to finish the job and retrieve the Kramml-zo from Franc and Abe".

"Precisely", replied Barak, "I am the Dark One, and I will have my revenge on the people of this world". Abe could see Conor retreat further but stopped at the doorway, falling to the floor. Abe could smell the blood, flowing freely from Conor's dying body as his life ran out.

11. Arresting Thoughts

Paul and Franc formed a strike team without further ado. Sheena and Rusty joined the twenty soldiers in the spaceship. Paul spoke to Joe's hologram, "Can I confirm that you heard every word of the discourse and can bear witness to Conor's murder?" Joe replied, "Affirmative. Barak has been deceiving us once again. The idea of the original Barak losing his mind in the long space journeys was untrue. Barak has deeper and more profound character flaws than we thought. In re-cloning him, Typhon recreated the monster".

Paul contributed to the discussion, "I don't think Typhon meant harm. He was following the old ways of his race, though I'm still not clear of his motivation. He believed, as we do, that Barak had become ill and gave him the benefit of the doubt".

Franc framed an open question to the team, "How do we engage Barak? Will the monks be standing with him?" "We have no way of knowing, we need to be careful", replied Rusty. "I suggest we hit the place in the early hours. We drop half the group into the roof surrounding the courtyard as the primary strike force, and deploy the remainder around the periphery, to enter the building from the outside or draw their fire. Suck it and see", proposed Sheena. "Is the wolf still in there?" she added as an afterthought.

"Abe is in the woods, he left when he could. He wanted us all to be a part of the decision to arrest Barak, rather than taking the law into his own hands", clarified Franc. "Good, he will be more use to us there, he can pick up any stragglers. They won't escape Abe so easily", expounded Paul confidently.

Sheena led the primary assault team, blue group, which dropped silently into the roof of the abbey. The team rapidly concealed themselves behind the twin minarets of Basilica St Benedict. Franc led the team which encircled the abbey, using the cover of buildings and trees wherever possible. Franc secreted himself behind a gravestone in the cemetery, by the main car park, it bore the words 'Klaus Benedict 1826', rather appropriately for a Benedictine abbey.

Sheena carocled the team on a private link, "Entered rooftop area, no visible signs of enemy. Moving in". Sheena waved her hand and the team removed rooftiles, cut the liner and slid into the building silently, she had trained her assault team well. Sheena took one last look from the top, secured her Kevlar vest, loosened her grenade belt, disabled her M16's safety catch, and dropped into the void. She was 58 years old and didn't look a day over 35. "She is good", remarked Franc to Paul, clearly impressed.

The void was largely empty, other than a few old papers and books. Much of the attic had been used as a storeroom as it was dry and available. Blue team moved onto the first floor starting with the Don Bosco Pastoral Institute. Again, the rooms were dusty and rarely used. The smell of mildew filled in the air.

Sheena and five of her team moved away from the basilica, leaving a group of five, led by her number 2, nicknamed 'Codpiece', as rear guard. They cleared each room, in every case expecting trouble, but being equally prepared for sleepy monks who needed to be placated after such a rude invasion of their privacy. Sheena reported, "Floor one clear, descending to ground floor".

Both teams took the staircases at opposing ends of the basilica. They had specific orders to clear the basilica last, as it had a large open space. Five minutes later, Sheena reported, "Ground floor clear. Green team, prepare to enter the basilica".

Franc moved his team in closer and surrounded the basilica building from the outside by the main door, "Green team ready", he reported succinctly. The team had found the building including the prayer rooms and dorms completely empty. It was deeply suspicious. There were signs of recent inhabitation, but no one had been in bed in the last hour. The beds were cold, the covers uninterrupted. Nothing was out of place. There were no spotters, lookouts or snipers. It was as if they had been expected.

Sheena clasped her hand into a fist and sent the message, "Engage". She and Codpiece ordered their teams to blow the doors and enter the basilica at speed, they penetrated the nave and ducked behind the pews on both sides of the chapel for cover as Franc's green team simultaneously entered through the main doors at the front. Paul found it strange the front doors were unlocked, Paul's team had charges ready to detonate them.

As Paul and Sheena quickly surveyed the area, they saw the monks sitting on wooden chairs near to the altar of the great basilica. A familiar slow hand clap filled the air, as Barak addressed the teams directly, "Welcome my friends, you are perfectly on time for the show. A little after 3am, how very predictable. It must be a great disappointment; I suspect you were hoping for a shootout. A nice little fight with your pathetic projectile weapons. I'm sure you had planned the engagement perfectly, my dear Sheena". Sheena looked at him and grinned evilly, "Come here baby, if you wanna good time".

Barak stood at the pulpit, with Herman Fürst at his side. Sheena breathed, "I see Barak has his chief sewer rat at his side". Fürst calmly walked over to the nearest monk punching him hard in the face, then smiled evilly. Cod reported from his superior vantage point, "There are no weapons visible, but the monks seem to be rigged, they are bound and may have explosive vests. Be careful". Franc called out, "Barak, you are under arrest for murder and treason. Come quietly and we might not have to gut you like the pig you are".

A dark presence appeared from outside the chapel windows, a low growl became audible. "Brought your pet with you Franc?" asked Barak. Paul stood and addressed the monks, "Abe knows what you did to his other clones, so I advise you not to mess with him. What are you doing Barak? These monks are your friends and colleagues, why would you want to hurt them?"

Barak laughed and dismissed the comment with a wave of his hand, "They are just pawns in a chess game. We now have lots of key pieces in the room, what fun! The monks have been injected with my rather unpleasant infection by my one true advocate, the stoic and utterly dependable Fürst. If any of them dies, then every living thing will die for miles, including you". Paul tried again, "But why Barak, this is fool's mate? We have embraced you into our community, we fought the Mbunalt together. You have a life here. Why throw it all away? It's pointless".

Barak gathered his thoughts, then addressed the group, "Revenge. You have destroyed my family, now I will destroy yours. We will all die here tonight; my hounds will destroy the rest of you. Forget your infantile plans to rebuild your havens in space, it will all be insignificant in a few moments. Allow me to savour these last few minutes before I execute you all. I am the Dark One, I am all powerful, see me and despair!"

Sheena whispered, "I have a clean shot". Franc responded with an urgent tone, "Don't, he's got this place rigged, he will have a dead man's switch, he's no fool". Barak lifted his arm, displayed a device and with a flourish engaged it. The team ducked their heads. When nothing happened, Barak looked at Fürst perplexed, "What happened, engage the device you fool?"

Fürst stepped forward and announced calmly, "I disabled the device. I also injected the monks with saline, so they have no infection to spread". Fürst smiled as he thrust his blade deep into Barak's stomach and twisted it, "Enjoy the exquisite pain of a slow death, my master. The monks expected no loyalty from you, they were dedicated to Typhon. Typhon was a good man, whereas you are a monster. When you killed my dear friend Conor, I swore to avenge him. Enjoy your torment, and your last moments before you enter hell".

Barak turned to Fürst and attempted a smile, but the pain was too great, "Did…you…think…I'd rely…on you? You…moronic stunted goat". Barak withdrew a concealed knife and cut Fürst's left femoral artery, blood spurted from his thigh. Fürst retaliated, withdrawing and thrusting his knife violently, pushing it upward into Barak's chest cavity, Barak fell limp to the floor. Fürst withdrew his blade, wiped the blood with Barak's cloak and sheathed it, then collapsed to his knees. Sheena ran to support him as the team began to untie the other monks. Fürst screamed through the bubbling red froth at his mouth, "Get out! He has infected me, the gutless bastard!"

The life was leaving Fürst rapidly, but his eyes still had a little light as he slumped on the floor, resting against the pulpit of the nave. The freed monks shuffled towards the exit doors. The monk who Fürst had punched paused to speak to him in his last moments, the monk asked him why. Fürst whispered, "I had to be convincing. I am truly sorry, but it was a necessary deception. In order to save everyone, I had to make Barak think I was loyal to him. I chose you as you are a good friend, I dearly value our fellowship. I hope that you would understand and forgive me".

The monk smiled a crookedly, "Do you treat all your friends this way Fürst?" Fürst eyes closed as he smiled at his friend for the last time. Sheena yelled, "Get out, the fruit is growing, we have less than a minute. You need to move, people".

Franc found the main door had been locked, one last trick from the master of deception. Sheena shouted, "Out of the way", she dropped her grenade belt at the hinge side of the door and pulled the pins, "fire in the hole!" The team hid behind the pews as the door blew, the front four rows were splintered and exploded. Luckily the Kevlar vests and helmets took most of the impact. One monk was not so lucky, he was impaled by a sharp door frame splinter through the abdomen. The others reached to help, as Paul screamed, "Leave him, there is no time!"

Two monks ignored the warning as the others left the building as fast as their legs would carry them. They headed into the woods, towards the spaceship. The breeze was blowing in their faces, which was a stroke of luck. However, luck was not an option. Joe had anticipated the worst and had landed upwind deliberately. The assault team entered the spaceship with Abe, the monks following close behind. They prepared for the short journey home.

The fruit exploded, exposing the two monks as they helped their friend to the doors. They made no sound as the invasive pathogen shut down their bodies and began to unpick their cells. Their bodies blackened and desiccated in seconds, they didn't feel a thing as they fell to the floor, the blackened husks of their bodies shattering on impact.

Mushrooms grew from the husks where their spine had been. The ship lifted and withdrew to a safe distance, the team observed from high in the sky as the spores killed all living matter in the area. The abbey gardens and a dozen rows of forest trees turned black and crumbled. The wildflowers in the gardens of the houses nearby became ash.

Paul addressed the group together in the ship, the monks agreed they would join the settlement in France. To a man, they had lost their appetite for the Bavarian mountains. The monks quietly shed their brown robes and Pareth-ng daggers. Paul looked at Franc and winked, "Our next task is locating six shroom dogs and putting them down humanely". Franc whistled, "That might be fun, especially when they bear fruit. They prove impossible to track, Barak made sure of that". Rusty chipped in, "Let's leave some poisoned meat out for them", he looked cheekily at Sheena who frowned at him, disappointed at the reference to her impure adolescence.

The ship landed at the commune in Rennes. Gerard greeted them and told the team to quarantine. Franc disputed his decision, as anyone who had come in contact with the spoor would be dead. However, he reluctantly agreed it was better to be cautious. Paul Carocled Joe, "We need to leave Earth as soon as we can, these wolves are going to cause trouble".

12. Too Much Interest

'Last Wish' live AI transcription

It's eight years into the mining operation, Franc and Sheena feel stir crazy. The same routine is killing them, so they try to mix things up. On alternate days they train as usual, but for the remaining days they attempt new activities. They had played crosswords, board games, cards, yoga, even attempted to compose music over the last few weeks. The latest activity is dancing. Franc hates it but will attempt anything to divert his thinking from his plight. Today the randomly selected dance is the Jive, the AI plays old rock and roll music and displays illustrations using old films from its complete archive of Earth's culture taken before the infection.

Sheena gyrates her hips awkwardly as they sway to the music. Franc stands on her toe, "Ow! You clumsy oaf", exclaims Sheena with a giggle. They try again and end up falling on the floor tangled round each other. Franc laughs, "How can you be so graceful in combat, yet be so clumsy when you are dancing?" Sheena pretends to be offended, "Me? Have you seen your dance moves? You look like the dancing hippo from Bed Knobs and Broomsticks doing a mating dance". "Jesus, how old are you?" asks Franc. "Eight years old, roughly. How about you? Actually, it was one of my mum's favourites, she was such a dreamer, like you", comments Sheena sarcastically.

They lie in a tangle for a while, gazing at the stars through the upper viewing port. Sheena smiles wistfully and plants a rough kiss on Franc's lips, "Always wanted to do that, don't know why". They both become troubled and separate their limbs but remain lying on their backs on the floor. "That was awkward", observes Sheena. "Yeah", replies Franc, "but it mystifies me as to why".

"I guess my memories are of Rusty and my kids. I feel guilty for having carnal thoughts for anyone else, I guess underneath the rough exterior I'm quite traditional". Franc ponders, "I feel the same way, I dearly love Lucy and the girls. The problem is I'm not actually that Franc, regardless of the memories I have. By now Lucy and the original Franc will be getting quite old, despite the pico-bots continually repairing their tissues. I am a different person, yet I feel so constrained by memories of someone else". "Yeah, it's not easy", whispers Sheena thoughtfully. They rise to try the dance moves another time and soon find themselves laughing again in a heap on the floor.

The ships autogalley produces two glasses of white wine, which they drink down rather too quickly. They then sit on the sofa, looking out into space. "This is a treat. I didn't know we could have wine", comments Franc. The autogalley clarifies that they are allowed alcoholic beverages, but in strict moderation as any change in behaviour may compromise their mission efficacy. "Compromise our mission efficacy", mimics Sheena. Franc reverts to the previous subject, "So if I am a different me, then Lucy and the kids aren't really mine. Why should I feel guilty? Why should I pretend to be Franc at all?" Sheena smiles, "Why don't we change our names, we can then be whoever we want. We can throw away the old chains and start afresh". Franc becomes enthusiastic, "We could, but I don't want to forget my past. I'll just embrace my memories alongside the new me, like a mutually beneficial divorce, if such a thing exists".

"Ok, from now on, I'll call you Sanchez. The old Franc is gone forever", suggests Sheena. "Ok, then I'll call you your old nickname from before you joined Summer Haven, JeT", offers Franc. Sheena warms to Franc's suggestion, "Yes, JeT. My real name is Jennifer. It was Rusty who started calling me Sheena to hide my old identity, he didn't want anyone finding out our true purpose liaising with the Swiss Guard. We were assigned by the Vatican to keep an eye on Paul and to assist, but we needed to fit in". Sanchez looks into her eyes, "I remember the story, how could I forget it. Your life was as harrowing as mine. JeT it is then. We are new people, we throw aside our old ties and allegiances, except for completing this tiresome mission. The folks back home are relying on us, and we owe them that much".

JeT laughs, "True, but when we finish, we are free from obligations, we've done our bit. We need to try to make a new life, somewhere out here". "Through the curtain", agrees Sanchez. "Yes, behind the curtain", affirms JeT, "we might even find our way home someday". Sanchez hums an old Wizard of Oz song, 'Someday Over the Rainbow' wistfully. JeT grabs Sanchez and looks into his eyes. They kiss and make love; it was hungry but sweet. Afterwards they lie together smiling. "I still feel a little guilty", observes Sanchez. "Yeah, me too. It'll pass", laughs JeT.

The bond grows fiercely strong over the following year. Time passes a little easier, but it is no picnic. Sanchez persuades the manufacturer AI to build a small starship, repurposing torpedo attack ships, allowing them to find a life when the cargo is finally dispatched. The manufacturer facilitates the request, as the quantities of organic Titanium involved are relatively small, and the mining drones had managed to gather an exceedingly good harvest. The large harvest unfortunately stimulates the interest of other passing ships.

The drones depart for their final mining expedition, a small green dome shaped vessel enters the solar system, appearing on the star map. The autopilot identifies the vessel as Baava, based on the knowledge imparted by the Kraalt ambassador. Further out on the map a Fosche Kallship is identified, it is heading on a bearing bringing it close to the red dwarf sun Gliese 876. The AI identifies the Baava vessel as potentially hostile, so Sanchez and JeT prepare the torpedo ships.

The Baava ship arrives two months later, transmitting greetings in universal language which the comms panel has been programmed to translate. "This is commander Ardv aboard the Baava vessel 'Gzand' from the solar system 'Gar4'. Please identify yourself". Sanchez formally introduces himself to the Baava commander and explains that his vessel is a human mining ship. Ardv expresses interest in the cargo and its nature. Sanchez explains that the cargo is metals and minerals for building a space station in their home constellation. Ardv becomes aggressive and demands a share of the harvest as a levy. Sanchez refuses explaining that the materials are critical to the survival of his home world. Ardv threatens to board the vessel, leading Sanchez to warn that any soldiers or their vessels will be fired upon. After a tense standoff lasting several hours, the Gzand retreats.

As the Fosche vessel enters the solar system, the Baava commander tries his luck again. JeT and Sanchez anticipate that both races aim to acquire the organic Titanium technology, and together they are prepared to fight for it. Within a week, the second vessel enters orbit and Ardv proposes a meeting. The commanders from both ships demand half of the cargo plus access to the technology to use the material. Sanchez respectfully declines and things turn sour.

Both ships launch boarding vessels, JeT and Sanchez launch the two torpedo ships. Sanchez approaches the four Baava vessels, as the Gzand opens fire with projectile weapons. JeT handles the larger Fosche landing vessel. Both torpedo ships attack fast and unpredictably, deliberately moving erratically, so automated gunners struggle to target them. The engineering lasers fitted to the torpedo ships rip open the hulls of the landing vessels like a hot knife through butter, within minutes the atmospheres in the main chambers of the Fosche ship is vented and the occupants are forced to adopt breathing apparatus. The main Baava vessel continues to fire, its attention now focussed on the torpedo ship. Sanchez's ploy is to distract them, to protect the mining vessel, but neither party wants to harm the cargo. The Aggt shields reliably deflect the ordnance, the mining ship takes no damage.

JeT flies in hot and low, ripping the underside of the Fosche vessel, which quickly engages its main engines in retreat. The Baava becomes more obstinate and continues to engage. Sanchez's vessel takes a hit to the main cabin and the atmosphere is expelled. Sanchez grabs a mask and straps it to his face, then puts the ship into a tight reverse. He flips the ship laterally, which physically hurts him due to the G forces, then strafes the underside of the Baava vessel brutally. Through sheer luck, he hits a critical zone on the enemy ship and there is a large explosion.

Sanchez perceives no sound from the detonation, as there are no air molecules to vibrate in the vacuum of space, but the flash is blinding, followed by a series of smaller flashes. The ship splits down the centreline and air pours out of the ship. The cadavers of the unprepared aliens float into space from the rents in the hull. There is a single survivor, a Baava female who has been quick enough or lucky enough to acquire a suit.

Sanchez couldn't leave the alien floating in space to die, it felt immoral. He uses his Carocle to communicate with the alien's comms device. Sanchez gives the alien instructions, "I mean you no harm. I will come in close, grab the tow line I throw you so I can take you back to my ship. You will be safe there". The alien responds acidly, "You will not take me alive, you human Kraac. I will kill myself before I let you torture me. Go back to the Crom and leave me be. I will see you in hell".

Sanchez realises she is an aggressive species, assuming he would harm her. He is lost for words; he has no idea how to convince her his promises are genuine. JeT had been listening, as she makes her way back to the Last Wish. "Just grab her anyway, she will come to understand". Sanchez considers this for a moment, "The problem is that in six months our mission will be over and there is no way forward. Our idea to take a small ship is not offering a her a great future". "It's better than certain death out here", JeT replies firmly.

The scan of the ship shows no other living lifeforms on the Baava vessel. Sanchez reels out the tow rope, but the alien refuses to grasp it. JeT opts to speak to her female to female, "Listen, you have nothing left here but slow asphyxiation and a painful death. Why not take a chance? I give you my word that you will not be harmed. We will only react badly if you try to harm us". The alien replies with words of cynicism, "I have heard about you, humans. You are murderers and liars; I don't trust a single word you say. The entire *Centriim* is awash with rumours of how you have destroyed spaceships with your dirty weapons and your war mongering. Your race has been at war with itself for millennia, now you are bringing your aggression into space and attacking the peaceful communities out here. Yes, we know about your Earth, we have been watching you for millennia. Don't think this attack will go unnoticed, the Grune are preparing for war. You will not get away with this, you Ganhas".

"The rumours are nonsense and misinformation. Humans live in peace with the Kraalt and Pareth-ng on our planet. We have suffered an attempted genocide, and we are facing extinction, our planet has been damaged catastrophically by alien races. We have done nothing but defend ourselves from attacks from off world people. We are the victims here. We are on a peaceful mining operation collecting raw materials to help save our race from extinction. Your ships attacked us. You demanded our property, and when we refused you opened fire. We have poor defences, so we were forced to attack as brutally as we were able. As I said, we are the victims here", argues Sanchez. "You lie. Your mission is not peaceful, you are stealing precious metals and minerals from the Centriim, and you are building a great warship. You cannot fool me, human. You are a liar and a cold-blooded killer", states the alien firmly.

JeT grows frustrated, "Ok, just leave her. She can freeze and suffocate. She is a bloody fool, and she is so bigoted and hateful, I'm not sure it would be a good idea to allow her on our ship. She would cause trouble and try to eliminate us".

Sanchez makes one last attempt, "What do you mean, steal. We are harvesting from an uninhabited exoplanet, light years from anything. Why do you consider us as thieves?" The alien carefully responds, "Are you really so stupid? The Centriim own this sector and all the solar systems within it. You need a permit to mine here. As you are mining unlawfully, we opted to claim one half of your product as penalty. My superiors explained this to you".

Sanchez considers the alien's comments carefully, "We were not aware of we were breaking any rules, we were unaware there was life in this quadrant. From your communications we assumed you were trying to steal from us, we were forced to defend ourselves. Look, come back to our ship, we can discuss this in a more comfortable environment. I promise you will be unharmed". "I would sooner die", replies the alien. "So be it", announces JeT calmly, as she re-joins the Last Wish.

Sanchez is still uncomfortable with letting the alien die, so he retracts the tow line, and engages the visor on his suit. He instructs the ship OS to eject him and take the torpedo back to the main ship. "What are you doing Sanchez?" whispers JeT in a tired tone. Sanchez ejects and uses his suit's propellants to move towards the alien female. He approaches her from the rear and grasps her spacesuit firmly. She objects violently but is unable to resist as he is behind her. Sanchez engages the suit's micro engine, propelling them back to the ship gently.

The alien complains and struggles all the way, but they enter the airlock regardless. Sanchez strips off his suit and attempts to help the alien. "Get your dirty ganha hands off me. The Grune will be here very soon, and you will pay for what you have done", she screams. She takes off her suit but retains a small breathing aid on the bridge of her nose to help with her respiration. She looks him in the eye, but she is clearly terrified.

The alien is humanoid but has a very faint blue tinge to her skin which is more prominent at her skull. This accentuates her large silvery eyes but is at odds with the fiery red bristle on her head. She stands a few centimetres taller than Sanchez but looks quite frail by comparison. The airlock opens and JeT stands by the door, her sword hangs loosely from her side.

"Welcome to the Last Wish. My name is Sanchez, and this is JeT", Sanchez articulates gently. Sanchez backs off and gives her some space. Sanchez's actions clearly surprise her, she was expecting to be physically attacked and possibly tortured. Sanchez grabs a coffee as proffered by JeT from the freshly brewed flask on the counter. He turns to the alien and offers her a cup, "I'm not sure if you will find coffee palatable". She takes the cup and sniffs it, "Is it a toxin?" but then she realises it was from the same pot JeT is drinking from. She sniffs it again, "It smells like the nut of a Jappa tree, it is bitter. She sips and finds it not unpleasant, then she continues to drink.

"My name is Phsang, I am from the Baava world of Baatra", she speaks softly. "I don't understand, I thought you brought me here to hurt me. To torture me for information. To experiment on me. I wasn't expecting to be offered a drink, it is considered a polite greeting in my culture, I am perplexed. Do you honestly mean not to harm me?" Sanchez explains the story of how Earth had been almost cleared of sentient life, and then how Earth itself had been damaged by the Pareth-ng. The complexities of the politics, but also how the community had found peace and lived in a makeshift harmony. Phsang is permitted limited access to the AI knowledge base to verify

Sanchez's story. Her distrust remains, but she starts to become more comfortable, her fears subside. JeT asks about the device clipped to the alien's nose, Phsang clarifies that her world has a similar mix of gases present in air, but she requires a different balance to breath efficiently.

As the days pass, Phsang learns much about humans and begins to fit in as much as she is able. She finds the exercise routines very odd, physical fitness is not a common pursuit of her species, their muscles do not atrophy with inactivity like the human body. Food becomes an interest to her, there are many analogues to her Baatran diet, but the flavours are more diverse. It takes her a little time to tolerate and become accustomed to the spices, but she starts to enjoy some of the new foods.

Phsang spends many hours studying Earth culture and their current challenges. She addresses Sanchez and JeT with her concerns. "It seems the Pareth-ng have caused numerous issues for Earth and its communities. Even when you embraced them into your society, they are causing devastation and upheaval. They are a barbaric race, who have learned to live in peace amongst themselves. However, when their families meet, they soon turn to barbarism". "True", replies JeT, "this is why the Pareth-ng chose to send each family to a different world. Those who remain are from a single family and they are working with us. They are helping us survive, their technologies are pivotal in saving our people".

Phsang reflects on JeT's comments, "My concern is your race is not space enabled nor are you mature, yet you have access to very advanced technologies, especially when it comes to waging war. You have fused technology from three of the most dangerous races, the Mbunalt pirates, the Pareth-ng and humans. The Grune will not take this lightly, you are a significant threat to the peace in our quadrant". The autopilot announces the approach of a Grune cruiser, it is a long way from their current position.

Phsang freezes, she pales as the shadow of another dark vessel materialises alongside their mining ship, as if appearing out of nowhere. "Perhaps you are not the most dangerous of races after all. That is a Zaarch Umbra, if they engage us, we face certain death", she whispers through clenched teeth. Seeing the reaction from their guest, JeT grabs Sanchez by the arm and indicates the torpedo ship bay with urgency.

"Wait!" screams Phsang, "For Ones sake, wait. You must not engage the Umbra; they carry terrible weapons. You have no possibility of even damaging their vessel, they will eliminate us in a heartbeat. If you can't run, offer no resistance. They tend to observe, evaluate and then they either destroy our vessel or will leave us be. We have no influence or control over their response.

This ship is unable to run, which is our normal protocol for encounters with the Zaarch". "The hell with that", replies JeT, but Sanchez gently places his hand on her arm. "We need to be careful, the Kraalt gave us the same advice. The Kraalt appeared to understand much of our technology, other than the polymorphic metals, which are no defence to us. If the Kraalt said don't engage, then perhaps it is good advice".

The Umbra appears like a darkness in the fabric of space, it occludes the stars, but no light emits from the ship itself, it is virtually invisible. JeT becomes frustrated, "Ok, if we can't fight then we should run. Let's gather up the Titanium we have and send it on its way and get the hell out of here". "We can't", replies Sanchez, "we need the last load. Ours is the second mining expedition, we are not sure if the third will arrive in time to save everyone on Earth. We must send back a full cargo; we are so close. We must take the risk". "One hell of a fucking risk", JeT raises her voice, "we might send back nothing if these bastards open fire on us". "I am aware of that", Sanchez whispers gently.

Nothing happens for two full days, but then something changes. The Umbra slowly eases closer to the mining ship. JeT becomes frantic, she feels it semaphores an impending attack. A moment before, Sanchez facilitated the drafting of an escape plan for them on the hull of the ship using a core-pen. The brainstorming session had gone nowhere, how do you plan if you don't know how close the ship is to the nearest inhabitable worlds? Much of the information in the data bank assumes the depictions on the Blaszalak force field curtain were real. The sector of the universe behind the curtain was unknown, clearly the Kraalt hadn't seen fit to include it.

Phsang works with the AI data vault, researching Earth's history. So far, she had not been happy to share information on the multiplicity of galaxies lying behind the curtain. The pen is suddenly wrenched from Sanchez's hand, there was no one present to exert such a force. The pen moves to the wall and writes:

> "All life's journeys are inevitably flowing to the Terminus
> The Zaarch seek the river, along whose course we depart

> I seek the small voice crying in the wilderness, we felt her call, it draws us in
> Where do we find the child? We need to locate the source of her gift
> You have one Earth hour to respond".

Phsang's jaw drops, "This is the first time the Zaarch have engaged in communication with another species as far as I'm aware". "They are obviously seeking something. They must presume we can help them in some way. But why?" replies JeT, "what do we have to make them think we could help?" Franc looks to the ceiling, "Well we had better figure it out quickly, or we lose everything". He pauses, then continues, "AI, do the Pareth-ng records show experience of contact with the Zaarch?" The AI confirms that although there has been contact, there has been no communication.

A total of three Pareth-ng ships have been annihilated by the Umbras. Pshsang summarises, "The Pareth-ng originate from far across the universe, therefore the Zaarch must venture the breadth of the entire universe. The missing piece in the equation are humans. You have some knowledge that they require. What could it be?" "I don't know, but the meter is running", points out JeT nervously.

"The first sentence in their writings discusses the Terminus, the end point. Is this the end of the universe, the outer reaches of everything? I suspect they know more than we do about that", offers JeT. Sanchez builds on her thought, "Are the writings referring to theology? Moving to the next stage of existence possibly". Phsang tuts loudly, similar to how a human would but it is more guttural, even rattly. "You presume the Zaarch are believers of the One? I don't, they only know how to kill".

Sanchez counters, "But you thought that about us, and you didn't understand us or our situation. Maybe they are desperate. Perhaps they have been searching for a long time and are getting frustrated".

JeT calms the situation using a distraction, "A small voice in the wilderness?" Sanchez considers, "I've heard a phrase like that before. AI, find me the phrases that appeared on my brother Joe's arms?" The AI recites the phrases in their English form:

- One of seven
- A voice crying in the wilderness
- As you sow so shall you reap
- Many are called but few are chosen
- The wages of sin is death

"The biblical reference to the voice in the wilderness shows they are warning people about the dangers of an important truth, but nobody is paying attention", adds the librarian function, "from the Earth Christian Bible where Jesus seeks guidance in the desert". "So why the small voice?" queries JeT. Sanchez continues, "We can assume the river refers to the path to the Terminus. Oh shit!" All faces turn to Sanchez to see the pain written across his features, "They are looking for Audrey".

JeT puts her arms around Sanchez, attempting to calm him, "Why Audrey?" Sanchez sits down and recovers himself, "Audrey hears voices. She is the one who called out to the not-dead and struck a bargain to save our race. She was just a child when she communicated with the spirits, hence the small voice. The Zaarch must have heard her call". Phsang calmly queries, "So they think Audrey knows the location of this Terminus?"

Audrey's protection is Sanchez's priority, but the Zaarch threat forces them to quickly consider their next steps. "I'm not going to tell them where she is", mutters Sanchez, "who knows what they plan to do with her. I consider her as my daughter...sort of". "What are our options?" asserts JeT, "We don't tell them, and we are destroyed, our community on Earth dies because they don't receive the cargo, including Audrey. Alternatively, we tell the Zaarch, send the cargo to Earth, and let Paul manage the issue, we can pre-warn him. Perhaps Audrey can provide some insight, who knows?" JeT was right, they had no option.

They pass the universal coordinates of Earth to the Zaarch using the note board; however, the Umbra stays precisely in position. The sensor array picks up three large ships closing on Gliese's solar system. "They are Grune. They could cause difficulties", observes Phsang, "but they won't approach whilst the Umbra is here, it's too risky for them.

A Moonlit Armageddon - Paul JC Edge

13. Beginning of the End

Bridget retrieved her walking stick and ambled to the front door of the Sanctuary, her main residence on Isola Salina. She waved to James, who was leaving to join the fishing party for the day. It was 6am and Bridget had not slept well, it was an increasing annoyance for her advanced years. Moving around caused discomfort, her arthritis was flaring up again. She was 112 years old, and she was very frail. Her son James only looked like a middle-aged man to her, but then she was no judge of age these days. She gathered some wildflowers and decided to take a walk to leave flowers on Joe and Enzo's graves. It was a lovely morning and promised a beautiful spring day.

The walk was less than a mile to the graveyard, but it felt like a marathon to her. Bridget was a determined lady, her grandmother's secret to a long life was plenty of fresh air, water and exercise. She was barely halfway when the siren sounded. She dropped the flowers and headed towards the centre. She turned the corner to the main square, becoming gradually aware of a presence in the trees. The wolf was dripping with water, clearly the beast had swum from either Sicily or the mainland. The red eyed dog smiled just before it pounced at Bridget, she had no chance. The lupine ripped her apart before the Guard opened fire.

The bullets had no effect on the beast, as it charged the men. The dog tossed the first guard around like threshing wheat, before turning on the others. One guard retreated as another bravely changed his magazine and continued to fire at the creature's eyes. The guard's aim was accurate, obliterating its eye, but the beast leaped angrily as it growled viciously. In his desperation, the marksman pulled the pin on his grenade just as the wolf's jaws closed on his torso. The grenade exploded inside the wolf's mouth, blowing its head apart. The beast fell lifeless to the ground, decapitated. Blood covered the cobbled stones of the square, as the locals emerged from their houses wailing as they saw what had happened.

A large black mushroom emerged from the wolf's spine. By chance, three more Guard arrived in the square before the fruit emitted millions of spores. Well prepared, the Guard located bags of sulphur which had been placed in strategic locations around the island. The Guard nervously emptied the sulphur onto the fruit and dropped the bag over the mushroom's head, tying it securely, taking care not to come into contact with the deadly toxin. They then began the arduous process of disposing of the large beast safely.

Paul and Franc were mortified at the news of Bridget's death. The penny dropped that the wolves Barak had released were hunting down their leaders mercilessly. Paul decided they should pull their key personnel into a single location, in order to protect them. "That may not help", explained Sheena, "we could end up facing the remaining beasts as a pack. I'm not sure we would be able to defend ourselves against all of them. So far, the wolves have been hunting alone and we have been successful. However, on their own they are more vulnerable, and we can take them down more easily". Paul considered Sheena's suggestion, "I agree, but on their own the leaders have no chance. We will die before the wolves are eliminated. This way we can prepare a trap". "Bait", observed Franc wistfully.

The AI endured an unprecedented breakdown following the death of Bridget. The core of its being was built in the form of Joe, including his memories and feelings, so the AI suffered terribly for the loss of someone it considered to be its wife. Eventually the AI recovered functionality and was able to function once more after feeling such raw overpowering emotion. The AI experienced the emotions associated with grief; it saw first-hand the value of human life and vowed to protect life at all costs.

Franc, Paul and Sheena made camp in the remains of the abbey at Mont St Michel. Pascal, Gerard, Ed and Joe planned to join them. Grawp and his lad Barn lived in the under chapel, having attempted to rebuild the abbey to its original splendour. In reality, it looked like a model of the original building built with a child's construction set, which deeply grieved Gerard.

The west coast of France was on the outer edge of the Eurasian plate and was at particular risk if the tectonic plates were to shift. Many havens were under threat, most of them sat on a boundary. Even Formentera, though not being on a plate juncture, could be completely wiped out by tidal waves. It would not be long before the havens would need to be abandoned for the relative safety of the more central land locked countries.

A day of tremors followed. The ground was starting to shift, and the plates rubbed against each other. In the years that followed the movement would increase causing multiple volcano eruptions at the boundaries destabilising the plates further. Oxygen content in the waterways would reduce as the dust spread, killing the majority of marine life too. The communities felt great trepidation as Earth shifted beneath them, they wondered if each day was their last.

The attack started at night. Two dark shapes were seen on the mainland, close to the broken causeway to the island. Paul waited at the front of the abbey with his brother. Ingress from the water would be problematic for the wolves, the rocks and castle walls were sheer. Paul chose to focus their large weaponry on the causeway and harbour as they were the most likely sites of attack.

Two wolves bounded down the causeway, leaping over the larger remnants of the old bridge. The Phoenix opened fire with its main cannon blasting pieces of rock apart as the large machine guns engaged from the walls of MSM. Rock was strewn in all directions, initially missing the wolves due to their pace. The shelling adapted to take account of their speed, and the explosions moved in front of the pack, as the crew learned to better estimate the speed of their target. The wolves intelligently varied their velocity, to avoid being targeted. Gunfire erupted from the harbour as three wolves swam into range.

At the causeway, Franc looked at Paul worriedly. "They will be here in seconds; they are not taking much damage, they are avoiding the ordnance", yelled Franc as he drew his Kraalt sword and ran down the hill. Franc reached the barricade as a wolf leaped clean over it, but Sheena was ready. She disembowelled the beast leaping over her head, her sword ripping through its underbelly. Even its Titanium skin couldn't stop the blade; it was infinitely sharp. It's steaming intestines fouled the cobbled street. The second wolf leapt the barricade as its injured packmate screamed in agony. Franc intercepted as it landed, decapitating it. The causeway cleared, so Franc and Sheena ran to the aid of the soldiers at the harbour. One soldier quickly doused the dead wolves in sulphur and waited to eliminate the threat of emerging fruit.

Sheena and Franc arrived at the jetty as Rusty launched an RPG at the leader, hitting its shoulder, knocking it aside. The blast had seriously maimed the animal but had not killed it. The wolf screeched; its blood covered the boardwalk. Another wolf leapt over its body, the gunfire having little or no effect on it. The creature tore into the soldiers at the waterside, tossing them left and right with its powerful maw. One soldier engaged the creature with a flame thrower, the lupine screamed in pain as it took him in its jaws. As the cylinder on the soldiers back was perforated by the animal's huge teeth it exploded, setting fire to the inside of the wolf's mouth agonisingly. The beast was instantly smothered in burning fluid, it leapt into the water and disappeared.

Franc dispatched the animal injured by Rusty's RPG using his sword. The third wolf hesitated and retreated to the safety of the water. By the time the Phoenix was in range to attack, the wolf had smartly followed the river estuary making it impossible for the frigate to follow it. It swam to the mainland at La Caserne and headed inland at speed using the buildings as cover. The AI followed the beast as far as the forest of La Ferté-Macé, but the wolf hid in the tree canopy until dark and then changed its trajectory.

Seven casualties were taken to the nave of the church for medical assistance, where there were well trained field medics on hand. Only two wolves remained, but they would be desperate, making them very dangerous. The wolves were unlikely to attack MSM again; it hadn't gone well for any of them. Barak was a coward, but in the form of a wolf he had convinced himself that he was invincible. He would seek revenge more carefully; the leaders would need to be cautious when they were forced to leave the protection of the island.

The damage to Earth had centred around destabilising the Eurasian tectonic plate, as many havens sat on its perimeter. The plate was sufficiently large to impact adjacent plates when it shifted. Barak had chosen his strategy well, the rumbles in the ground were not centred merely around the edges of Europe, the Kraalt had detected minor quakes on the bordering North American, African and Pacific plates. The structure of the planet was becoming more unstable as the years passed.

The first sign of serious trouble was the appearance of a new volcano in the ocean, which erupted near the northern Philippines and was the largest recorded eruption in history. Its silicic magma volume of ten thousand cubic kilometres was not unusual but it was a warning of things to come. The bomb was primed, and the clock was ticking. The magma was silicon rich, and the Kraalt made a point of harvesting the material, it was as easy as picking cherries off a tree.

The resulting dust cloud covered half of Asia, but luckily it had little or no impact on the nearest haven. Paul and his teams had no choice but to ignore the issues on the planets crust and focus on preparation for the evacuation. The Kraalt manufactured breathing apparatus and the havens prepared safe areas with air filtering as a precaution.

Four years later, a second volcano appeared north of India, the centre of its crater completely destroyed Paro in Bhutan, where the initial test of the Kramml-zo artifact occurred, the eruption was smaller than the first, but more explosive sending gigantic mafic lava bombs high into the air and pounding nearby countries. The igneous rocks were of special interest to the Kraalt, as they were rich in silicon, oxygen, aluminium, sodium, and potassium, no useful minerals were wasted.

Summer Havens botanist, Phil, worked with the bots to corral wildlife onto the havens, and gather DNA samples from every living entity. The mammoth task was akin to boiling the ocean, but Paul was very specific that Phil should apply the pareto principle, by focussing on the most important species and their food chains.

14. Beyond The Curtain

'Last Wish' live AI transcription

Phsang looks at the vague translucent outline of the Umbra through the upper viewing port. JeT anxiously makes preparations for the arrival of the last shipment of cargo from Gliese 876d. Sanchez monitors the growth of the new discovery vessel at the stern of the ship. All is quiet, the Grune vessel remains at a safe distance, due to the threat of the Zaarch Umbra. Sanchez transmits the coordinates of Earth to the Umbra and worries he has made a terrible error of judgement. His action may be the first step to the destruction of his family and friends, but then without the Titanium they are unlikely to survive.

The cargo merges into the humungous ball of material attached to the underside of the ship. The ship has trebled in size due to the processed Titanium becoming part of the Last Wish's expansive hull. The accelerator is primed with the calculated return vector, plus the self-destruct instruction. The time of departure is set, the countdown clock starts, Sanchez and JeT have one hour to make their escape.

The wait is tense, Sanchez attempts to pass the time by watching old Tex Avery cartoons, another relic held for posterity in the data vault. Phsang watches the display with a curious expression, she is utterly baffled by the animation. Sanchez laughs as a large chicken traps the farmyard dog in a shed. JeT becomes annoyed, "Sanchez, turn that shit off. We could all be dead soon; I don't want Foghorn Leghorn to be my last thought". Sanchez requests the film to stop, "If this baby blows, the last thing to go through your mind will be your cute ass".

The three enter the cabin of the newly grown discovery ship, the necessary supplies are transferred by the maintenance bots. The inside of the vessel is identical to the ship they have been living in, except for its reduced dimensions. They strap in as the mining ship departs. The cargo laden mining ship morphs to a long thin dart shape, to allow entry into the narrow accelerator. Sanchez watches, as the ship enters the tube, which glows florescent green, as it reaches the halfway point it is catapulted to near three quarters light speed. The ship appears to elongate as it moves away, an optical illusion as the reflected light takes longer to reach their eyes as it accelerates.

In a heartbeat, the Umbra follows the mining vessel into the accelerator and vanishes. "What the hell?" shouts Sanchez, "Tailgating isn't supposed to be possible". The ship responds, "The accelerator was reconfigured to point at the sun Gliese ten milliseconds after the mining ship departed, but the Umbra entered before the configuration changed. It will follow the trajectory back to Earth. The self-destruct mechanism will engage in 3-2-1" The accelerator glows green and implodes silently, there is no vibrating medium in space to carry the sound of the explosion. All that is left is a football sized blob of organic Titanium, which is retrieved into the body of the ship's hull.

Sanchez is concerned as he considers Earth's fate at the hands of the Zaarch, as if there is not enough worry, the ship announces that one of the three Grune cruisers is inbound. JeT calmly asks, "Can we outrun them?" The autopilot announces that the propulsion systems are of a similar nature, although the cruisers have more engines to counter the significant additional mass. It is likely the discovery ship could outrun the cruiser by a small margin but evading them is improbable. Supplies and food would become an issue over time. JeT turns to Phsang, "Will the Grune welcome you aboard their vessel?" Phsang smiles, "The Grune are not a physical lifeform, they are AI. They are peacekeepers for the Centriim, but they have facilities for search and rescue missions. They will provide me with safe passage to the Centriim, but if you come into tractor range, they will capture you". "What will happen if we head into the Centriim?" queries JeT. The alien responds curtly, "You will be allowed to dock, then you will be detained, awaiting processing by the Grune. The outcome will be the same, it is inevitable. They will charge you with theft and murder, both of which carry a life sentence. Your bodies will be held in stasis until the day you die, it's not a pleasant outcome. I will be unable to help you, I fear".

Sanchez looks at the floor, "What the fuck? Let's take our chances out there!" Jet smiles at him, "But what about Phsang, we can't just kidnap her, it wouldn't be right". Sanchez ponders, "We'll drop her at the Centriim and escape however we can". Phsang looks at Sanchez with concern, "You would risk your life to return me to my people? To my great shame, I have misjudged you terribly and for this I will always be deeply sorry". Phsang bows awkwardly to Sanchez and then to JeT. "Let's do this", announces JeT, "Autopilot, set a course to intercept the curtain". JeT grasps Sanchez's hand, they kiss briefly but passionately and settle back into their chairs as the ship accelerates on a course avoiding the Grune but passing through the very centre of the Blaszalak Curtain at full speed.

The ship exits the vagueness of the curtain, the Grune ships pursue a fraction of a parsec (a few hours) behind. The Grune struggle to manoeuvre their large capital ships quickly. As the abstraction recedes, a new constellation becomes visible. Phsang moves to the viewing port and points to the Collbra and Darikk solar systems. "Collbra is the main centre for the Centriim, around which the Grune, the Baava and Mbunalt worlds are in orbit. Darikk has an unusual mix of races living on its worlds, including the Fosche".

"There are five other solar systems comprising Centriim, but the others are more distant, and are difficult to observe from their viewpoint", Phsang explains. "Where is the safest place to leave you Phsang, somewhere quiet but with transportation?" asks Sanchez. "I wouldn't select somewhere quiet, you will be too conspicuous", counters Phsang, "they will observe unusual activity more easily. I recommend you make port on Space station Aal, orbiting Aalwa. It is the habitat of a multitude of races, you will be almost invisible, though we will need to disguise your ship, the shiny Titanium is striking. You will have a few hours to drop me off and be on your way before the Grune arrive. From there you can hide in the asteroid belt encircling the phosphorescent moon of Zetal for a time.

Zetal is the Mbunalt home world, so avoid leaving the area of the moon if you can; use the asteroids for cover. The Grune are currently on the other side of the curtain, and you will not be observable by them until they cross its threshold. If you keep moving, it will buy you time before they reacquire your energy signature. When things quieten down, move to the nebula of Grizs, where scanners are useless. After a few months, the Grune will lose interest and move on. Your ship will be monitored at all times in each vicinity, so it is important not to draw attention to yourselves. Blend in and stay safe".

The ship morphs to assume the shape of the Kraalt cone shaped vessel and changes to grey. The journey to Aal will take several weeks, so they relax and resume their usual exercise schedules. JeT and Sanchez take turns choosing old movies to watch in the afternoons, much to the amusement of their alien passenger. It is a long tedious journey, but their experience at Aal space station proves to be the diametric opposite.

The ship monitors the docking protocols using information from the Kraalt knowledge base. The problem would come during the docking procedure when the AIs interface and access to the ship's data is declined. When the ship lands, the game would be up. The ship adopts a unique ID by replicating the call made by another inbound docking vessel. The technique is likely to fail but worth the risk, they prepare a malfunction cover story as a contingency. The plan is to land, let Phsang disembark and then exit quickly.

From the viewing portal, space station Aal appears like a heavy metallic belt fitted snugly around the black moon's circumference. Phsang explains the appearance is deceptive, the truth is the station occupies the entire moon's interior, as a result of the moon's continued excavation over time. The appearance is utility, the visible ring has docking ports around it at regular intervals.

The station is home to a complex cocktail of species making it easy to be inconspicuous. The Grune retain tight control, although safe it isn't completely crime free, and it's possible they are classified as renegades. They need to be on their guard. Phsang describes Jet and Sanchez to the control centre as humanoid (or Baava equivalent) automatons; they aim to pose as androids.

The ship approaches port and begins negotiations with the port automation which immediately flags an exception. The ship is allowed to land in the bay, but a welcoming party of unusual looking aliens awaits them in the port. Phsang identifies the three waiting beings as Ferte technicians. They appear slender and humanoid, but with multiple rings forming a neck.

Their eyes large and intelligent, they appear to be armed. Phsang takes the lead, the Carocles translate the conversation. Phsang takes the initiative, "I am Phsang Kele-alla, I am a member of the Baavan consulate. My ship was destroyed, I was rescued by a human mining expedition from Earth, beyond the curtain. This ship does not understand the correct protocols, hence the exception. Please could you unsecure the bay, I can vouch for them". The Ferte lower their weapons. Sanchez notes a number of turret apertures distributed around the roof of the bay close up. The port appeared to be well armed.

Phsang leads them through the rough bay via the airlock doors. Sanchez and JeT wear suits to hide their appearance and help them breathe the heady nitrogen rich air. They carry weaponry as a precaution, though Phsang is curious when they strap the Kraalt swords on. Phsang removes the respiration device from the bridge of her nose and takes a deep breath of the fresh air.

Beyond the bay, the enclosure is gigantic. The walls are glowing blue, and the space is featureless other than a long line of docking bay blast doors. A huge variety of humanoids pass by. They appear to have somewhere to go, but it's hard to determine where in the bland surroundings. Phsang explains that the entire facility operates using a concept similar to 20th century Earth's virtual reality.

Implanted tech allows the participants to experience the facility akin to their own home worlds, and the need for expensive furnishings are not required. She wishes them the best of luck and disappears through an oblique doorway on their right. JeT feels Phsang was eager to leave their company. Sanchez looks around bewildered, "How do they know where to go? What do they do?" JeT responds curtly, "I'm not going to explore, we don't have time. Let's get the hell out of here before the Grune detect our presence".

"If you mention the name of a demon, then it shall appear", states Sanchez dully, as ten androids enter the space, nearby lifeforms move away, anticipating trouble. The Grune are tall and appear stocky, their body panels seem to be loosely attached to their limbs and tend to move around fluidly as they walk towards them.

Their faces are a hologram, displayed above their torso. Their hands carry long staffs. "Cattle prods", comments JeT. "I bet they are no ordinary cattle prods", replies Sanchez. He addresses the Grune, "Good afternoon, I am Sanchez from the planet Earth. This is my companion JeT. We are merely passing by, just leaving actually". The Grune leader speaks in clearly articulated human English, "The Grune are aware of you, you are fugitives. You have been conducting illegal mining operations without necessary authorisations, destroying a Baava ship, the Gzand, plus inflicting significant damage to a Fosche Kallship, the Kalo. You are convicted to lifetime incarceration".

"Fuck this!" shouts JeT as she draws her Kraalt sword, Sanchez quickly follows suit uncertainly. By the time he engages the Grune, Jet dissects three of the androids who simply freeze. Jet spins and takes the legs from beneath another, as Sanchez blocks the staff of a fifth, which cuts the end of the staff clean off. He then parries and severs the torso of the attacker. All hell breaks loose as a claxon sounds and there is the sound of marching metallic feet from the other side of the enclosure. JeT cuts the arms from another assailant in a double slashing move, turns and stabs an android that had manoeuvred behind her, the sword snags as another Grune lunges at her with its staff. Jet falls to the ground apparently lifeless, as Sanchez dispatches the remaining Grune.

Sanchez draws his Sig and opens fire on the approaching guards, they halt and raise transparent shields. He holsters his weapon and checks JeT; she has a weak but regular pulse. He hoists her onto his shoulders in a fireman's lift and runs for the docking bay. As he sprints, he instructs the ship's tactical AI to move the Aggt armour to the front of the vessel. Sanchez had ensured much of the Aggt from the mining ship was repurposed to their vessel, as they were likely to need its defensive capability.

Sanchez boards the ship, and lifts JeT into a pod. "Let's get out of here ASAP", Sanchez orders the autopilot. A loud voice bellows that they are forbidden to leave, as blue strobing lights rotate around the bay, lasers scan the front of their vessel. The ship lifts and reverses out of the docking bay.

Turrets immediately open fire with projectiles. The ordnance ricochets from the Aggt, damaging the bay as the ship shrugs off the attack. "Leave them a gift", Sanchez orders. A cylinder is deposited on the floor of the bay as the ship departs, it rolls into the mouth of the bay and explodes. The pre-prepared cylinder contains two kilograms of HMX (cyclotetramethylene-tetranitramine). The tactical AI indicates that a quarter of a kilo of the explosive would destroy an Earth commercial airliner, the selected charge of 2kg has eight times this power. The entire bay erupts into a fireball as the discovery ship leaves the space station and heads indirectly for the asteroid belt encircling the phosphorescent moon of the Mbunalt home world, Zetal.

15.   A New Dawn

The brothers tracked 'A New Dawn' hurtling across the solar system. By the end of April 2060, the ship arrived in Earth's vicinity in the opposing orbit to the moon. The ship had processed 0.889×10^{22} kg of organic Titanium. The mass was considerable and could be seen by the naked eye on a clear day.

The hybrid AI initiated the control modulation which implemented the construction plan, triggering the organic Titanium to grow the structure of the space station. Pascal had explained the process to Paul as being similar to the cell structure of the human body, but without cell replication itself. Stem cells in the Titanium instructed local organisms to form, and bond to create the overall structure. Paul viewed through a telescope as the mass expanded into a spherical superstructure, at such a growth rate, the sphere would be formed in a matter of days. A thumbnail calculation estimated the diameter of the moon haven to be a third of Earth's natural moon, around 600 km across.

Its mass was less than the moon, so propulsion was required to synchronise the elliptical orbits. Joe explained that the haven would not be a perfect sphere, like Earth it would be oblate, the best geometric approximation being a Cedano Spheroid. It would be slightly flattened at the poles to optimise the space with acceptable gravity.

Paul showed Franc the emerging superstructure via the telescope, "It's going to be enormous, like a mini planet. I still don't understand how we will transfer the islands onto the crust, insert the oceans and ensure gravity holds the structures in place. The gravity on the moon is a sixth of that on Earth, and the new haven will be smaller and have less mass. I just don't get it". Paul frowned, "Nor I. But Ed assures me the basic concept is sound and has been tried and tested elsewhere. I understand the Titanium has the capability to hold the island in place, but how do we extract the island in the first place. An island the size of Salina wont float, it is the tip of an underwater mountain. I hope the scientists have calculated this correctly".

Franc pondered, "They are keeping the final design close to their chests and refuse to share it with the wider team. Why don't they just put the plan on the table and explain it?" Paul whistled, "It makes me think that the concept will freak us out. They would rather show us than tell us. It will probably blow our tiny minds". Franc laughed, "I just hope we can find a semblance of life when all this is over". Paul looked more serious, "If we survive, I can live with a few surprises and compromises".

Paul's wife, Kate brought over two large mugs of coffee. Kate was in her late 90s but looked remarkably well. The introduction of the pico-tech into the human bloodstreams had extended their lifespans, Paul and Franc had aged more gracefully due to their Pareth-ng biology, which leant itself to the technology. After all it was specifically designed for their alien genome.

By the end of the week, the sphere superstructure was in place and its shiny mercury-like reflective surface was clearly visible in the daytime sky. As the sun went down, the Moon Haven lit up brilliantly, reflecting the light of Sol and extending the daylight by almost an hour.

Joe gathered the wider team to review A New Dawn's ship's log. It was a solemn occasion; everyone knew the ending would be tragic for the crew. Joe read a summary aloud and presented fragments of video to illustrate the events to the gathering.

The ship had arrived in the constellation of Eridanus on June 2nd, 2049, and mining had commenced immediately. Command passed to Franc three days later. Franc and Sheena started training on the torpedo ships and reached full physical fitness after three months. Four years later, the Kraalt visited the ship to identify their purpose and left without any issues. The Kraalt were not enslaved by the Mbunalt and operated independently. They explained that the Mbunalt who invaded Earth were pirates. An additional three years later, the facility was visited by a black vessel with no life signs aboard. Franc chose to ignore the vessel, which remained alongside the ship for three months, during that period Franc and Sheena postponed torpedo ship practice. The dark vessel left the sector, making no contact whatsoever. Ship assumed benign.

After ten years of mining, the cargo was becoming sizable and was starting to attract attention from outsiders. A grey Fosche cylinder shaped vessel arrived, and the operation was visited by three humanoids. They had a very similar in bodily form to human and Pareth-ng, but bearing three eyes, two in the normal human position, the addition eye cited below, replacing the nose. The third eye was not optical, its purpose was unclear. The emissaries seemed nervous, and rather fidgety. They sensed any small movement as a potential threat, and Franc and Sheena were forced to restrict their movements.

The Fosche attempted to negotiate a technology transfer, they became aggravated when Franc politely refused. Franc explained the purpose of their harvesting mission, but the news fell on deaf ears. The situation became heated, resulting in Franc ordering the visitors to leave the ship.

The Fosche Kallship remained in orbit for four days, when negotiations failed, they issued threats and attempted to board the ship. Franc and Sheena dispatched seventeen boarders using rifles and in close quarters the deployed the Kraalt swords. The Fosche proved no match for Franc and Sheena, the enemy could not get close enough with their electric lances to properly engage them. The Fosche ship powered up energy weapons and threatened to open fire.

Franc decided to enable the accelerator and leave immediately. The Titanium harvest was sufficient to allow the mining ship to return home with the cargo. The AI had warned that the accelerator must not be left for the Fosche to take control, so two precautions were made. The first was to redirect the trajectory into the heart of the sun, Epsilon Eridani as soon as the ship passed through. The second countermeasure was for the accelerator to self-destruct soon after.

When the Fosche sensed the accelerator was warming up, they targeted it with their weapons. Franc and Sheena launched torpedo ships and attacked the Fosche ship, as the New Dawn slipped through the accelerator. Sheena's torpedo ship was vapourised on the first attack run, but Franc inflicted significant damage to the enemy vessel as he strafed the hull at close quarters with the engineering lasers. His flight path was so unpredictable, the Fosche struggled to target him. The New Dawn passed through the accelerator and commenced its return journey. It remained unlikely that Franc would survive the encounter, as the torpedo ships had limited range and only a few hours of life support.

The meeting delegates looked to the ground sadly, in respect for Franc and Sheena's clones. Franc and Sheena exchanged a look, they were unsure of their feelings. Their clones had achieved their mission, but their lives had been hell. Sheena carocled Franc privately, "I hope our ending will be as dramatic". Franc smiled at her, Sheena was seventy-eight years old, but had lost none of her fight. She was of human DNA, however the pico-tech had extended her life considerably, although she looked old and tired these days. Her son Tank was nearing his fiftieth birthday, and he was a fine man. Strong and agile, but with the sound judgement of his father, Rusty. Her daughter had sadly passed away in her teenage years, due to a tragic accident.

Paul shared a beer with his brother, "Listen Franc, there are other races out there, who would like to get their hands on the new hybrid Kraalt and Pareth-ng technology. When we build our new haven, we will need to be able to protect ourselves". Franc agreed, "I'll talk to Joe, we probably should consider building some warships, as a precaution. It was a wise move to change the coordinates of the accelerator before it self-destructed. Hopefully the Fosche will not know from where we originate. I hope the only races that have detected Earth are the Mbunalt pirates and the Pareth-ng, and the latter are either living as a part of us or are dead".

Joe searched for the remaining wolf with little success, like Barak it was adept at evading detection. There had been sightings to the northeast of Beauné in Burgundy, by a scavenging party gathering wines from the Loire valley and in Burgundy. Their task was to obtain samples of specific grape varieties, but unofficially they had collected large supplies of wine too.

In the village of Nuits-St-Georges, a recognisable dark shadow passed by the camp at dusk, it had other interests than attacking a small party. One of the accompanying soldiers observed its significant infra-red signature, the beast was seen to be limping slightly and appeared bloated and lethargic implying the beast could be in the later stages of pregnancy.

The team felt more optimistic, they could see Moon Haven taking shape, though no one had an understanding of how it could accommodate them. The plans to lift the havens into space seemed impossible too, but the drilling and the deployment of the Titanium continued unabated. Anything seemed eminently possible when they had watched the Kraalt build a Titanium moon in the sky. The remaining folk in the haven worked hard to keep the cattle fed and the plants fertilised, crop harvest was imminent and there were insufficient hands to gather the food. All bots were deployed gathering wildlife and DNA samples.

Paul and the teams retreated to the havens early in the fall, the designated islands for transfer were in good shape for the move. Additional cattle were herded post-harvest, the team began shipping the livestock to Anglesey and the Isle of Wight, which would act as large farms in the new haven. Drake and Jake spent much time planting trees and plants to generate additional oxygen and collecting valuable farming equipment for the new islands.

16. Apocalypse

As more volcanos erupted along the European continental plates, the scanners detected 'A Last Wish' incoming with a significant cargo. There were cheers as Joe shared the news, it had been a ten year wait with substantial trepidation since the superstructure of the haven had been completed. The third volcanic explosion was eleven times the size of the eruption of Vesuvius, which destroyed the city of Pompeii. They created significant dust clouds, but they were distant from the surviving population, so had marginal effect. However, the Arks were prioritised in those continents before precious species suffocated.

There had been good progress with the population of the Arks, the bots had returned from the major continents and had obtained genetic samples of flora, fauna and animal life. For a human task force, this would have been an impossible feat, but the tiny bots appeared like winged ants, so very few animals paid them any attention. They had collected ten percent of the target sample set, and their work continued. The Kraalt had worked with the Pareth-ng to construct six Arks, each a large archive capable of storing the samples for each continent. They sat in the centre of each continental plate, and when the air became clear they would deploy, creating clones of lifeforms incapable of surviving the disaster. Regardless of the survival of humans, the Arks would rebuild the Earth to its former magnificence.

Months later two more volcanos erupted, causing a small shift in the plates. The resulting tidal wave hammered Asia and

Australia. The dust made it impossible to breathe, many animals suffered with coughs and lung infections, some died. It was a small taste of things to come. Soon more volcanoes would erupt, triggering the apocalypse.

Paul, Rusty, Franc and Sheena were contemplating events sat around the campfire, they had worked hard with the team gathering animals and critical plants for the havens. Sheena addressed the obvious elephant in the room, "How can the Kraalt take ten island clusters into space and just drop them onto that big silver sphere and make it work? Then there's the question of the seas and oceanic life. I'd like to know what the hell is going on, it's our survival at stake here".

Paul agreed, "Me too. I know they are already drilling beneath the islands to insert an organic Titanium superstructure beneath the waterline. They are planning to encapsulate each island in a bubble, to retain the atmosphere and animal life. They will use the repaired engines from their ten beached spaceships to lift each island in turn". Rusty smiled, "Yes, but those engines power the ships at near light speed with two hundred big heavy Cros and their armour on board. I guess they plan to retune the engines to provide slow powerful thrust, rather than the high-speed transportation they are used to". "Turn a Ferrari into a Land Rover", laughed Franc.

Franc became serious, "But the gravity of that silver bubble won't be enough to keep us stuck to the surface of the moon. I simply don't understand how they will resolve that. Joe refused to elaborate; he assures me that all will become clear when the time is right. Really bloody helpful! I hope they know what they are doing". Paul added, "I was expecting to be living on the inside of a rotating wheel, like in the movies. I guess anything is an improvement on that". Sheena looked sidelong at Rusty, "I'm not living in any shitty hamster wheel, save that for the fucking rats!"

As they sat, the group became aware of a presence watching them. They hadn't seen anything, it was just a primal feeling that a threat was lurking, something large and dangerous. The sensation passed but returned the following night. Rusty was on watch. With age his thought process was slower, but he was no fool. He raised his weapon and thumbed off the safety, "Wake up guys, there something out there".

Lucy was working with Colletta and Audrey to improve the garden on Vulcano. They were the only people on the island other than Abe. Lucy relied on her daughters to do most of the work, due to her advancing years. They missed Franc, who rarely had time to return to the island these days. Her daughters shared Franc's alien blood which gave them a longer lifespan. Despite Lucy aging faster than Franc, he said that every day he shared with her was a gift, and every day he loved her more.

Bridget and Lucy had become firm friends over the years, Lucy took Bridget's death badly. She berated the Guard on Salina for not protecting her, which was unfair. Lucy had apologised, but she still harboured a grudge which niggled her from time to time. She worried about Barak's wolves living out in the countryside, she knew they were vicious and nasty like Barak, not kind souls like Abe.

In the night Audrey woke, and gently padded next door to wake Colletta, "Somethings up", she commented. Colletta connected to Audrey using her Carocle to see their father asleep in the tent by the fire on the Scottish mainland. Paul and

Sheena were with him, and a handful of soldiers. Sheena was on guard, wide awake, "Sheena, the wolf is out there", Audrey warned. "I know, I can feel it. I just tried to roust these lazy buggers, but they are sound asleep", replied Sheena. She shook Paul and Franc again, "Wake the others, we have incoming". Paul and Franc stood quickly, reoriented and gathered the others.

The team stood back-to-back in a tight circle awaiting the attack, but it didn't come. They went back to their tents and fell asleep leaving Paul on watch. Another warning came in from Audrey, Paul roused the team again. It was much easier to wake them the second time. There was movement in the undergrowth, but again no attack materialised.

Sheena urged the team to form a hunting party, but Paul resisted; he knew they would not catch the wolf if it ran, it was too fast. Hunting the animal in the dark was a risky business. It was impossible to sleep in the face of impending attack, so they sat around the fire awaiting dawn. Sleep found them eventually, they had planned to stay awake and hadn't agreed who would take watch. Audrey assumed the role; she had observed the error and sensed their tiredness.

Audrey woke her father as the wolf attacked. The beast was probably hunting Paul but had mixed up the scents, Paul had loaned one of the team an overcoat. Franc leaped towards the beast shouting the others, as the wolf ripped one of the outer tents open and gorged on the man sleeping within. When the beast realised his mistake, he discarded the severed cadaver, looked at the gathering and charged.

Paul opened fire with his Glock, as the others gathered their weapons. Ignoring the others, the beast made a beeline for Paul. Sheena took the wolf's hind legs as it leapt. It hit the ground a metre from where Paul was stood, ignored the profuse bleeding and used its forelegs to crawl. Paul backed up as quickly as he could but tripped over a tent guy rope, falling flat on his back. The dog closed the distance quickly but slowed due to blood loss. Franc leapt onto the wolf and rammed his sword between its shoulders, missing its heart by a fraction. He withdrew his sword by slicing sideways through the shoulder of the animal, to make a second attempt. The beast was in reach of Paul, its huge slavering maw stretched for his legs.

The lupine looked into Paul's eyes with hatred, as he emptied his magazine into the monster's left eye as it lunged. The wolf grabbed Paul's left leg and tugged him close, so it could close his mighty jaws around him. Francs second strike was true, and the best fell. In its last seconds it continued to stare at Paul with its right eye, Sheena rammed her sword directly into its brain. She shouted, "Get the fuck out of here!" Already the mushroom was growing as Franc called, "Run into the wind, the spores will blow the other way".

The mushroom exploded, and spores were sent high and wide. But Franc's advice was sound, and although the slowest of the team were only ten metres away, the spores didn't touch them. Many spores flew into a small clutch of elder trees and gooseberry bushes. In the light of the campfire, they could see the trees turn black in seconds, and one of them fell. They left the tents and equipment, for fear of infection and returned to the haven. "That's six down, only the injured one to go", announced Franc.

As predicted by the Kraalt, the chain reaction of the remaining volcanoes began. Each threw clouds of dust into the air, and the choking mist reached as far as Salina and northern France. The survivors were forced to wear respiratory masks to keep their lungs clear. Everything was covered with a dusting of carbon and rock, but not severe enough to harm the cattle or crops, providing they were diligent.

The threat of a major shift in the tectonic plates was worrying for everyone, time was quickly running out. A shift would destroy Salina and Summer Haven, and their hopes would be shattered. The sand of the hourglass was running out, people wished life would get easier. The first sign of hope was the arrival of 'A Last Wish' towing a huge quantity of organic Titanium.

17. A Last Wish

'A Last Wish' hurtled across the solar system, carefully tracked by the brothers. It was 10th September 2081 when the ship arrived in Earth's orbit, close to the haven superstructure. The ship had completed the processing of a mammoth 2.04×10^{22} Kg of organic Titanium. The mass was enormous and was visible from Earth without the need for optics. Immediately the hybrid AI continued construction of the haven, to the pre-programmed design.

A Pareth-ng discovery ship gathered a significant portion of the precious cargo and transported it to Earth on a steady glide path, the ship morphed massive wings to slow the descent through the atmosphere. The Titanium was to be used to prepare the land masses for travel, and to contain large portions of the oceans and their wildlife as they were assimilated into the sphere.

Paul and Franc reviewed the transcription of events from the Last Wish. The imminent threat of the inbound Umbra vessel which tailgated the Last Wish proved to be a grave worry for them both. The only ray of hope was the fact that Franc and Sheena's clones seemed to be trying their luck in the wider universe. "Good luck guys", whispered Paul to the skies. "Second that", breathed Franc.

Events were becoming critical, there was little they could do to mitigate the risk of the Zaarch. They needed to focus on the evacuation as Earth's defences were weak, they were only armed with their wits. Despite the fact that the Umbra entered the accelerator a fraction of a second behind the Last Wish, it failed to materialise immediately. There was no sign of it, even after a couple of weeks had passed.

The communities consolidated in the USA near Wichita in Kansas. It was deemed the safest place, at the centre of a very large land mass. Paul, Franc and Joe oversaw the transportation of large bubbles containing portions of the Artic, Atlantic and Mediterranean oceans. Vast silver-coloured bubbles encapsulated cross sections of sea, coral and sea life as they were transported to the sphere in the sky.

In the Mediterranean, an army of bots had helped nudge numerous whales, seals, dolphins and fish into location before they were drawn into the sphere. The bubble gently lifted out of the sea causing the water levels to drop a couple of centimetres at the shore, showing the scale of the operation. The water level soon returned to normal as water flowed in from the Atlantic and the Indian Ocean via the Red Sea. The sphere gradually eased into the sky. Paul was transfixed as the bubble lifted into the stratosphere, like a hot air balloon. Thirty hours later, the bubble rendezvoused with the larger sphere and disappeared. The sphere changed form to a more familiar egg shape as it returned to continue its task with the next stretch of ocean.

The operation was repeated many times, it was over a month before the bubble formed over Summer Haven. Paul and Franc felt of little help, as they stood on the shoreline at Polbain on the Scottish headland watching the waves of bots cajoling birds, bees and other fauna into the radius of the slowly expanding sphere. As the bubble emerged, the bots assimilated into the surface of the bubble, their work complete. Joe joined the brothers, the rock beneath the three small islands started to crack and shake. The ripples in the waves accentuated the vibrations, as the islands gently lifted into the air.

"I hope it all stays in one piece", commented a worried Paul, the tension evident on his frowning face. Joe put his arm around Paul's shoulder comfortingly, "Don't worry. The main supporting structures have been strengthened; the buildings have silver veins running through their structure. They will hold, but a little dust may be shaken loose by the vibration. We have been forced to disable the wind farm; the propellers may have an effect on the simulated winds in the new haven. I will bring them on line one by one and monitor the impact, if they are needed. The updated solar panels and Kraalt power sources will provide the energy we need until the sphere is complete. They have devised an infinity battery to power most of your devices. They mimic your battery technologies and fossil fuel engines. The skin of the sphere will absorb sufficient energy from the sun to provide all our power needs in the longer term, when the final cargo arrives".

Franc watched his brother, as Paul monitored the ascent of Summer Haven into the sky. A dark brooding nimbus threatened rain and minor storms. The bubble was soon enveloped by clouds and the Carocles displayed a graphic of the progress as visibility was poor. Franc smiled at Paul, "Happy Birthday brother. You don't look a day over a century". Paul smiled back, "I just wanted to live long enough to see this happen. See our people safe, so I can retire happily". His thoughts then turned to his family. Kate had been rejuvenated by the introduction of the Pico tech into her body, but she was nearing the end of her life. She did not have the long lifespan of the Pareth-ng. Paul's face turned sombre. As if reading his mind, Franc intercepted his thought, "She has lived a long and good life, there's still a few miles on her clock yet".

It took five days for each of the nominated islands to be levitated into position. The last of the mining ships was reputedly preparing to return to Earth but would take almost half a century to arrive. The new haven would not be fully complete until the last of the precious cargo was merged into its mass. The planned defensive warships would not be ready until sometime after.

In the short term, a rag tag fleet of three modified Mbunalt ships would be all they had. The Pareth-ng vessels had been plundered in order to start the build of the haven itself.

A day prior to the departure of the last community, Paul and Franc watched the last island, Anglesey, take to the sky. The pair of road bridges to the island had already been severed, the large Menai bridge remaining in place as the land mass lifted, swinging violently in harmonic motion caused by the ground's vibration. They observed the slow progress of the balloon until the clouds enveloped it. As it had lifted from the crust, the waters surged from the ocean and the Menai straits. The ocean roared into the hole which remained where the island once existed.

The brothers slept in their tents, though sleep was hard to come by. In the morning they built a small blaze and dined from fire roasted tins of beans and hunks of heavily buttered bread. They found the skies clear, though the wind was icy. Franc huddled into his jacket as Paul looked through the telescope. "Why are you using that old thing, you will get a better view using the Carocle". Paul retorted jokingly, "We need to try to keep our old ways going, you never know when technology will fail you". "I heard that", muttered Joe via the Carocle. Paul responded jovially, "Looks like our brother is still in there somewhere".

A discovery ship arrived as the last island, was assimilated into the moon. Paul watched the great bubble as it passed through the perimeter of the sphere. The brothers boarded the spaceship via the silver ramp, with Joe close behind. The ship lifted into the sky without delay, they took their seats and strapped in for the journey. Joe's voice took on a more excited tone, "Let's unveil our blueprint for survival, I suspect I have quite a surprise in store for you". Franc smiled, "You haven't cloned our families again, have you?"

The following day, Joe made the brothers aware of a vessel approaching Earth at high speed. It was identified as it crossed between Earth and Sol; it had been disguised due to the complete shadow that obscured it. The ship slowed as it approached Earth, it dropped into Earth's gravity well and commenced orbit. From the data interfaced from the Last Wish, it was identified as the feared Zaarch Umbra. Joe scanned the ship and found no signs of life, as per the information provided by the Kraalt ambassador. The ship sat in orbit, ominous and silent. Joe attempted to communicate with the vessel but there was no response of any kind.

It was a little after midnight, Audrey sat bolt upright in bed in the makeshift home they had made. Colletta was in the next room with her husband, Eddie. Eddie was fast asleep after gathering the last of the crops. Lucy had passed in the fall, almost a year ago. She had a wonderful life, the funeral was bittersweet for them all; her father, Franc, had been heartbroken. Lucy would have been 108, but Colletta's mother was a clone, her physical age was only 79. It was hard to keep track, age was becoming nebulous. Colletta and Audrey had mixed DNA and had a longer life expectancy than their mother.

Colletta was instantly aware that her sister was troubled. She popped on her Carocle and asked Audrey if she was ok, but there was no response, it was like she had gone offline. Colletta slid silently out of her bed and slipped into Audrey's room to find her sitting. "Are you ok Sis?" Colletta asked gently. When she received no response, she grasped Audrey's hand and attempted to connect minds with her, but she was unresponsive. Colletta slipped back into her room and quietly opened her drawer. She grasped the Kracz-el empathy device and connected it to the front of her Carocle, then headed back to Audrey's room.

The room pulsated in electric blue as Colletta reached out to Audrey. She found herself stood on the deck inside a black spacecraft, Audrey stood before her, looking into the eyes of a dark shrouded figure. Audrey screamed, and they found themselves in each other's arms in Audrey's bed. Ed ran into the room after hearing the piercing sound to check if everything was ok. Abe sat outside Audrey's window; he too was aware something wasn't quite right.

"What was that?" asked Colletta, mortified. Audrey replied cautiously, "I'm not quite certain. The man said the Zaarch are looking for the Terminus, where all life flows. He had heard my call, when I was a young girl, and had been searching for me. He said there were three such termini in the universe, and the Zaarch were unable to find them. He claimed he needed my help".

18. The Last Goodbye

Franc and Paul looked through the main viewing port as they neared the recently completed moon. The spheroid rotated around the pole axis, though it was hard to see the reflective outer surface rotate. It was a familiar mercury like substance, similar to the Pareth-ng discovery ships. Paul whispered to himself, "I still don't get it". He looked over his shoulder to the dark menacing Umbra, sat silently in orbit. It felt like it was watching them. Paul and Franc's ship passed the perimeter of the spheroid near to the pole and through a long shaft into the environment within. Nothing could prepare them for the scene that unfolded before their eyes.

The vessel entered the airlock cavity in the centre of the sphere, and the ship lowered towards the sea. In front of them was Summer Haven and the Summer Islands nestled in the ocean as should be, though there was no Scottish mainland nearby. Paul and Franc's jaws dropped open as they exited the ship as if in a dream, they felt the familiar rough knotty grass beneath their feet.

Paul and Franc sat on the stone wall near the smithy in silence. Joe pointed upward, to the horizon which curved upwards into the sky. Clouds obscured the view, but they could make out the form of the Welsh island of Anglesey rising up from the horizon. The sky was slightly darker, the sun was not illuminating the entire sphere simultaneously.

Joe explained, "We have created an inverted planet. It's like a Dyson Sphere, but it has a smaller artificial sun at the centre. A Dyson Sphere is a concept really, its magnitude is too large create to build in real terms". "What the hell is a Dyson

Sphere?" Franc queried. Joe explained, "It's an enormous sphere erected around a sun, in order to harvest all of the energy radiated". "That's crazy, the sphere would be the size of an entire solar system", contended Paul. Joe continued, "Yes, but it's not feasible with current technology. We have built the new world on the inside of the sphere, so its rotation will create the same gravitational pull as on Earth, but as centripetal force from the rotation.

We have built the main rotation superstructures and service zones in the vicinity of the poles, where the gravity will push objects sideways. Concentric rings surrounding the poles allow the bots and the Kraalt access to the main mechanisms. The artificial sun in the boom at the centre of the sphere casts sunlight onto a third of the circumference, to retain a normal daylight cycle. The sphere rotates at a different speed to Earth, but the sun also needs to rotate, in order to keep the day and night cycles correct. The size of the aperture in the sun reduces in the winter months, and the heat reduces a little. You will find temperatures here are a little warmer than Scotland though". "Thank God for small mercies", muttered Franc.

Joe continued his introduction, "The sun is offset so it's nearer to the Tropical pole, allowing the other pole to be cold. We have located Iceland at the colder side, obviously, and surrounded it by a section of the Arctic Sea with its natural inhabitants. We have organised the oceans into giant swim lanes. The lane nearest the Arctic pole contains the Arctic Ocean, whereas this swim lane holds a portion of the Atlantic. Next is the Mediterranean, then finally the South Pacific.

The rings are separated by a flexible membrane. We have located the Summer Islands, Anglesey and the Isle of Wight in the Atlantic; the Aeolian islands, Barbados and Formentera in the Mediterranean; The Pacific ring contains the Japanese Obe Islands and the Indonesian Island of Sabu. If the Sun was not obscuring our vision, you would see Salina behind it at the highest point in the sky, some 1000km away along the circumference of the circle".

The concept was mind blowing for the brothers. Franc asked, "How do you power all of this?" Joe explained that the outer skin of the spheroid collected the energy from the sun when the Earth was not occluding it. Tides and currents worked differently than on Earth, the Coriolis force is reduced, but the gravity of Earth, the Sun and the Moon affect it differently too. The membranes allow the sea to flow between each other, but in a controlled way so the ecosystems will not cross-pollinate.

The winds are different for the same reasons and are marginally gentler than on Earth. Air pressure is comparable, but high-pressure zones move around to create winds. Mature trees have been transplanted to optimise the CO_2 and Oxygen balance maintain good air quality. There is sufficient vegetation to support life for three times as many lifeforms as are currently present in the haven.

"This brings me to the compromises", explained Joe, "the outer shell of the spheroid is not at full strength. It is vulnerable, we are we awaiting the third cargo of Titanium to bolster it. We do not have a fleet to protect the haven from external interference. The three retrofitted Mbunalt warships will suffice for now. Movement between havens is via boats or the discovery ships, but I recommend keeping their use to a minimum.

We have deployed the frigate, the Phoenix; it is waiting in port at Salina. However, we have replaced its dirty nuclear reactor with something a little more sustainable. We have also refitted additional ships for the use of each of the islands. Don't worry about crossing the semi-permeable membrane, it is self-aware and will avoid contact with your ships". "How can a membrane be self-aware", enquired Franc. "Everything is linked into the AI, to me", replied Joe.

The brothers were dumbstruck, but soon recovered as the discovery ships started to ferry in the communities. There was work to be done and people to manage, which was always a challenge. A process always worked well until people were involved.

The Kansas communities were last to be collected, once their accommodation was complete. There were just over two thousand people, to be ferried to their new home in the six remaining discovery ships. The spaceships had expanded their hulls to accommodate 350 people on each. Sheena had been forced to coerce people to encourage them to board the ships quickly. The individuals were nervous about leaving Earth, they worried about their belongings and their families.

The first three ships had arrived safely, but the departure of the final three was proving problematic. A small band of survivors were spreading propaganda concerning the reality of the apocalypse. They promoted a conspiracy theory that scared the remaining people. "The aliens are shipping us off Earth so they can take it for themselves. I don't want to spend the rest of my life in that big fur lined coffin in the sky. I'm staying here, who's with me?" announced one of them, a tall farmer called Unwin.

Sheena walked directly up to the protagonist and punched him in the mouth. The man doubled over in pain, screaming "She hit me. The bitch hit me". Rusty smiled at his wife. They hoped they may have a few more years together, if these idiots would get on the damned ship. The crowd became feisty following the violence, and no amount of straight talking would urge them to board. Rusty decided to use negative psychology and announced, "Ok then, we're going now. You can stay here, no problem. Good luck". He turned smartly and boarded, reaching for Sheena's hand.

As Rusty's foot touched the silver ramp the world shook violently. The tremors were getting worse. Sheena yelled, "The plates are shifting. You need to get on board now! This is your very last chance. Soon, a super tsunami will be heading this way. The Carocles displayed a view from deep in the Atlantic Ocean; they could see massive dust clouds rising into the sky. They almost felt the rumble as the sea receded from the shoreline; in the distance they could see the mother of all waves heading towards the shore.

Rusty's Carocle estimated that the wave was 2.2km high. Persuasion was no longer needed, the remainder of the community fought to board the ships in panic. The last ship lifted as the wave hit the east coast. It swept across the land, destroying the tower blocks and bridges. All sign of humanity was eradicated for a hundred miles. The city of Philadelphia was no longer visible, the wave continued across several state lines deep into Pennsylvania and Ohio, smashing everything in its path.

Even in the spaceship they could hear the crack of the plates shifting violently, the geo-activity was escalating quickly. The ship moved over the Atlantic, nearing the European continent. A huge chasm had appeared between Spain and Africa; the water rushed in to fill it, the two countries halted and then smashed together. A giant spume of magma and steam sprayed from great ruptures in the Earth's crust; cast into the air at various points along the rift. Dust filled the air as the ship left Earth, visibility was poor until the ship left the atmosphere behind.

The ship's viewing port showed the blue sphere of their world being consumed by a grey dust cloud. The people aboard were terrified, they saw their world being torn apart by huge fiery rifts as the land masses moved, smashing into each other. The passenger's faces looked distraught as the familiar blue hue of Earth was completely enveloped by dirty grey. The world and everything on it had been destroyed, Barak had achieved his heart's desire.

Audrey was strapped into a seat in the shuttle adjacent to Colletta and Ed. Tank sat in the rear with Abe, occupying a large part of the cargo space. As they approached the large metallic sphere, her eyes focussed on the large dark ship close to the horizon. As their shuttle left the Earth's atmosphere, the Umbra became animated and moved on an intercept course to their transport. Colletta immediately informed her father, who was unable to acquire a spaceship in time to provide support, all vessels were occupied transporting people, ocean, animals and insects to their new home in the sky.

The Umbra moved in front of the shuttle in a broadside position. A voice rang out in Audrey's Carocle, her sister listened in, it spoke a single directive, "Join us". Audrey closed her eyes and concentrated, like before her spirit was summoned to the bridge of the black ship, looking into the eyes of the dark cloaked figure. Colletta observed, connecting to her sister's visual data stream. The ship was vague, its features blurred in and out of focus. The bridge of the ship was occupied by several dark cloaked figures, sat at consoles with a multitude of dimmed displays and controls. The screens moved in and out of focus continually. The ship's changing insubstantial nature gave Colletta the sensation of motion sickness.

The four Zaarch crew joined their leader, who continued to contemplate Audrey eerily. The leader reached out to touch her cheek, Audrey gasped with the sensation of coldness. Colletta was surprised Audrey could breathe in this alien vessel, but soon realised Audrey was not actually there. Somehow her consciousness had been transported, but her body remained on the shuttle.

Finally, the leader spoke but Audrey's Carocle was unable to translate, the language was arcane. The figure appeared to recognise the issue and spoke directly through the Carocle's mind to mind connection with no effect. Audrey suddenly realised her error, and spoke to the man using her spiritual ability, "Hello my name is Audrey. I don't understand how I can help you". The dark figure smiled, but by doing so looked fell and grim, "It is a very great honour to meet you Audrey, we have travelled a long way to find you". Colletta continued to observe, shaking, she was terrified, "It's okay", Audrey whispered.

The grim figure continued, "We have been seeking the Terminus for millennia, but so far we have been unsuccessful. No race has been able to help us, but we are hoping you will, we sense your abilities, you are our only hope. We followed your race's ship 'A Last Wish' across the galaxy to seek you. A human called Sanchez helped us". Audrey was confused, she couldn't remember anyone by the name Sanchez, despite it being her surname. Colletta nudged her, "It's Dad's clone, from the mining ship. He must have given them your location. He wouldn't have done that, if he wasn't worthy of our trust". Audrey looked at her sister, "I have no idea what a Terminus is, let alone where it is".

Colletta addressed the alien through her sister, "My sister will need some time to consider your request". "Some would say we have all the time in the world. However, we are tired, and we desire to move through the portal with alacrity ourselves, our patience is wearing thin", the gloomy figure responded. Colletta continued, "Please tell us a little more about the Terminus, so we can understand the object you are looking for?"

The last remaining wolf in Barak's pack looked sullen and walked towards the east with its tail between its legs, she was injured and despairing. Her maw was painful and her coat heavily damaged from the fire. Gone was her opportunity to thwart the escape of Earth's people to their new haven. There was little time remaining before dust would saturate the atmosphere. The lupine ran for its life, back to the mountains of Bavaria. The wolf coughed to clear the dust from her lungs, she pressed on relentlessly. Heading towards the centre of a tectonic plate bought her more time. The dust was spreading from the edges, the gigantic tidal waves were unlikely to reach this far inland.

The ground shook as another terrible tremor twisted Earth. A dead tree fell in her path, the wolf instinctively changed course to avoid it. By the end of the day, the wolf could see the distant mountains in the dusk light, her journey was nearing its end. She ran through the night until she could see the outline of the crumbling abbey with the hazy sun setting behind it.

The wolf sprinted into the building through the broken doors, headed to the nave where she perceived a terrible scent. Not the smell of rotting flesh, something far worse, a smell of disease and the unnatural. She almost choked as she exited the basilica, heading to the entrance of the crypt. She took care to avoid the poisoned vegetation and cadavers and to avoid disturbing the spores.

The cellar door was slightly ajar, she pushed her nose into the crack and pushed the door open. The wolf closed the door behind her, pulling the old oak door back into place with her teeth. In the darkness she managed to find her way to the pod, which illuminated and opened as she neared it. She climbed inside and circled to prepare her nest, her ears pricking up when the ground shook again. Awaiting hibernation, she could feel the kick of the tiny puppies within her uterus. She smiled and went to sleep, as the lights switched off in the pod. Fast asleep, she was unaware of the ground's upheaval and the collapse of a section of the abbey roof above her.

IV. Epilogue: New Moon

"Give me a lever long enough and a fulcrum on which to place it, and I shall move the world".

Archimedes

In late September 2083, the Moon Haven became fully operational and housed the remaining human race, plus the other alien families which formed Earth's communities. Life was almost normal, when one became familiar with the horizon extending in a curve upward, into the light of the bright sun above. At night, rather than observing the stars and moon, the section of the sphere experiencing daytime became faintly visible. From Summer Haven, on some nights Paul could make out the outline of Isola Salina amongst the Aeolian Islands in the sky vertically above them.

Their new home delivered its promises as Earth failed. No longer could Earth be called the blue planet; its surface was a murky grey, the atmosphere was saturated with dust particles. Life had ceased on one of the most beautiful habitable planets in this sector of the universe. Hope remained in the orbiting haven, though the brothers lived in fear of the impending threat from the black spaceship holding position next to the space station.

The Umbra had been both silent and motionless since the Moon Haven was commissioned. Earth's leaders racked their brains to assist Audrey in her quest for the information the Zaarch desired. There was a shared feeling that the hourglass was running out. Paul knew this single ship could destroy everything they had built. Their first Pendragon class warship was not complete, Paul lacked the confidence that the Umbra could be defeated, if the Centriim feared the Zaarch as they did.

Paul paced the Summer Haven atrium, feeling increasingly stressed. Franc had no answers for the Zaarch regarding the Terminus, "Can we buy more time? Could we tell the Zaarch that the Terminus is on Earth, but we are forced to wait until the volcanic activity calms down?" Paul replied sadly, "I doubt they are that ignorant. If it worked, what then? We are merely buying more time, but facing the same ultimate outcome, plus they will know we have lied to them". Franc looked at his brother's time worn face, "It could buy us a century, if we play it right. By then, we might find a solution. They are looking for Audrey for a reason". Paul countered gently, "They came looking for Audrey because your clone sent them. It was his only option to buy time to complete Moon Haven. It doesn't mean that she is able to help them". "But they heard her call, she used her gift, her ability as a medium to connect with them over such huge distances. It can't just be a coincidence. The Zaarch are noted for their brutality, yet they are waiting patiently. We need to buy more time", asserted Franc.

Joe was asked to focus his processing power on finding the Terminus. After two months of endless data mining and analysis, Joe presented his meagre conclusions to the leaders of Moon Haven. They had gathered in Summer Haven Atrium, with Audrey and Colletta. The huge outline of Abe was visible at the rear of the room, the third member of the atypical triad.

Joe took to the podium, "I'm afraid I do not have good news, the information I will present is incomplete and leads our computation to no obvious conclusions". The team in the room started to chatter nervously, until Joe continued. "Although it comes from Latin, the English dictionary definition of the word Terminus is a final point in space or time, an end or extremity. We cannot be sure the Zaarch apply the same meaning, though by context they chose the English word when they communicated to Audrey.

Their communication is not a Carocle translation, it was a direct connection between spirits. We can only assume the Zaarch are looking for the end of the universe, or metaphysically the end of life in this phase of existence. Our knowledge base contains nothing, actual or implied, about either of these options. Only our theology refers to the 'end of phase' as being death itself".

Joe offered the audience a little comfort, "There is no information about the Zaarch or their nature. Encounters with their race demonstrate they will not attempt to communicate; they bring destruction in seemingly arbitrary attacks. The only contraindication is they communicated with Franc's clone, they somehow understood he had knowledge of Audrey. Why is Audrey so important to them? Audrey is a very special person, her gift differentiates her from the rest of us, her ability to speak to the spirits of the dead. The one assertion I can make is the Zaarch are seeking the place whereby one can move to the next life".

The wolf recited via the Carocle the opening and closing stanza pairs from Keats' poem 'La Belle Dame sans Merci'. Those in the room listened carefully, as when Abe chose to speak, it usually had meaning and led them to a new direction of thought.

> O what can ail thee, knight-at-arms,
> Alone and palely loitering?
> The sedge has withered from the lake,
> And no birds sing.
>
> O what can ail thee, knight-at-arms,
> So haggard and so woe-begone?
> The squirrel's granary is full,
> And the harvest's done.
>
> ...
>
> I saw their starved lips in the gloom,
> With horrid warning gapèd wide,
> And I awoke and found me here,
> On the cold hill's side.
>
> And this is why I sojourn here,
> Alone and palely loitering,
> Though the sedge is withered from the lake,
> And no birds sing.

Colletta queried, "I don't understand Abe, what are you trying to say?" Audrey looked at her warmly, "He wonders if the Zaarch are not living beings. He speculates if they are the spirits of a race long lost, palely loitering as Keats writes. Are they trying to find their way to the next life, like the Shrooms? Surely there can be no other piece that fits this puzzle".

Paul seized the thought desperately, "The Well of Souls, it always comes back to that infernal place". "On the contrary Uncle Paul, it is the place where souls move on to the next plane of existence. It's not somewhere to be feared, it's a place we must all visit one day. It's as natural as an autumnal breeze or the first smile of a new-born baby", replied Audrey evenly. Paul followed the thought, "How can we take the Zaarch to the surface of Earth, given all that is going on? It is treacherous". Joe explained, "The discovery ships can fly in Earth's corrupted atmosphere, they simply can't fly aerodynamically. We can survive in the suits, for as long as the oxygen tanks and the air recycling operate. Visibility is poor, and there is the danger of volcanic eruption, which we can mitigate by monitoring seismic activity".

The Zaarch accepted the theory, although Audrey carefully positioned the idea as not being a certainty. The expedition departed the following day, crewed by Paul, Franc, Joe and Audrey. They were accompanied by the drawn figure of the Zaarch leader, wearing a black cloak concealing his grim frame.

As ship entered Earth's atmosphere, optical visibility was almost non-existent. The dust laden air was voluminous like a terrible smog from industrial ages long past. Joe displayed the outlines of the damaged world from below his sensors. They neared Europe and could see the extent of the land mass movement below them. The continental plate had shifted, pushing England into the central land mass, and the Mediterranean ocean was completely absent, Spain and the most southern European countries butted up to Africa. The plates continued to move, and lines of volcanoes spit magma into the air around the boundaries. Audrey could sense Mother Nature's absence, her cries lost in the turmoil.

The ship neared Israel; it was hard to differentiate between the countries. Joe had extrapolated Jerusalem's location based on the plate movements. They closed on the location; Paul could make out the ruined city. The walls and buildings were rubble. The task of locating the rock would be exacerbated by having to trawl through masses of debris. The team suited up and agreed to leave the ship at the valley of Hinnom, so they could attempt to retrace their path to the Dome of the Rock.

After disembarking, the ship left the ground quickly and retreated to a safe distance. Luckily, there were no active volcanos nearby. "You can't even see your hand in front of your face down here", shouted Franc. He quickly switched to the Carocle for communication, the winds were howling, driving dust and sand into their visors mercilessly. Paul fought his way to the position of the old gate, he brushed the dust from some of the larger rocks to confirm they were in the right place, the ancient Zion Gate.

They climbed over ruins to head towards the Moslem quarter. It was slow work, but it was possible to recognise the scene. Their Zaarch colleague walked amongst the dusty ruins effortlessly with his hood drawn across his face, the sand assaulting the heavy cloth of his rippling cloak.

Franc whispered to Paul on a private channel, "That guy gives me the creeps, do you see the way he looks at us with those empty eyes?" "I think he looks sad", replied Paul, "who knows what he has been through or what he is feeling". They weaved their way into the main square of the dome. Paul uncovered a large piece of stone from the desecrated temple showing a fragment of the symbol of Baphomet. Drawn on it was the pentagon from the centre of the pentacle with two ominous eyes. The wailing wall was destroyed, a part of the wreckage surrounding them.

Audrey led the way to Abraham's rock. The temple was ruined, covering the rock with rubble. The earthquakes hadn't affected the rock's fundamental structure. The team uncovered the rock and the entrance to the well. The stairs were damaged but remained in place, they removed rocks and rubble from the staircase to make them passable. It took two hours to clear the way, but they entered the chamber beneath the rock with sufficient air remaining in their tanks. The hooded figure questioned Audrey, "What is this?"

Audrey pressed her ear to the rock and asked the Zaarch leader to copy her action. She could hear the voices clearly but wondered if he was experiencing the same phenomenon. The figure removed his cloak, exposing his skeletal body, then walked directly into the face of the rock and disappeared, much to the surprise of the team. After a short period, he reappeared and redressed in his cloak, he looked solemnly at Audrey nodding once before he vanished.

Joe reported the Zaarch Umbra had immediately departed Earth's orbit. One last message filled Audrey's mind, "Find Kevin, the one known as 'The Torch', he needs your assistance. He will help you with your unwritten story, the remainder of your life".

"The Zaarch are embarking on a quest to find their kin, to help them find their way to the Well of Souls and on to the next life", explained Audrey. "That's quite a sacrifice, it could take them a very long time", observed Paul. Audrey transported the others back to the haven, then went in search of 'Kevin' with her father.

The brothers tracked the third mining vessel, 'Inspiration', streaking across our solar system. It was 19th April 2133, when the ship arrived in Earth's orbit close to Moon Haven. The ship carried 3.01×10^{22} Kg of organic Titanium integrated into its hull. On arrival, the AI retrieved a large portion of Titanium to bolster the outer skin of the spheroid. A Pareth-ng discovery ship towed a significant percentage of the precious cargo and took it to the 'shipyard' on the moon, ready for construction to begin with the growth of a new warship.

Paul manoeuvred his wheelchair into the Atrium and looked at his brother warmly, his face wrinkled and worn, "I'd always hoped to live to see this day. We'll be 160 next month, but I'm not sure if I'll live to see the next". "I feel so tired", replied Franc leaning on the desk for support, "my legs are shot". Franc sat down with a thump, Colletta brought him a drink of hot nettle tea.

It had been a long time since their wives and friends had passed on to the next life, but their children remained, the reluctant leaders of the haven. "When Moon Haven is up to full strength we can stop worrying", laughed Franc. "Yeah, I think I'll worry until the day I'm in my grave", retorted Paul. "There's life in the old dog yet", said Franc with a twinkle in his eye.

Joe joined the group as they reviewed the ship's log from the 'Inspiration'. There was disturbing news, which Joe wanted to avoid making public. The mining expedition to 55 Cancri E had been a great success, but the Grune had caught up with the team. Franc and Sheena's clones had died defending the harvest. Clearly this would worsen future diplomatic relationships with the Centriim.

Paul pulled his blanket over his knees, "It's getting cold, its seeping into my old bones". Franc chuckled, "That's nothing, remember how cold it used to be before the move. The wind would cut through you in the winter, it was horrid. I'm used to warmer climes. When we moved, the Kraalt made the island more temperate". "Praise them for small mercies", responded Paul.

Fifty years later a little of the blue colour started to return to the planet we called Earth.

Paul J.C. Edge's new series 'Razed Earth' depicts an alternative path through the events depicted in the Summer Haven series. The first novel in this new series is: Terminus

Printed in Great Britain
by Amazon

49808654R00274